THE GATHERING

The Queens of Magra Book 1

GAIL MERRITT

The characters and events portrayed in this book are fictional.

Any similarity to real persons, living or dead, is coincidental and not intended by the author.

ISBN M0D2091023242

Cover design and maps by KaeDeNoki,

Image by Hazel Wastnedge@NightCafe

for Julia

'Semper in Cordibus Nostris'

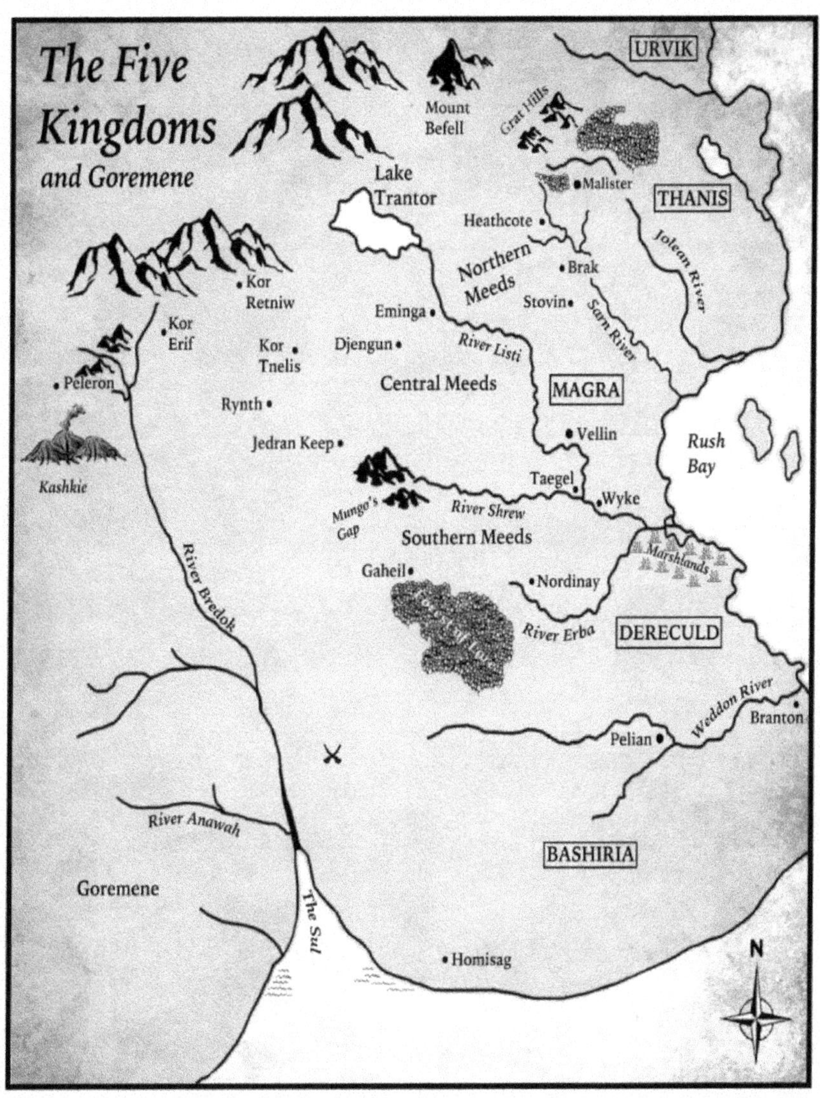
The Five Kingdoms
and Goremene
Mount Befell
Grat Hills
URVIK
Lake Trantor
Malister
THANIS
Heathcote
Northern Meeds
Brak
Jolean River
Kor Retniw
Eminga
Stovin
Sarn River
Kor Erif
Kor Tnelis
Djengun
River Listi
Peleron
Central Meeds
MAGRA
Rynth
Vellin
Rush Bay
Jedran Keep
Kashkie
Taegel
Wyke
Mungo's Gap
River Shrew
Southern Meeds
Marshlands
Gaheil
Nordinay
River Bredok
River Erba
DERECULD
Weddon River
Branton
Pelian
River Anawah
BASHIRIA
Goremene
The Sul
Homisag
N

6

The Gathering

I. Encounter

Where should I begin this account of my history? Should it be with my childhood? I doubt it, for I was a precocious child, often spoilt by those who cared for me and cherished by a patient and wise father. Should it commence with my wedding when I was adored and admired by all? It was a time of much celebration and posturing, a time of pretentiousness and personal delusion. I revelled in my achievement, my ambitions fulfilled. I shimmered in my own glory and was blinded to everything except what I had accomplished. Foolish girl!

I will not start with my fall from grace, the painful journey to the North and incarceration. No, I shall not begin with such misery, for I wish to render an accurate and balanced view of my life. The fearful desperation that I felt in those early days of my exile might well taint my recollection of the events that were to follow.

Instead, I shall begin with an encounter, an unexpected meeting that pleases me to retell.

It was daybreak. Dawn's ribbons were fading on the eastern sky beyond the ghostly hills. With their heads in cloud and their feet in the meadow mist, the peaks of The Grat Hills floated like a land of spirits, but on that morning, their nether world held little interest for me. The forest enthralled my senses. Dew dampened the hem of my gown and brushed my ankles. Even though the sharp chill in the air shortened my breath, it was my favourite time of the day. I was out in the woods picking wild herbs to enrich Martha's stews, and I relished their aromas as I plucked their stems. Wild garlic, nettle and lesser celandine leaves were already in my basket, and I knew a hollow, carpeted with rampant mint, where thyme and sage grew among a scattering of stones. I suspected that these stones were the ruins of some crofter's home in times past, the herbs the only remnants of a vegetable patch. I was often grateful for their legacy. On earlier foraging walks, I had come across a spindly rosemary bush, and thanks to my pruning, it now stood sentinel on the rise above the ruins. Its perfume filled my nostrils as I cut sprigs using Cedrick's wool shears. Martha would not loan me her precious kitchen scissors.

Such was the hierarchy that drove our daily lives. The kitchen provided ready pleasure for us all, and therefore, Martha had to be obeyed and frequently praised for her efforts. Though her rations were often meagre, she produced appetising meals that rivalled any magical potion conjured by a wizard. Besides which, we all loved her despite her acid tongue and sharp temper. In times of sickness, she would tend us like a wise mother, but if we invaded her kitchen, she was likely to scold us worse than her tirades to her unproductive chickens.

Martha's brother, Cedrick, was the closest thing to a bailiff within our little domain. He cared for our larger beasts and supervised our small company of field workers. They were drawn from the nearest villages or were Cedrick's relatives. They worked hard, ate the same fare as we did and had their share of the mead we produced. At lambing or harvest time, we worked shoulder to shoulder. We often agreed that our small community was a model of equality from which the world outside might learn. Of course, that would never happen because out there, beyond the river, beyond the boundaries that had become my world, was greed, pride, and ambition. We had all but banished those notions from our minds.

I did not hear him approach, and he stood watching me in silence until a slight shift in his stance caused me to look up.

"Forgive me," he said in the thick accent of the region, "I did not mean to startle you, but you are on my land."

I gaped and hurriedly looked back towards the east. The ruins must lie beyond the line of stones that marked the boundary. It was not hard to trespass in the woods. The marker stones could be missing or overgrown. I had often spoken to Cedrick about it, but he simply shrugged. In my innocence, I had wandered further than I intended. The punishment for trespass was at the discretion of the landowner, and in all the years of our exile, I had never met our neighbour.

"I am Lord Elderin of Brak, and these upland forests all belong to me, except the little patch that circles the Castle of the Lady." The Castle of the Lady! That's what the local people called the grey towers that I knew as Roth Manor, or more recently, home. He took half a step towards me.

"By your dress, I suspect you are from that place, so I will honour your mistress by not exerting a fine for your folly, but I would know your name."

My name? Oh, folly, my name. "Kate, my Lord, it's Kate!" I gave him a belated curtsey, then marvelled at my own foolishness for doing so.

"Well, Kate, your trespass is forgiven," he smiled. It was an honest, open smile that creased the corners of his eyes and formed small dimples in the corners of his lips. Thick, nutbrown hair framed a clean-shaven face, a sign that he cared little for the courtly fashion of beards. It was a face worn by the elements, thin, sun-kissed and quick to express his thoughts. His tunic bore the emblem of Brak and was made from fine wool and leather.

"You search for herbs?"

"For the kitchen at Roth," I answered and showed him my basket. He glanced down at the contents before reaching for my right hand. When I gave it to him, he turned the palm upwards.

"But you are not a cook!"

"No, My Lord." I hesitated with my explanation while he was already following his own logic.

"You are a gentlewoman, and The Lady needs good companions." He smiled again. Grateful that he was not pursuing my trespass, I smiled too.

"Well, Lady Kate, you may visit my forests whenever the fancy takes you. You have my permission and protection." He lifted my hand and kissed the back of it. Experienced as I was in courtly manners, still I blushed and felt the urge to run away, not because I was afraid, but because I had the need to giggle, like a young girl. He took my haste as fear of being late.

"'I often walk here at dawn," he called after me. "Perhaps we shall come across each other again, Mistress Kate."

"Perhaps, My Lord!" I blurted it out, giving him a swift curtsey before hurrying back down the track towards the boundary markers. I didn't slow down until I was out of the woods. My heart pounded, and I was grinning foolishly. I was still grinning as I crossed the courtyard and slipped into the kitchen with the herbs.

What a saintly existence you must think that we led at Roth Manor! Indeed, compared to the lives we had known in the royal court, we lived simply enough and with little ceremony. But our days were filled with activity, working, undertaking tasks that were not unpleasant, and our rewards were comfortable days that we enjoyed, and evenings warmed by good companionship.

There was music and poetry, and sometimes we would sing long into the darkness, valuing our pleasure over the value of the tallow we used. But that encounter with Ross, Lord Elderin of Brak, had left a strange impression upon me, and I found myself collecting herbs more frequently than I had done before. This drew several comments from Martha, but if my other companions suspected more than a predisposition to taking early morning walks, they said nothing. It was the first but not the last time Lord

Elderin and I found ourselves in the same part of his forests. We said little, content to observe the morning, while gathering sprigs of this and that for my basket. I suspected it was not to gain knowledge of the herbs that he came, for after one such forage, Martha's eyes widened as she held up a clump of ragwort.

"What's this? Trying to give us all a bellyache?"

"Perhaps she was distracted!" Grace rolled her eyes as she took the offending weed and threw it on the fire, where even its burning was slightly acrid. "At least she brought the basket back." I could tell from Grace's suppressed grin that I would be quizzed further about my dawn dalliances. Perhaps my eagerness to collect herbs had become suspicious, but Grace would wait until we were alone to probe my motives. It was fortunate that other events would occupy our minds before her inquisition.

The following morning, I was back in the woods, carelessly adding sprigs of mint to my basket in the light of an early sun. The forest smelt fresh after the rain of the previous day, and the musk odours of the ground were pleasing.

"Good morning, Mistress Kate!" Ross Elderin said, climbing down into the hollow. In heavy travelling clothes, with a sword hung from his belt, he wore the same open smile that I'd found hard to dismiss from my memory. "I have been hunting with Lord Anard, and I am on my way back to my home in Brak. I wondered if you might be here."

"You came here, My Lord, before returning home? What will your wife think?" The remark was clumsy, but his admission had surprised me.

"She would be jealous… if I had a wife," his left eyebrow lifted as he smiled, "but as she has not married me yet, then she can hardly chastise me." He pushed his wayward hair from his eyes. They were hazel, almost dark gold in the forest light and accustomed to merriment. He offered me a buttercup. "I thought about you while I was hunting."

I laughed. "That is a strange thing to confess!"

“It was strange for me too. The hunt usually fills my mind, but as I rode along, I began to notice herbs and flowers in the hedgerows, and I thought about you.” He reached for my hand, and I allowed him to take it. He kissed it gently. “Have you visited our wood while I have been gone?”

“Every day,” I confessed, and knew that I was blushing. We regarded each other, neither of us knowing what to say next, then a hunting horn sounded and he winced.

“My people are eager to be home.” A second kiss was planted on my hand. “Until tomorrow, Mistress Kate!”

We parted, and I found my legs were a little wobbly as I walked back towards Roth. I chastised myself for behaving like a silly girl. I was not young, and neither was I silly. Usually. Well, not for a long, long time.

There were three horses in the courtyard. They had been ridden hard and were still steaming as Martha’s nephew, Jack, attended them. I went in through the kitchen door, and Martha looked up.

“There’s men here from Vellin. You’d best get up there.”

II. VISITORS

I heard their voices as I changed my gown. They were below me in the hall, male voices and one familiar female voice, Rosamund, Senior Lady in Waiting to the queen. Faithful, stalwart Rosamund, who had followed her queen into exile, forsaking her pleasant life in the court. She was speaking calmly to the agitated young men who were all so eager to deliver their messages. As I climbed slowly down the back stair, my hand tracing the curve of the stone walls, I could hear Rosie offering them refreshment, and the ensuing silence meant they were accepting it. Her back was to me, watching the three young men eat hungrily, so I sat on the steps until I felt they had been given enough time to eat. Then I went in.

"Ah!" she beamed, relieved to see me, as small talk was not the reason why Rosamund of Thanis was valued as a lady in waiting,

"Gentlemen, Her Majesty, The Queen!"

I offered my hand, and each came, bending at the knee to kiss it, while Rosamund introduced them. For a brief second, I remembered the last time that my hand had been kissed.

"This is Lord Heathcote's knight, Sir Stefan," Rosamond said as the bulky knight rose from making his obeisance. He wore the purple, heathland colours of his master and the insignia of The Palace Guard. Heathcote was the oldest of my husband's councillors.

"Master Flyn Norton, nephew to Lord Norton of Camlan and this is …" She paused, uncertain of how to introduce The Mantle, who had not given her his name.

"Lady, I am a messenger from my lord, Conrad, Master of Mantles." He bowed. "My name is not important, only my message." He bowed again.

"And what message would that be?" I smiled at them all.

Faced with delivering their news, all of them became reluctant. Finally, Flyn Norton, who so resembled his uncle Tertius, with his chestnut curls and dark eyes, took a deep breath. "Madam, we have been sent to inform you that your husband, the King, is dead."

The room fell silent. I think Rosamund might have gasped, but apart from that, there was not a sound.

The birds had stopped singing, and even the kitchen noises from below were stilled. I felt my rib cage sink towards my feet, drawing ever tighter on itself as it fell, until there was an empty space where once my lungs and heart had been. I could breathe while my eyes swam with sudden images of a young lord, his long blond hair shimmering in the sunlight as he rode towards me, a single red rose in his hand. He leapt from his horse and drew me into his arms in one swift movement, planting a hot and hungry kiss on my eager lips.

Then I recalled the disappointment in those same eyes as he looked down at the body of our firstborn. The pain was followed by anger and recriminations. In his rage, he would often tell me that I should be dead beside our baby son. From that moment, his eyes had turned from me. He gave his love to others. I was no longer welcome in his bed, then in his palace, and finally in Vellin. I was dragged from my apartments in the night and bundled into a closed carriage, like a criminal. The next thing that I saw as I stepped from that bone-shaking box was Roth.

Flyn Norton fidgeted, drawing me back.

"Thank you, gentlemen, for your message. You may rest before your return to Vellin. I shall write a letter to each of your masters thanking them for their thoughtfulness." I went to the window to feel the morning breeze. The room, it seemed to me, was hot and airless. "You may tell them all that I shall arrive in Vellin in four days' time, after I have put my household in order. I intend to bring a small retinue with me, for we have a royal funeral to prepare."

"To Vellin, Majesty?" Rosamund came to my side. "You intend to go to Vellin?"

I patted her arm before addressing the three young riders. "Now, if you will excuse me, sirs, I would like to be alone." I did not wait for a reply but escaped to the staircase and my chamber with as much dignity as a sudden widow could summon. There I composed the three short messages in a steady hand, steadier than it had any right to be. I was a widow. The word meant nothing. I had been without a husband or a title for too long. I did not dwell upon his loss, but for the kingdom, it could be devastating.

I sent the notes down to the young men who were enjoying my household's hospitality, no doubt relieved that their interview with the cast-off queen had been brief.

I lay on my bed for a long time watching the shadows move across the ceiling. I could not cry. The King had robbed me of my tears long ago. I felt nothing. No, worse than that, I felt empty. I am obliged to go to Vellin in order to publicly mourn the man who had banished me from his side over twenty years ago.

Well, I could do that. Had I not been trained to do such things? I was the daughter of a king, the granddaughter and great-granddaughter of kings. My lineage went deeper than a broken marriage. I must assume the role that I had been trained for. I would be a royal widow that they would all remember.

After watching the young Mantle point his horse in the direction of Vellin, the first of the messengers to depart, I returned my writing table and began to draw up plans for my husband's funeral.

The household was subdued that evening as we shared our meal. Those destined to accompany me to Vellin did their best to hide their excitement from those I had selected to remain at Roth. We all knew that I needed to rely more heavily on those remaining than ever before. They were the keepers of all my secrets, and our destinies were closely entwined. Rosamund understood this when I told her that she must be mistress of the estate in my absence. I had no idea what awaited me in Vellin, and I would not risk the safety of those I held most dear until I judged that it was safe for them to follow, or I returned to Roth. We retired to my chamber together to discuss the details of her custodianship over a goblet of mead.

"There is much to do if you are to be in Vellin in four days," Rosamond said as we concluded our planning. She drained her cup and sighed. All our plans had been laid, and it was time to retire.

She spoke in a softer voice. "I did as you bade me and sent the message to Lady Lamfrik at Stovin by way of the young nephew of Lord Norton." Rosamund was accustomed to knowing all my thoughts and plans. "Was there any particular reason why you chose Norton's messenger and in such secrecy? Could I not have asked any of them to deliver the note?"

"Tertius Norton and I were childhood friends. His father was Chamberlain to my father. We grew up together. Of all my husband's councillors, I trust him the most, not because he is a paragon of virtue but because I know him too well. By asking his nephew to perform a small task for me, I have also sent a subtle message to the uncle - I still trust you, Tertius." I had not seen The Lord of Camlan for twenty years. I wondered if he would understand the significance of The Queen breaking her journey at Stovin.

Lord Lamfrik's wealthy manor, with its oversized hall, had been little more than a fortified farm, but it stood on the edge of a garrison town where the elite royal cavalry was based. It had profited from the garrison's continual need for food and ale, and Lamfrik had built his fine keep and cavernous hall from the proceeds. It was three hours ride from Vellin if the rider was young and rode at a gallop. It was to Stovin that Tertius had been sent in haste to begin his military training when we…

Well, all that was a long time ago but perhaps he felt some lasting fondness for me, as I did for him.

"This is the Tertius who wrote the poetry book you have in your chamber?" Rosamund's eyes widened. She had begun to brush my hair, as sisters might do while sharing their evening secrets. In our household, the duties of my ladies had long ago ceased to include the necessary preening of their queen. I could brush my own hair and even repair my own gowns and gardening britches.

"The same," I nodded. "As my husband's chamberlain, I doubt that he has had much opportunity to write poetry in recent years.'

"Oh, Madam!" Rosamund was suddenly gleeful. "Do you think he …?"

"I think he will remember a past that we both share, and that he might be a useful friend when I reach Vellin. Of course, he might have forgotten such childish things and be just another ambitious politician. Remember, he is married to a wealthy and influential woman and thoroughly soaked in courtly intrigues. I would like to think not, for both our sakes. I can only hope he has not forgotten me completely."

"He would not do that, Madam." She drew my hair away from my face as I studied how the years had changed my features since the days when I secretly met Tertius Norton in the palace garden. She asked, "Will you stay in bed a little longer tomorrow?"

"No!" I spoke too eagerly. She regarded me thoughtfully but said nothing. "I shall miss my walk through the woods and would like to do it one last time before I leave," I explained. "I doubt that I will be able to gather wild herbs in Vellin!"

It was foolish of me. I should have anticipated that The Lord of Brak would also have heard of The King's death and would be occupied in making plans of his own. The woods were empty that morning, except for rosemary, sage, and thyme. I gazed beyond the ruined croft to the boundary stones and felt that emptiness. For years, I had found solace in my morning walks until the day I encountered Ross Elderin. Since then, he had occupied more of my thoughts than was his right, and now I must put him out of my mind in favour of Tertius Norton and the court politics of Vellin.

I had little time to brood over my disappointment. Rosamund had already assembled gowns and the few baubles I had been permitted to keep. She demanded my agreement on which to pack. I reminded her that I would be travelling in a small carriage and would not have pack animals following in my wake. Cedrick had mustered the most able-bodied of our men and equipped them with what armour and weapons were on hand. This motley company was to be my royal escort, and while I appreciated my bailiff's concern for my safety, I doubted they would be much defence against an unlikely assassin. The last evening at Roth was more miserable than I could have imagined. I knew that I was leaving all that I loved and had grown to love in Rosamund's safekeeping, but the separation would be painful. We were all reluctant to go to our beds, preferring to talk, to reminisce and to avoid all thoughts of the morning.

In my chamber, I conjured images of my childhood and the Vellin that I remembered. The memory had faded so, from lack of use, but I could picture the young Tertius Norton with his chestnut curls that framed his head like a crown and his dark brown eyes, cow eyes my father had called them. My father had not approved of my fondness for the son of his chamberlain. A royal marriage to a Norton would have given the rolling hills of Camlan too much power in the eyes of other envious fiefdoms.

The men of Camlan were already too proud and powerful. Instead, my father looked to the young men of his precious cavalry to settle on a husband for his fourteen-year-old child, a child who had been trained in the art of kingship, not for her own sake, but so that she would be able to advise and support her husband, the future king. My father was a great and noble king. His people loved him, but he was not a good judge of prospective husbands. Prowess in the lists and the geniality of the barracks were not qualities easily transferred to the role of husband, or even king, for that matter. Brodik, for all his golden hair and bronzed muscles, was a brute, and it was not long after our wedding night that I knew it.

I dismissed thoughts of my marriage. It rested on the same cold slab that a dead king now occupied. There would be an appropriate time to mourn both. I fell asleep imagining the scent of mint and the damp fragrance of forest litter.

We waved until our arms ached, long after we lost sight of the grey towers, we waved to our tenants as we passed their farms. Then we lapsed into silence as the landscape, turned grey by steady drizzle, slipped gently past us. How different to the threatening thunder of the night when we arrived at Roth, fearful of lightning. I had grown to appreciate the tempestuous weather of The Northern Meeds, and perhaps the limp landscape outside our carriage was a foretaste of our reception in the capital.

There were four of us within the carriage and two manservants riding with the driver, young Jack and another of Cedrick's cousins. Grace sat facing me, her head deep within her book. Rosamund, her cousin and I had both considered her as my best choice to fill Rosamund's place. Like Rosamund, Grace had gone into exile with me, and although she was not as close to me as my dear Rosie, she was my friend, as well as my servant. Indeed, I rarely considered the ladies of my court as anything but friends and never as servants. Lady Grace had been raised at Court and knew all there was to know about courtly manners. She would manage my small company without my supervision, and I could rely on her discretion. The cousins shared the same pale skin and blond hair, now fading elegantly to grey. Slender and serene, her fondness for reading had been responsible for encouraging our whole household to read both for pleasure and to broaden our education. When the number of children at Roth started to increase, Grace was the natural choice to tutor them. We also shared a sense of humour, and it was often Grace who could detect when I had something on my mind. She felt my eyes on her and looked up from her pages. I smiled and returned my eyes to the passing forests. She immediately returned to her book.

Shana, the youngest member of my party, sat next to me. She was the orphan of two of my tenant farmers, both dead in a barn fire when the girl was a babe. Martha had adopted her with the idea that she could train the child in the kitchen, but it quickly became obvious that my ladies had no intention of allowing the pretty creature out of their company. Shana had been welcomed into the growing number of children and was a favourite amongst all the adults. Perhaps we had all spoilt her a little, but her cheerful and open nature endeared her to all who met her. We loved her thick, curly black hair that forever escaped from the confines of pins and combs. She would sing her way down corridors and sit until dawn, eagerly finishing some delicate needlework. Shana had been overjoyed to be included in our company, as she had never been much further than the market in Brak. Trying to contain her excitement, she began to chatter to the final member of our company, who was happy to answer her eager questions.

Lady Judith of Pellian had also followed me into exile, but her presence had not been welcomed, at least not at first. Like me, she had been cast aside by Brodik. She had been one of his first mistresses, installed in a small house close to the palace only weeks before our marriage. He had sent her to Roth as my personal gaoler, and in those early months, she was responsible for locking me in my chamber at sunset, and she accompanied me everywhere, often bemoaning the fact that he had not already released her from her task. Only when winter came, our first winter in a damp and leaking wreck of a prison, when food was scarce, and fuel for our fires was hard to come by, did our relationship change.

We had all been in a sorry state, starving and without hope. It was then that I took charge, summoning more courage than I thought remained in my heart. I wrenched the key from her hand and threw it into the moat. I bade her follow me, handing her an axe and taking up one myself. Rosamund feared that I intended to fight some sort of ridiculous duel with Judith, but instead, I went into the forest and began hacking at a sapling. My efforts were full of anger but ineffective, and I soon paused. Lady Judith, tall and statuesque, like some ancient war goddess, with fire in her eyes, just smirked, so I stepped aside and bowed to her. She raised her own axe and dealt the tree a mighty whack. The axe planted itself firmly in the trunk, and she gave me a triumphant grunt. I acknowledged her success and, triumphantly, she began to make headway in demolishing the tree. In no time, we were dragging it back to the yard outside the kitchen, where she began to divide the trunk while I detached the branches. Others came out to help. I returned to the kitchen with an arm full of kindling. The door was ajar, and I could hear their labours as I stoked our pitiful fire.

"Couldn't swat a fly, that one," Judith crowed as they worked.

"A queen shouldn't be expected to use an axe!" Rosamund countered.

"She's weak!" My husband's discarded mistress announced. "I had to do it. I chopped the whole thing myself."

"Ah!" nodded Rosie.

"What's that supposed to mean?"

"A queen doesn't have to know how to use an axe," Rosamund explained, "She has to know how to get someone else to use it and make them feel important when they have done so. That's what a queen does."

After that, Judith began to join us for our evening meal instead of eating alone, and gradually she became one of us. She was an asset. No one was better at organising Cedrick's work crews when there was something to be done that did not fit into their normal animal husbandry or farming tasks. Under her guidance, they built a bridge across the river to shorten our journey to market. She supervised our tenant farmers into a cooperative so that we could get the best prices for all our produce. She even persuaded the tenants to plant diverse crops for sharing and crops that would bring in more profit rather than those that their families had always subsisted on. But her favourite pastime was learning the skills that my father had taught me. I showed her how to wield a sword and use a bow. In no time, she had outstripped me in skills and strength, and so while it was my custom to gather herbs for cooking and medicinal use, it was Judith's delight to set out before dawn to hunt venison for the pot.

Now she was coming with me back to Vellin, back to confront memories of that life she had once been reluctant to leave. At first, she had refused to come, insisting that they needed her at Roth. I convinced her that I might need her more in Vellin. She would be my sword arm, the protector of the Queen's person.

"You have the tongue of a fox, Majesty!" She had shaken her head when I told her. "You know I can't resist that challenge, and a pox on any man who tries to lay a finger against you while I'm there!" Looking across the carriage at Judith, who was gazing out of the window, I wondered what thoughts and fears passed through her mind. I suspected they were just as confusing as mine. We had both been very different people when we left Vellin.

The fiefdom of Stovin belonged to Lord Lamfrak, a man who preferred the solitary, stoic existence of a scholar to the gregarious nature of his court, filled as it was by officers and noblemen affiliated to the cavalry. His wife, Lady Greer, presided over his great hall while her husband spent his days in his library.

The arrangement appeared to satisfy them both.

It was Lady Greer who strode to greet us in her crowded inner courtyard, her thick corkscrew curls escaping from the braids wrapped about her ears. It appeared that the cavalry itself had left the barracks to take up residency among the gaudy tents of the troubadours and whores, the purveyors of pies and trinket sellers. Shana blinked, her eyes wide with amazement as we threaded our way towards the great oak doors of the hall. Inside the throng was no less thick, and the air was heavy with the smoke of roasting pigs.

"As you see, Majesty, there are many others here tonight." Lady Greer waved her arms helplessly. "It will take my cooks the whole night to feed them all, but have no fear, your supper awaits in the rooms prepared for you and your ladies."

"Who are all these people? Why are they here?" Shana asked, avoiding a pair of legs that jutted out from under a table.

"Why? They are all on their way to Vellin for the King's funeral! The lords will gather there to begin the excessive ritual of claiming their right to the throne, and every footpad and pedlar able to walk will flock there to entertain and rob the crowds." Lady Greer took my arm and ushered me to a stone stairway. I saw Judith stiffen, but it was not the time, nor the place to stand on royal ceremony. The throngs that had claimed hospitality that night had overwhelmed Lady Greer and her servants.

"My bailiff counted forty lords and their retinues, then he stopped counting," she confided. Lady Greer left us at the threshold of the chamber she had prepared. It was her own, with a great bed wide enough for all of us. It bore the faint odour of her husband's pet hounds. Theirs was not a love match, but the joining of two great families for the betterment of both. Lamfrak and Greer soon found that although their appetites differed in many things, they quickly became appreciative of each other's strengths and so lived in happy liaison with each other.

The supper was tasty, mutton pies and fish from the manor lake, followed by dainty pastries seasoned with honey. We fell upon it with little delicacy and washed it down with rough ale. Three of us took to our bed immediately, but Judith was restless and announced she would go down into the hall to listen to gossip. I hoped that the temptation of free ale and the company of men would not sway her from my service. I should have been more trusting. When she returned, she sat at the end of the bed and told me of the rumours.

"There's a strong following for the Lord of Camlan. They think he will demand the crown, but Lord Strewan has his supporters, too. Some fool was saying that The Mantles planned to take over the whole country and kill as many lords as they could catch. I even heard that there was a prophecy concerning the Lords of the Green Isles returning to claim the land." At my side, Shana stirred in her sleep, and I stroked her hair gently.

Judith grinned. "It is like a bear pit down there. There's a wrestling match and card games everywhere. Some of the cavalrymen are holding a cock fight in the entrance, and the lords are mingling with the common people until it's hard to tell them apart, save for their fine clothes." She paused, listening to the clamour below. "I did recognise Lord Elderin, of Brak. He's here too, though I always thought he had little love for The Royal Court."

I tried to control my face, showing just an appropriate amount of interest in a neighbour. Thankfully, Judith had consumed enough ale not to notice the slightest change in my expression

"He asked me if Mistress Kate was accompanying The Queen," she laughed.

"And what did you say?" I knew that the question had fled from my lips far too urgently, but Judith shrugged.

"I said yes! Though I'm sure we have no Kate at Roth." She guffawed and slapped my leg. "And there was a whole crowd of Mantles in a little huddle, all muttering and whispering to themselves. I went over to chat to them, but they are so proud and protective of their virtue that they just fell silent until I walked away. Rude morons, that lot!"

"I wonder why Mantles are here," I asked, eager to divert Judith's attention away from the mysterious Mistress Kate.

She yawned. "You can bet they're up to no good. I wouldn't trust that nest of charlatans and their magic further than a cross-eyed pig can spit! Still! We'll find out in the morning!" With that, the ale defeated her, and she curled up, fully clothed, across the bottom of the bed, and slept.

Indeed, in the morning, we found out why Mantles were at Stovin. Their senior presented himself at the door of the chamber, the same man who had brought the news of Brodik's death, this time with a message from Conrad, Master of Mantles himself. In his neatly crafted message, he begged the privilege of providing an escort to Vellin for the royal party. They were instructed to protect us with their lives and suggested that we make haste to depart before many of the revellers awoke. The thought of Mantle protection did not inspire my confidence, for I had assumed I did not need protecting at all, but I agreed to the proposal and badgered my ladies to make haste. We were dismayed to find our driver and his cousins drunk and snoring with the rest, so after thanking Lady Greer for her hospitality and asking her to send the men back to Roth when they were sober, we continued our journey, our coach driven by a Mantle. As we proceeded southwards in the grey dawn, I began to wonder if my bold gesture to return to Vellin might place us all in danger.

III. Vellin

Our escorts were courteous but hardly convivial. They flanked our carriage but made no effort to communicate with us except when we needed to pause for Judith to relieve herself. She was sporting a headache and spent most of the journey sitting with her eyes tightly shut. The clouds were heavy and threatened rain, but since the day was mild for the time of year, we rolled up the heavy curtains that shielded us from the wind and prying eyes. A few miles from the city, we began to notice that small crowds of people had gathered beside the road. At first, the groups clustered in the centre of their villages, but as we progressed, they spread out from the villages along the high road. They stood quietly, their heads bowed, the men bareheaded, the women and sad-eyed children.

"They're here for you, Majesty," Grace said softly in her lilting Thanis accent that reminded me of the sea and salt-laden winds.

Outside our coach, the silent throngs watched us pass and then shuffled back to their lives. Even when the rain began, we saw them standing beyond the veil of drizzle, and all the time their numbers were increasing until they lined each side of the road, a human palisade sometimes five or six deep. Occasionally, they threw wildflowers. Otherwise, they were still and silent, and all I could do was peer out at them from my small carriage window.

Our escorts appeared to be as shaken by their number, bemused by their stoic composure. I was humbled by their presence. By the time we reached the city gates, the people filled the streets, and every window seemed to hold a solemn face. Blacksmiths stood before their smithy, an innkeeper and his serving girls rubbed shoulders with merchants from the market, children huddled in the mothers' skirts, their faces pinched with the cold, and off-duty soldiers held their helmets under their arms.

The vast open square before the pale walls of the citadel was thick with people, and the Mantles struggled to make a path for the carriage.

"Stop here!" I called the senior Mantle. He looked doubtful, but the driver had reined in the horses at the sound of my voice.

"Madam, this is a dangerous place!" The Mantle advised.

"I thank you for your concern, Sir, but you have seen the people. There's no danger here. I beg you, take most of your men and wait on the other side of the gates. You may leave a couple as my escort, for I intend to walk through the gate. The people have waited a long time to see me, in foul weather, and see me, they shall."

He bowed low and gave the order, then helped me to step down from the carriage. A gasp went around the square as the coach carrying my ladies clattered through the opening gate. I faced the people of Vellin, their queen, back from exile and in the black weeds of a widow. Slowly, I lifted my veil.

"I thank you, all of you!" I called and heard my voice echo down the alleyways towards The River Listi. In the silence I heard sobbing.

"A blessing on you, Queen Katherine!" a man's voice yelled.

There was silence, then the crowd took up his blessing, some cheering, some slapping the sticks and staves they carried. I listened and nodded to show them that I understood, and we stared at each other, my people, and their queen. I loved them for their love.

Slowly, I replaced my veil and walked through the gate, which began to close after me. The cheering and blessings continued as I made my way up the steep causeway towards The Citadel, the castle that I was born in and had thought would always be my home. It was a homecoming that should have gladdened my heart, but there, awaiting me on the broad steps, leading to the ornate doors and marble vestibule beyond, was my welcoming party, the King's Councillors and Conrad, Master of Mantles.

"Majesty, welcome! The people have all come out to show their sorrow for their departed king." Heathcote, the oldest if not the wisest of my husband's advisors, bowed low and kissed the hand that I offered to him. He had changed little, gaunt and thin, his hair longer than I recalled. He had grown to prominence in my absence, perhaps through his shared pleasure in hunting beside my husband. His manor was to the north of Magra, and since his rise in prominence, it had been successfully managed by his wife, Lady Maud.

"It would seem to me that they wanted to show their love, not sorrow, for their queen," Tertius Norton said. Shorter than Heathcote, tall beside Strewan, and younger than both. He took my hand, which I had been preparing to give to The Master of Mantles. "Welcome back to Vellin, Your Majesty. You have been too long away." His eyes were mischievous, just as I remembered them, though the face around them had aged and the brown curls were now thinner and faded to the colour of weathered wood.

"It was not of my doing, Tertius, as you well know." I smiled at him quickly and then turned back to The Mantle.

"My Lord Conrad, I must thank you for your kind gesture. Your escort from Stovin was greatly appreciated. I do hope that you will invite me to visit The Talarin soon. I have fond memories of The College of Mantles under your predecessor, Lord Jollian."

"It will be my pleasure, Madam." Under Conrad, the Mantles had transformed from a homely collection of magicians, ridding kingdoms of plagues and conjuring weather, to the austere warrior magi that had formed my frosty escort. I did not doubt that they continued to perfect their magical arts, but wondered if the nature of their powers had grown darker under Conrad's elevation to leadership. I was grateful when he quickly excused himself, although he promised to return later for a private conversation with me. That left me with the remaining three men who had wielded the power behind my husband's throne.

To be sure, they had done it successfully. The kingdom was wealthy and healthy. The governance of the fiefdoms was fair, taxes were well within the purse of manors and cities, and, for the most part, people seemed content with their lives. All this was due to Heathcote, Strewan and Camlan. They had also proved moderately effective in keeping the King's excesses in check.

There was little left of his own wealth. Indeed, he had spent most of mine, which had become his at the time of our marriage, but the councillors had kept his spendthrift hand well out of the country's purse. So, the Treasury flourished.

"You must be tired after your journey. We have sent your ladies to occupy the chambers we have prepared for you." Strewan had intended to usher me to the great staircase, but I made for my husband's favourite room, only second to his bedchamber. It had been my father's library, and his books, dusty from lack of use, still decorated the walls. One wall had been cleared and on it hung the trophies of my husband's greatest pleasure: deer heads, wolves, bear and smaller trophies of badger and fox. A small arsenal of his favourite weapons was displayed beside the hunting trophies. I mused that if the heads or lower body parts of his many paramours were to be mounted here also, it would leave very little wall space unoccupied!

"I am weary, My Lords, but also anxious to hear what preparations you have made for my husband's funeral?" I sat in my father's favourite chair, now threadbare and as uncomfortable as ever.

Heathcote answered. "We have had the King's body embalmed. The Mantles took care of that, and it lies in state, in the royal tomb below our feet." He hovered over me, a gaunt, bony man with large knuckles and bushy eyebrows. His face might have once been kindly, but now it was so old and wrinkled it was difficult to detect any expression at all. "We thought that the entombment should take place in two days with a solemn feast in The Citadel for the lords and perhaps extra alms for the poor and sick."

"Is that all?" I looked from face to face and when Strewan nodded, I sighed heavily. "Then it is not enough My Lords. Brodik was your king, entitled to a king's funeral."

"We thought that as he left no heir and that any further celebrations might inflame the situation and …" Strewan's voice withered away to silence.

"He was The King." I rose from my father's uncomfortable chair and went to the corner of his desk. How often had he reminded me on this very spot of the due that should be given to The Royal House? I now reminded my husband's councillors.

"A dead king should be seen by his people. He should rest in The Mantle Sanctuary at Throdin and from there be brought down the river by royal barge. His coffin should be drawn through the streets by black horses and then placed in the tomb."

"But...," Heathcote licked his thin lips, "he wasn't very popular towards the end."

"That's immaterial, Lord Heathcote!" I felt my fists tighten. "He was The King."

"It's a very difficult situation, Your Majesty," Strewan whined. "We want to get this over quickly, not because we disrespect The King, but because of the unrest it might cause. We want to send the crowds home as soon as possible. A city full of people, thick with lords and their private militias, it is asking for trouble. Someone will insult someone else. The brawl will become a riot, and before we know it, there will be civil war!"

"I thought the general opinion was that a civil war is inevitable," I replied, trying the chair my husband had placed behind the desk. It was uncomfortable, too. "And I am sure that even the most uneducated dolt clearing slops from an alehouse knows that my husband did not name a successor. Any uprising and challenge for the throne will not depend on the quality of the King's funeral."

Lord Norton of Camlan came to my side. "How should we bury your husband, Madam?"

I gave him a weak smile. "As I have said, Tertius, the sanctuary, the barge, the solemn procession to The Citadel and the entombment. Then, in the evening, food should be distributed, and coins given to the poor. All orphans are to be fed in The Citadel courtyard, and a feast should be held for the lords and their retinues. I have already sent mead from my own estate to toast my husband, enough for every fiefdom. The morning after would be a perfect opportunity for an audience with all the lords in The Great Chamber. You may then address them with your plans for the succession… if you have formulated them."

The three of them looked blankly at me. Of course, they had not considered anything beyond their own hunger for the throne. Did they expect me to return to Vellin without a thought in my pretty little head? Did they not suspect that I would want to give my husband a king's funeral?

"How many days would it take to complete such an undertaking?" Camlan was warming to the idea, or trying to gain favour with me, or both. That was something about Tertius that I suspected would never change. He was his father's son and had learnt the art of political persuasion and pragmatism at an early age.

"Four days," I told him confidently. "I have already sent messengers downriver to Wyke, where my father's barge is kept. It is being restored and painted as we speak, and should be brought up the river under the cover of darkness, drawn by horses. It will be moored on the river below the sanctuary at Throdin the evening before the funeral. The body must be taken to the chapel as soon as possible, tonight, if it can be done. I am sure Conrad would be only too delighted to provide an escort and an honour guard to remain with The King until the body is put on the barge. I will accompany the barge back to Vellin and through the city."

I turned to Lord Strewan. "You, My Lord, have a reputation for organising memorable feasts. As a great kindness to me, would you undertake to organise the banquet and alms for the poor?"

"Most certainly, Majesty. It will be my honour. I will have special bread baked to be distributed throughout the city, too." Strewan was also well known for his obsequious deference.

Heathcote was not going to be outdone by Strewan. "Then I will undertake to supervise all the other arrangements for the day, My Queen. You may be assured that all will be in readiness. You must not distress yourself about anything."

"Bravo, Majesty!" Camlan applauded after the other two had scurried off to begin their preparations. He sprawled in my father's seat. For a moment, he was the same charming boy I had once known. "Give them something to think about, and they'll forget the bigger concern they had when they came into this room."

I stretched back into my husband's uncomfortable chair. "You credit me with too much guile, Tertius. I simply want to give my husband a fitting funeral."

"I would have thought burning him in a tar barrel might have been a more fitting end, after all the wrongs he has done you."

I offered him a fleeting smile. "I doubt if that would impress the people of Magra, or the lords. The country should unite, even if it is only for a few short hours, to mourn the passing of a king. No one cares what kind of husband he was." I stood. "And now I am truly tired and would like to see where my ladies have put my things." I started for the door and then stopped. "Where is The Lady Alice? What have you done with her?"

He appeared flustered for a moment. "I have done nothing to her."

"Where is she?" I repeated.

Tertius looked alarmed. He shook his head slightly. "She's little more than a child, Kate. Let her be. I'll have her gone from the palace today."

"Where is she?" I demanded slowly, advancing on him.

"In The Rose Tower," he answered, his head bowed.

"Don't worry, Lord Camlan, I have no wish to harm her, but I would like to look at her. I have one of Brodik's mistresses in my service already. Perhaps I should gather them all together and create a sisterhood!" I swept past without looking at him. He still smelt of the polish he applied to his leather doublet and his horse's saddle.

On my way to The Rose Tower, I passed my guest apartments. I knew where they were because I could hear Shana laughing. It was a welcome sound in the impersonal air of The Citadel. They were unpacking our trunks, but my young lady-in-waiting had found a black cape like the one worn by The Mantles, and she was marching about with strands of hair under her nose like a moustache. They ceased their merriment when they saw me.

"Forgive me, Lady, I meant no disrespect!" Shana curtseyed.

I placed my hands on her shoulders. "And I saw none, just a young woman cheering her companions. Although I doubt Conrad, Master of Mantles, would appreciate your impersonation." They had already begun to unpack familiar things and arrange them about the room, spreading tapestries and coverlets on the bed.

"We have much to do ladies, and I have tasks for you all, so please make haste and turn this barracks into a queen's apartments. I shall be with you soon." As I passed one of the great mirrors that my father had imported to please my mother, I paused. The last image it had offered me was of a young girl, flushed with joy as she prepared for marriage, her red hair bound in braids and bright-eyed. Now I saw a middle-aged woman with skin that had been weathered by northern winters and hair fading quietly towards grey.

The Rose Tower had been a favourite haunt of mine as a child. It was a slender structure with a small room on each of its four levels and was topped with a roofed parapet. The second-floor room opened out to a narrow garden, which also served as a private entrance to The Talarin, The College of Mantles. As a girl, I had been allowed to use this doorway whenever I chose, but now I discovered that it was locked from the Talarin side. My memory stirred. My father had caused that door to close and the realm beyond to be forever forbidden to me. How strange that I had forgotten so much. I rolled my hand over the smooth brass doorknob. Such memories! But I had something I must do first before allowing myself to evoke the past. I climbed higher in The Rose Tower.

When Alice opened the door, I could see that she had been crying. Her red-rimmed eyes were ringed with dark shadows, and the expression of horror that spread over her pretty face when she saw who had knocked on her door was pitiful. She immediately dropped into a deep curtsey and remained there even after I had walked into her chamber and positioned myself against her weak fire. The room was damp.

"You need a larger fire, Lady Alice, or you will catch a chill." She whispered agreement but remained on the floor. This delicate waif was not what I had expected. My husband's taste in mistresses had varied over the years that we had been apart, but for the most part, he had shown a preference for voluptuous, tall, big-breasted women, amazons who often matched him in height and sexual appetites. This wisp of a girl with her thin face, large violet eyes and straw-blond hair must have prompted something other in Brodik's mind than simply lust.

"Oh! get up child, do, or I shall be forced to come down to your level if we are to have anything like a reasonable conversation, and my knees are not happy to be pressed against such a cold stone floor." I sat in one of the two chairs that had been placed by the fire and threw two logs into the flames. She looked alarmed. "I will have more wood sent to you, if that is your fear," I told her.

She rose to her feet but waited for me to beckon her to sit. The discomfort in facing me was almost too much for either of us to bear. This young girl had been my husband's mistress for almost two years. Rumours told of a besotted king who had lavished gifts upon this dainty creature and was a fool to her demands. The urchin that faced me hardly seemed capable of such capricious behaviour.

"How old are you, child?" I asked.

"Fifteen, Majesty." She sniffed.

"I married him when I was fourteen. Did you love my husband?" The question appeared to surprise her, and she blinked but gave no immediate answer, so I repeated it.

"I," she hesitated, then muttered, "he was the king."

"That's no answer! Did you love him?"

"Yes!" Her eyes dropped to her hands on her lap.

"And did he love you?" Her eyes fluttered up to hold mine for a brief moment, then went back to her hands.

"No." She seemed to be struggling with a memory or perhaps how to put the memory into words. "He never loved me. He told me that. He liked my body. He said it made him feel young." Ah, was that her charm? Did she remind him of his earliest conquests? He often boasted of deflowering all the young virgins on his father's estates.

"And did you like his body?"

She gasped. "You can't ask me that!" Her indignation was real.

I stood. "I was his wife, his queen, your queen! Of all people, I alone have the right to ask you that. He had promised his body to me, but he gave it to you and all the others before you. I have every right to ask you."

I knew I was standing over her, and she must have felt threatened. After all, I could have her banished, or worse. The man who had protected her was dead. By making certain that she had no friends at court, he had isolated her. She had been his property, now the chattel of a dead man. She looked down at the stones close to my feet and drew one deep breath.

"I didn't like his body. It was old. He was heavy. Sometimes he was rough and hurt me." She looked up at me, squarely, into my eyes for the first time. "But he was the King, and I had been given to him by my father. When I tried to run away, he beat me with the flat of his sword. So, I accepted my fate and decided that if this was to be my life, then I must live it as best I could."

She bit her lip. "I had always dreamed of being a good wife, with children, and being the mistress of my husband's home, but fate had given me to The King. I didn't want to spend my life feeling miserable, so I did what I could to please him. I played his games, and sometimes it was almost like love."

"And the other times?" I asked in a soft voice.

"He forced himself upon me."

Defiance and challenge spread across her face. She understood that we shared far more than just the man. We had shared the torment that he could inflict. Her body had not been one to relish but to ravish and conquer, over and over again. I resisted the impulse to gather her into my arms. Instead, I went to the window, giving her time to regain her composure. Or was it to help me to retain mine?

"What will you do to me?" she asked in a small voice. What indeed? Clearly, the councillors had anticipated a vengeful retaliation, at least Tertius had, who should have known me better.

I returned to her and allowed my first smile to warm the room a little. "I will do nothing to you, Alice. Enough has been done to you already. You are free to do whatever you wish to do."

She blinked with disbelief. Her jaw dropped, and her lips began to quiver.

"But where will I go? I cannot return to my family. I have no friends. What shall become of me? All I know is how to be a whore." Her eyelids struggled to contain the tears escaping down her cheeks. How dearly I wanted to throw my arms about her.

"Shush!"

Her clear understanding that she no longer had a place in the world drowned any fear she had of my wrath. How well I knew that despair!

"You may stay here if you wish." I sat and faced her, reaching to take one of her hands in mine. It was icy.

"I have need of a lady-in-waiting. I can think of no better choice than someone who has often been allowed to observe the politics of the court without taking part in them. You do not have to decide at this moment, for we have other things to discuss, but you are welcome to come and meet my ladies and share our evening meal. There are also beds in my antechambers that are warmer and more welcoming than this one."

Lady Alice was bewildered by this turn of events, so I pressed on with my next proposal. "I am determined that my husband will be given a king's burial and have arranged for his body to rest in The Sanctuary of The Mantles before it travels down the river to be entombed. Will you come with me on the eve of the funeral and hold night vigil by his body? I want the people to see that we, you and I, are at peace with each other and are sisters in our mourning."

This was all too much for the girl, and she began to sob.

"It is important for both of us, Alice," I told her, rubbing her chilled little hand. "Everyone will see that there is no animosity between us and that I accept you. This will make you less of a target for those righteous fools who forget that you had no choice in your fate, and it will help me to be seen as the noble and forgiving queen."

"If," she bit her lip, "if you wish it, I will certainly come." She rubbed her eyes, then suddenly looked alarmed. "I don't have a dress for funerals."

"My ladies can help you there." I stood and offered my hand.

"Come with me now and meet them. One of them has a great deal in common with you. She was my husband's mistress too!" Alice stopped and looked at my face, trying to detect some sort of lie or cruel joke, but when she saw me smile and nod, her eyes widened. "You do not jest?"

I shrugged. "I do not."

She allowed her drawn little face to find a tentative smile and willingly took my hand. As we made our way back down the

Rose Tower, I wondered what Judith would make of her and, indeed, what Alice would think of Judith.

This was all too much for the girl, and she began to sob.

"It is important for both of us, Alice," I told her, rubbing her chilled little hand. "Everyone will see that there is no animosity between us and that I accept you. This will make you less of a target for those righteous fools who forget that you had no choice in your fate, and it will help me to be seen as the noble and forgiving queen."

"If," she bit her lip, "if you wish it, I will certainly come." She rubbed her eyes, then suddenly looked alarmed. "I don't have a dress for funerals."

"My ladies can help you there." I stood and offered my hand. "Come with me now and meet them. One of them has a great deal in common with you. She was my husband's mistress too!"

Alice stopped and looked at my face, trying to detect some sort of lie or cruel joke, but when she saw me smile and nod, her eyes widened. "You do not jest?"

I shrugged. "I do not."

She allowed her drawn little face to find a tentative smile and willingly took my hand. As we made our way back down the Rose Tower, I wondered what Judith would make of her and, indeed, what Alice would think of Judith.

IV. Farewell

I had been correct in assuming that Conrad and his Mantles would relish the opportunity to display their importance to the throne by escorting the king's body to their sanctuary at Throdin. They agreed to provide an honour guard both during the hours of darkness and later when the body travelled down the river to the city. The Master of Mantles also furnished us with a fine, black carriage to transport myself, Lady Alice, Judith, and Shana to the sanctuary.

We arrived at twilight. Light was still in the sky, but dark, scudding clouds promised a starless sky and rain. It was hard not to notice my companions' reluctance to be in such an austere and lonely place.

Perched on a cliff overlooking the river, the sanctuary had been a place of worship long ago when the Old Ones still ruled such wild places. Judith looked about her as if she expected some fiend to come out of the night to terrorise us, or was she afraid that Brodik's shade still clung close to the empty shell it had once inhabited? When I looked at the pinched faces of Shana and Alice, I wondered if I had been wise to bring them, but the services they were to perform, one to play the part of the forgiven mistress and the other to prepare me for my performance as the mourning widow, I knew their presence was essential.

When the Mantles first commandeered the ancient site, they removed the old altars and shrines, replacing the earth floor with an ornate mosaic of the pentangle, the five-pointed star which represented their own inner circle of powerful men, The Souran. Conrad commanded them as Silver Mantle, the wearer of the cowled cape embellished in silver, but the identities of the other members of this clandestine cabal was a closely guarded secret. There were rumours that the king's councillors were involved, but I doubted that, having known that in my father's time, the remaining four Souran members had been itinerant magi, only returning to Magra when summoned by Silver Mantle. They spent their lives moving through the kingdoms and beyond, gathering knowledge and safeguarding land and people. I could not believe that Conrad would change that custom. He alone ruled in Magra, training his elite warrior-magi in the secret world within The Talarin.

Beside the sanctuary was a small alms house, maintained by Mantles and offering accommodation as well as rudimentary healing skills to travellers. Two palettes were prepared for Judith and Shana. Alice and I reluctantly left them there, finishing off a supper of mutton stew beside a warm fire.

Our escort of six Mantles arranged themselves around the rough plaster walls of the small sanctuary. With their heads bowed and eyes closed, resting their hands on the hilts of their broadswords, and the dark shadows of their uniforms shuddering in the candlelight, it was easy to imagine them as stone statues from the past. Holding hands, Alice and I approached the open coffin in the centre of the room. My husband's face was peaceful in death, a testament to the embalmer's skill rather than a true reflection of how he had looked in life. He was dressed in chain mail, and his helm rested between his feet. His pale blue surcoat was decorated with the black boar of the Lords of Gaheil, his mother's family, and above his left breast a small, rampant, yellow lion encircled with laurel leaves, my family crest. I doubted that Brodik had ever worn such a garment and wondered if The Mantles had included the lion as a mark of his kingship. I touched it gently. Alice shivered, hovering at his feet, afraid to approach, but I wanted to look down on him.

"You've grown fat and paunchy, husband, and that rose in your cheeks and nose is from too much wine." I placed my hand on his cold cheek as I whispered. "Late nights, gambling, and drinking have fashioned apothecary bags under your eyes! You look old and worn. Yes, worn like an old carpet. Do I surprise you with my candour, my dear? Surely, you did not think I would say you look calm and regal?"

"Oh! Truly, you do look pleased with yourself, so satisfied with your life, so completely certain that you have been successful. Popular! Effective!" I leaned in towards his face, the perfume of embalming oils not unpleasant.

"But you are not victorious, my love. You defeated no one. Your only battles were in the bedchamber with defenceless women, and even in those skirmishes, you won nothing, no heirs, no lasting memory of your mediocre reign. But you knew that, didn't you? That's why you kept conquering, even when your power had all but shrivelled away." I looked briefly at Alice, but she remained in the shadows well away from the body.

"You used a young girl, little more than a child, to make you feel powerful and all the while, my poor dear monster, you had no idea, had you?" My voice was little more than a whisper as Alice drifted away, taking her place on the cushions provided for us.

"There was a victory, Beloved, and it was not yours but mine! Yes, it was mine. Poor, weak Kate, who would have followed you into the darkness of death if you had asked her, when we were first married. I have the victory, not you. You cannot harm me now, and it is time that I showed both you and my father that his teaching did not go to waste. Kingship is an art that you did not care to master, but I have. Oh, how I wish you could see it happening, but that is your punishment. You won't see it." I kissed his forehead and then took my last look at the man whose cruelty and neglect had so shaped my life, in ways not even he could know.

No Mantle sentry stirred. Perhaps they had heard my words, ready to recall them before Conrad, but it was unimportant. I was surely a resentful widow venting her bitterness on a lifeless body. I sighed, and in the gloom, sat beside Alice, my husband's last victim. Above us, the walls of the sanctuary rose into darkness, quivering and trembling in the flutter of candles. I held her hand and waited for the long, dark hours to pass, my thoughts not on the reign of a dead monarch but on those I had left behind in Roth, those whose lives would be changed by the death of this unfamiliar body.

Conrad arrived before dawn. He entered the sanctuary quietly and appeared surprised to find me standing beside the coffin. The cold of the floor had seeped through the velvet and brocade cushions. I had risen to bring life back into my tingling legs. Alice lay fast asleep, wrapped tightly in my cloak.

"Forgive my intrusion, Madam, but it is almost dawn." He bowed low. It was the first time I had ever seen him exhibit deference. "I sought to wake you, but I see you were determined to maintain your watch."

"I am not as resolute as you imagine me, Master Conrad. I did sleep a little, and I thank you for all that you have organised for us here." The light was growing slowly, and I could see the young men around us standing to attention in the presence of their leader. They too had dozed and were resisting the urge to yawn.

"I did not rouse your ladies, but the kitchen servants are preparing a warm porridge for breakfast. No doubt, your women will wish to help you prepare for the river journey." He offered me his forearm, as a prince escorting his lady might, and I lightly rested my hand on it. We walked out into the chill morning air, savouring the view of mist and river below us.

In the rosy skies of the coming dawn, the fearful beauty of Throdin becomes apparent. Shards of rock rise out of the fast-flowing river as it skirts the base of the promontory, creating currents and eddies. Tenacious trees and shrubs sprouted from the crevasses, and small finches flitted among the branches. We watched in silence, each of us locked in our own thoughts. Conrad noticed my reaction to the cold, damp atmosphere and removed his silver cloak as he spoke, gently placing it around my shoulders. The gesture surprised me, and the reaction on my face amused him.

"My predecessor spoke very fondly of you, Madam. After his retirement, I would often visit him in his rooms and spend the evenings in pleasant talk. He liked to recount his small memories of your childhood and how you took delight in visiting the Talarin. He did confide that you also took instruction from him."

"Master Jollian was like a second father to me," I said, pulling the cloak closer about my arms. The material was unfamiliar, at once comfortable but also strangely unsettling. This was the emblem of his office, revered by all who knew the power of The Mantles, and yet he gave it to me to protect me from the cold dawn.

"He once told me that you had …" He paused, then faced me. "You were an unusual girl."

It could have been the coldness of the dawn, or perhaps my old limbs reacting to their stiff state, but I felt the touch of ice inside me. His dark eyes fixed on mine, and I feared what I should say next. Could this man really have the power that the Mantles of old exercised?

"I think I learnt some trickery from him that amused my father." I dismissed the event but suspected we both knew that what had happened in the Talarin during my visits to Master Jollian was far more startling than a trick to please my father.

Indeed, it had not pleased my father. Reviled words, when delivered in my father's voice, were spat from his mouth. Most dread of all was 'witchcraft'. All children knew old tales of wicked witches, with their evil spells and of their gruesome ends. My trick had brought the end to my visits to The Master Mantle and the arrival of a tutor who spent long hours drilling me in the skills my father knew I would need. When I was older, I sometimes wondered what the difference was between that loathed word 'witch' and that revered title 'magus'. Of course, I knew. The magi were all men.

Conrad touched my arm. "If you had been a young man, after such a demonstration, you would have been invited to join our number."

Recognising that he must have known the truth of the incident, I gave him a side-long glance. “If I had been a young man, I would have been a king!” It was the first time I had seen amusement and gentleness in his stormy grey eyes.

After a long moment, he removed his hand from my arm. “Know that you will always have the protection of The Talarin.” The warmth in his face was gone. He gave me a stiff bow and returned to the sanctuary to issue new orders to his men.

I found myself thinking of this new, gentler yet somehow disturbing Conrad, while Shana and Judith prepared me for my journey down the river, accompanying the body of The King. It would be our last journey together. My ladies knew the importance of this morning, and they used their arts to turn a country matron into a regal mourner. Alice tried to help when she could, and I was pleased to see my ladies treating her as one of them.

When all was ready, Judith and Shana returned to Vellin in Conrad’s carriage. The Mantles moved the coffin to the barge down the narrow steps hewn into the rock. Alice and I followed cautiously. A slip would mean falling headlong into the torrent below or being impaled upon the pointed shards of rock rising from the riverbed. The narrow path ended at a wooden jetty, carefully constructed to offer boats a safe passage well away from the torrents that swirled at the base of the pinnacles.

At the wooden jetty, Alice took her seat at the back of the barge. Conrad took my hand to help me aboard. I turned to thank him, and instead of releasing my hand, he kissed it. Long after I was seated behind the body, long after Conrad had watched us leave the shore and had turned his horse towards Vellin, the turmoil of my hand being kissed unsettled my composure.

Had I not been kissed on the hand before? Why, it was only a few days since Ross Elderin had done the same thing. Was I so easily moved? Why was it that Conrad’s lips on my skin had shot tingles through my body and shortened my breath? I admonished the foolishness of such thoughts and focused on the marble-faced body before me. Today, the people would expect a queen in mourning, and I would not disappoint them.

The six oarsmen from Wyke guided the barge into the middle of the river's flow. They knew that their labour would be lighter there and the barge would have a passage clear of sandbars. My Mantle escort faced the riverbanks, their solemn, silent guard only broken once when a mallard, disturbed in the reeds, flew out suddenly. One young man, as startled as the duck, let out a cry and stepped backwards, almost toppling into me. I gave him a brief smile as he rushed to regain his position and his composure.

The river carried us downstream at a stately pace as the dawn broke and the mists thinned and lifted. The air was still, and only our movement through the water encouraged the black standards to flutter above our heads, death ravens escorting the soul to the shadow valley of The Old Ones. On the riverbanks, the trailing willows in spring bud and the tall rushes waved softly as we passed.

Here and there, short wooden jetties thrust into the stream and on every jetty, the people of the river had gathered. Others waited on their long boats, tethered to the banks the previous night. Gradually, as we drifted southwards, the crowds lining the banks swelled. Some had waded into the shallows for a better view. They threw flowers that joined us on our journey, and we became a flotilla of petals. From bridges, they tossed blooms, their forlorn faces gazing down at us. By the time the first riverside wharves of Vellin came into view, it seemed that half of Magra was at the water's edge. They watched us pass in silence, sometimes in tears. Others began to follow our passage, keeping a respectful pace with the barge along the towpath, their movement mirrored in the calm stillness of the river. Only the oars disturbed the surface as the barge turned gracefully landward to reach the final jetty, decked in King Brodik's standard of a raging boar.

The crowd stood motionless as the body in its coffin was transferred to the back of a flat cart, gilded and adorned for the occasion. They joined behind us in procession as King Brodik passed through his city for the last time. Every street was a sea of faces, young and old, noble and pauper. There were more flowers, some rushing forward to place them on his body, while others threw them before the horses' feet. By now, a pale sun was high in the sky, shrouded by a blanket of translucent cloud.

"Bless you, Queen Katherine!" a voice called out, and it was answered by muted agreement. As we neared The Citadel, the throng was so great that there was hardly room for the horses to pass. The Mantles began pushing the people back, and I feared that their actions might incite anger, so I hurried quickly to the head of our procession, touching the arm of the Senior Mantle as I passed.

"Gently, I beg you," I spoke softly, and he nodded. We proceeded to The Citadel Square in this fashion. I walked ahead of the horses, and the Mantles flanked the cart.

The great space before the gate had been reserved for the lords with their gaudy retinues, whose banners and flags fluttered in the gentle breeze. It was a colourful pageant for such a sombre occasion, out of keeping with the subdued dignity of the common mourners, but I scarcely noticed them. The lords must wait for another day. The Citadel gates opened, and the cart passed through. I turned back to the people and bowed my head slowly towards them, once, in humble thanks, before the gates were closed.

The councillors and Conrad were waiting on the steps. "Welcome back, Majesty." Tertius bowed low, and Heathcote was beaming.

"Quite remarkable, Your Majesty!" Strewan fluttered like a plump, annoying moth. "I had my doubts about such a lavish affair, but I have to admit it all went beautifully."

"Indeed, it did." Conrad came to my side, and I hoped that none of them could see how his presence flustered me. "My Lady, I take my leave of you." He reached for my hand, and I feared that he might kiss it again. Instead, his hand held a key, which he passed to my palm without the others seeing. "As Castellan of the Talarin, I was entrusted with this and believe it was once yours. It should be so, again." He bowed to the councillors and strode away.

"Extraordinary fellow!" Heathcote exclaimed as I slipped the key into my pocket. "Madam, allow me to escort you to your rooms. You must be exhausted and hungry, too. The entombment can proceed without you. You will need to conserve your strength for the evening's banquet with the lords."

"It is my duty and my wish to see The King join his predecessors, Lord Heathcote." I waited for him to offer his arm, and we all followed the coffin down to the cellars below the castle. It would be brief and without much ceremony. Alice was also present as they lowered Brodik into the stone sarcophagus and covered him at last with a carved likeness of himself, but as a younger, warrior king. Each of them felt compelled to offer a final complement then they lapsed into dutiful silence. I ran my hand gently along the larger sarcophagus of my father beside my husband, but I did not linger. Neither did the councillors. They returned to my father's library with me, leaving only Alice to shed a final tear either for herself or the man she sometimes cared about.

"Madam," Strewan waited for me to sit in my father's chair, 'all is prepared for the banquet this evening, but…" He hesitated, looking to Heathcote for help.

Heathcote stooped towards me. "Madam, we were wondering what you propose to do after today is over." He tilted his head slightly, waiting for a reply.

Tertius was more direct. "What he wants to know is when you will be returning to Roth?" He perched on the edge of the desk. I was sorely tempted to push him off, but I simply nodded.

"I have given my plans very little thought, gentlemen," I lied, "although you may rest assured that I intend to remain in the palace until my husband's successor is found to ensure the peace." They appeared to be divided in their emotions about that news, so I explained.

"I assume you are all concerned about the threat of civil war, and I share your fears. The people are also afraid of what might happen. You saw how eager they were to welcome me. I am their symbol of stability, someone who has been distant from courtly intrigue and power. They see me as someone that they can trust. I doubt any of the lords will wish to show their hand through force while I am in mourning. This should give you gentlemen enough time to hold your discussions, or whatever you need to do to prevent blood being spilt."

Heathcote nodded slowly. "It might work," he conceded.

"There are some very power-hungry men in Magra," Strewan's eyes narrowed. Was the little man thinking of his own bid for kingship? Would a figurehead queen keep an uneasy peace long enough for him to gather a larger following?

"I think it's a good idea." The Lord of Camlan appeared to have few doubts. He already possessed a well-equipped private army. Even as a child, Tertius had keenly felt his obligation to restore Camlan's power, and through his careful management of its lands and townships, he had brought prosperity back to the valley of the Listi. I admired him for it, but it did not give him the right to be a king.

I could see that Heathcote and Strewan were less convinced, so I tempered my words. "Of course, My Lords, if you feel that I would serve Magra better by returning to Roth, I will follow your advice. My lands in the north prosper, and I have no wish to hamper your difficult task with my presence."

Heathcote straightened his back to its great height. "Majesty, your understanding of our predicament could only come from someone who has been aware of the government of The Five Kingdoms since birth, and we are grateful for your experience and your offer. We welcome your wise and calming presence. After all, this is your home."

"So, is it your intention to attend the meeting of The Lords?" Strewan ventured, his scheming weasel's eyes were little more than slits in his chubby face.

"Only if you advise it," I smiled humbly. "Naturally, I would not participate in your deliberations. I would be there solely as an observer."

"But perhaps an observer who could continue to share her observations with her husband's councillors?" Heathcote was almost grinning. Ah! He had found a use for the queen. She could be their spy.

"If Master Mantle Conrad would not object to my presence?"

"What if he does?" Heathcote gave me a paternal shrug. "The Mantles have no official power in our assembly."

"But it is ultimately their right to name the new king," I corrected him. "Or are you planning to waive that ancient custom?"

Heathcote stiffened. I did not need a Mantle's insight to see that he at least had considered such a possibility. "Rest assured, Madam, there will be a naming ceremony by The Mantles, shall we say, their participation will be restricted to that ceremony. The lords do not require the College of Mantles' superstitious nonsense to divine our next monarch. We can do that for ourselves."

Tertius spoke, "Of course, Your Majesty is mindful of the traditions behind the naming of a new king, and you are quite right in your wish to see such ceremonies continue. The people expect no less, and we have no desire to change that. It is simply that we feel that the lords should have the final say in the selection." So Tertius, despite his acknowledgement of the role performed by The Mantles, was also eager to discard time-honoured traditions. These men, who had steered the country to prosperity and peace, risked everything they had achieved because of their own ambitions. I needed time to consider how that would affect my own future and safety. I thanked them for their understanding and support in honouring my husband in death, but craved time to return to my chambers before the evening's feasting. As I left the study, I had one more request to make.

"My father loved this room. It was his sanctuary and a place where he could speak freely with his councillors, such as your father, Tertius. It was a place of contemplation, of calm and solemn decision-making." I waved a hand in the direction of my husband's trophies. "These are out of place here, don't you think? Dead relics of a dead king! Could we not remove them?"

Heathcote promised it would be done that very day, and he was true to his word. The next time I entered the room, the bare wall was covered with tapestries. Even the chairs had been exchanged, but were no more comfortable than those they replaced.

Back in the comfort of my apartments, I had little time to enjoy the warm bath my ladies had prepared for me. Grace had already arranged the gown and jewellery for the evening's banquet, and Shana set about redressing my hair as soon as I perched myself on the stool before the mirror. Shana always chattered away as she worked. Over her shoulder, I could see Grace shaking her head, so I asked what troubled her.

"This banquet!" She looked to Judith, who nodded for her to continue. Clearly, there had been some discussion before I arrived. "You had little rest last night, Madam, and tonight you must face the whole court. I worry about your health."

"I am grateful for your concern, ladies, but you forget that after I have graced the high table and accepted their profound expressions of sorrow, I shall be encouraged to leave so that some decent drinking, gambling and goodness knows what else can take place."

I had no illusions. "My greatest fear tonight will be trying to keep a serious face as they tell me how pleased they are to see me back in Vellin, all those stout and noble gentlemen who lifted not so much as an eyebrow when I was ejected from Vellin. It will be amusing to hear them say how much they respected my husband and how they will miss him, particularly the ones who covet his crown."

"I have a few scores to settle on my own account!" Judith concurred.

"Not tonight," I warned her. "There will come a time for you to exact your own revenge, dear Judith, but not this night. Tonight, we will be the epitome of reconciliation. Smile sweetly on them all, but keep any daggers in your mind."

"I don't trust these scheming men!" Judith insisted. "I will keep a dagger in my kirtle too, just in case. If someone so much as gives you a cross glance, I shall be ready for them."

Grace chuckled. "Have no fears, Judith, they will all be on their best behaviour tonight. The Lady of Roth has set them such a fine example of decorum. Nothing will happen tonight."

As fate determined, something did happen at the banquet, which did disturb my sleep, but it had nothing at all to do with any fear of meeting the pretenders to my husband's throne, and therefore, I had not been prepared for how deeply it affected me.

V. Banquet

Legend says that the great hall in the palace at Vellin was constructed not by the craft of the stonemasons but by the arts practised in The Talarin, that the College of Mantles designed and built it during one midsummer's night, while the king and his court were in the forests of Wyke hunting boar. A Bashirian legend about the same event says that construction took over four hundred years and was entirely due to Bashirian slave labour. Everyone from the architects down to the wretches who dragged the enormous stones from the quarries in The Meeds was said to come from Bashiria. It is hard to give credence to this second version of events, as Bashiria has no stone building of note in the entire kingdom. Their local fiefdoms prefer to demolish any predecessor's lodges in order to construct their own. These have traditionally been of wood, which is plentiful, and mud, which is abundant in a land of marsh and forest.

When I was very small, my grandfather, King Rolland, would tell me a different story. He said that The Mantles stole their tale from the truth, that the whole of the castle keep had been built by The Old Ones in the time of the first true king of Magra, Kelin of Ulomsk, the legendary warrior chief from Urvik. They had taken much longer than one night but had indeed moved the pink granite slabs from their quarry in The Meeds without the aid of man or beast.

Whoever built the great hall, it was constructed of cubes of granite, the length of two men's arms, above which were smaller slabs and finally vaulted galleries of stone and wood with pointed arches. Niches lined the walls, adorned with the statues of previous kings, including ancient Kelin. The flags of the two hundred fiefdoms hung from the beam and tile ceiling.

Entry into the hall is via a walled courtyard with stone and wooden colonnades on all sides. Few can pass through the lofty bronze doors without marvelling at the intricate reliefs of ancient warriors and flying creatures. Servants come and go from twin arches on either side of the chamber, one which leads to the kitchens, the other to the upper galleries and the rest of the palace. I had descended the great stairway connecting the royal apartments directly above the hall many times, first behind my father and later on the arm of my husband. On the night of his funereal banquet, Tertius, Heathcote and Strewan escorted me down them.

They were dressed in the livery of their lands: Strewan in a surcoat of soft mustard and blue of The Eastern Marshes; Heathcote, as his name implied, in the dark red of the heather which grows on the moors of The Northern Meeds; Tertius wore the ancient purple and white of Camlan. The men of Camlan find it hard to forget their past, when the whole country paid homage to the king who ruled Camlan. The men of the rich farmland had been powerful then, and none would challenge their power, just like the great hall we stood in, it was the power of The Old Ones.

As a boy, Tertius could make me laugh, his bright eyes sparkling with enthusiasm, as he proclaimed that he would one day restore the seat of power to Camlan. Perhaps that was why my father was so fearful when I showed a preference for his company. A struggle for power between Camlan and Vellin was not something my father would want to see in a kingdom he cared so much about.

My sombre grey gown stood out among the gaudy colours of the lords and their companies, just as Grace had intended. "They need to remember what the occasion is, my Lady, at least while you're among them,' she insisted.

I wore my mother's jet necklace and the matching crown that had been made for her by the artisans of Sarnmouth, who fished in summer and made exquisite jewellery from the black coal that washed up from the sea during winter storms. As I passed by where Grace sat with the other ladies-in-waiting and their escorts, she nodded encouragingly. Tonight, we were all on display. I noticed that she had enlisted Flyn Norton, the young nephew of Tertius, to accompany Lady Alice. It was a wise choice. Since delivering news of my husband's death, Flyn had become a favourite with my ladies, and it was clear Alice enjoyed his company.

Before the feasting began, there was the presentation of each lord, sometimes together with his spouse or a handful of his minions. For most, it was a brief salutation and bow with perhaps a thoughtful comment from me, their queen, but for some, it would be the first time that we had spoken since they watched me leave the city, imprisoned in a dark coach with my gaoler, the Lady Judith. She had pleaded not to attend the banquet, and I was happy to agree. It would be a painful reminder for all of us, and while I felt no need to ease the consciences of the lords involved, I felt that Judith should be spared the experience.

Those same lords and their ladies passed by me in a haze of woollen surcoats and richly decorated gowns, those highborn princelings of The Five Kingdoms. The King of Dereculd, my closest relative, my cousin, Delion, was delighted to finally meet me as much as I was to finally make his acquaintance. He was a young man, the son of my father's younger sister, who had been a small boy when I was exiled to Roth. Dereculd remained the richest and most prized fiefdom in The Five Kingdoms and was traditionally held by The Royal House.

If Delion had been a different man, he might well have challenged for the crown, but he was content in his present state. A serious, scholarly soul, he had founded a great seat of learning in his palace for philosophers and mathematicians. When Delion spoke of it, his face glowed with his passion. He wished only to enrich the lives of his people through the development of thinking. He paid great attention to the histories and honoured local ancient cults, such as The Sisterhood of Hope. He had enriched their secluded island retreat with his own wealth. With curling chestnut hair and soft green eyes, Delion had no wife but had brought three young scholars with him, and although their long eyelashes and athletic limbs had drawn the attention of many of the courtly matrons, it was certain that they only had eyes for each other and for Delion. It was clear to everyone that Delion could never be a serious contender for the throne.

"Your Majesty, we have brought a gift for you, a product of our humble labours!"

This was how Ransom Frain introduced himself before the herald could announce his name and title. The powerfully built man with thinning curly hair and eyes of palest grey bowed as he spoke and opened a small box in a graceful gesture for one so muscular. The box contained a belt of fine gold filigree work, certainly crafted by the finest goldsmiths in the land. It demanded to be touched, and I complied, feeling the curves and spirals dotted with inlaid gemstones.

"Mine Master Frain, I assume!" I smiled and offered him my hand to kiss. "Your smiths have surpassed themselves. It is a most beautiful and fitting gift, and I shall be delighted to wear it. Magra is grateful for all the treasures that The Mine Masters of Rynth bestow on our people."

"I am honoured to see the delight that it brought to your eyes, Majesty!" He towered over me, but there was a reassuring gentleness in his manner. "I hope I will have occasion to speak with you again before I leave the city. The Mine Masters wish me to convey their sadness at the loss of the king, and to pledge themselves to Magra's future sovereign." He held my hand for a brief moment too long, as if to press home some message, but I could not grasp his implication. I was still pondering on the strange look in his unsettling pale eyes when I turned to face the next in line.

"Lord Elderin of Brak!" The herald announced, and my hand was offered and taken before I realised who it was who stood before me. I could not hide my delight and beamed at him.

"Majesty!" He said stiffly.

"Lord Elderin!" I knew that I was gushing, "It is good to see you again."

"Indeed, Majesty?" He spoke the title with apparent distaste. His face remained unsmiling, and he looked at me as if I were a stranger.

"As a neighbour of some years, sir," I stammered. My ribcage tightened, and so did my throat. I felt I could not swallow.

"Of course, yes, as a neighbour!" Ross Elderin bowed slightly and kissed my hand, then released it as if to move away.

"And are you well, Sir?" I asked quickly, unsettling the herald who was already prepared with his next announcement. I wanted to keep Ross Elderin a little longer. I needed to see his smile and know that all was well between us once more. He looked impatient to be gone.

"Quite well, Majesty," he nodded coldly, "as I see you are. And how is your lady in waiting, Mistress Kate? How does she fare?" There was no humour in the question. His eyebrow rose slightly, and there was a snarl on his lips.

I said quickly, "Kate misses her friends, Lord Elderin."

"Then you must school her, Majesty, not to treat her friends so poorly and play unkind tricks upon them." He bowed again and stepped back, giving the herald enough time to interject with his next introduction.

Whoever that next lord was, I have little remembrance of him, his face, his wife, or his words of wisdom, if indeed he had any. My eyes and my mind were fixed on the back of Ross Elderin's head as he moved away from me, through the hall and back to his place at the opposite end of the room. He neither slowed his step nor glanced back at me as I concluded the introduction ceremony and took my place at the centre of the high table.

He must have felt my eyes on him as the first course of river trout arrived, and whenever I could escape from conversations, my attention went back to his table. Not once did his eyes drift up towards the high table. He was not subdued nor making merry, but was involved in the discussions that flew around him. He joined in when an animated discussion ensued, and he flirted with the portly matron across the table from him, but there was never a glance across the hall to see what I was doing.

Not even the harper, who took up his place in the very centre of the hall and regaled us with ballads of the old times, could keep my attention from straying to Ross Elderin, and despite the sumptuous feast that Strewan had provided, I felt hollow and empty.

The mere thought of those cold, frost-sharp mornings in the woods threatened to bring tears to my eyes, and I struggled to banish them. I should have told him the truth. I should have sent him word. I should have sent for him and explained. Now my folly had lost his good opinion, and I longed for his good opinion.

"Madam, you do little justice to the venison," Heathcote observed as he poured more wine for himself. I declined his offer to fill my glass.

"My dear lady," Tertius leaned towards me and gently placed his hand over mine, "are you not well?"

"A little overcome and tired," I confessed, although my reasons for feeling as I did would have surprised him. "I will retire to my chambers now, if you will excuse me, my lords."

I rose to leave the hall and was astonished to see every diner stop, some with their knives to their lips, and stand. Elderin's admonishment for his treatment had been so distressing that I had momentarily forgotten that I was a queen. The people who now stood looking at me were doing so because this was expected of them. If I chose, I could keep them standing there for as long as I wished. No one would resume his meal until I either sat or departed. I thanked them for their attendance and bade them enjoy their evening in memory of their king. Then, instead of scurrying away through the servants' arch as I had intended, I walked slowly through their middle. I gestured to my ladies to remain behind, but Grace stubbornly fell in behind me as I returned to the foot of the great staircase. I coolly passed by Ross Elderin, who now gave me his full attention. I neither acknowledged him nor any other, but climbed back to the warmth and safety of my apartments with all the dignity I could muster.

Later, when the pins in my hair and the grey velvet gown were removed, and my ladies were gathered in the ani-chamber, I confess, I cried. Of course, my ladies, hearing me through the thin door, believed it was the sorrow, the delayed realisation of bereavement, and the intensity of our days in Vellin that had overwhelmed me, and I allowed them to think that. There was no one that I could tell the truth to, and I missed Rosie. I might have opened my heart to her, and she would have curled beside me in the great bed, giving me warmth on the cold and lonely night. Instead, I slept fitfully. I dreamed of the woods, the herbs and wildflowers that grew there, but Ross Elderin was nowhere to be seen, neither do I think I searched for him. The dream was of home, those who waited there for me, and the simple pleasures that would no longer be mine.

VI. LORDS and LADIES

There were many sore heads the next morning, and many heads would struggle to see any of the morning. My own mood was sombre, and I was grateful that everyone around me moved carefully and quietly. As soon as I could, I escaped to the garden of The Rose Tower to walk in the river mists as they rose from the Listi. It was chilly pausing beside the deserted ramparts, but the strange light of the mist lifted my spirits. I relished the view down upon the shrouded river and the tops of trees. Through gaps in the mist blanket, I saw the small waterfall and close by a barge horse cropped grass.

"I hope it is a good morning, Lady!" said Conrad as he joined me at the wall's end.

"It is," I nodded, "but I confess to being nervous about this meeting with the lords. Perhaps they will think it impertinent for a widowed queen to attend."

He laughed, rich and honest laughter. "You are the dowager queen! It is your right to attend. We have no king, and until we do have one, you are the only regal personage on hand. You should have no doubts about your right to be there."

"I don't," I said, trying to sound confident, "but they might have doubts and strong objections."

He put his hand on mine as it rested on the pink granite, his skin warm and comforting against the cold stone.

"Why should they? You are there to give dignity to an occasion that otherwise might dissolve into childish bickering, if not utter chaos. They should welcome your presence. After all," he gave me a sideways glance, "you are not a contender for the throne. If you were, then you would be a very dangerous opponent."

He looked out across the mists, his eyes steady on the invisible horizon. He knew well that his words carried a deeper message that neither of us was able to voice. The words of the Mine Master the previous evening came back to me, and I felt my rib cage tighten. With an effort, I copied his stance, and we stood there in silence. Each one of us quickly became aware that we were listening to the voices in our heads, his voice and mine, without speaking, but sharing thoughts. It was a silent dialogue so honest and intense that I could not maintain it. I turned to face the garden with an involuntary gasp.

"So?" he spoke softly.

"So!" I replied, trying hard not to panic.

He faced me, the hint of a smile on his lips, his eyes gentle. "You know that I am always at your service. Whatsoever befalls you now and in the future, you can rely upon my support."

"Thank you." The mist was clearing, but a damp chill had seeped into my body. "Will you always be able to do that? I mean, slip into my mind?"

"Only when you allow it. It is the same for both of us. I have not tested how distant we can be before our thoughts cannot be shared, but I know that in the past, kings and their Mantles could converse across the kingdom. I suspected it was possible for us.

"Your father and Master Jollian could do it across Vellin, and you, yourself, as a child, heard Master Jollian from within the palace when he called from The Talarin. He told me himself, although he doubted you were aware of it as a child. I hoped it would be possible." He faced me, tentatively resting his hands on my shoulders. "It was once the way that a king was selected."

I opened my mouth but said nothing. I needed time to think about what had just happened. Conrad had conveyed so much in those few thoughts, mind to mind. He'd known my thoughts, and more, he'd known my heart and all the secrets there. He had accepted my secrets as his own and pledged to protect them. Most dangerous of all, he had known my plans, plans still in their infancy, hesitantly forming in my head. Unclear thoughts and aspirations that had existed in the back of my mind for a long time, fading with improbability and flaring again with the Mine Master's words. Conrad had known them before I had shared them with him, with anyone. How could he have known? More alarming, it seemed they were his plans too, the plans of The Souran themselves, who, so it would appear, still preferred their own methods of selecting a monarch. I did not doubt their loyalty, but I feared their involvement. I felt vulnerable and, not for the first time, doubted my own resolve.

"You have others who will stand beside you, powerful others who recognise the importance of a strong and just monarch."

His hands slipped from my shoulders, leaving them tingling, as my hand had tingled from the touch of his lips. We parted with no further words, after he had planted a chaste but no less disturbing kiss on my forehead.

The morning rolled by quickly, although I was too distracted, thinking of Conrad and his words, not to mention the internal turmoil caused by his touch. I tried to relish the pains my ladies took to prepare me for my first encounter with the lords.

Over a white shift, I wore a plain black gown, embellished by Shana's embroidery, matched with the simple net caul that tamed my red hair. I hoped I looked disarmingly modest, yet undisputedly regal, as I stood before the blackened oak doors of The Council Hall, with my councillors beside me. Tertius squeezed my hand and then withdrew his own. The doors opened, and the babble of nearly one hundred men flowed out past me. The noise subsided as they became aware of my presence, and a subtle murmur accompanied my procession into the centre of the room.

The granite chamber was almost a perfect cube in shape with arched windows high up on three sides. Heavy pennants bearing the emblems of the fiefdoms hung below the windows, and in the centre was a square table, large enough to seat every lord. Grandfather told me that the wood came from the forest beneath the ground, the forest in the heart of the world. Wherever it came from it was wood so unlike any that I had ever seen, ghostly white like the marble of a tomb.

Using Vellin as its centre, seating roughly corresponded with the geographic location of the fiefdoms. Each seat was identical, save for two. The pale, beechwood chair with its familiar pentangle identified the place reserved for The Master of Mantles, and on its left was the ebony throne of the monarch.

I sat in the ebony chair. Conrad was right. No one objected. Few could, as there were only two of us in the room who bore the blood royal, and Delion, recognised as a king in his own right, quickly seated himself on my left, followed by the councillors. Gradually, others took their places until the table was filled except for one seat. That belonged to King Freon of Urvik. He was sick and had sent messages of sympathy and apology. Conrad, at my side, told me that he had seldom travelled south to Vellin due to a weak constitution. He told me in my mind.

Heathcote began the proceedings, relishing his opportunity to drone on about the lords' ancient rights to assemble before their monarch. I looked around the table at the faces, some familiar, some unknown, the faces of men whose word was law amongst their people. Some I knew by reputation to be ruthless and vengeful. Others, like Elderin of Brak, were respected by their tenants and serfs. Brak had prospered under Ross Elderin's stewardship. He sat at the far end of the table, his eyes lowered, his hands resting on the polished surface of the nether-world table, such long, slender fingers, his thin face grave and unfathomable. I wondered how well he had slept last night and immediately felt Conrad shuffle slightly in his seat. I did my best to block him from my mind and caught the faint smile that disturbed his lips.

There was no confrontation that day. Perhaps Heathcote's and then Strewan's tedious speeches had dulled their enthusiasm, or perhaps it was the surfeit of wine and mead from the previous night. All those present swore an allegiance to their unofficial brotherhood, affirming their loyalty to Magra and honouring the power of the throne. It was then that Conrad rose to his feet.

"My Lords," he began, "the process by which a king is chosen has always been an honour bestowed upon the College of Mantles. King Brodik left instructions that he wished this tradition to continue." He looked to the councillors, who nodded their agreement. "Therefore, all those of high birth who lay claim to the throne are commanded to set out their claims and present them to The Souran within three months of this day."

"Three months?" Strewan spluttered.

"It is the appointed time," Conrad informed him before continuing. "Three months from this day, all should gather at The Field of The Pentangle, where the new monarch will be crowned, and all will swear allegiance."

"And what do we do in the meantime?" someone called out.

Conrad's words were measured but firmly delivered, "The King's Council remains intact and will continue to function as it always has. You may all return home in the safe knowledge that The Souran will make their choice fairly from the lodged claims. I see no other need for haste. However," he rested the fingertips of his right hand on the table and leaned forward slightly, "if you wish to appoint a figurehead to represent The Crown, I see no better choice than Her Majesty, Queen Katherine."

There was stunned silence, and although we had known each other's thoughts, when the words were said, they caused me to face him with a sudden look of alarm.

"Bravo!" Ross Elderin called from his place at the northern end of the table. "Why not have the queen? The people seem to like her. They appear to trust her, and it should keep them happy."

I glared at him but felt Conrad's foot close to mine, pushing at my ankle. Since I had blocked my mind, he was trying to control my responses in other ways. I decided to allow his thoughts back into mine.

Others echoed The Lord of Brak's sentiments. It could do no harm. Everyone respected The Queen. She would probably do a good job. She'd drawn quite a sober and respectful crowd on her way down to Vellin and at the funeral. Why not?

I smiled appreciatively at their kind words, and when it seemed appropriate, I offered my thanks for their trust. Heathcote, Strewan and Camlan all proclaimed the meeting as successful, and the company left with some measure of satisfaction.

Among them, there would be those who would be preparing their claims. Others whose claims were less strong would be plotting their strategies, considering allegiances, or even how they could offer their support to retain influence over their chosen candidate. What Ross Elderin was thinking about was unclear. He gave me a quick, cold glance as he left.

Even Conrad, Master of Mantles and I were making plans as we left. He had promised to meet with me again, on the morrow, on the battlements. We both knew there was much to discuss. I was grateful to my ladies for preparing a scented bath for me before they left me alone with my thoughts. I suspected that my earlier distracted grumpiness had convinced them to keep away from me for the time being. Judith and Grace sat mending and sewing by the window while Alice and Shana went off together, happy for a few hours of freedom. I was pleased to see them enjoying each other's company.

Later, before the light of the day was lost, I walked in the palace gardens, not the Rose Tower Garden but the flower garden that gradually and naturally turned to woodland before it ended abruptly at the steep cliffs of the Angirat. It was a place less frequented than the other formal lawns and beds, and it reminded me of Brak, and the gardens of Roth. I was lost in thought when I almost fell over the man before I saw him stooped over a climbing rose that had escaped its lattice support and was spreading across the pathway.

"It's Gwillem, isn't it?"

"It is Majesty," he bowed.

"I have been meaning to ask the councillors where you were. You were always at my husband's side. I had expected to see you when we reached The Citadel."

"I was like my king's third arm, Madam, but since there is a king no more, there's little use for a king's manservant. No one seemed to know what I should do, so Lord Strewan said I should retire. He said it would be for the best. I was granted life tenancy of a small cottage in the walls of the palace, but it doesn't feel right for me to just be idle. Not used to it, you see. Can't just stop doing things. None of the other gardeners seemed to bother with this little place, so I've taken it on. There's quite a bit of work to be done."

"There will be a king again soon, Gwillem," I assured him. "Then they will need a man of experience like you."

He laughed. "Nay, Lady, the new king will have a new manservant. Us older ones have to make room for the younger fellows. It's time I stepped aside."

"And all your wisdom and experience?"

He laughed even louder. "I didn't listen to experience when I was young, so I don't expect them to listen, either. They'll have to learn just as my generation did."

"So, if I asked you to teach a younger man all the wisdom that you have acquired, you would refuse?" I watched as he gently fastened the rose back against its supports. He had grown old in the years that I had been away, but his hands worked deftly to secure the thorny branches.

He stopped and looked into my face. "Are you serious? Do you expect the new king to have his servants trained by me?"

"I was thinking more of a young squire that I know who would benefit from your sound advice about courtly manners and responsibility. He is a fast learner, but I fear he needs someone older and wiser to curb his enthusiasm. Someone who is accustomed to influencing a younger man without causing offence or shaking his confidence."

Gwillem joined me on the stone bench. He was chuckling. "That's a skill I have perfected, Madam. Why, I had to watch for my head when I first served your husband! He'd cuff me about the ears or punch me full in the stomach for my mistakes in the early days. His temper was that short! He sobered. "Pardon for my rude words!"

"He wasn't opposed to boxing my ears or slapping me hard in the face, either!" I told him. "You know that. I remember only too well the day when you had to come between us to save my life."

He nodded. "Aye, I recall it. Wild he was sometimes, and always full of regrets afterwards. I know full well why he gave me that cottage."

His pain blighted his face, and he rubbed the side of his nose as if to redirect the growing tears in his eyes. It was a pain that we shared and one that I had thought I would never recover from, but I did. I took his hand.

"Breaking your silence would not have saved my baby, and when I was sent to Roth, louder and more influential voices than yours were silent too."

"Bad business, it was!" He agreed and sighed. He was quiet for a minute and then asked, "So there's a young squire you need trained?"

"Yes," I told him, "the son of a member of my household. He's a clever lad, and I think he could do well if he had the right man to train him. Would you take care of him, Gwillem, as a favour to me?"

He agreed to meet again and discuss the practicalities, then hurried off to burn the discarded rose branches before nightfall. My mind went back to that terrible night when wine had driven my husband's rage so far that he had beaten me and killed the child within me. The misery of that time still brought tears welling up inside, but time had lessened the pain to a dull ache, and since my removal to Roth, other joys had restored my spirits.

I had accomplished another part of the minor project that I had set for myself, small though it was, against the mountainous wave of tasks ahead. Satisfied, I wandered through the wood at the edge of the cliff in a better mood. The updraft from the cliff disturbed the branches closer to the edge, and the evening sunlight was coating the trees with gold that shimmered in the breeze. From the edge of the cliff, standing above the dizzy drop, I could look down on the jagged rocks below. They, too, glowed in the sunset. Dragon's teeth, Grandfather Rolland called them.

King Rolland could touch the mind of a Master Mantle across great distances, and my father shared a bond with Master Jollian. Did I wish for that kind of power, that connection? I was unsure. The thrill of showing my father how easily I could use my mind to lift and move his enormous war shield was still tinged with bitterness when the act had caused him to fly into a rage. For me, it had been a child's prank to show how clever I was, but to him it was wizardry in the hands of a girl. It was a thing to be squashed, exorcised from memory, a wicked display that disappointed and saddened him. I spent many weeks afterwards hard at my studies to show him that the incident would not be repeated.

Would Master of Mantles, Conrad, be a dangerous ally? Was his friendship and indeed his obvious encouragement of my Mantle magic a snare, a trap to be avoided? Perhaps I should move carefully before trusting him completely, and yet he knew so much that if he wished, he could already use me as a pawn in his own quest for power. My mind zigzagged from one thought to the next until I almost collided with a man who rose from the bench he had been sitting on.

"My Queen, forgive me for intruding upon you in your garden, but I wished to take my leave of you as matters in Rynth call me away." Ransom Frain's bulk blocked out the evening sun and forced me to sidestep on the path in order to see his face more clearly.

"Mine Master, you leave us so soon?" I indicated that we should sit, as I hoped that I would not feel quite so dwarfed by his bulk.

"Alas, there are always matters to be dealt with in Rynth. Since our trade in iron and coal with Goremene has increased, we have been hard pressed to extract enough ore, and five new mines are to be cut this summer."

"I had no idea that we traded so much with King Florian," I admitted. "Do we trade with other kingdoms?"

"Minor quantities compared to what we presently send to Goremene." His face never betrayed his personal opinion about how much had been sold to the south, but his next comment was carefully constructed. "Of course, your husband, the King, approved the transaction. I believe it was keenly bargained for by Lord Norton, who was very eager to strengthen the ties between our two kingdoms."

"King Florian is the Lord of Camlan's brother-in-law," I told him, "and I know his wife returns to her brother's court regularly to keep herself informed of the current fashions and to buy fine linens and silks."

"Then I can understand why it would be advantageous for Lord Norton to broker such a contract." Frain nodded.

"But neither of us can understand why there would be an advantage to Magra by selling our raw materials to Goremene, so that they can then sell them back to us as products crafted in their workshops. Our goldsmiths would welcome the patronage of our own countrymen, would they not?"

Ransom Frain's eyes sparkled. "That is my opinion, Majesty."

"Perhaps all such contracts should be reviewed when we have a new king." I stood. I did not wish to pursue this conversation further.

What could I do, and how could my opinion be worthwhile? I was just a figurehead queen. Such conversations must wait for the next true monarch.

"Indeed, Lady!" He rose. "I only hope that your husband's successor sees it as we do. Goremene is a powerful neighbour that grows stronger thanks to the low price they pay for our ores."

"Have the Mine Masters already chosen their candidate? I thought I heard such a rumour." We had walked to where the path divided, one way returning to the palace while the other led to the main causeway down to the town.

"Indeed, we have!" He laughed. "But I am not at liberty to discuss our choice with anyone, not even you, My Queen." He took my offered hand, bowing low to kiss it, and I marvelled again at his graceful movements for one so large. "I take my leave of you, Madam, and hope that I might speak with you again at the announcement of The Mantles' choice."

More than ever, I hoped that Tertius would not become king. All that power going to Camlan and into the pocket of Florian of Goremene made me fear for what would befall the rest of The Five Kingdoms and Vellin itself.

I watched him walk slowly through the gardens and turn beyond the hedge of yew trees.

VII. To Business

When their business concluded, the lords and their hangers-on trooped back to their fiefdoms. With their exodus, the good people of Vellin returned to their normal lives once more. When the barges on the river carried coal to the coastal marshes and fish to the markets of the town, the daily routines of the palace resumed as if the royal personage of a king still guided their necessity. Cooks ordered the same vegetables from the market stalls. The sentries changed and lounged about in their barracks or frequented taverns, indulging in the fleeting pleasures offered there. I watched it all from my chamber windows and marvelled at what little had changed with the ending of such an important life. Brodik had ruled without touching their lives at all, and now, for the common people throughout Magra, life went on as usual.

I was not idle as the figurehead queen. I wrote letters to Roth, telling them of our splendid funeral, of the people's demonstrations of fondness for their queen and of how the lords had nominated me as their figurehead. I allowed my ladies to refurnish the royal apartments with such simple draperies and comforts as befitted rooms now occupied by women. Tertius, who was responsible for the Royal and State purses, watched on and said nothing, but his thoughts were so obvious I felt that I should speak to him about our purchases. We walked together in the roof garden that connected the palace to The Talarin.

"I have funded the changes from my own fortune, Lord Chamberlain, revenue garnered from The Roth estates." I began simply.

"I did not ask, Madam." He wore that bemused smile he used when pleasantly tolerating someone's company.

"You didn't, and that is to your credit as a gentleman, but you wondered where the money was coming from, all the same, as you should. As keeper of The Crown's purse, it was important for me to explain."

"I simply wondered," he admitted, carefully choosing his words, "why you were going to all the trouble, as your stay will only be for a short time?"

I stopped and faced him. "A short stay?"

"Three months, Katherine! I know you see it as your home, but we'd all assumed you'd want to leave when the new king starts his reign." His eyebrows were drawn together in concern. My future must have been a topic discussed by the councillors when they met in private to consider what would happen when The Mantles' decision was made.

I nodded my head. "Of course. Naturally, there will be a new king. The comforts I have assembled will benefit the new monarch, or perhaps his wife."

"My wife would require a great deal more than the homely embellishments befitting a country squire," he shrugged, "if Camlan is successful in the ballot."

"Then I shall take my country comforts back to Roth. Do not concern yourself, Tertius, Roth is large enough to warrant further embellishments."

His discomfort showed he could at least appreciate that returning to my place of exile might not be particularly appealing to me.

"You don't have to go back there. You could go anywhere. Perhaps you could go to Dereculd, to your cousin? You could come to Camlan, but I doubt Lady Norton would be happy for you to be there. My wife likes to be the centre of attention, and a displaced queen would be too much competition for her."

"I understand." I dug my fingernails into my palms. The last thing I would wish to do was to outshine Lady Norton, even if I was just a queen who was no longer a queen. I changed the subject.

"Have you heard rumours about who has nominated themselves as my husband's successor?" It was an obvious question to ask because he gathered intelligence from throughout the kingdom. His spy network was well known. But this was beyond even his reach. The Talarin kept the secret close and, despite his efforts, Tertius could not be certain who had presented their claim. He placed my hand on his forearm and patted it gently.

"It is difficult. No one manages to fossick information from inside those walls," he admitted, nodding in the vague direction of the Talarin. "Anyone with common sense should realise that some of us have more experience to draw upon and would therefore be the most appropriate choice. However, some foolish churls are making loud noises about their claims, armed with the most superficial arguments. Lord Clairstow insists that the king had promised to make him his heir after their last successful hunting trip together. Taegel and Gaheil both claim a very tenuous relationship to The Crown through several marriages a few generations ago, and even the mine masters are said to be giving support to their own favourite, whoever that might be."

"What happens if The Mantle choice isn't the popular choice among the other lords?" It was a question that I had been careful to avoid asking Conrad during our daily conversations. Sometimes the discussion went on within our heads, but more frequently these days we made excuses to meet and either wander the gardens or walk beside the Listi. I already knew everything that Tertius had told me, and more, about the noises being made up and down the Five Kingdoms. I also knew that the number of claims grew by the day. Very soon, there would be more contenders for the throne than peasants to serve them.

He squeezed my arm. "Heathcote is convinced that nothing will happen until the Mantle announcement. He thinks that your presence has bought us some additional time before the private armies start gathering." Such irony! How gratifying to have been of some use, and how kind that the councillors acknowledged my contribution!

"It is a great pity that I cannot be of more help," I told him, as we sat on a bench that overlooked the river. "Thank you for reminding me that I must begin to consider the location of my future home, although I've always thought of this as home, but I suppose that is no longer the case now."

"We did think," he began, but paused, uncertain about how to continue. I encouraged him. "There was a suggestion," he talked to the stone of the parapet at the edge of the cliff, "that perhaps a marriage to you might be a solution. Strewan is quite keen on that proposition, either for the chosen candidate or perhaps a foreign prince."

I tried to control my temper. He waited as I appeared to give the suggestion some serious thought. "I can see his point," I lied. "It would mean that I could stay here, wouldn't it? Oh, but what if the new king already has a wife? That solution would be impossible then, wouldn't it?"

Tertius' face was so grave that I had to force myself not to laugh. The enormity of the current crisis and the threat of civil war were perfectly real, but for all their stalwart management of the royal purse during my husband's reign, these very intelligent men could find no answer. Of course, that was because they all had their own self-interests to think about. It was no secret that all three of the councillors had submitted their claims. I wanted to scream at him as he reassured me that they would consult with me about my future. Instead, I calmly thanked him for his candour and watched him leave.

So, among my possible futures was the likelihood that I would be offered as a bride to some foreign royal personage, or to an appropriate but insignificant lord. For a fleeting moment, Ross Elderin's face came to mind, but of course, he was not what my councillors had in mind. True, he had expressed no desire to become king but was probably too popular among his peers not to be seen as a threat by the would-be kings. Strewan, with his pink, fleshy body, obviously saw my foreign marriage as an excellent solution. I felt sick at the very thought. Alternatively, I could retire quietly to practically anywhere that I wished, as long as it wasn't near Lady Norton. What a bright future they offered me!

Had I accepted their view of my future, I would have been more than eager to scurry back to Roth, where I had amassed a comfortable fortune from turning a derelict castle and its impoverished lands into a productive and pleasant estate. But I had other images of Magra's future in my mind, and I, too, needed a little time to draw them closer to reality. I only hoped that other lords were as reluctant to be the first one to seriously challenge for the throne as the councillors were.

I was so enveloped in thought that I did not see Conrad standing on the threshold of the doorway into The Talarin until he coughed loudly.

"Forgive me, Master Mantle! I was distracted. I was unaware of you." I smiled.

"Clearly!' He moved to join me as I sat on a stone seat. "I am accustomed to those around me always being aware of me," he admitted. "I assume Lord Norton was apprising you of the current state of affairs regarding the succession."

"Apparently, my presence has given everyone a little more time to consider their aspirations and make plans." I faced him. When he smiled, as he was doing at that moment, he had a handsome face with a high forehead and fine features. His skin was touched by the sun, and his neatly shorn raven hair and beard were well-kept and fitted him as trimly as his fine woollen surcoat. “One solution that some favour is my marriage to a foreign prince or a minor lord.”

“A lord of your choosing?”

My laugh was bitter, “Gracious no! Of course, I could just return to Roth and leave them all to their own fates.”

“But you won’t.” He stood. “You promised to visit us. Come now, and we can talk.”

He offered me his hand, and I took it. It felt warm and strong, no stranger to labour, but it was impossible to know whether that work was in perfecting his swordsmanship or tending the beasts and gardens of The Talarin’s farm.

“I do both!” he replied to my unspoken thoughts, answering more than I had been contemplating. “Sometimes your thoughts are so clear that I hear them even when I am not intending to listen to them.”

“That is an unfair advantage,” I told him as we passed through the narrow-arched door and into the Talarin’s smallest tower. The air was cooler inside the stone walls, but not unpleasant, and there was a strange but not unfamiliar smell, a mixture of leather polish and herbs.

“I can only apologise and remind you that your thoughts remain with me. No one else will ever know them. I can train you to protect yourself better, but that will take time.” He guided me down a narrow stair and into an airy room, well-lit by the great leaded windows overlooking a courtyard, deserted now, but containing all the paraphernalia familiar in a knight’s practice yard.

“Ross Elderin!” he said as he poured goblets of mead for both of us. “He has begun to fill my mind, and I can only think that you are putting him there.”

He held up his hand cheerfully. “Believe me, I do not wish to know your heart, but his face has appeared in my head before I sleep. It has been quite unsettling.”

We both laughed.

I apologised. “I am fond of him and perhaps my thoughts go to him at the end of a day filled with courtly intrigues and giving alms to the poor.”

“Do not dismiss your visits through the town. The people love you, and the lords know the people love you. It will keep you safer than any number of well-paid spies and bodyguards. They are your defence, and one day you may need that love.” He drank and tilted his head to look at me. “Does Ross Elderin love you?”

“Gracious, no, but I thought he cared for me. At least, I think he did, but he is not my concern at the moment. You know I have others that I need to protect. I am fearful that I cannot accomplish my plan, and yet I know that I must do it in order to save my kingdom. The lords appear determined to have their civil war, and I must be just as determined to stop them.”

“That is why you are here.” He handed me a scroll. It bore The Mantle pentangle and The Royal Seal of The Palace. It was a document setting out my claim to the throne. I looked up at him, alarmed.

“I drafted it myself and require you only to read it and sign it.”

I put it down and reached for my glass, but he stopped me, dropping to his knees beside me. He gripped my hands as he spoke. “Katherine, you know that you must do this. They will never take you seriously if you do not.”

“The lords will never take you seriously if you choose me.”

“We have time to change their minds, at least to change the minds of some of them, but you must be willing to play your part.”

His hand was on my knee, and I tried hard not to think about it.

"From now on, you must become the king your father meant you to be. You must attend the Council meetings and give your opinion. I shall naturally support you. You must continue to be seen and loved by your people, but also you must begin to charm your lords. They see you as the dowdy widow, the forsaken wife. It is time to change all of that. I believe you should begin to hold court, give banquets and even a tournament. Invite the wives of the lords. Lady Norton would feel very flattered if you invited her, but not too often. I have heard that she is a selfish and ill-mannered woman."

I reached for my glass and drained it. Lady Norton's reputation had reached even Roth, and she knew only too well that Tertius and I had been close when we were young. "Is that all?" I tried to joke.

"No." He stood and returned to his seat.

"You should come and train with us in The Talarin. There is one woman amongst your ladies, Judith of Pellian, who would benefit from our training for combat. She impressed the officers who comprised your escort, and they would be willing to train her."

"You do know that she was Brodik's mistress?" I felt I should warn him.

"She drinks like a cavalry trooper and fornicates with any man willing." He leaned forward. "I know about her, but she will find that we are made of sterner stuff here and cannot be easily corrupted."

"I will put it to her," I agreed. Judith had been restless of late, and she missed her opportunities to supervise her estate workers. Perhaps training to be a knight might appeal to her. "Do you intend for me to train as a knight too?" I asked.

"A little combat practice would be beneficial just in case the lords decide to destroy themselves in a civil war. I know that your father taught you as a child. But I also wanted you to be here to learn the skills of a Mantle."

I watched him pour a second glass of mead for both of us. I took the glass and looked up at him as I spoke. "I would like that more than the sword play. My father did tutor me in weaponry when

I was young, but I lacked the strength. I only ever truly mastered the bow. I am not a warrior, but I valued my time spent with Master Jollian. It has remained very dear to me, and although I don't practise Mantle arts, his advice on dealing with others has always benefitted me.'

"Then we will use your training time to develop your agility in body and mind." He looked into his glass. "I also wanted to spend more time with you." His eyes met mine, and I felt my blood colour my face.

"I cannot deny that you stir something in me that I had thought was long obliterated by my training here, but it is not for that reason that I want to know you better. It is because throughout my years of study, the ancient connections, the almost mystical links between kings and mantles have fascinated me. Your father and Master Jollian had a long and powerful friendship, but your husband dismissed all thought of such a relationship. Between you and me, I sense that we have something deeper than a simple sharing of minds."

I blinked, unable to respond. I had no knowledge of anything deeper than what we already experienced, and even that was alarming.

"I have frightened you, forgive me!" He rose and went to the window. There was the noise of men assembling, the clang of equipment being distributed.

"Not frightened," I followed him. "Uncertain. You forget that I am coming to terms with many things, Conrad. After years of careful restraint, my emotions have been pulled in a hundred directions over these past few weeks. Ross Elderin may have awakened them, but you, you touch something deeper and unknown that I need time to accept." I placed my hand on his forearm. It was the first time that I had dared to touch him. "I will return to you, with Judith, and I will endeavour to fulfil everything that you have suggested, but it still fills me with dread."

He looked down at me. “Only a fool has no fear.” Our faces were so close I could see the light on the grey hairs appearing in his beard. He moistened his lips and then whispered. “And if we ever kissed, perhaps I would be tempted to relinquish my vows.”

I stepped away from him. “You are a dangerous man, Conrad Silver Mantle!”

There was mischief in his eyes. “My dearest lady, your thoughts truly need protecting!” He offered me his hand. “Come sit at my table and let us begin with a lesson on how to defend your thoughts from teasing Mantles, but first, sign your rightful claim.”

I sat and used the quill he offered to me to claim my right to my father’s throne, wondering all the while what my father would have thought about that.

Judith’s enthusiasm was greater than I had expected when I told her about Conrad’s offer. She wanted to begin training the very next day, but I had other business to attend to, so she had to wait for two days to meet her training partners.

Meanwhile, Grace was eager to transform me from my drab greys and blacks into a widow of purples, violets, and subtle blues. She changed my hair and insisted that I should get a little more sunlight on my face to bring back my natural colour. I allowed them to preen and fuss in between my visits to the alms-houses and the preparations for restoring the official court calendar.

Tertius was not particularly pleased when I invited his wife to visit Vellin. He was flattered when I told him that it was important for such a close friend of The Queen to present his wife, otherwise there could be talk. He, I reasoned, would not wish to sully my reputation in any way. The whole conversation caused great amusement among the other councillors. I suspected he had his reasons for keeping his wife in Camlan. Shana often related palace gossip to me, including rumours that he kept a young mistress in a quiet part of the town.

I had always detested attending my father's court. Sitting listening to the sycophantic knee-kissers or indulging in conversations about fashion, the price of wool, births, deaths and marriages and whose wife was sleeping with whom had bored me even when I was a young girl. My father had insisted that I must attend to learn, and he had been pleased when I had acquired the skill of appearing to listen intently to one person while sampling the conversations of several others. Perhaps it was a Mantle skill we both shared.

My first court went moderately well. The ladies examined my new gown, and I listened to the wool merchants explaining how the upland sheep produced heavy duty woollen yarn while the placid flocks of Magra had the finest and most prized wool for garments. I even found that I could learn much about the secret allegiances when three lords presented their simpering wives to me. The ladies were only too eager to share their gossip with their queen, who quite clearly understood what it was like to be the wife of a minor lord. Everyone was delighted to be invited to dine with me, and Conrad's presence, constantly passing mental comments about the other guests, made the evenings bearable. I felt ready to meet Lady Norton and invited her to court.

Conrad continued to teach me how to protect my thoughts from him. It was easier than I expected, and we finished our session with some simple listening. I remembered Jollian teaching me this when I was a child, but I'd been too impatient to succeed. Conrad helped me to listen to the whole person when they spoke, and he prepared some exercises for my use during my next court. Then we went down to watch Judith wielding a broadsword. She could already best some of the men.

"Silver Mantle tells me that you can also use a sword, Your Majesty." The sword master spoke to me during a break in their exercises.

“Alas, sir, I was a bitter disappointment when it came to swordsmanship.”

“You should try a smaller weapon, Your Majesty.” Judith was breathing heavily after her last bout. Her opponent had defeated her, but gave her a hearty slap on her back as consolation. Conrad confessed that she had exceeded his expectations and was becoming a favourite among the men. I was pleased to see that it was for skill and not any other reason.

“Try this one.” The sword master handed me a shorter, lighter weapon with fine filigree work on the handle. Before I could object, Judith began strapping protective pads around my chest and arms. I felt like a sausage. The sword master was happy to parry with me at first, then began to seriously test my agility and my memory. In a short time, I was out of breath and eager to stop.

“I can see you have talent, Majesty,” he told me, “but we will need to work hard on your fitness. I will see you again at the same time tomorrow?”

I looked to Conrad, who explained, “Sword Master Tory understands that you may have other commitments, but he will be available for your lesson, should you wish to have it.” I nodded, still recovering my breath, and held out my weapon to the sword master.

“It is yours, Lady. I forged it myself to suit your size.”

“Sword Master Tory is skilled in many disciplines,” Conrad said.

“A craftsman should be prepared to fashion and use his own tools,” Tory said simply, gathering up his clutch of weapons and equipment, leaving me still holding my sword.

“He is a temperamental artist sometimes, but his skills are exceptional.’ Conrad offered his arm. “You may keep the weapon in my day room if you do not wish to return to the palace with it.” Thus, my beautiful little sword remained in Conrad’s room.

I did attend two sessions with the Sword Master Tory, who was indeed a hard task master but also a quick wit and an amusing companion. I never left his presence without a smile on my face. A week later, preparations for the delayed annual spring festival began, and Lady Norton arrived for her presentation at Court.

Majolica Norton was the youngest sister of Florian, King of Goremene, Magra's closest neighbour to the southwest, across the narrow stretch of water called The Sul. With two brothers and three older sisters, young Majolica had found it hard to satisfy her ambitions within her father's court. When he died, and her elder brother took their father's crown, she became a commodity to be traded to reward some faithful functionary or sent off to marry a minor prince. When a young emissary from the Court of Magra arrived, she seized on her chance to escape. In Tertius, she found a kindred spirit. He, too, was ambitious and eager to acquire power as well as wealth. They were married with all the elaborate ceremony the elegant court of Goremene could muster. Now she governed Camlan in her husband's absence. She was efficient but not well-loved by the people who feared her periodic anger at poor harvests or storm-damaged dykes that required large expenditures for repair. She taxed everyone and everything to afford and wear the finest gowns that Goremene could create.

There was no humble curtsey when Tertius's wife and I finally met. She dipped slightly and began to speak to me before I had addressed her. I raised an eyebrow to Tertius and began to walk further along the line of introductions. She swallowed the rest of her sentence and glared after me. Later, as I sat watching the assembly, I noted she had gathered a small cabal of women about her. I decided it was time that Majolica learnt who the queen was.

"Lady Norton!" I approached her little knot of ladies and interrupted her sentence. The other women curtseyed, but Majolica was angered by my arrival. She glared at me. I bent towards her.

“It is a pleasure to see you here after so long, my dear. Tertius has told me so much about you.” I took her reluctant arm in mine. “Come sit with me and let us talk. You will excuse us, ladies.” The others curtseyed again, and I guided Majolica to my private table.

“Your Majesty, I was quite upset that you didn’t…” she began quickly, but I held my hand up to silence her.

“Dear Majolica,” I smiled, “please remember that at court it is polite to allow the monarch to speak first. Then you may answer.”

“I know that!” she snapped, “I have spent my whole life in the court of the Kings of Goremene, and you are no monarch, you are simply a widowed queen who will soon be replaced!”

The room fell silent. Her voice had carried far more than she had intended. It was a quality certain parts of the room had and, if used wisely, could silence or encourage talk.

“Please continue,” I told them all, “Lady Norton and I are becoming acquainted.” The room pretended to return to its own business, for what could be more important than watching a widowed queen school and aspiring one? Majolica glared.

“Now, where were we? Oh, yes, I am a worthless widow keeping the seat warm for the next queen. Perhaps you see yourself as that queen, my dear? Of course, you do! Why not? You look every inch a queen and could be a great asset to your husband. It is such a pity that you have begun so badly.”

I folded my hands on my lap and waited. She said nothing. It took no great Mantle skill of listening to detect that she was furious with herself. I was merely a pitiable creature trying to retain her fading shreds of dignity until the new king was crowned.

“Can you forgive me, Madam?” she began, “In my excitement, I forgot my manners and then, being a stranger to court, I compounded my error.”

“My dear Majolica,” I patted her hand, “it is forgotten. We should be friends, you and I, for the sake of Tertius. It would not look well if we were seen to bicker. How was your journey? I hope your accommodation is comfortable. You look very beautiful in your gown. What divine material!"

Throughout my conversation with Majolica Norton, I could feel Conrad chuckling. He almost allowed his mirth to show in his face when she confessed her jealousy towards me. Of course, now that she had met me, she knew there was nothing of which to be jealous. Her husband had loved me when I was young and beautiful, but that was a long time ago. When she talked about their months of separation and her hard work to maintain Camlan, about her oldest son, who had been sent to Goremene to be taught the skills of knighthood in his uncle's court and about the small, lonely house in Vellin in which Tertius lived, the house that he had told her was too shabby for her to stay in, I found myself truly pitying the woman. She had a lonely life in Wyke. Her three younger children were her only joy. Her husband had his young mistress in his love nest in Vellin, while she had nothing but the management of Camlan to occupy her days. It was to her credit that she herself had not strayed and taken a lover. I pitied, and I respected her a little more.

"You must come and meet my ladies," I told her, standing. I bade the courtiers to continue without us. A group of musicians was setting up to play, and as we made our way through the palace, we caught snatches of their music.

"The palace is larger than I imagined," she told me as we climbed to my chambers. "Of course, my brother's palace in Goremene is much larger and the furnishings richer, but this is a very pleasing place." I very nearly retorted that I hoped she would find it comfortable when she became queen, but I held my tongue.

Grace, Alice, and Shana made her welcome and fussed over her clothes. Later, they insisted on unbraiding her fine golden hair to discover how it had been arranged. Within a short space of time, Majolica Norton, Princess of Goremene and wronged wife of a man I had once loved, was invited to dine alone with the ladies of my inner circle, and all hostility towards me had melted away. Even the harsh lines that spoiled the corners of her sensuous lips had smoothed a little, and over wine and venison she laughed a great deal. That night, she slept in the royal apartments. Where her husband slept, and who with, was not my concern.

VIII Rynth

During the early summer, my days were divided between the duties of being the figurehead queen and my precious lessons in the Talarin. I must confess that Judith fared far better than I with her swordsmanship, but Master Tory did praise my agility and determination. In truth, I spent less time in his practice chamber than I did at Conrad's table. I learnt to stretch the natural skills I had inherited from my father and I enjoyed sitting with Conrad, discussing the day, or simply sharing our thoughts. Unlike Tertius and his fellow councillors, Conrad required nothing from me except my company. For a few precious moments each day I was merely Katherine.

Another delightful time each day was breakfast with my ladies. As the summers in Vellin are warm, we took to eating on a small terrace above the wilderness garden. Grace presided, reminding me of the day's business and distributing tasks for the rest of the household. She had also discovered Gwillem planting herbs in his garden, herbs given to him by some northern lord, he told her, including rosemary, which the lord had said was a particular favourite of a lady he had once known. I suspected, I hoped, it was from a particular northern lord who might have partly forgiven me for my treatment of him. Grace immediately drew Gwillem into our circle, treating him as her own personal advisor, and he would often join us at the table, the only man in our little company. I knew I would be sorry to see him leave when he set out north for Roth.

One morning, he was explaining the medicinal qualities of the common onion, and Grace agreed, saying that she had used an onion and lemon preparation to reduce her freckles, as Heathcote and Strewan arrived. They were both red-faced, and Heathcote clutched a sealed scroll which he thrust into my hand. It bore the seal of The Mine Masters, and I broke it open and read.

"There have been enormous explosions and fires in the mines in Rynth. Over two hundred miners are dead, and others are trapped below ground." I relayed the content of the scroll and shared their shocked faces. Strewan muttered something about a terrible disaster and sending our commiserations, but I cut his meanderings short. "How long would it take to ride to Rynth?"

"Madam, who would you send and for what purpose?" Heathcote asked.

"Myself, of course!" I glared at him. "And the purpose would be to let the people of Rynth know we care."

I turned to Grace. "Judith and I will leave as soon as possible. Please prepare." Judith and Grace both nodded and left. To Heathcote and Strewan, I added, "Gentlemen, you must inform the Court and deal with things here in Vellin until my return."

Tertius and Conrad arrived at the same time but from different directions. The Lord of Camlan openly opposed to my making such a foolhardy journey. The ride would take several days, and by that time, the dead would have been put in the ground, and the mines reopened.

"Let the Mine Masters deal with this, Madam. They are the power in Rynth," he counselled.

"The journey would be arduous, but it would remind the people of distant Rynth that they are still part of Magra and that their queen cares about them." Conrad addressed his comment directly to me and ignored Tertius, who was by his side.

"And who will escort you, Madam?" Heathcote was doing his best to at least sound supportive, although I could tell that he also felt it was an unnecessary gesture.

I looked to Conrad. "I would volunteer myself, Madam," he faced me, "but Mine Master Frain would not welcome any Mantle presence in his territory. Rynth has always been closed to The Mantle Order."

I persisted. "Judith and I will ride there alone, if necessary!" That drew all manner of protests from them all.

"Might I suggest a small escort of reliable but inconspicuous men who have distinguished themselves in the past without making an open show of their valour?" Conrad spoke calmly, and when he went on to say that Queen Katherine had undoubtedly made up her mind to travel and that it was their responsibility to ensure her safety, the councillors capitulated. They even agreed that Conrad was the best person to select such a company, as he also had secret knowledge of all claimants to the throne. It would not be fair to send such a person on this errand, away from Vellin, at such an important time. I suspect they also thought that if any ill did befall me, then they could quickly place the blame squarely on Conrad's head.

By afternoon, Silver Mantle had gathered his chosen volunteers together. He explained that he made it his business to know who was presently in Vellin, and so it had been a simple matter of seeking them out with the proposition. I was a little surprised to hear that none of them had refused the commission, but an even greater surprise was in store.

"They await you in the courtyard, Madam. The Lady Judith is with them." Conrad escorted me to the stables. I found Judith grinning like a stuffed piglet, her hands firmly gripping the reins of our horses. She wore her manly riding clothes, made for her by Grace from leather prepared in our own small tannery. Beside her, but not grinning, was Ross Elderin. Conrad anticipated my reaction before we reached them. "Next to Tory, he is as skilled a swordsman as any in the kingdom or beyond, and we both know that he will do everything that he can to protect your person."

The other three men were unknown to me. One, Thorfin of Dereculd, I found out later, was a favourite of my cousin, Delion, and wore a quiver of arrows over his fine doublet. His handsome face had a steely quality about it, easy to smile but in a secret and knowing way. The second was a mountain of a man called Weld, who came from Thanis. I was told nothing else about him, and as we rode through the lands west of Vellin, I doubted that his taciturn manner would allow me to find out much more unless he divulged it himself, which seemed unlikely. Last of all, there was Soldin Meganor of Alodia, with skin the blue-black colour of midnight and watchful eyes that pierced through your skin to your core. Soldin, Judith, confided as we rode through the late afternoon in weak sunlight, was a skilled killer with any number of weapons, but his favourite was the knife. She did not disclose how she knew that, and I did not ask. The man made no effort to bow to me but helped me into my saddle. As we travelled, he always rode at the back and rarely spoke to anyone.

***

The mines of Rynth lie in a cluster of shallow valleys in the western corner of the lands known as The Southern Meeds. Many types of ore are extracted by The Mine Masters, and the land is scarred by wooden mine heads and open-cut wounds, whole cliffs of exposed rock and rich ore seams. The miners lived in small hamlets close to their work, and over the years, their masters had erected fine mansions on the higher ground. There were no large towns in Rynth. The mining guilds operated their own farms where the wives of the miners could earn extra money. Not that the mining community was poor or underpaid. Their health was also important to The Mine Masters, who provided better care for their men than many of the generals in my husband's army, my dead husband's army, my army, at least for a short time.

We travelled west until sunset. Small streams punctuated our journey, and the rolling hillsides were rich in lush pastures and game. The Southern Meeds are less populated than their northern cousins. A string of market towns spreads across the Northern Meeds, towns like Brak, Anardis, Heathcote and further south, Stovin. Since leaving the farmlands of Vellin, we had seen only the occasional cluster of farm buildings.

It appeared that Ross Elderin led our party, for it was he who determined where we should make our camp after consulting with Soldin Meganor, who seemed to know this part of the world well. Thorfin had charge of our supper, and Weld maintained our fire, leaving Judith and me free to compare our saddle-weary bones and sore bottoms. If we had expected an evening of shared camaraderie, we were disappointed, for no sooner was the meal over than our travelling companions turned to their blankets and slept. Judith shrugged after trying to engage Thorfin in a conversation about Dereculd, but the young man's taciturn answers left her in no doubt that he wished to sleep.

"This escapade might be considered foolhardy by some." Ross Elderin poked the embers of our fire. The night was warm, with a sky full of stars, and we were the last two to take to our beds.

"That's what my councillors said, but I couldn't ignore what was happening in Rynth. I felt I should go there and try to help. You will ask what I could do to help, but…"

"Your being there will help," he said. "The miners who have survived will appreciate your gesture, I'm sure. What I can't understand is why The Lord Mantle was so eager to place me at the head of your escort. Surely, he should have sent a troupe of his black knights to ensure your safety."

"Apparently, there's some uneasiness between Mantles and The Mine Masters," I replied, eager to be holding a conversation with Ross again. I was sure Conrad had selected him for many reasons, including knowing full well how I felt about him. "Besides, he knows that no one would defend me more ably than you."

"You spoke with him about me?" The Lord of Brak's eyes widened. "So, the pair of you could laugh at my stupidity?"

"I didn't tell him about Kate, no, not that!" My eyebrows lifted, insulted that he would think that I could do such a thing. "I told him that we were friends. I didn't need to tell him how close we might have become because he already knew." I reached and touched his arm, but he pulled away and shook his head.

He muttered, "Don't trust The Mantles with all their magic and potions.'

"He knew about you because he could communicate with me, mind-to-mind, as my father could with his Silver Mantle," I explained.

"But you're not a king. How could he know your thoughts?" He leaned towards me. "My lady, you should not trust him! It's trickery, and he probably knows about us because he has spies everywhere."

"In the forest at Roth?" It pained me a little to have to explain. I suppose I had expected him to accept my abilities as easily as Conrad had accepted them. "Lord Elderin, I have the blood royal and come from a long line of kings, all of them able to share thoughts with their Silver Mantles. I could even do it when I was a child, and it's not just him knowing my mind. I can also know his thoughts." I could see the concern my revelations caused, but I pressed on. "I can also block him from my head. For example, right now, he can't know our conversation."

Ross Elderin looked up at the sky, then back at me. Did he believe me, or was he thinking this was another deceit? "You should still be cautious. Let's hope they choose the new king quickly, and then you'll be free of all this intrigue."

I desperately wanted to share the same secrets with him that I had shared with Conrad, but the time was not right, so I simply nodded and hated myself for it. He would see it as another deceit if I became queen.

He grinned, "At least Silver Mantle had the good sense to let me pick your escort."

It was Ross Elderin's turn to surprise me. He had known each of these men during his time serving the king, my husband, and had learnt to trust them with his life. He now trusted them with mine. I looked at them all, curled in their woollen blankets and hoped they would not have the need to demonstrate their skills.

The following morning, we were riding before dawn, and Soldin Meganor assured us that we could reach Rynth the following day if we rode until after sunset. So, we rode, all that long day, and never has every bone in my body cried out for rest. By the time we enjoyed the wild boar that Thorfin provided for dinner, I thought only of sleep and oblivion from the aching soreness in my back, buttocks, and thighs. With another clear night sky above us, I found it hard to sleep despite my weariness and was surprised to discover Ross by the fire, warming a pot of mead.

"Lady Kate, a tankard of mead?" He straightened up as he spoke. In the dark, with the fire creating strange reflections on his face, it was hard to detect his mood, but as we had talked the previous evening and had exchanged occasional words during the day, I assumed he was trying to mend the rift between us.

"In truth, Ross," I replied, "I had expected to fall asleep quickly after such a day of riding."

He looked up from his small cauldron. "If I were in my woods, I would pick you valerian to help you rest, or rosemary for remembrance and rue for sorrow."

"I would sooner have honeysuckle for devotion." I took the warm cup he offered to me. I faced him, looking into those nut-brown eyes so accustomed to laughing.

"Would that be the queen or Mistress Kate?" He sat closer to me.

"I know the queen is glad of your devotion, but it is Kate who holds the mead." I wanted to tell him so much more. Instead, we both faced each other without a word. Then, when words came, they rushed out from both our mouths, and we laughed.

"I went to find you in the woods before we left Roth." I gabbled. "I wanted to tell you who I was and to apologise for not telling you sooner."

"I was already on the road to Stovin," he apologised.

"Since then, there's been so little time for anything." I waved my arms hopelessly. I wanted to make everything right between us." He didn't reply, watching the flames dying around the red coals. The silence came again. "I enjoyed being Kate," I said, uncertain of what he was thinking, longing to open my heart to him, to tell him everything.

"I enjoyed meeting her." He reached for my hand, and I gave it willingly. "But what now, uncomplicated Kate? How can I face my queen and not think of those cold mornings in Brak?"

"I want you to think of them. I think of them, even when I should not be thinking of them, wondering what would have happened if the king had lived."

He drew closer to me. "The King would have died eventually. Perhaps it was good that it ended when it did before you were forced into greater deceptions, and I made a fool of myself by professing my love."

"Might you have done that? Was that possible?"

He released my hand, and his voice was dull when he spoke.

"Who knows? But what might have been is now gone forever. You are the queen, and I'm a minor lord from The Northern Meeds. We will stare back at each other across The Council Table, or at functions in The Great Hall, and I will bow and kiss your hand, then we will pass out of each other's lives again."

"I don't want that to happen!" The urgency in my voice made his eyes widen. "I don't want you to pass out of my life."

His hand rested on my shoulder. "My dearest Kate, my brighten-the-morning-and-give-sunlight-to-my-day Kate, you are The Queen, and neither of us can escape that. When this journey is over, I must return to Brak, and you must be the beautiful, unattainable mother of your people." He touched my cheek, and I pressed my face into his hand.

"I won't always be queen." My voice was little more than a whisper.

He drew me to him once more, encircling my shoulders with his arms. "That is a day that I shall wait for."

He held me close until the fire lost its heat and glowed red, as the stars turned slowly in the ink sky. I closed my eyes, wishing that I could stay in the warmth of his arms forever. We neither kissed nor spoke the thousand things we might have said.

Reluctantly, as the night grew colder, we parted. He left me, and I curled into my fur cape, alone beside the embers, and in that starlit wilderness, I had never felt so lonely or so bereaved. I allowed the tears to cloud my vision and slowly closed my eyes in sleep. The widow, the mother of her people, he'd said. No widow could feel more loss than I felt at his words. No mother was ever so alone.

The first sign we had of Rhyth was in the sky the following morning. As we rode over the crest of a hill that led down to a landscape of rolling hills and valleys, a strange pall of dark dust hung in the air, like the smoke from a fire, except that it did not rise from the ground. It simply sat among the sparse clouds. There was the smell of soil and dirt, and the air itself, cloyingly thick, it dried the backs of our throats. As we drew closer, a mist clung to some of the shallow valleys, and there were fires burning, buildings, like impoverished corpses blazing unattended, sometimes fire appeared to be burning in the ground itself. We rode through the first mining encampment in silence, searching for any signs of life. The mine appeared to be deserted, and so did the cottages in its shadow. We dismounted and stood gaping, unsure what to do.

Suddenly, the door of the dilapidated tavern opened, and a strange creature appeared, wiping a dish with a grubby cloth. He was filthy, from head to foot, covered in dust and grime until it was impossible to discern the colour of his clothes or his hair. The pale circles around his eyes were the only indicators of his skin colour. We did not introduce ourselves.

“Everybody’s over at Wheel Silverleaf,” he said, by way of introduction. “Just done a shift at Solace, me-self. If you’re passing through, best turn back the way you came and bypass Rynth altogether. There’ll be no hospitality in these valleys for a while.”

“We are from Magra,” Ross Elderin began, then looked to me for affirmation. “We seek Mine Master Frain. Is he at this Wheel Silverleaf?”

“He is, and every other able-bodied soul in the valleys. They took out two hundred dead this morning from Wheel Solace, but Silverleaf’s got ‘em stumped.”

“How many mines have been affected? We were told it was just one?” Ross helped the man to sit. He was clearly overcome with weariness and despair. Weld relieved him of his bowl and cloth, and Judith went to the well to draw water for him.

“The water’s bad!” The innkeeper yelled to her. “Full of dust, like everything.” He coughed and pointed to the inn. “There is mead and ale that’s drinkable. Help yourselves.”

We did so while we listened to the man’s account of what had happened. There had been strange rumblings underground for many days, and then, in quick succession, every mine suffered a disaster. Some had cave-ins, the timbers suddenly gave way and at Solace, the chambers were flooded. Then, at Silverleaf, the land above the mine began to crumble into the mine.

The man shook his head in disbelief. Silverleaf was the most recent mine. No cost had been spared to make it safe and comfortable for the workers. Indeed, men did their best to be allotted to it, and competition was fierce to work the Silverleaf seams. Now even the surface was unsafe to walk on, and the rescuers were at a loss as to how they could reach the ones below. By the time this last disaster had occurred, there were few left to mount a rescue as they were still bringing out the injured and dead from the other mines. That is why even the tavern owner had been called upon to do his shift at Solace to free a more experienced miner to join the rescuers at Silverleaf.

“Where is this Silverleaf that you speak of?” I spoke for the first time, and the man regarded me with distaste.

“No place for a woman!” He spat dust from his throat, then turned to Elderin. “Best leave your wife here, sir, and you and these four gentlemen go on to the mine alone.”

“I have no wife, and these three gentlemen are the bodyguards of our lady, Queen Katherine, and the Lady Judith of Pellian.” Ross Elderin drew himself up, suddenly every inch a lord, and glared at the fellow. “Now, which way is it to the mine that Your Queen asked you about?”

The man’s eyes grew wide, and he stumbled to kneel before me. “Beg pardon, Majesty! I meant no offence, but the valley is a fearful place, not fit for a person such as yourself.”

“Let me be the judge of that, Master Taverner.” I gestured to him to rise. “This is not the time for courtly manners. I wish to go to Silverleaf, if not to help in the rescue, then to find out how best we can help survivors. I expect Mine Master Frain would wish to speak with me if he knew I was here.”

“Then I’ll take you to him, Your Majesty. You can ride a little further, but when we reach the village of Silverleaf, you’ll have to leave your beasts and walk. The ground’s unreliable, and the beasts can sense the danger. There’s been no end of cattle and ponies lost when they panicked and fell down a hole.” He looked for agreement and then raced to collect four large wineskins and a large basket of bread. “For the men over there.” He indicated the bread. Then he set off towards the valley road at a trot, and we followed.

The taverner was a good guide. He set two young boys to watch over our mounts once we reached the outskirts of Silverleaf, warning them that if they felt the ground move, they were to go back down the valley towards safety and take the horses with them. Then the innkeeper took us through what had once been a very prosperous and comfortable village, now little more than countless piles of rubble and smouldering wood. None of us spoke. Bodies lay unattended everywhere, nearly all of them with a large circle of red daubed on their backs. The taverner explained that this was a miner's mark to signify a corpse. Those without a mark were clearly alive, but without help, they would surely gather their own circle before night fell. Some were women and children. Judith questioned why they were not being helped.

"Everyone's at the mines. Once we get the living from under the ground, we'll turn to the ones above ground," the taverner explained. "It's our law. Near dusk, when the rescuers come this way, they'll check for their own and take them back to their homes."

"Are there no places of healing?" Judith persisted, recalling the Mantle rest houses for the sick.

"Not here. We don't care for Mantles." The taverner stood on the edge of the town, looking to where the Silverleaf mine had been. All we could see were deep wounds in the land, some dark holes, as if a giant hand had poked fingers into the fields and some long, narrow chasms where earth continued to tremble and slither into the depths.

"Silverleaf was the first mine to have men trained in healing skills, and they used to work over there." The taverner pointed to the left beyond the road. Nothing remained but a few low walls and, in another hollow, what might have been parts of a roof. Behind it, appearing to straddle the road was the structure of the mine's poppet head, tilted dangerously, the machinery dislodged and partially suspended over a sunken trench that stretched for two fields' width in every direction.

"That's what is left of Silverleaf." The taverner murmured.

I began to understand why the animals had been so fearful. The ground felt brittle and unstable beneath our feet as we walked, and there was a strange movement, almost as if the ground itself shivered at the touch of our feet upon it. I looked at the faces of my companions and was comforted, for while they were certainly alarmed by the crackling of the soil, like ice on a spring lake, they paid no heed to the tremors when they came. When we reached the first chasm, which stretched halfway to an exposed cliff where other miners had extracted ore many years ago, the tremor was so strong that I dropped to my knees until it was over.

"My lady?" Ross was at my side immediately, raising me to my feet.

"The trembling ground is frightening. I felt my legs go weak when that one reached its height." I was grateful that he delayed releasing me immediately, and with his arm about me, he helped me walk beyond the fearful place.

"You feel the ground tremble?" he asked when we joined the others.

"Don't you?" It was a foolish question, for I had seen from their reactions that they certainly could not and were clearly concerned about my nervousness.

"She's got the gift," the taverner said mildly, not feeling the need to slow down.

"What gift?" Soldin Meganor's rarely used voice was deep.

"The best miners have it," our guide explained. "They can feel the earth. It warns them about danger. The Queen has the gift. We should listen to her. If she feels something, we need to do what she does. Many a mine gang was saved by a captain with the gift." He smiled at me, and I could tell that although my companions perhaps doubted my bravery, in the taverner's eyes I'd joined the ranks of the mining elite.

We found Ransom Frain on the edge of the great chasm, supervising a team of men desperately trying to construct some sort of wooden framework.

"Majesty! You do our valley a great honour!" Frain bowed low, depositing dust and dirt from his hat as he removed it. This was a very different Ransom Frain from the proud, wealthy schemer I'd met in Vellin. He wore the same dowdy and dust-encrusted garb as his men and had clearly done his shifts down mines over the past few days. His eyes were red-rimmed through lack of sleep, and his bald dome sported scratches and bruises to testify to his involvement.

"The news that came to Vellin did not prepare us for what we have seen here, Mine Master. How can we help you?" I offered my hand to be kissed and collected my first smear of coal dust in return. I hastily introduced my company, and Frain was about to send messengers to his house to have rooms made ready for us. I stopped him. "We mean to help. That is our intention, not to be an additional burden to you. What has to be done?"

Grateful, he began to explain how his engineers had determined that the ground was too fragile to try to dig out survivors and that constructing a small lift, large enough for a few souls at a time, might be the best option. They had already started to construct the winching mechanism, but then found that they couldn't get their equipment near enough to a suitable hole. The original shaft was distorted, so they'd decided to use one of the chasms that had opened above a mine tunnel.

'Unfortunately, we've had two men badly injured trying to take even the smallest cradle across the ground, and the whole place is becoming so fragile that we've decided that we can only send a lad with a single seat. He'll have to get down there and report back to us."

Frain pointed at a small boy, dirty as any of them, sitting apart from everyone. He was quietly crying and wiping his nose on his arm. That part of the arm was the only strip that appeared the colour of flesh. He looked about nine years old. My heart ached.

"Surely something else could be done?"

"He's a good lad. Looks after the ponies usually. He's been in the mines for two years, so he knows what he's about, but the little fellow is afraid of being down there alone. Frightened of the dead, and of the gods of the deep places."

"Poor child, is there no other way?"

"I could try to crawl across."' Judith immediately offered, and one by one, so did the rest of my escort, except for Weld, who had already spotted where he was most useful and had ambled over to the men constructing the winch tower, offering his strength to help their construction.

"I will not risk your lives." Ransom Frain shook his head. "Besides, the last man who went was about your size, Lady Judith, and he broke both his legs falling down the hole. Luckily, he was strapped to the injury seat, and we were able to winch him up."

"And the boy's parents, what do they say?" Elderin would not be satisfied.

"Both dead. He's an orphan. That's why we chose him." Two men were now speaking to the boy whose whole body shook as he sobbed. I could not stand by and watch the small child being reminded of his duty to the mines. I went and knelt beside him.

"Hello, young man, my name is Kate. What's your name?"

"Tom!" He stuttered between sobs.

"The Mine Master tells me you're a very brave boy to be doing what you're about to do. Only you can do this, Tom. The whole of Rynth is relying on you."

He sniffled. "I don't want to be a hero. I'll die. They'll come for me, the dead 'uns will, and take me with 'em down to the deep places. I'm frightened. I can't go."

He was shaking, and I put my arms about him. This shocked him, and he stood, pulling away. To my surprise, he was as tall as I was. He clumsily returned my embrace and whispered. "Please help me. Don't let them send me. I'll die, and I don't want to be alone down there." The ground trembled again, and I released him. He had not felt the movement, but his frightened face tore at my heart. Frain and Elderin were beside us.

I turned to Frain. "Master, do you have clothes like this boy's that I could wear? My riding gown is not appropriate for where we are going."

I watched the slow realisation of what I was suggesting creep over his face. Ross was quicker to anticipate my plan and muttered, 'no' several times before I held up my hand.

"Judith is too heavy, but I might not be. If I go first, that will show Tom that there is less to fear. I will be down there with him, and he can tell me what we must do when we get there." I looked to Tom, who nodded furiously.

"No, My Queen, I must refuse." Frain's voice rose, and I sensed his fear. "There is great danger, and I could not accept the responsibility for your person. I could never face the world if harm befell you."

"And I could never face my people if I did nothing to prevent more deaths when I could have helped." I placed my hand on his arm. "I suspect that the taverner has told you that I have 'the gift'. If I have, then it is perhaps fate that brought me to this place. Who better to go down there than someone who can feel the earth?" Frain shook his head and was turning to Elderin to seek his support, but I had not finished.

I took him aside. "I know that you have little love for The Mantles, but I have been visiting Silver Mantle, Conrad, since returning to Vellin and have learnt much about the connection between royal blood and Mantle mysticism. Perhaps other senses grow without our knowing. Perhaps I sense the movement of the ground as animals can sometimes do before great disasters. Ransom Frain, I would never wish to undermine your authority in Rynth, but I will command you, as Your Queen, if you force me."

"Majesty!" Judith interrupted any further discussion. She had a bundle in her arms and a woman at her shoulder. "This is Agatha.

She is a miner's widow and the mother of a young miner who is trapped down there. He's thirteen years old but short for his age, so she tells me, and she's been standing here since the news reached her with clean clothes for him to wear. She wants you to have them."

Agatha was grey. Her hair and face were the colour of fire ash, and her eyes had been drained of tears long ago. She thrust the clothes at me, gave Ransom Frain a look of disdain and returned to her place beside the knot of relatives waiting for news. I thanked her and went with Judith to find a suitable place to change.

When we returned, the debate about my suitability for the job had been concluded. Elderin had convinced Ransom Fain that I could be very stubborn and was known to be very unpleasant if I didn't get my own way. I noticed that Thorfin, the archer from Dereculd, had set about tending the injured with a confidence and apparent knowledge that showed he had dealt with such matters before. I wondered if that was how he had met the Lord of Brak. Soldin, his eyes bright and his deep voice maintaining a cheerful banter, had organised a make-shift kitchen and people were bringing pots, pans and even vegetables to him. He called to me as we passed. "There'll be hot soup for all those you get out alive. Find plenty, or the food will go to waste!"

Tom's spirits brightened when he saw me with the boys' tunic tight across my chest and the too-long leggings carefully strapped about my legs. The boots were too big, but we had wrapped my feet in rags to fit them better. Ross and Frain both tried to stifle a laugh but found that they couldn't.

"I don't think I shall have my portrait painted in this particular garb," I told them. It brought a brief light moment for the anxious onlookers. Their hours had been miserable for so long that any humour was welcome, if short-lived.

"You're going to have to crawl on your belly over this patch of ground. The men who went before left those markers to show the path they took. Stay between them." Frain and I were standing at the edge of the solid ground while the engineers fastened the rescue seat to my back. It appeared to be little more than a wider version of the common swing seat with additional leather straps attached to support the injured. 'It's really crumbly once you pass that small rowan bush, so be ready for a fall. Grip these straps, and we'll lower you down. If you're lucky enough to get to the wider opening, then turn around and go down feet first, facing the wall closest to you. That way, you can see any obstacle or hazard that might stop your descent.'

The seat was in position, and I had been shown how to unfasten it. When the engineers returned to the winch, Ross placed his hand on my arm quietly. I could not tell him how much that small gesture gave me the courage to attempt what I was about to do. Frain went on with his instructions.

"When you get to the bottom, and your feet are firmly planted on solid ground, give the rope three firm tugs. We'll pay out a little more rope and then wait until you're out of the harness before giving us one big tug. We'll then pull the rope and harness back for Tom to follow you. If you feel that you can't go further and would like to come back, give one tug on the way down."

I nodded and accepted their words of encouragement and then turned to face the chasm. I dropped to my knees and then rested my stomach on the ground. I had only crawled a few feet when the ground shuddered, and I saw the small rowan bush disappear.

IX SILVERLEAF

With each crawl, I felt the ground sag a little, and my muscles tensed. I tried to anticipate the moment when my weight would send me plummeting after the rowan bush. Before I reached the edge, I looked back at the crowd gathered around the perimeter, all watching me crawl along like a baby, except with less grace. I spotted Tom. Even at a distance, I could see his hands gripping the barrier rope, his knuckles white. I edged to the right because Fain thought the ground would be firmer there. Just in time.

The ground beside me crumbled away, leaving a canyon with me on its very edge. The rope between me and the winch dipped a little over the edge. I decided to edge a little further, hoping that the subsidence didn't continue because if it did and I fell, with the rope following the path of the canyon, I would swing wildly in the new crevasse rather than slither down a hole. I preferred to slither. I reached the edge, carefully turned my body, and began to lower myself down. Suddenly, the edge crumbled, and as I fell, I heard the gasps and cries from above. The jolt took my breath. I shut my eyes and gripped the ropes as I swung, promising never to take such a risk again. Lucky for me, the winch men knew their job well and lowered me gently, the swing decreasing as I descended, concentrating on the walls of the chasm.

The soil smelt moist. Roots poked and scratched my arms and legs until soil gave way to rock and the air grew cooler. I watched the layers of rock move past my face, and the light became twilight. The sounds of the surface were muffled and far away now. My ears ached from the ringing in them. I tapped the phosphorus tube, which the miners used to illuminate their world, and its light was welcome as the day faded. If I looked directly up, I could still see the sky, but it was like a narrow window in the mouth of the darkness below.

I tried to keep focused on the walls but found myself questioning the reasons for undertaking this journey, not to mention risking my life in this rescue. It had been impulsive, and perhaps it was a petulant reaction to my councillors' lack of concern. Certainly, Conrad had not advised me against it, but he was also quick to excuse himself from involvement in anything concerning Rynth. Yet something had filled my mind as soon as I heard the news of the disaster, and I knew that this was a journey that I had to undertake. If it was my destiny to perish here, I felt that I had followed my instincts and would meet my fate with courage. Not that I felt particularly courageous when my feet stumbled on the ground, and I toppled into the dirt.

Staggering to balance myself, I tugged three times on the rope, and when it became slack, I removed the seat and sent it back to the surface. It was only as I watched it ascend that it crossed my mind that I was alone down here, with no way of returning to the world above except for that wooden seat and the reliability of Ransom Frain. If he chose to, he could remove Magra's queen by simply doing nothing. The thought was chilling. I cast it aside, promising my more prudent self that I would try to avoid such risks in the future.

It would take some time before I expected to see Tom at the chasm rim, so I used my green glow block to look about me. What I saw did nothing to lift my spirits.

At first, I thought they were rocks. The fallen earth and vegetation had camouflaged everything at the bottom of the chasm. I saw the small rowan on its side, where it would no doubt die. I was on my way to stand it upright when I trod on something soft. It was a hand, the hand of a dead miner. That was when I began to notice them all. All dead, shrouded in black earth, grass sods and the brittle rock that had killed them. Faces were visible but more like stone than flesh in their blanket of soil, and I tried to avoid looking at them. Then one of them moaned as Tom's legs came into view, dangling over the edge of the opening above us.

I have never felt so inadequate. The man said his leg was broken, and I could see blood drying on his head and arms. He coughed and struggled to speak. I told him to stay quiet.

"Who are you?" he rasped.

"Kate!" I told him. "Lie still! Help's coming!"

"Others!" He struggled to point. "Down tunnels. Still alive. Can't move." Then he fainted. His chest still rose, but I could not rouse him.

Tom had brought better lights as well as bandages, strapped to the seat. I ran to help him as he reached the bottom. He was far more prepared than I was. When I told him about the man, and with much effort, we both managed to fix the man in the harness and give the signal to the winch men. I watched our survivor slowly rise. Tom was already systematically checking the others with a small mirror and placing a white cloth on the ones he found breathing.

"Have you done this before?" I asked him.

"No, but the Mine Masters make sure everyone knows what to do. Master Frain gave me a good ear bashing, afore I came down. We'll get this done, right? You're not going to faint, are ye?" He slapped my arm cheerfully.

"I'll try not to," I answered with more certainty than I felt.

He went to the opening of one of the tunnels and yelled down it, then waited. There was no sound.

"Here!" a voice said from under a lot of rubble. We rushed to uncover the speaker. It was a young man whose legs and arms had been trapped. His head was also bleeding, but once we'd removed the rocks, he appeared to be able to stand. "Young Tom!" he laughed as I hastily bandaged his wound. "Good to see you, Tom and you, Miner." He appeared to be lost as to how to address me.

"Kate!" Tom helped him. "Her name's Kate and she's a friend of The Mine Master." Tom and the miner appeared impressed. I smiled weakly as Tom prepared to guide the man to the seat.

“Nay!” The man laughed. “You’d do better by sending some of these others afore me. I’m fit enough to help get ‘em into that contraption.” He looked up. “There see, the crafty buggers up yonder have sent down two seats, so we’ve got twice the passengers!”

So it was that we began dragging our living to where we could put them in the seat and send them skywards. One seat leaving as another arrived. Tom handed me the mirror and the strips of white cloth.

“You finish off checking them, Kate, then take a big light and search the tunnels. If you hear the timber poles creaking, come back quick.”

We had cleared a space in the centre of the chasm, but there appeared to be plenty of others in the recesses. I hoped that I would find survivors, but at first, there only appeared to be the dead. Using the mirror, I checked most carefully. On and on the process went, painfully slow for the survivors. We quickly lost track of time.

I came across a smaller fellow who was face down but whose back appeared to rise and fall. I turned him over to check him, and his cap fell away, revealing a tumble of black hair. It was a woman. I must have gasped as the sound brought the miner over to where I was kneeling.

“It’s a girl!” I stammered.

“Aye, Kaylette Briggs,” he said, gently lifting her in his arms. The movement made the girl cough violently and vomit the dirt she had swallowed down his chest. “Had a good sleep, ‘ave you, princess?” He wiped her mouth with his hand. “This one next, Tom!” He carried the girl to the waiting seat and fastened her in, all the while reassuring her. His gentleness touched my heart. When she was on her way, he smiled apologetically. “Always had a soft spot for her.”

“There are women down here. I thought the women worked on the farms.”

"Most do." He helped me turn over a heavy man. Sadly, he was clearly dead. I closed his staring eyes, the only part of his face that was recognisable as a face.

"Wives all work over there, but young women, especially headstrong, independent ones like Kaylette can earn good matrimonial money down here. 'Cept she's in no rush to tie herself to anyone.'

"Oiy!" Tom called us back to task and poked me in my arm. "There's children an' all." He pointed to a huddle of small mounds in the darkest corner. It could have been a horrible moment, but as it was, the five young boys in their early adolescence had been fortunate. Someone, perhaps one of them, had protected them with a wooden pallet and a sheet of heavy tarred canvas. Most had little more than a broken bone or a sore head.

An empty seat returned with sealed pitchers of water and a metal box with bread and cheese. Tom and the miner insisted that we take our refreshment.

"Kate!" The miner beckoned me and confided as he broke the bread for us all, "If they think we should have a break for a bite to eat, then we must need one!"

I had more of an appetite than I had imagined, even with hands covered in grime and soil. The water and bread were eaten greedily before we resumed our task. We shared it with the young survivors who waited patiently for their return to the surface,

The miner, whose name was Jem, appeared to know most of our survivors and gave each one of them a cheery word if they were conscious and if they were not, he spoke to them anyway. We found some, more dead than alive, people, both Jem and Tom shook their heads at, but sent them to the surface anyway.

"Families want something to grieve over. Even if they don't survive, we'll get them all out, if we can." Tom nodded in agreement with Jem's comment.

Then we found Drin. He was a truly large man, surviving despite being half-buried under soil. He wheezed and spluttered as Jem fed him water, and gradually, he recovered. His cuts and bruises were fearful. Nevertheless, he was able to stand and assist with the loading.

"Now we have two of us here, Tom, you can start searching the tunnels with Kate." Jem put his hand on Tom's shoulder. "Safer to have the two of you do that together."

I could see that Tom was disappointed. I suspect he would have liked to return to the surface after all the younger boys had left. We had been binding a broken leg to a pickaxe before the miner, his leg and the axe rode to the surface. The miner in question was very pale and begged to go up without the make-shift splint, but Jem insisted.

With a shrug of his shoulders, Tom took hold of a large light and nodded for me to follow with one of the medical chests. "C'mon, Kate! Sooner it's done, sooner we get back up there."

"You know you're going to be a hero after this, Tom."

"I'll think about that once we've done." His expression was determined. "We could still be buried alive if that cut collapses much more."

We chose the widest tunnel first and quickly found pockets of people, small groups who had either been caught by a rockfall or overcome by dust. We conducted our checks with the mirrors quickly and tagged the living. There appeared to be more survivors than dead in this tunnel, which lifted our spirits. In the space below the chasm opening, Jem and Drin continued to load the chairs until Jem joined us in the tunnel.

"All the living are out from in there!" he said, handing flasks of fresh water to us both. "Drin's just waiting for the next chair, then he'll be along to do the heavy lifting."

More food and stores had been sent down, together with better lights. Night would be upon us before too long, and our task was far from finished. Two of the tunnel survivors, a man and a young woman, both coughing from lungs full of dust, bruised and bleeding, insisted they should remain below and began to help Jem and Drin carry the living back towards the waiting chairs. They were joined by two other men, dazed and limping, who had followed the sound of our voices. They pointed down one of the narrower passages and said everyone else working with them had been buried under fallen rock. They had scrambled to move the rock and called the names of their comrades, but there had been no response.

Just before sunset, an event we could only imagine in the fading but rosy light, hot food came down, the soup that Soldin and his volunteers had prepared and crusts of freshly baked bread. An oilskin pouch also arrived, and Jem took it solemnly. It was the list of miners working down Silverleaf when the world disintegrated around them. Jem knew most of them by sight and name, and he began the task of marking the dead, the survivors and the current missing. The list went back to the surface with the next chair passenger, and I realised, watching them rise, that the hole had continued to crumble.

The vegetation that had fallen was being trampled into the floor of the cavern, and I noticed the rowan, still with its root ball intact, resting on the ground. Impulsively, I handed it to the next chair occupant.

"When you get to the surface, tell Mine Master Frain that Kate would like this replanted where it can grow in safety. Like you, it was a victim of this day." The man looked bemused but nodded and held on tightly to the little shrub. I watched it rise back into the world above as we savoured the warm broth and vegetables. I knew I would never taste such a delicious or well-deserved meal again.

Jem sent us all down more tunnels before the night fell on us. We found a few battered souls and a sad group of children who had been too terrified by their ordeal to leave their protective overhang. Behind them, the passage was blocked by rocks and the occasional cold limb of a miner. Tom told me that if the Mine Master thought it too dangerous, the bodies would be left where they lay. The living should not be sacrificed for the dead.

"The Mine Master is right, but I do not envy him the responsibility for making that decision," I said as we helped the children back to the cavern. It had been decided to stop the chair during the hours of darkness and start as soon as the new day dawned. Blankets and woollen hats had been sent down, which we shared among the children and fed them the last of our soup.

Tom and I shared a blanket, and although I was certain that I would not sleep in such discomfort and cold, I found myself waking as the first chair of the day arrived. Tom and Jem were already awake and unpacking the hot bread stuffed with eggs and ham that was to be our hearty breakfast. The children fell on it with relish and as the first of them went to the surface, he was too busy devouring his food to feel afraid of rising up on the chair.

"You should go up next, Kate," Jem told me as the last of the children was being strapped in. "There's nobody alive down here that we've found, so we can load the dead. It might take a few days to do that."

"I won't say that I'm eager to stay," I smiled, feeling the grit in my mouth. "I'll help you bring the lights we set out in the tunnel back into here while I wait. You might think of sending Tom back up there before me."

Jem nodded. Tom had watched the other children leave with envious eyes. He tried hard to disguise his feelings. He now sat on a rock, looking dejected, for he was also aware that loading the dead would be their next task. I thought about calling him to help me gather up the lights, but decided that Jem should have him ready for the next chair when it came. I set off down the wide tunnel, collecting the small lights into the heavy burlap pouch in which they had arrived.

I could still hear the distant murmur of their conversation when another voice vibrated through my head and made me stumble. At first, I thought it might be someone trapped, but the voice wasn't a scream or a moan, and it spoke no words. It was in my head and everywhere around me. The tunnel itself appeared to be shuddering, and I fell to my knees, wondering if these would be my last moments alive before the roof of the cavern collapsed.

The voice persisted, laden with misery and anguish. As it called me to it, small flecks of light came up the tunnel towards me like snowflakes caught by a breeze. One danced past my face, and in the faint light it shimmered. I caught a second one in my hand and was amazed. It was a leaf, a tiny silver leaf, delicate and perfect. I turned it over in my palm, fascinated, but my attention was reclaimed by the urgency and misery in the summoning voice. It drew me back to my feet, and I staggered through the hail of leaves, not aware that I had dropped the mining lamps, seeing only through the ethereal light of the leaf shower.

The tunnel narrowed and twisted as the leaves tossed and danced in the eddies of the strange breeze that neither touched my face nor ruffled my hair. All the while, the voice guided me downwards. I call it a voice, but it was no sound I had ever heard, yet I knew it summoned me.

I turned a sharp corner, dodging a hail of leaves, only to find myself slipping and slithering down a steep drop, and as I tumbled, I had the impression of falling into a great open space, a dark void. Winded, I lay in the dust, dazed but aware of the whispering around me, and the voice was stronger now, demanding my attention.

There was vague light, but where it came from, I could not tell. It is hard now to describe my feelings during those first few seconds in that place. I was afraid, of course, but I was also mesmerised by the beauty that surrounded me. Trees, vast arching branches of trees, laden with the same silver leaves spread out in every direction, their limbs bending gently, stirring the air, whispering. I wandered between their huge trunks, dazed, wondering if this was a dream or that I had fallen to my death and here I was in the shadow valley of The Old Ones. The voice broke into my mind. Still calling, it drew me to itself, until we faced each other.

In a space, the very centre of this forest, rose a giant among giants, a tree whose girth was wider than the turret towers of Vellin and whose bark glistened in its own light. Was this the fabled tree, one of The Old Ones itself, that could bridge the void between all living things?

I believe it was, and in the immeasurable amount of time that it took for The Great Tree to plant a thousand images in my mind, I knew why it had summoned me there. I dropped to my knees and vowed to do its bidding.

The mines were too close to this sacred grove and must be closed. In return, new ore seams would be shown to the Mine Masters, drawing them away from this valley, which must be left untouched. I had seen images of what would happen if this warning went unheeded. All Magra and even the land beyond would suffer if the great silver forest was disturbed.

The tree was content with my pledge. It knew that it came from my heart, the heart of a Royal Mantle. A single silver leaf fluttered down to me. I was told it was a token of our covenant, a promise made between us. Before I could ask any of the questions that flooded my head, low branches offered themselves to me, and I was commanded to climb. The trees passed me, one to another, as I rose above the forest floor, feeling giddy at the speed with which I was moving, being passed with such gentleness, a mote in the presence of the mighty, yet I knew no harm would befall me. I was deposited at the mouth of the tunnel, and the voice bade me farewell. Then there was silence.

As I hurried back to join the rescuers, I felt the ground shudder again, and from the dark behind me, I heard rocks crumbling. I broke into a run, ignoring the pouches full of lights and only stopping when I reached the cavern.

Jem and Drin gave me a strange look when I told them that there had been another rockfall, but their faces paled when the ominous cloud of debris followed me. The tree had granted them time to remove their dead, but no more than that. We all saw the faint glint of silver flicker through the tree roots that surrounded the cavern mouth. The miners both agreed that I should leave first.

We embraced each other before the ground crew hoisted me up very gently. I blinked as the light grew stronger and almost lost my balance on the seat when all those remaining at the site let out a great cheer as my head appeared. They were still cheering as Ransom Frain placed a thick, woollen blanket about my shoulders and hurried me away from the crowd. They all surged forward to touch and congratulate me. The rest of my journey from Silverleaf to The Mine Master's mansion was hazy, although I remember Judith was crying and laughing, and Ross Elderin was silent, his face showing the strain that my hours down the mine had caused him. He helped me into the Mine Master's carriage and held my hand a little longer than was necessary. He squeezed my fingers and smiled full of concern and relief. I was glad when I was shown to a private room to rest. I confess that I might have slept in my dirty boy's clothes if Judith had not informed me that she had ordered a bath for me. Once clean and in bed, I slept until she returned to light the torches and stoke the fire. I asked her to tell The Mine Master that I must meet with him immediately.

X The Field

I was to meet Ransom Frain in his private study, but when I arrived, it appeared empty. Therefore, I had the opportunity to admire the room, which was as large as my father's study and held documents that spoke of a world far wider than the mines and their operation. He allowed me to browse before announcing himself with a cough.

"You have an interesting collection, Mine Master." I smiled at him.

"You have something of importance to say to me, Majesty. The hour is late, and I will be at the mine at dawn to see our dead brought safely back, so you will excuse me if I ask you to be brief." He looked weary. Judith had told me that neither he nor Ross Elderin had slept since my descent into the mine.

"Then I, too, will dispense with pleasantries." I began to feel in the pocket of my borrowed bedgown. "When I went to collect lamps in the tunnels, I had an encounter."

I showed him the single leaf that had been given to me.

"There are others down the mine, others living there. They have lived there for many long years before ever we and the mines existed." I showed him the leaf. "They have been disturbed and need your excavations to stop."

His eyes widened as he studied the leaf.

"We have a twin to your leaf." He held it to the light of the lamp. "That one is silver of a rare purity we could never achieve, but the leaf is much more, and I suspect this is one also. Our alchemists told us that it contained the remnants of life. It was found on the body of one of our engineers who excavated the first seam for Silverleaf. That's how the mine got its name."

I had no idea how Ransom Frain would react to what I had to say. He was a miner, a man of commerce, and no doubt would dismiss the ancient beliefs quickly. I supposed that the mere mention of The Great Tree would have him laughing at my gullibility, and it might well be the end of my credibility as a possible leader of my people. Nevertheless, I had vowed to tell what I had been told, initially without mentioning The Old One. I explained that the mine was too near a sacred place and that the inhabitants of that place wished only to protect themselves. In return, they had vowed to show The Mine Masters better places to create new mines. However, Silverleaf had to be sealed.

"And how did these beings communicate to you, Your Majesty?" I could not detect a hint of sarcasm or forbearance on his part, so I pressed on.

"Trees, Mine Master, they were trees, but only one communicated with me, in my mind." I saw his eyebrows rise. "I have a little Mantle skill, inherited from my father, and the tree must have recognised that."

He said nothing but went to a broad, oak cabinet, which appeared to contain very old volumes and turned a small lever. The shelving was separated to reveal several bottles of what appeared to be wine and a golden liquid which I did not recognise.

"I think we may both need a small drink of this." He poured the liquid and offered me a small glass. The liquid burnt the back of my throat and made me warm. "A drink distilled from crops that grow in the northern wastes. Please sit, Queen Katherine."

I allowed him to guide me to a very comfortable chair, and I found myself wishing there was such a chair in my father's study.

"You communicated with The Old One." He shook his head at the irony. "When many a Mantle has tried to find one, and fewer have been addressed by one. You have been in the presence of The Great Tree."

I took a deep breath of relief. He believed me.

"I suspect it would have chosen anyone who went down that tunnel. It was desperate to convince someone that the mining should stop in that place." I sipped the elixir, which was beginning to taste less fiery and smoother. "It was the most beautiful place. The trees made the wind, which scattered their leaves. The leaves guided me to them."

"You are wrong about The Tree choosing anyone, My Queen." He poured a second glass for himself, but I declined. "Only those with Mantle skills could communicate. I am impressed. Of course, I had heard the rumours of your current friendship with Silver Mantle and of a certain shield being lifted by the mind of a small girl."

"A small girl who was severely chastised for it," I replied, bitterly.

"Nevertheless, I thought Conrad was exaggerating."

Again, he was on his feet, walking across the room. Here, he opened another concealed panel in the wall and took down a garment, swirling it about his shoulders, allowing it to settle there and fall in familiar drapes to the ground. The fiery red of the material and the familiar pentagon emblazoned about the hem and left breast brought me to my feet.

"Forgive me, Queen Katherine, for my rather theatrical introduction to my other self." He chuckled, no doubt laughing at my stunned face, then he bowed low. "I am your servant, Majesty!"

"My Lord, Red Mantle!" I took his outstretched hand, and he kissed mine.

"I get to wear it so infrequently. My life here demands that no one know of it."

"Conrad said that the Mine Masters don't appreciate Mantle interference in Rynth," I spluttered.

"No more, we don't, and Conrad has been at pains to keep my secret, so I must ask you to also be a member of that conspiracy. It serves The Souran well to have a member of their council in Rynth, keeping an eye and ear on the lands distant from Vellin and the kings who might cast a greedy eye on The Five Kingdoms. It serves the mines well to have a Mantle with deep understanding of the fires below the surface, although it would seem that on this occasion you were the Old One's chosen messenger."

"Not by my choice, My Lord!" I pointed to the elixir bottle and held out my empty glass.

He chuckled. "I am glad you came. According to Jem Molder there are many alive now who wouldn't have been without you." We sat facing each other, allowing the liquid to soothe our minds. I began to feel sleepy once more.

"The young boy, Tom," I said, admiring the intricate patterns on the glass, "what will happen to him now?"

"He's being treated like a hero and will dine well on it for some time. He'll go back to his job with the ponies or be offered work above ground, if he prefers."

"Where does he live? You said he was an orphan."

"He is, but no doubt some family whose breadwinner has been saved this day will take him in. Orphans have a pallet to sleep on at the mine and are fed by the mine cooks. Tonight, he's in a bed along the corridor from you. He's had his first bath, which he didn't like, and he ate a hearty meal of chicken, pie and fruits, which he did like."

I leaned towards him. The Red Mantle robe shimmered in the firelight.

"I'd like to adopt him and take him back to Magra with me if he is agreeable to it. We have raised several children at Roth, and they would welcome another boy. I would make sure he receives a good education, and I will help him to gain a place in whatever he might show an interest in and aptitude for.

"That, Madam, is a wonderful offer you are making, and we will put it to him in the morning." He stood. "Now I must away to my bed and you to yours."

"Your secret is safe with me, Master Mine Mantle. Thank you for sharing it and this fine drink that you have introduced me to, but I also feel that if I do not get to bed soon, I shall fall asleep on your library floor!"

"The elix comes from the lands of The Kashkie, to the west, and in a land of volcanoes, it is rightly called firewater. I will send a bottle to you in Vellin."

He removed his robe, folding it with care, returning it to its secret cupboard, then he escorted me to my own room.

I slept soundly, and by midmorning we were on our way back to Vellin, with Tom riding a pony and frequently reassuring himself that he was not dreaming by asking each of the company in turn if I truly was Queen Katherine.

I had not anticipated the news reaching Vellin before us. Instead of slipping quietly back to The Angirat, crowds came out to meet us, cheering and waving, escorting us through the town until the gates of The Citadel closed behind them. Ross Elderin took his leave of his queen that very night, riding back to Brak with a letter from me to Roth. It gave a brief account of my visit to Rynth and, in a separate note, told Rosie to prepare for my visit. Less than a month remained before the lords would gather at The Field of the Pentangle, and I had to face my own doubts before confronting all of their scorn and doubt. I needed to return to Roth to gather my strength.

I had intended to leave Shana and Alice behind in Vellin, but both pleaded to travel north. Young Tom was eager to see Roth, so our company was a large one, escorted by Weld, Thorfin of Dereculd and Soldin Meganor. The three of them showed no urgency to leave my employ, and Thorfin expressed a wish to witness the events at The Pentangle. Perhaps that was the reason that they all stayed, although access to the kitchens and the training yard of the Talarin might also have helped. Grace archly pointed out that Judith was spending a lot of time in their company.

We travelled without fanfare, choosing to form a camp each evening rather than seeking hospitality at a manor house. At some other time, I think my councillors might have objected to our mode of accommodation, but they were all too busy preparing their own claims to the throne to notice what I was doing. Conrad was satisfied that I would be safe in the care of my hand-picked bodyguard.

When we arrived at Roth, they tumbled out to greet us. I had never felt so happy to see the stout towers rising up from the river. By evening, when Rosie and I sat beside the fire, my spirits were lifted as she questioned me for more details of everything that had happened since we were last together.

"The Lord of Brak seemed very eager for the day of The Pentangle to come." Rosie gave me a sidelong glance. "He seemed to think you would be content when you are able to relinquish your crown to your successor."

"He said that?" I leaned towards her.

"He did, when he presented us with a brace of grouse.' Rosie stood and moved to the table where we always kept a bottle of aged wine for an occasional treat. She poured a second glass of the Kashkie elixir for both of us. "He is a good man, don't you think?"

I took the glass she offered to me. "Yes."

"And not unattractive, for his age?"

"He's very attractive to me, yes."

"Enough for you to…"

"Rosie!" I leaned over to touch her hand as she sat beside me. "Our plans have not changed, nor will they. Ross Elderin is everything I could wish for in a man, but fate has seen to it that I must get a crown before I can ever contemplate the love that he could offer me." I gulped the wine, grateful for the warmth it gave my throat. "If I fail to gain the crown, then all our futures will have to change, and even if I hoped to win him, he may feel differently."

"Tell me about the boy, Tom." Rosie was astute enough to realise that a change of subject was required.

I might have tossed and turned all night thinking about The Lord of Brak, if Silver Mantle's thoughts had not demanded that I clear my head of such things and allow myself to sleep. I marvelled that he could reach me from so far away until he confessed that he was close by, at Heathcote, on his way to The Field of the Pentangle to meet with the other members of The Souran. They would make their selection and begin preparations for the arrival of the lords. Did I really feel his hand gently touching my hair and stroking my temples until I slept?

I spent my short time at Roth talking with Rosie and Grace, introducing Tom to the children, and watching him enjoy playing like a child, as carefree and noisy as the others. But the pleasure of watching their innocent games filled me with foreboding and regret that all that might have to change. All too soon, gowns were repacked, farewells exchanged, and we were on our way north, towards Heathcote and then westward towards the mountains.

Brak was quiet when we passed through it, the lord having already made his way to the high plateau below the Grat Hills.

The Field of the Pentangle was a long-revered place of ancient magic, where the Old Ones taught the ancient Mantles their skills. Many miles from any town or village, the green pasture, flat and without shrub or tree, spreads out from a cluster of standing stones, a circle of fifteen stones with five tall granite monoliths marking a pentangle. A single low building at some distance from the stones is the only other feature of the field. This open meadow would be transformed when the lords assembled to greet their new monarch.

As we climbed higher towards the plateau, we could already hear the sounds of a vast gathering. I could see the rising excitement in my young companions' eyes. When the plateau finally came into view, the ancient stones were lost among the lords' gaudy tents and banners. The silent plateau, the haunt of hawks and rabbits, had been transformed into a city of canvas, shivering and flapping in the strong afternoon breeze that blew down from Mount Befell, stark and white in the distance. Spread before us were the banners of the fiefdoms, the pale domes of the Marsh lords, dark cloth cones of the men of the Southern Meeds and the slanted roofs of the Northern Meeds encampment. The drapery of the standards fluttered, halyards clanking cheerfully against wooden posts, and everywhere was colourful and full of sound and movement, particularly beyond the encampment where eager young knights practised their skills. I could sense Judith beside me, leaning forward in the saddle to watch the activity.

Mantles were on hand to guide us to our designated space, and with Weld's help, Thorfin organised the erection of our canvas tents and awnings. Rosie unpacked the furs and rugs that would protect us from the cold while Soldin set up our kitchen. During his stay at Roth, the master knife-thrower had managed to charm Martha into letting him supervise our food while we were staying at The Field. I was told several times not to interfere with all their preparations and was thankful when a servant from The Mine Master's encampment brought an invitation to Ransom Frain's tent.

The Mine Master, resplendent in his finest brocade and bear fur, was already entertaining others. He ushered me to a comfortable chaise and introduced me to his guests. Polin Dukas, a bright-eyed old man with a silver beard and hair that brushed his shoulders, with more creases in his skin than furrows in a new-ploughed field. He spoke softly and talked as much with his hands as with his voice. In contrast, Arun Tenregor, robed in dark furs, said little, his grave features hardly betraying any emotions, but I could feel his eyes on me as I talked with the others. It was not an unpleasant feeling as I felt no animosity towards me, just his interest in what I said. I found Dlin Edgebar the most talkative of them all. His dishevelled hair and laughing eyes shone as he quipped about the weather, the lords' wealth of accoutrements, including Lord Clairstow's pack of hounds, and the musicians that Lord Mandrisoil had insisted should be given a special camping plot for themselves.

"I find the excesses of some of these noblemen to border on the obscene when their serfs have so little."

"You speak as if you know their manors well, Sir Edgebar." I ventured.

"I do, Queen Katherine, for my work necessitates that I travel through the kingdom and sometimes beyond. For example, I was in Roth last winter and had the good fortune to stay a few nights in your travellers' guest house. I was very impressed with your generosity to strangers."

"We usually have surplus to our own needs, Sir, and are very happy to share when we can."

Ransom Frain stood as Conrad entered. His guests did the same.

"Majesty!" Conrad came to my chaise, and I, too, stood, not through deference but to meet him face to face, though his face would always be some way above my own. He bowed as he kissed my hand. "I trust your time at Roth was pleasurable, even though your sleep may have been troubled." We both delighted in our shared secret.

"What news, Lord Silver Mantle?" Ransom Frain returned to his seat as Conrad joined me on the chaise.

"All our claimants have arrived, and we may begin the ceremonies before nightfall with the announcement of their names." Conrad looked at me. "Are you prepared, Majesty?"

"There will be those who mock your claim, and some may become hostile. Are you well-protected?" Ransom Frain gave me a warm smile, but there was genuine concern in his voice.

"I am." It suddenly occurred to me that both these members of The Souran were speaking openly before the other men, and all at once, I knew who Dlin, Arun and Polin truly were, lords, perhaps, but much more. My thoughts must have been very transparent, for Arun Tenregor put his finger up to his lips as he beamed at me. We talked a little longer, but the afternoon was passing.

I took my leave of The Souran and hurried back to my camp. I felt honoured that they had revealed themselves to me and recognised what great trust they placed in me. My ladies had been busy preparing my clothes, purple for majesty, cream for honesty and blue, my family colour and for warmth, a surcoat of kidskin, embellished with silver leaves. If I were to be regal, then I would have to look every inch a queen. As they dressed my hair, the doubts about this perilous path I had chosen flooded my thoughts. I held many lives in the balance. Suppose I failed them? Had I even considered what might happen if the civil war began here? In my head, Conrad's reassurance did little to calm my anxiety. Grace and Rosie cast their critical eyes over me and pronounced me ready. Soldin Meganor, in his finery, a red surcoat over black velvet breeches, escorted me to the stones, followed by my household.

The Pentangle had been cleared, and the lords clustered beyond the stones in a great circle. A way was opened for me by The Mantles, and Conrad escorted me to a small seat at the foot of a wide dais on which five chairs were placed. He left me sitting there, and some of the lords called to me, some with a greeting and some with a sharp barb or humorous quip about looking for a new job after the selection. I smiled and nodded, knowing that many of them were just as anxious as I.

A fanfare sounded, and the assembled crowd quietened. As I looked about me, my eyes met those of Ross Elderin. I returned the smile he gave me. My heart sank. Against all the valid and honourable reasons why I sought the path opening for me, the emptiness I felt overwhelmed me. The Kate inside me mourned.

Through the crowd, the Souran came, garbed in their elaborate Mantles, their faces hidden. Only Silver Mantle's head was bare, his cowl resting on his shoulders. Behind him came tall Black Mantle, stooping Blue Mantle, elegant, giant Red Mantle and lastly, Green Mantle, his body moving easily as he took his seat. Silver Mantle called for the lords' attention and began by explaining the process that had brought us all to The Field of the Pentangle.

Thirty-two lords had presented a claim to the throne, and as a mark of respect, they would all be called to stand before their peers. When all had been presented, the day's ceremonies would end, to be resumed shortly after dawn when the final five would be asked to speak before their assembled peers. This was why Ransom Frain had asked me about my personal protection. He feared for my safety during the coming night.

Silver Mantle began to read out the names slowly, and those named took their places on the dais, facing their peers and with their backs to The Souran. I watched each of my councillors make his way up the steps, Strewan with eagerness, Heathcote carefully, looking about as he climbed, and Tertius striding, supremely confident that he, and he alone, would be chosen. Thirty-one men, their hearts filled with hope, dread, elation, and confidence, faced their peers.

"Katherine of Roth, daughter of King Severin, grand-daughter of King Rolland, great-grand-daughter of King Peregrin and of all previous kings of the House Roth.'

I got to my feet. Conrad watched me walk carefully up the steps, to the accompaniment of gasps, whoops, cheers, and jeers. I swallowed hard before I turned to face the lords. Again, my eyes met those of Ross Elderin. He was not smiling. He turned away and was lost in the crowd.

Beside me, Lord Clairstow shook his head in disbelief. "You are making a mockery of this, woman! How dare you? When I am king, I shall send you back to Roth, where you belong."

I was still shaking by the time I reached our encampment and was grateful for the warm mulled wine that Rosie had waiting for me. I retreated to my small chamber, listening to the voices of my household. Some had already gone to explore the great gathering. Others were eager to join them. Rosie and Grace remained behind, with Thorfin and Weld, and they spoke quietly as they shared the wine. That night, a lavish banquet had been planned, but I was in no mood to celebrate. It fell to Rosie and Grace to bully me into attending.

"Long hours have I spent on the gown, and I will see it worn!" Grace and my ladies had been looking forward to the evening, and I could not deny them that pleasure. It was perhaps their greatest triumph to date. The gown in question was deep blue and embellished with golden royal lions. Simple in its style with few embellishments compared to the gaudy creations worn by the few other ladies present, but it fitted so perfectly, and the clever cut caused the full skirts to swirl as I walked. When I appeared at the entrance of the large pavilion, every man inside stood, and I was thankful to see more friendly faces than I had expected. I knew it was not Clairstow's foolish remark that burned into my memory of the presentation, but the anger and betrayal on Ross Elderin's face as he turned away from me. It was pain that I had anticipated, but far more acute than I could have imagined. It was a pain that must be conquered. My goal rested within this elaborately decorated tent with its banners and ornate table decorations.

"My Queen!" Heathcote bowed low. "You radiate majesty in every step that you take."

"Such a transformation, Majesty!" was all the breathless Strewan could manage.

"You put every other woman here tonight in your shadow." Tertius pressed my hand to his lips and held it there for an uncomfortably long time. Of course, his own wife had remained in Wyke, enabling him to shower me with such obvious affection.

"You look radiant," Conrad told me in my mind as he guided me to my place.

In truth, I enjoyed the evening, dividing my time between dancing a measure with some of the lords and speaking more earnestly with others. I drank and ate little, knowing that this would be my only opportunity to win others to my cause. I left before the gaming and drinking bouts began in earnest. As my ladies and I walked back to our tents, we all felt that the night had been successful.

I woke suddenly. It was dark within the tent, but I could hear whispers, and someone was moving about behind the tent. At first, I thought it might be a drunken lord relieving his bladder, but the gleam of a blade piercing and then slicing through the canvas told me it was not.

I was on my feet, backing away from the canvas, searching about for the dainty sword that Sword Master Tory had made for me. My fingers found it just as a pair of hands gripped the canvas, ripping it apart. I must have screamed as I lunged at the intruder. He yelped and withdrew, but a second man was climbing into the gloom of my tent, his dagger in his hand. There was very little space to swing the sword, so instead I threw my quilt over his head. This gave me time to step out of my bedchamber and into the main portion of our tent, tripping over Weld, and waking him. The man ignored Weld and came after me. By now, our whole tent was awake, Judith reaching for her blade, Grace standing as protector of my ladies. All this I saw, before Soldin quickly dismissed the killer with his own knife.

Our commotion had awakened The Mantles in their tents, and Dlin Edgebar, his identity no longer hidden from us, suggested that I would be safer in The Mantle Sanctuary, the low building some distance from the stones. With my ladies carrying what they could and escorted by Mantles, we hurried around the very edge of the camp to be greeted at the sanctuary by Conrad. He ushered me into the small chamber where the senior Mantle would have slept and watched in silence as my ladies made a comfortable bed for me. They would sleep outside the room with the rest of our company. Conrad waited for me to settle into my bed before he sat on the ground, his back to the door.

I shivered. “I wonder how many of them want me dead?”

“It could be thirty-one of them, but I doubt most of them would have attempted to do it.” His eyes were heavy. “Try to rest, there is still time for sleep.” I lay on my back, looking up at the rough timbers above my head.

“The floor must be cold; would you like a coverlet?”

“It is nothing.”

We lapsed into silence. I had ceased to tremble, but the pain of betrayal in Ross Elderin’s eyes crept back into my mind. I could not hide it from Conrad, although I tried. He came to me immediately and held me tight as I cried. I felt as though I would weep forever, but eventually my sobs subsided, and he loosened his grip on me. He moved towards the door.

“Please stay. I know I should not ask it of you, but tonight I need your strength.”

He returned to the rough bed, smoothing away the wetness on my cheek. “It will be sweet torture.”

He lay above the coverlet, his arms about me, holding me tight. His mind calming mine, his hands stroking my shoulders, my back, my cheek. He bent and kissed my forehead, his lips lingering on my skin. He knew my mind and lowered his mouth to mine in a kiss so full of longing and passion that I felt the air leaving my lungs.

I woke with the memory of his kiss still on my lips, or had I dreamed it? He was gone, and the clatter of pans and voices beyond the door told me that it must be almost dawn, although the chamber was still dark.

The dew was heavy on the grass as we made our way to the stone Pentangle. After the noise of the previous night, the tents were hushed. People moved quietly about their business, and even the colours of the pennants mellowed in the early light. We were all shadows creeping to the ancient rocks. The Mantles already waited to escort the five most eligible candidates up the steps, one candidate for each of The Souran. It had been rumoured that each would choose a different lord, but I doubted that it was true.

My councillors loomed up out of the dark, intent upon one final attempt to dissuade me. Heathcote began. "Madam, it would be impossible to even contemplate. There has never been a sovereign queen."

"Just because it has not happened in the past, Lord Heathcote, does not mean that it is not possible or preferable." I tried to sound calm and confident.

Heathcote persisted, "The people wouldn't like it, and neither would the lords. It would be totally alien to them."

I sighed with resignation.

"Forgive me, Madam. As your senior advisor, I speak only what I must."

"There is nothing to forgive, Lord Heathcote." I patted his arm. "Tell me, did you enjoy the mackerel pie last night?"

"Indeed, Madam!" He brightened at the change of subject. "I had never tried mackerel pie before, and it was most surprising …" He stopped, realising that he had fallen into my trap.

My smile was gentle. "Just because you hadn't eaten it before, it did not lessen your enjoyment of it!"

As I spoke, I was intercepted by a young Mantle and escorted to the platform. I did not search the crowd for Ross Elderin. Unlike the previous evening, my mind was clear and tranquil. I took my place at the end of the line. Lord Taegel's distant marriage connection had earned him a place, and Lord Wickstead, a distant cousin of my husband, had also qualified. Strewan beamed at me as I passed him, no doubt reminding us both of his suggestion of a royal marriage, possibly to his wife's nephew, who had been complaining of the family's inertia in gaining more power despite Strewan's closeness to the throne. Beside Strewan was Tertius. He leaned towards me.

"I heard a rumour that there was some trouble in your tents."

"It was not a rumour. Someone tried to kill me."

His eyes grew wide. "Katherine! Are you safe? Was anyone hurt? Did you catch the villain?"

"He's dead, no one else came to any harm, and I am well, thank you."

In turn, the five of us standing on the platform, including Tertius, addressed our peers, reminding them of our claim and telling them how we would rule the land. None of the speeches was memorable, not even mine, but at least mine was honest.

We were instructed to kneel and lower our heads. Even my father, the natural heir, had to receive his crown in this manner, bowed and kneeling before Silver Mantle. There had been no other challenges to King Severin, as he was the only surviving son of King Rolland.

We waited, with only the sound of the wind on the ocean of canvas and the slapping of banners against their poles. It was bitterly cold. Even wearing my warmest woollen dress and fur-lined cape, the wind bit at my flesh and made me shiver. As silence descended, the crown was carried around the circle of the stones, then up the steps. Many crowns are embellished with precious gems and detail. This was plain, a circlet of gold, a ritual crown cast in Urvik to crown the first king, Kelin of Ulomsk, and passed on to every king after him. Legend says that it was cast by the Old Ones themselves. In the hands of Silver Mantle, it caught the first rays of the sun as he lifted it high; the gleam of the metal was strong enough to cast a mirror image on his dark breastplate. With our heads still bowed, he walked slowly along our line, circling us twice, each time slower than the last and on the third circle, he paused behind me and placed the crown on my head. I felt the weight of it, the weight of kingship, embodied in gold, a weight my forebears had known, placed on their heads in the same manner on the same freezing plateau.

He placed his hand on my elbow to raise me up. “Queen Katherine of Magra!”

To my astonishment, a full-throated cry of approval rose from the lords and their retinues, many rushing forward to voice their congratulations. If not for my vigilant bodyguards, they would have swept up the steps and engulfed me. With Soldin and Weld shielding me and an escort of Mantles barring their way, Conrad guided me back to the sanctuary.

Around me, my companions celebrated. Everyone talking at once, jubilant at our success. Only Conrad, standing on the threshold, understood the turmoil inside me. I had accomplished the unthinkable, becoming the first queen of Magra, the unlikely monarch my father had trained me to be, without expectations of fulfilment. Yet, the hard task lay ahead, to prove myself worthy of the circle of gold on my head. Without words, Conrad urged me to relish the moment. The future must wait a little while.

My ladies had already set out my gown for the great celebration being prepared in the huge tent, erected by the Mining Guild. Rosie and Grace had planned this for a long time, and even I was impressed by their efforts. The gown, white and blue, adorned with embroidered lions and silver leaves, was flattering and yet free enough for me to lead the celebratory dancing. My mourning was over. At least that was what happened. Kings had never publicly mourned their wives, and as monarch, the business of governing took precedence.

An honour guard of knights lined my path from the sanctuary to the tent, now decked in the blue of The House Roth; garlands of ivy signifying fidelity were placed on the rough trestle tables for the lords to wear. At the high table, a hurriedly assembled wreath of wildflowers indicated my seat. This had been intended as a banquet to celebrate a male king, and poor Heathcote offered his abject apologies for his oversight. Some wives were present but of no consequence beyond their decorative value. I have little memory of what we ate, except for the pears poached in a brandy sauce, which was delicious and a Heathcote tradition.

I had determined that it would be politic to dance with all my councillors. As I danced with Strewan, he had puffed himself up with eagerness when I suggested that he would be perfect to preside over my coronation and subsequent celebrations. Heathcote had been pacified by my reassurance that I would always seek the good advice of my most trusted councillors. As for Tertius, he was charm itself, as elated and eager for my reign as if he had orchestrated it himself.

"I have so many wonderful memories of you and I when we were young," The Lord of Camlan said when we were dancing together.

"So, have I, Tertius,' I assured him. "It wasn't my doing that ended those happy times."

"And now you will be allowed to choose your consort." He let his hand linger on my waist a little longer than the measure dictated.

"I have no intention of choosing a consort," I told him. "I think with such excellent councillors and with the help of The Mantles, I have no need of a man to fill that post." I felt him stiffen a little.

"I believe we may need to discuss that when we return to Vellin. Taking a husband would be beneficial in many ways for you. He need not be a lord. There are several unattached princes in other kingdoms who would be delighted to marry you."

“But any husband would expect to wield the power, whereas without one, I have the opportunity to gather the opinions of three men with a lifetime of experience in governing a country.”

Not even my flattering explanation seemed to satisfy him. “The lords will expect you to take a husband, if only in name.”

I stopped dancing. ‘I don’t want a husband, Tertius. I’ve had one, and we both know how that ended. I intend to be queen without a consort.’ I realised that other dancers were noticing us, so I resumed the steps. Tertius had clearly been formulating plans inside that scheming brain of his. Perhaps he had already made a short list of potential candidates. I refused to let him dampen my spirit. If I could dismiss Ross Elderin’s disapproval for this evening, then I found the Lord of Camlan’s suggestions were easy to disregard.

Once I had done my duty and danced with as many lords as I could, I gratefully left the celebrations.

XI FOREIGN AFFAIRS

The return to Vellin would be a more permanent move this time. Back in Roth, I spent time discussing the move with Rosie, Grace, and Judith. Rosie, cautious as ever, thought we should not move the younger members of our extended families until the lords had completely accepted my authority. I reluctantly agreed that my original group of ladies-in-waiting would return with me, while everyone else remained in Brak. It was the safest approach for all our sakes.

If I had expected to slip back to The Angirat without fanfare, then I had underestimated Lord Strewan's enthusiasm for the task I'd set him. The people had been informed of my triumph and the day of my expected return to Magra; hence, they lined the route. Last time, they had shown their respect for a grieving queen. This time, they were loud and excited to welcome their new monarch. Strewan had even insisted that my final day's journey would be in an open carriage so that the people could see me. Thankfully, the weather was fine. Thorfin, Weld and Soldin travelled behind me on horseback, followed by my ladies. Rosie suggested that they wear the livery of my household, the blue and gold of my family, but I gave them the option to choose their own attire. All chose leather jerkins. Weld's was plain. Thorfin wore blue leather trousers to match his jerkin, with a new quiver bearing the royal lion. Soldin was resplendent in a black leather ensemble, enlivened by a long surcoat of blue and yellow brocade. At every turn, people approached my carriage with flowers and mothers rushed up with their infants in their arms so that I might touch them.

This time, the reception on the steps of the palace consisted of just two councillors, Conrad and Strewan. I congratulated Strewan on his arrangements, then used my mind to tell Conrad that I would like to see him in my study. Yes, my study. No longer my father's or my husband's, but mine. It was hard not to feel a little triumphant about that, and as is so often the case, when I met with Conrad, his news clouded my brief elation.

"Most of the lords are already preparing to travel to Vellin for your coronation, but a few will be missing." He sat facing me in one of the two comfortable chairs that had accompanied us from Roth.

"I think I can guess one of them." It still stung that during my few days at Roth, my early morning walks in the woods had been alone.

"Oh, he's coming!" Conrad folded his arms. "But urgent business in Camlan will keep Tertius Norton away, although he is sending his wife."

"Well, that's a comfort!" I scowled, then succumbed to guilt at my own pettiness. I sighed, "I suppose it will be pleasant to see Majolica again."

"Heathcote is suffering from gout and can't leave home, while four lords who supported Lord Clairstow's bid have all found reasons why they cannot be present." Conrad relaxed. "The pleasant news is that your cousin, Delion of Dereculd, is bringing a large entourage, part of Strewan's entertainment, and I understand that everyone in Rynth who can be spared is making their way to Vellin. The Mine Masters will be bringing your new crown with them. The old crown has already returned to the Talarin for safekeeping. The three other absentees are all old, infirm or both."

"Lord Norton seemed quite resigned to my being chosen when we danced. He even hinted I should take a consort." The idea amused me, but Conrad was unimpressed.

"He's not the only one. There are rumours that several lords might want to charm you during the coronation period. If they couldn't win the ballot for king, then they'll charm the queen and gain influence that way."

"Just let them try!" I told him.

"Then there are the other kingdoms. All five will be represented."

Conrad gave me a list of the various royal persons expected to arrive for the coronation. I already knew some of them but our neighbours to the south and west were strangers to me. Of particular importance was The King of Goremene, Tertius Norton's brother-in-law and ruler of our wealthiest and most powerful neighbour. Goremene was a large country with an equally large army. It was separated from The Five Kingdoms by a narrow stretch of water, which had probably protected us from invasion in the past. I would have to be very careful when dealing with Florian the First.'

"He's an excellent dancer and singer, apparently." Conrad said reading my mind. "But he's no fool and he might think having a queen in Magra would be a good opportunity to test the waters for invasion. His last acquisition was the island of Rhion, which he gained through marrying the princess. Sadly, the poor girl died, but the island is still his." Conrad handed the list over to me. "All the royal visitors will be housed here in the palace."

"Conrad, there is another matter that I'd like to talk to you about. Old Gwillem served my husband for many years. I would like him to go to Roth, with a small escort, for he is no longer young and I would hate something to happen to him. I have a pupil for him, someone who would benefit from Gwillem's experience. I have already spoken to him about teaching the boy."

Conrad relaxed, even crossing his legs. "Ah yes," he nodded, "the ever-faithful Gwillem, of course. I will send two of my gentlemen to escort him. The young man is very fortunate."

Once our meeting concluded and Conrad returned to the Talarin, I visited Gwillem and told him of my arrangements. The old man was happy to be considered useful and was more than willing to make the journey to Roth after my coronation.

I was grateful that Strewan was too busy to spend time ingratiating himself with me when I passed my approved guest list back to him. I was impressed with his thoroughness and thanked him for his invaluable help. Looking around the small room he had appropriated as an office, I suggested that if there was a larger space he wished to occupy, then I would be happy for him to do so. The delight on his face was quite humbling. I had always regarded him as the least effective of the three councillors but with the absence of the other two, he was rising to the occasion. We parted, both smiling, which was a bonus for us.

As I was propelled along in the flood of elaborate preparations, the endless fittings for my gown, the approval of new coinage, the mountain of menus, floral decorations, and briefings about the crowning ceremony itself, I had little time to think of much beyond the event. It confronted me, like a pair of stout oak doors, barring me from thinking very deeply about what lay beyond the morning when I would be laced into the elaborate confection of a dress, preened, polished, and escorted to the throne room of the palace.

Breakfast that day was shared with Grace and Judith, a bowl of Martha's porridge, a glass of apple juice and some precious tranquil moments, although I knew in the room above us Alice and Shana were preparing my transformation. Grace's advice to relax, placing myself in their capable hands worked to some extent but as my mind wandered thoughts of Roth and Brak surfaced. Why had I risked everything I had there for a chance to be queen? Would being queen satisfy me? Did I truly believe I was the best person to fill that role?

"Your fears are natural and essential. The path you tread is fraught with failure, but your destiny calls. Who better than your father and his Silver Mantle to prepare you for this day? Remember, the victory is already yours and today you take your rightful place. Tomorrow will bring new challenges. Leave them there. It is not their time." Conrad's thoughts assailed me.

Like a troupe of fumbling mummers, each gathering armfuls of voluminous material, Shana, Alice and I chaperoned my dress up the narrow stair to the throne room. A simple white shift, covered with a surcoat like no other. The deep blue of The House Roth, the colours of the Five Kingdoms embroidered on the long trail, the delicate golden lion on the bodice and about the hems. Once in position, my ladies hurried away to the side entrance to occupy their seats. I waited outside during Strewan's welcome speech and then Conrad's announcement of my entrance.

I entered, taking very little notice of who I passed, as I concentrated on not falling over. It was a blessing to be able to sit through most of the ceremony. When the crowns were produced, the assembly gasped. I was familiar with the traditional coronation crown, the plain, heavy circle of gold that I wore at The Field of the Pentangle. It had been worn by every King of Magra. Choirs sang as Conrad, resplendent in his silver and black armour, placed it on my head, then removed it, which was fortunate because it threatened to bypass my ears and drop directly onto my shoulders. My own crown was entirely different.

I had not seen it until the moment Strewan placed it on the small dais beside me. It was an exquisite example of Rynth craftsmanship, a delicate circlet of silver, with tiny silver leaves that swung freely and a golden filigree lion at the centre. One huge stone, a black opal, was placed under the lion's front paw. The opal is a gem most prized by miners for its rarity and black like the mines they work in. The crown felt light on my head and fitted perfectly. I later heard the story that the crown's size had been fashioned using the miner's cap that I had worn during the Silverleaf rescue, but I think that was just a whimsical tale.

The presentation of the other kings of The Five Kingdoms, my cousin, Delion of Dereculd, delicate and handsome in a silver surcoat, Arolan of Urvik, wearing the ceremonial robes of an ancient warrior, Xerio of Thanis, in the colours of the sea, and twin princes representing their father, the aging King of Bashiria. Their gaudy attire was almost painful to the eyes, but their smiles compensated.

The ancient ceremony of oath-taking by the lords followed. Strewan announced each lord, who placed their hands between mine and repeated the oath of fealty. No other conversation took place, which was a relief, except when it came to Lord Elderin of Brak, whose eyes never lifted from the floor. I wanted so much to explain why I was here on this uncomfortable throne, but I would have to wait. Perhaps I might never get the opportunity to tell him.

When the formal presentations ended, it was time to circulate for my first conversations with my subjects. Following protocol, the kings of The Five Kingdoms came first and without exception, I felt encouraged by their words of support. Most of them were old enough to remember my father, and none of them felt the need to talk about my husband.

Delion of Dereculd embraced me warmly.

"Cousin!" he squeezed my hand in his, "I cannot tell you how pleased I am for you. This was always your destiny." He leaned towards me. "Even if you have stolen my dear Thorin from me!" He straightened. "I forgive you, and he can't stop singing your praises. I might steal him back for a few days while I am here. Then he is yours once more."

I remembered King Arolan as a small boy who visited Vellin when I was twelve. He was a sweet little fellow with a mop of blond hair. Now he had no hair but still had an open, friendly face. We laughed about the time he spilt honey all over the floor of the great hall, and thanks to me, my father's dogs had licked it away before anyone important found out. Likewise, King Xerio had visited Vellin many times as a young man and had been one of my father's choices as a possible suitor for my hand. He walked with a slight limp, incurred during a hunting season in the Northern Meeds.

The gaudy twins from Bashiria dressed alike and were hard to tell apart. They were both enthusiastic about their kingdom's history and praised the first Magran kings for giving them a homeland after their perilous escape from Goremene. I knew a little of how the dark-skinned slaves swam across The Sul, to the semi-desert of Bashiria and of how they were welcomed and helped by Magra. It was one of the more enlightened actions of my royal ancestors. I would have loved to talk longer with them, but Strewan was moving me on.

After the kings came the visiting royalty from other lands. First among these was Florian of Goremene. His sister, Majolica, wife of Tertius Norton, was a beautiful woman, so I should not have been quite so startled by King Florian, but I was. His features were fine, slightly angular, with high cheekbones and violet blue eyes that fixed steadily on you when he spoke. His eyelashes were long and dark, as was his curling hair. His closely trimmed beard suited his face, and his figure hinted at a healthy, active life.

"We should have met long ago," he said, taking my hand and kissing it. "I had no idea that your husband had neglected such a beautiful wife." He looked at me through his eyelashes. "I would not have done so."

"It is my pleasure to meet you, too, Your Majesty," was all I could answer.

"We should not be parted for so long again. You must visit us, and I intend to visit you often." My hand was kissed once more. "Let us speak again before I leave."

I had to take a deep breath before meeting the King of the Kashkie. Adleb the fourth was dressed in orange and pink with his face painted blue. The face colour made his teeth dazzlingly white.

After the kings came the representatives of the City States, some a single individual and some, like Rynth, a small group of the most influential citizens. Ransom Frain bowed low as he kissed my hand and congratulated me on my coronation. Eventually, Strewan announced that formal introductions were complete and that the assembly should move into The Great Hall for the feast and entertainment.

The last time that I sat on the dais, facing a room of diners, was when I had been the grieving widow. I felt no less daunted by the evening ahead. I could not see him, but I knew that The Lord of Brak had been placed at the far end of the room, and I had very little time to search for him before the festivities began.

Strewan had transformed the room with tapestries and more candles than I thought the kingdom could produce. The long benches for dining were arranged around the walls to give sufficient room for the cavalcade of entertainers that my eager councillor had employed. Dancers from Kashkie followed a troupe of acrobats from Bashiria. Then came clowns from Urvik and a choir from Thanis. From Rynth, miners performed an agile stepping dance through two sets of poles placed at right angles to each other and held close to the ground by other miners. In time to a small drum, the poles were drawn together with a loud clap, then separated while the men walked through them. One false step or delay would have resulted in a painful injury. We all stopped eating as the tempo increased, anxious that surely someone would be trapped, but none of the men was harmed.

On my left, my cousin, Delion, clapped enthusiastically when the display finished. "That was amazing and quite frightening. I might have to introduce it to my court. That should keep everyone on their toes." He turned to Strewan, seated on his left. "That was a remarkable display, Lord Strewan!"

"I take no responsibility, nor praise for that item, Your Majesty." Strewan leaned forward and looked to my right, beyond Conrad, to where Ransom Frain grinned. "Mine Master Frain suggested the item, and it sounded intriguing."

"Perhaps I should include it in the training for our novices. Your company should demonstrate it to our students." Conrad gave Ransom a cheerful wink.

The floor was then cleared, and a single seat heralded the final item on Strewan's list of entertainments. It was a harper who had accompanied Delion's party from Dereculd. My cousin whispered, "I hope you like him. I do, very much."

The man was slight, and although beyond his prime, he moved with easy grace to where his instrument and a small canvas pouch on a stool had been placed. Before he began, his dark eyes scanned the room, and when they focused on me, I felt a strange fluttering in my rib cage. A momentary smile played on his lips before he began to play.

The room grew silent. Eating and drinking paused. The music, wistful and melancholy, flowed over me, filling the vaulted galleries above with vague, lilting echoes, and I was once again in the woods of Brak, the scent of lavender and mint surrounding me. An overwhelming feeling of happiness, tinged with regret, filled my whole body. I could do nothing but listen, enchanted by the harpist's poignant music.

When he rested his hands on his knees, the echoes of his last notes still floated in the galleries, and the whole room paused for a moment before responding with enthusiasm.

"What did I tell you?" Delighted, my cousin squeezed my arm. "Master Findin's music is so evocative. It reminds me of the surf breaking over the rocks on the coast, below my lodge."

"For me, it was the seabirds calling on the wind as it whips across the marshes." It was clear from the catch in his voice that Strewan bore deep affection for his home.

I turned to Conrad, about to ask him if the music had touched him, but the look in his eyes told me that it had. Was he dreaming of his home in the Green Islands, or was some other memory stirring his controlled emotions? Sitting on his solitary chair, the musician had moved his harp to one side and taken a small flute from his pouch. Again, his eyes met mine, and he winked as he played his first note. Not a reflective, lilting piece this time, but a jovial, cheeky jig that had feet tapping and guests reaching for their wine and mead. Throughout his performance, his eyes were merry, but despite loud calls for more, the musician simply bowed to me, gathered up his instruments and left the hall through the doors to the kitchen.

"That was masterful!" Strewan declared, "And a fine way to herald our own musicians for dancing!"

My marshland councillor had been very thorough in preparing me for the protocols of the evening. Strewan had emphasised that as monarch, it was my duty to begin the first dance and my partner must be the most important man in the room, recognised by his status. Never one to rely on others to ensure success, he'd whispered "Florian!" to me as we waited for the tables to be cleared.

The music began, and I obediently walked across the dais to where the King of Goremene was already standing, waiting. I doubt that Strewan needed to tell him that he would be my chosen partner. From the look on his face, it was his unquestionable right. I offered my hand, and instead of just taking it, he lifted it to his lips.

For the commencement of the evening, Strewan had insisted on a stately and elegant basse. It was also mercifully short. When the music ended, I expected Florian to escort me back to my seat. Instead, he remained holding my hands in his, facing me. That confused the other dancers who had joined us. They adopted a similar pose until the second measure began.

"Sometimes, it is simply fun to see what others will do when you do something unexpected," he said.

"Isn't that a little cruel? They looked so surprised." I spoke over my shoulder as I circled him.

"I give no thought to their embarrassment." He dismissed the idea with the flick of his hand. "I wondered what you would do."

"It would have been rude to leave you standing alone." I countered. "What else could I have done?"

"A queen might well have walked away, but you are still growing into your new role." He held me tighter than my dancing partners normally did. "Of course, I would have been bitterly disappointed if you had left me. By staying, you have shown me that you might be attracted to me."

The music ended. "Then let me leave you in no doubt about my feelings," I spoke as I turned away from him and took two steps before he was beside me, taking my hand.

"Marvellous! You have spirit. I admire that quality in a woman." He persisted. "I can't wait to meet you again. Perhaps tomorrow?"

"Perhaps!" I spoke as I left his side and approached Dlin Edgebar, who looked shocked that I had chosen him.

"I am not a dancer, Your Majesty!" the poor man spluttered as we took to the floor.

"Neither am I, My Lord, so, we should be perfectly matched." We bowed to each other as the dance began. Neither of us spoke through the intricate twisting of interlocking hands, but as the gentle promenade began, I asked him, "You told me that you have visited The Northern Meeds in your travels."

"Indeed, I have, many times. It is one of my favourite areas. I travel throughout The Five Kingdoms, but there are certain places that I enjoy for their own sake." He watched me twirl.

"Master Mantle, Jollian, once told me that Green Mantles could converse with animals. Can you?" We were promenading again.

He missed a step. "Of course not, I'm just a traveller."

"I know you to be Green Mantle," I said softly, as we circled. "But if you wish to deny it, I understand. Nevertheless, if you are, your skills are much appreciated by me. The land and the beasts that inhabit it are close to my heart, too. I often wished that I could converse with animals when I was a child, that is."

"It is not a hard skill to learn." He spoke as we sidestepped. When I moved to face him, he added. "Not for someone who could levitate a war shield!" It made me laugh. I would have said more, but sadly, the dance ended, and new music announced the next measure. Strewan had included the popular progressive dance, which required partners to form two circles, the gentlemen on the outer and ladies facing them. When the pace changed, the ladies sidestepped away, towards the centre, while their partners moved on. The process was repeated after a simple swing with the new gentleman before he, too, moved on. It normally created some merriment, even among carefully controlled courtiers. This progression continued until the music transformed into the new dance. Of course, in less formal occasions, much jostling and changing places was an accepted part of the process. However, this was a very formal occasion.

The look of discomfort on Ross Elderin's face when we came face to face, and the music changed, were enough for me to suggest that perhaps he could escort me to the courtyard for some air. He was reluctant, but he followed me. At first, we said nothing, looking out across the river to the fields beyond. He took a deep breath, and we both spoke at once. His nod deferred to me.

"I wanted to apologise to you for everything. I never intended any of this to come between us." I wanted to take his hand, but was afraid he would recoil.

"Your ambition would always come between us. Back in Brak, you never told me who you were, and then you agreed to be the temporary queen. You risked your life going down a mine without consulting me, when I was responsible for your safety, and now, here you are, the elected queen of your people. My congratulations! Isn't that what I am supposed to say? It's your destiny. I hope you find a consort who can make you happy." He turned away.

"Ross! Please don't go!" I pleaded. "There are things I need to tell you, things I want you to know so that you might forgive my behaviour." He ignored my plea, bowed quickly, and walked back into the hall. It was a moment of utter misery for me. I closed my eyes and leaned back against the cold stone.

"He'll be back. He can't help himself. He's in love with you." The voice came from the other side of a pillar. I was surprised to see it was the musician. He sat on the floor smoking a pipe, a plate of chicken bones beside him.

"And how would you know that, Master Harper?" I folded my arms and looked down at him.

He lifted his face towards me, those eyes still bright and piercing. "Because of all those present, his was the only other mind that took him to a forest smelling of wild herbs."

I scoffed, "And how would you know that?" Inside, I felt that same fluttering I had felt during his performance. I shifted my stance to appear more in control than I was. "Are you a Mantle?"

The idea amused him, and he snorted, "That bunch of ill-conceived mongrels! If my kind had not extended their amorous adventures to your kind, Mantles wouldn't exist, and no, I am definitely not a Mantle."

"As it happens," I boasted, "I have some Mantle powers myself."

"Oh! My compliments to you!" He flattened his pouch on the ground and indicated that I could sit on it.

"Who are you? Master Findin, isn't it? You're certainly no simple musician, even if the King of Dereculd thinks you are."

"A charming young man, King Delion." He faced me as I sat. "Who do you think I am?"

"Are you an Old One?" I was not even sure that I believed in the old myths about those powerful magi, but I had always dismissed the stories about The Great Tree until I saw it with my own eyes. Could this musician really be a powerful magus? I doubted it.

He feigned indignation. "Well, Old One, indeed! I've always thought I was somewhat spry for my age, all things considered." He puffed on his pipe and asked me a question in return. "What kind of a monarch do you intend to be? The mean, peevish kind who impoverishes their kingdom and people, for their own gains, or something a little more interesting?"

"I want to be a good monarch." I had no idea why I was spending time talking to this stranger instead of returning to the hall, but I answered him. "I want to bring my people together, to give them better, happier lives and to have peace. I want to leave the throne better than I found it."

"Ah, yes!" He nodded, tapping out his pipe on the wall and pushing it back into his pouch. "It's important that you leave a sound legacy for your successor." He stood. "Time I was off, but we'll see each other again, I expect."

To my horror, he suddenly disappeared, along with his belongings. In his place was an owl, which flew off into the night. At that same moment, Conrad came out onto the balcony.

"Your Majesty? Is everything well?" He came to my side, concern on his face. I asked him if he believed in The Old Ones. "Not really, although I know many who do. Why?"

I looked into the night where the owl had gone.

"No reason, except that I think I might have just met one. He flew off in the form of an owl." I didn't wait for his response but went ahead of him, back into the hall. The night was still young, and I had more people that I should dance with before it ended, excluding Conrad, who never participated in the dance. I felt suddenly desperate to put The Lord of Brak and Findin the harper out of my mind, at least for that night.

XII SOUND ADVICE

There were many sore heads the following morning, and servants tiptoed about their business. My ladies had all enjoyed their evening, some through dancing and others, like Judith, from too much mead or whatever it was that I saw her sharing with Soldin Meganor as they sat together on the stone stairway that led to The River Gate. Shana had danced every dance, and I found her dancing alone well after the changing of the watch. We talked for a while, then I sent her off to bed. Grace told me that she was still snoring long after we had broken our fast. While we sat together, enjoying the morning sun, Grace also told me that young Flyn Norton had spent the whole evening with Alice. I suspected they might, and I was happy for the girl. The dark shadow of my husband was receding into her past. Flyn might be related to Tertius and share aspects of his youthful appearance, but the younger man was more open and honest than his uncle.

I did not have time to recollect much of the previous evening because Strewan had arranged several meetings for me, some in the company of himself and Conrad, some alone with departing guests before they returned to their homes. It began well enough with Conrad setting out new plans for my protection and the resumption of my weapons practice with Sword Master Tory. I would continue to strengthen my bow arm, struggle with my short sword and now also learn how to handle a knife, for my own defence. True, like most women, I carried a knife in my belt, but solely for dining purposes. In future, I would be instructed by Soldin Meganor on how to use it as a weapon.

Our royal guests each took their leave in their own way. King Adleb hugged me enthusiastically, while the twin brothers from Bashiria promised to send me a copy of their research into their country's past. I have it still. The Kings of Urvik and Thanis departed together, reminding me that although they both knew Vellin well, I had never visited their palaces. I promised that I would. The free cities, including Rynth, were farewelled as a group, all except for Mine Master Frain, who was remaining longer as my guest, in order to spend more time in the Talarin.

That afternoon, Strewan had scheduled a pleasant boat ride on the river for me with King Florian. I doubted it would be pleasant and offered a bribe to Polin Dukas to summon torrents of rain to prevent the excursion from happening. But it did.

We occupied a curtained shelter at the back of the royal river barge. It offered privacy while we were able to view the outside world as it drifted by. It did not surprise me when the master of the small vessel pointed out that my husband used the boat frequently when visited by certain courtesans. I suppose I should have been grateful that the large divan had been replaced by individual seats.

At first, we sat opposite each other, and our conversation was inconsequential. He asked about my exile, the state of the country and the rumours about my visit to Rynth. I asked him about Goremene, his court, and his people. We shared anecdotes about his sister, Majolica, before we lapsed into watching the river and commenting on the weather.

Then he moved his seat beside my own. 'I'm pleased we could spend more time together. I feel that there is a natural attraction between us that must be explored.' He took my hand. 'I think we could make each other happy and bring benefits to both our kingdoms.'

'What benefits would I bring to my Five Kingdoms by becoming your queen? You have already told me that in Goremene, women have few rights, not even to own property or travel unaccompanied. How would that benefit The Five Kingdoms?' I wanted to discuss his proposal with honesty, although I had no intention of accepting it. Even Strewan had agreed that it would not be a marriage of equals. I would be subservient to Florian, and The Five Kingdoms would be vassal states to Goremene. Even if the other kings kept their titles, they would all be subordinate to Florian.

'Surely, you can see that trade would increase across our borders and The Five Kingdoms would have the protection of The Goremene Army.' He gave me a benign pat on the hand. 'Besides, there are other things in life than sitting in a gloomy castle worrying about the peasants and next season's harvests. You are still a beautiful woman, and although I am a widower with one child, I require sons. We could have a wonderful life together. I would shower you with beautiful things. Ask my sister. My court is lavish, and you would be at its centre!' He seemed to think I would readily accept and sat back in the seat, looking pleased with his offer.

Where to begin? How could I explain diplomatically to this man that handsome and charming was not enough, that surrounding myself with pretty baubles was of no consequence and that providing him with children was the last thing on my mind.

'I am flattered by your attention, Your Majesty, and would welcome your continued friendship, but I cannot accept your offer of marriage. As a woman, I might have been delighted to make a life with you, but as a queen, the High Queen of The Five Kingdoms, my first, my only priority is the governance of my realm. I accept that trade with your kingdom is beneficial to us, and I hope that arrangement will continue, to both our benefits, but marriage to you would subjugate not only Magra but every other kingdom to the laws of Goremene. I cannot permit that.'

While I struggled to try and explain all the differences that prevented any possibility of uniting with Goremene, he stood and paced about, twice thumping the supporting wooden posts of our shelter. That futile gesture alone would have alienated him in my mind. It reminded me of Brodik. He would pound inanimate objects to soothe his frustration. Then, when that failed to dissipate his anger, he would pound me, or sometimes Gwillem. I had lost one child to his anger. I was not remotely tempted to offer my womb to another intemperate king. Instead, I sat composed while he railed at my short-sightedness. Finally, he returned and sat facing me.

'I could have made you happy!' He frowned. 'But no matter. You have made up your mind. I will accept that. I do have one request to make before I leave you.' He moved back to my side. I was grateful that he didn't reach for my hand. 'I have not seen my sister's children for a while. I would like to travel back to Camlan with her. Do I have your permission to see the Nortons?'

I remember feeling quite relieved by his request. 'Of course, you may. It would comfort me that the Lady Majolica enjoys such a fine escort, and I am sure the children will be happy to see you.'

After the intense conversation of earlier, it was pleasant for both of us to chat about simple things, his Norton nephews, his sister, Majolica. His eyes softened as he spoke about his own daughter. It had been a disappointment, to be sure, when she was born, but a source of delight to her father ever since. Perhaps because of the way he spoke about his child, I agreed to visit his palace someday and meet the young lady myself. We left the boat arm-in-arm. I was thankful that this ordeal was over. Before she left, Majolica visited me. She understood my decision not to marry her brother and confessed that in my position, she would not have done so either. I embraced brother and sister the following morning and watched their company cross the Listi in the direction of Camlan.

My daily session with Sword Master Tory went better than I expected, and I was climbing back up the Palace Gate staircase when Conrad intercepted me. He asked me to join The Souran in his office. There they all were, thankfully in their normal clothes and sitting informally beside the fireplace. Ransom Frain gave me his seat and went to stand beside Conrad.

By the window, Arun Tenregor, Black Mantle, turned towards me. 'So, Your Majesty, now that you have been crowned, what are your plans for the future?' Tall and pale, he moved his thin body with grace. With his slick black hair and long limbs, he reminded me of a heron standing in the shallows.

'I would dearly like to tour Magra and the other kingdoms. So many of our vassal kings pointed out that my husband rarely left Vellin, except to hunt. He became a remote figurehead to many of our people. I want to be more visible to my subjects. After that, I would like to review areas where we could do more, from giving more financial help to cities, to your own hospices, to innovators, to exploration.' I stopped, seeing their growing smiles. 'I'm not sure exactly what I'd like to support in that manner, yet.'

'It is early days, my queen!' Beside me, Dlin Edgebar stroked a ferret. It often travelled with him in a special pocket of his green mantle. 'But I commend your ambitions, and I certainly agree that The Five Kingdoms should all have the opportunity to see their sovereign. It is on such occasions that you and any advisors who accompany you can begin to appreciate any problems or good practices that might benefit other parts of the realm.' My thoughts must have been very transparent, for he added. 'As you know, I travel a great deal and would be honoured to accompany you.'

Polin Dukas crossed his legs. 'I see the kings are already circling you like hungry sharks. I expected Urvik and Thanis might see themselves becoming King of Magra and sincerely hope you sent that over-confident whelp from Goremene packing!'

'Her Majesty has no need of a husband.' Conrad gave the old man a pat on his shoulder as he stood behind him. 'Your Majesty, we are always at your service. Touring The Five Kingdoms is an excellent idea and long overdue, but it will require careful planning and preparation. I suggest we raise it when all your councillors are back in Vellin.

'They were not here for the coronation?' Ransom Frain's eyebrow raised.

'Apparently, Heathcote is sick, and Camlan had urgent business to deal with at home.' Conrad made no effort to hide his antipathy towards both men.

Polin's hands brushed the air. 'They are both still licking their wounds over not being chosen king. I was pleased to see that Strewan has seen sense and made the best of his mistaken self-importance. I think Your Majesty has greatly improved my nephew's personality. I don't know how you have achieved it, but he does seem less fractious and argumentative, even towards his relatives.'

'Your nephew is Melchus Strewan?' I was surprised. I could find no similarity between the softly spoken old man and the fastidious little organiser, whose obsequiousness had diminished since I became queen. I had only seen the annoying side of Strewan before that. His handling of my coronation had impressed me. I could even tolerate his frequent reiterations about the necessity for a consort without wanting to strangle him.

'He was an annoying child, forever whining about something, but he seems to have settled down.' The old man's face creased in a smile.

It was well past noon when I returned to the palace. Outside, the day was warm, and after I attended to some documents that my lone councillor had prepared, including a list of suitable consorts, I escaped to the sunshine of the gardens.

Taking air in the wilderness garden later that afternoon, I came across Master Findin, sitting on a bench smoking his pipe. He looked up as I approached, and a small, red cushion appeared on the bench beside him. We said nothing at first. He was content to puff on his pipe. I sat and stared out across the river, watching the farmers in the distance preparing for harvest.

He regarded his pipe and then addressed his question to it. 'So, will you be entertaining distant princes?' When I didn't immediately answer, he went on. 'Can't think why you'd bother, except to satisfy the three mewing cats you call councillors. There's a perfectly good man for you, and you know it.'

I gave him a disparaging stare. 'Perfectly good, and not wishing to ever speak to me again.'

Still addressing his pipe, Findin observed, 'Well, you know why that is. He doesn't trust you.'

'Why should he?' I didn't have any defence. 'He thinks I've deceived him.'

'Well, you did!'

'Not on purpose, but when my husband died, things happened so fast.'

Findin shrugged. 'Therefore, what do you intend to do about it?'

I got to my feet. I had better things to do than be told all my faults by this annoying musician.

He looked up at me. 'I'm only trying to make you realise what you have to do, if you really do care for this man as deeply as he cares for you.' He didn't move, and neither did I for a moment. Then I sat down again. He put down the pipe.

'My dear, whether you like it or not, I am here to help you, as I am bound to you by our ancestry. I know deep down something is gnawing at you. You know it, and it will continue to fester inside you, like an open wound. Tell him!' He gripped my hand. 'Open your heart to him. Tell him your secrets. Let him help you. The throne can be a lonely place, and very soon, you will need all the support that the two most important men in your life can give you. You are fortunate indeed that although both desire you, one is restricted by his ridiculous calling.'

I knew he was right. I had intended to do exactly what he proposed on the night of my coronation, but Ross did not wait to listen. I doubted that he would ever listen to me again. I tried to put him out of my mind, pouncing on something else that Findin had said. 'You say you are bound to me by my ancestry.'

'Our ancestry,' he corrected me. 'Long ago, one of my kind foolishly sought the affection of a young woman. He deserted her, of course, but she bore a child from their union and, in doing so, lost her own life. Unfamiliar with the deep remorse he felt, he swore to protect all the offspring of her descendants. Thus, I sit here giving you advice, like an old uncle.'

'You don't quite look like an old uncle,' I told him.

'Oh! I thought I'd carried it off rather well.'

I told him that he was far too impudent, self-confident, and quick-witted to be an old uncle, not to mention that wicked twinkle in his eye. I said that I suspected that he was also an outrageous flirt. 'Of course, I am, and will continue to be. I delight in human company. I always have. Now, think on what I have told you.' He stood.

'Are you going to change into a bird again?' I teased.

'No.' He lifted his nose in the air. 'I am going to walk out of this garden like any other man would.' He set off down the path, and when he was half along it, he vanished.

Part of me wanted to go rushing to Conrad to ask him what he knew of The Old Ones and share what Findin had told me, but the old man was right. Conrad was a Mantle, and their order denigrated belief in The Old Ones, likening it to fables and homespun ideas about fairies and dragons. It seemed Findin held a similar poor opinion of Mantles. I knew Conrad cared for me, and perhaps it was fortunate that his position as Silver Mantle had prevented either of us from allowing our relationship to change. If Findin spoke the truth, it was an Old One's love for a mortal that brought about the powers that I possessed. Wouldn't it be ironic if The Mantles acquired their skills in the very same union?

Heathcote returned to Vellin a week later. He requested a private audience with me, and from his appearance, I could see that this illness had not been simply a fit of petulance as a result of not being chosen as king. An ashen pallor spoke more of his health than he could ever say, and I immediately asked him to sit.

'My Queen, I must apologise for my absence at your coronation.' His hands and lower arms rested on the chair so limply that I feared he might faint.

'My dear Lord Heathcote, your health is more important to me than your presence, even in Vellin. Should you not rest for a few days after your journey south?' I realised just how fond I had become of him, despite his reluctance to accept my abilities, even as a temporary sovereign. I knew all his restraint came from his devotion to the kingdom.'

'Nevertheless, I should have made the effort, but my wife insisted that I remain at home until the fever passed.' When Heathcote spoke of his wife, he gave a fond little smile.

'Then the Lady Maud should be congratulated for her good sense. She has my thanks.' I had an image of Maud Heathcote in my mind, from when she last visited Vellin, a strong, no-nonsense woman that I could relate to immediately. She had apologised for not accompanying her husband to Vellin during his years as councillor, but, as she put it, she had a manor to run, people who relied upon her and not a great liking for the frippery of court. My years at Roth had taught me how hard it was for wives left to undertake all the responsibilities of their lands while husbands were absent.

Heathcote nodded. 'She told me you'd understand, over and over again.'

I stood. 'I cannot say that I have not missed you, because I have, which is all the more reason for me to suggest you take time to recover from your journey before resuming any duties. Strewan can cope, has coped far better than I had given him credit for, and nothing is urgent enough for you to threaten your health. Return when you are recovered.'

He had difficulty regaining his feet. 'I suppose Norton and Strewan can manage without me.'

I held on to his arm to steady him. 'Norton has not returned from Camlan. He was also absent from the coronation.'

Heathcote's eyebrows raised. 'Had he been taken sick too? My infirmity was due to gout, which has plagued me for years.'

'He is well, as far as I know. He had important matters to deal with in Camlan.' I could tell from Heathcote's expression that he also found that excuse hard to accept. I walked with him to the door, where his manservant waited. He looked bent and old as they slowly made their way down the corridor.

Rest and care restored Lord Heathcote quickly, and within a week, both he and Strewan were badgering me to consider suitable consorts once more. In a moment of weakness, after a particularly gruelling training session with Tory, I agreed to see the list of their choices, stressing that I would probably refuse them all. It was late afternoon when they met with me. I had slept badly the night before and was steeling myself to be patient and unbiased during the meeting.

Marriage to me would elevate any man to High King. At the top of Strewan's new list of candidates was my childhood acquaintance, Arolan, King of Urvik, which Strewan thought might please me as I was already acquainted with him. I sternly reminded Strewan that the suggestion was for a consort, not a new king. I noticed a look of satisfaction pass over Heathcote's face as he turned to Strewan. Clearly, the old man had tried to explain that to Strewan before our meeting. Undaunted, Strewan moved on to the next candidate. King Xerio of Thanis had a younger half-brother. I looked at the information set out before me and rolled my eyes.

'He's fifteen years my junior!' I folded my arms. 'Is there anyone who is remotely my age, whom I might get along with, if only moderately?' Strewan began to shuffle his papers.

'What about him?' Strewan handed me a tiny portrait. The man's hair was turning grey, but he had a pleasant face. 'The eldest son of the Mazak of Kor-erif. The family is extremely wealthy, and they've capably ruled the city for seven generations. His younger brother is being groomed for leadership.' Strewan bent a little closer. 'Different mother, and the new Mazakasa is very influential.'

'So, what has this one been doing if he isn't going to be the next Mazak?' I was trying to be cooperative, although part of me just wanted to refuse any suggestion of a consort, even one who did look friendly. How could I trust any consort not to rally others against me?

'He's a studious man.' Heathcote had been given a chair, although he protested. He was completely healthy once more. 'I have read some of his papers on astronomy and animal anatomy. I think he was quite relieved when his stepmother produced a son.'

'Then what sort of a consort would he be?'

'A quiet, helpful one, who would not care to usurp your throne, providing you let him get on with his experiments and writing.' Heathcote folded his arms to match mine.

Strewan erupted with a dramatic sigh. 'This is the nephew of the King of the Kashkie!' He hurriedly put the next candidate's information forward. 'Wealthy and the right age.'

I read a little, then looked up at Strewan. 'He already has a wife?'

'The Kashkie are allowed to have two.' He added, 'You would, of course, be his principal wife.' I pulled a face and tossed the King of the Kashkie's nephew to the floor.

'There are some highborn princes available on The Green Islands, two on Inserfal and one on Beregstar. I could send an envoy to them with a portrait of you.'

As I scowled at Strewan's suggestion, Heathcote leaned towards my desk. 'What about one of the lords, Your Majesty? Since your selection as queen, a lord could not aspire to be king, yet he would be respected, even by those lords who are currently keeping away from Court.'

I looked down at my hands. 'I wish I had your faith that a lord selected to be my consort would not try to usurp my throne. My husband was a lord before he became king, and I did not fare well in that marriage, so you will forgive me for not rushing into a second liaison with a lord.'

They were both silent. When I looked up, neither of them spoke, so it was up to me. 'However, I understand your reasons for a consort, and I shall consider it.' They both looked disappointed. 'And Strewan, if you wish to invite the Mazak of Kor-erif's eldest son to visit Vellin, I shall make every effort to judge him fairly as a possible consort. After that, then perhaps I will consider a lord.'

I had no intention of marrying the discarded heir to the Mazak, but it would satisfy them for now, and I had other things on my mind. Since Findin's last visit, I had struggled to drive Ross Elderin from my mind. I knew I had treated him unfairly. I should have told him who I was as soon as we met, but I didn't. I should have told him about my aspirations for the throne, but I didn't. Perhaps if I selected him as a consort, he might agree, but deep down, I knew very well that he wouldn't. I folded my arms on the desk and rested my forehead on them. A whole hour later, Grace found me there, fast asleep.

'Majesty!' she whispered, then louder, 'Kate?' I blinked at her. I might have asked how long I had slept, but there was something in her worried face that told me she had more urgent concerns. When she was sure I was awake, she stepped back. 'Majesty, the Lady Majolica Norton has arrived. She's waiting for you in your solar.'

I slowly got to my feet, a little confused. 'Majolica Norton?'

'Yes, Majesty. She came alone, without an escort.' Grace continued to speak low as we went to the door. 'And she's badly bruised.'

'Did she fall from her horse?' I was still trying to imagine why she would be here, at a time when Tertius was clearly staying away.

'Her clothes are not soiled and,' Grace put her hand on my arm, 'her wounds look more like a severe beating rather than a fall.'

XIII TREACHERY

Majolica Norton was surrounded by my ladies when Grace and I arrived in my solar. When Majolica turned to face me, I could not hide my shock at her appearance. There seemed to be very little of her face that had escaped the battering. Judith was dealing with the blood from her nose that appeared to be broken, certainly swollen, and misshapen. Both eyes were purple, one half closed, and her lip was cut in several places. She had lost two teeth. From behind, I had already noticed the blood in her hair and two places where hair had been pulled from her scalp. When she saw me, she became tearful, and I could do nothing but hold her trembling body tightly until she calmed.

Alice gave her a beaker of warm honey and milk and urged her to sit down. After sipping the warm liquid, she was ready to speak.

"Forgive me, Your Majesty, for my appearance. I have ridden all the way from Wyke without stopping, except when my horse needed rest."

"Who did this to you, my lady?" I held her hand as Judith continued to carefully untangle her blood-mattered hair.

Majolica did not answer at first. So, we waited. She winced when Judith touched parts of her scalp. Eventually, she passed the goblet of milk to Alice and faced me.

"Tertius did this." She looked at her hands. "It is not the first time that he has quenched his anger on me, but this time, I suppose I should have expected it because I disagreed with him."

"No man has the right to do what he has done." I could not hide my anger. I knew only too well what Majolica had endured.

She sighed. “The beating is not why I have come to you.” She fought the urge to cry. “I have come to warn you, and …” Suddenly, her face dissolved into total misery. “He has taken my children away from me! He threatens to send them to Goremene!”

I gripped her hand more firmly. “We won’t allow that. Majolica. What is it that you come to warn me about?”

She did her best to compose herself. “Forgive me, it is hard not to dwell upon my poor children.” She took a deep breath.

“My husband and my brother intend to take the kingdom from you.” She waited until that statement had settled in the air. “Tertius had expected to be made king. My brother had expected this, also. When he failed, Florian came here to woo you. When that failed too, they decided it was time to use force. They intend to attack Vellin. Tertius will become King of Magra, and Florian will become High King of the Six Kingdoms.” She blew her nose, making it bleed. We all waited while Judith did what she could to stem the flow.

“I know what a devious creature my brother is, but I couldn’t believe it when I heard his intentions.” Her eyes appealed for an explanation. “How could Tertius ever agree to such a plan? You grew up together. He loved you, I know, because he has yelled it at me often enough.”

She sobbed. “I told him he was a traitor to his queen. We argued, and then he began hitting me.” She put her hand on her cheek, feeling the length of a deep cut. “He was like a madman. He yelled that I was unfit to be the mother of his children and that I would never see them again. He dragged me to my feet and then pulled me down the staircase. I fell, but he pulled me along like a sack of oats. I bounced on every step. I was still pleading with him to stop when he pushed me out of the door, into the night, kicking me several times. Then he had the door barred to prevent me returning.”

I felt nauseous. My own past rose inside my mind, yet for all Brodik’s violence, he had never treated me so terribly. Judith put a steadying hand on my shoulder and asked Majolica, “Didn’t anyone help you?”

“Yes. Oh, not while I was taking the beating. They wouldn’t dare. But as soon as my husband had bolted the door, one of my ladies and my groom came out to see if they could help. They wanted to take me into the kitchens and clean me up, but I knew I had to come to tell you as soon as I could. They promised to make sure that my children were safe and well, then my horse was saddled, and I left.” The telling of her tale had completely exhausted her, and she wept.

Grace and Judith escorted her to a private room, and both insisted on staying with her. Judith was pleased that Majolica ate some soup, and they persuaded her to bathe before she retired.

During the early part of my conversation with Majolica, I had alerted Conrad, who listened, through me, to everything she said. Shortly after the poor woman took to her bed, I sat in Conrad’s room, thankful for a glass of the Kashkie firewater.

“It took great courage for her to decide to ride here. The poor woman is worried she will never see her children again.” I curled my feet under me, sitting on his chaise beside the fire.

“I felt your own pain as you listened.” He sat beside me.

“I can’t believe that Tertius Norton could be party to something like this.”

“Can’t you?” He drank. “I suspect that the man who tried to kill you at The Field of the Pentangle was probably sent by your friend Norton. It’s no secret that he’s in the pocket of Goremene. Even his mistress is from there. She probably spies on him for her former master, King Florian.”

“I can’t believe he would betray me, like this.” I cupped my chin in my hand.

"Perhaps your father saw his true character." Conrad rested his hand on my forearm. "Perhaps he was eager to divert your affections to someone more trustworthy."

I sighed, "Well, we all know how successful that was, don't we?" We both kept our thoughts to ourselves until my foot cramped. While I winced at the pain, he knelt in front of me and began massaging my foot, keeping the toes tipped towards my head. The pain subsided, and I thanked him. I had moved further along the chaise, my feet resting near its end, so he sat on the other side of me. It seemed a natural move for me to rest against his chest, his arms loosely around me.

"We must try to rescue those children," he said, "King Florian left the day before Lady Norton was beaten. He is making his way through the Southern Meeds, so he could not have taken the children with him."

"You know where he is?" I turned my body slightly.

"The Mantles like to know where strangers are, just in case." He paused. "I suspect that the Norton children are still in Wyke. I think he was just trying to frighten his wife, but if he is planning some sort of attack on Vellin, then he might send them somewhere for safety, so we must act quickly."

I allowed myself to relax on his chest, my head just below his shoulder. In the early days of my marriage, Brodik and I would often sit together by the fire, just like that. "How can we rescue them?"

"I know three or four men who could enter a fortified manor without being detected and spirit the children away." He touched my hair. "It will be done." I closed my eyes and might have slipped gently into slumber, but he gently pushed me up to a sitting position. "And I need to set it in motion before the dawn." He helped me to my feet, then looked down into my eyes. "King Brodik was a fortunate man." He kissed me on the forehead and led me by the hand to the door. "Do you wish me to have someone escort you back to the palace?"

"No, unless…" I stopped myself from saying unless it was him, but he knew what was in my mind, just as I knew his own thoughts. He kissed my hand, slowly, then turned me towards the palace. He saved us both, but as I made my way back to my solar, I wondered what would have happened if I had stayed. Or if he had followed me.

The following morning, Conrad joined me with Heathcote and Strewan, who listened with grave faces as I told them of Majolica's heroic ride to warn us and of Norton's treasonous alliance with Goremene.

"I never trusted that smug, conceited popinjay!" Strewan's eyes screwed tight, and he clenched his fists.

"I didn't like him, but I never thought he could be a traitor." Heathcote's eyebrows threatened to meet above his nose when he was angry or perplexed. "He's always managed the king's accounts very efficiently." He corrected himself. "I mean, the queen's husband, as was."

"The weather is already turning, so I doubt anything will happen this year. Goremene and Camlan will both need time to prepare. Presumably, they won't act until spring. In fact, I suspect Norton might have brazened it out and returned to Vellin." Conrad remained standing, all energy this morning. "His wife's departure will have unsettled him. He doesn't know where she is. He might suspect that she'd come to the queen, but he doesn't know."

Conrad turned to me, "I suggest we don't tell him. I know you can rely on your ladies' discretion. We will hide Lady Norton for her own safety until we can unite her with her children. That particular mission is already underway."

"But if he comes back, how can we prepare ourselves without him knowing? Fortifying the city can't be done in secret." Strewan hunched his shoulders, already trying to think of ways to strengthen our defences.

"Hopefully, it won't come to that." Conrad pointed to the map of The Five Kingdoms, spread before us. Vellin is a difficult place to defend, all except the Angirat. If it comes to a siege, the lower town will have to be sacrificed. At this early stage, we don't know their plans. All we know is what Lady Norton told us.

'I suggest that we wait a little longer to see if Norton does return. He'll do it soon if he's going to do it. Meanwhile, a better plan is for The Queen to begin her shortened journey around The Five Kingdoms, giving plenty of opportunity to assess the strength of each lord, their willingness and ability to supply men and equipment, as well as detect any Norton allies. Shortly after Year's End, we should have a better idea of our own combined strength and if it's enough. We should let Delion of Dereculd and the Lords of the Listi deal with Camlan, while the main force moves south to engage Goremene's larger army. I believe that we can prevent them from reaching Vellin."

It had been the most unanimous meeting I had witnessed between my councillors. Each offered improvements to Conrad's plan, but the main thrust was accepted. Strewan was eager to prepare plans for a tour of the kingdom and even suggested that he liaise with one of my ladies. I introduced him to Grace. Her reluctance to spend time with a man she had always thought was an oily, sycophantic cretin was not auspicious, but after their first meeting, she had to admit that he was incredibly organised, and not once had he strayed from their task.

Majolica slept most of the day, during which time Judith stayed at her side, even forgoing her training session with The Mantles. I was not so privileged. Tory had sought me out and escorted me to the Talarin.

"Master Mantle, Conrad, has told me that you will need all the skills that I can teach you before the turning of the year, so let us not delay." He handed me my sword. It was not my worst day, but it tired me more than usual.

Grace and Strewan presented their itinerary for our journey after two days of hard work. To convince Tertius Norton that Majolica had not arrived in Vellin, we would first travel down the Listi through Camlan to Dereculd. Then we would go west, across the Southern Meeds to Bashiria. Turning north, we would visit Rynth and the free cities of Djengun and Jedran. If time and the weather permitted, we might go as far west as Kor-erif. Turning north-eastward to appraise the kings of Urvik and Thanis of our plans, we would travel south through the Northern Meeds, where I intended to spend the turn of the year. To return to Vellin would mean passing through the swampy Central Meeds to complete the circle. Much would depend on the weather and the condition of the roads. A royal court does not travel lightly, although I intended to pare down some of Strewan's list of lavish accompanying luxuries.

On Majolica's sixth day with us, when her face was beginning to heal and her spirits were calmer, Conrad came to my chambers.

"Your Majesty," he bowed. "We have some guests, just arrived." He beckoned into the corridor, and in came Majolica's children. They cried for joy to see their mother, and she cried thankful tears to see them.

"I don't know how you did it, but I will be forever in your debt!" She looked up from hugging them, all of us touched by the emotions of those rescued and their mother.

The eldest child, a girl, came to me and curtseyed. "Majesty, the men who came for us told us that you had organised our escape. My father is not bad, but we missed our mother. We heard them quarrelling, and Mama's screams, and we were frightened."

"Your mother was worried for you." I raised the girl to her feet. "I see that you are as brave as your mother. What is your name?"

"Flora, Your Majesty." She was suddenly aware that the whole room was looking at her, and she blushed.

“Well, Flora,” I glanced towards Majolica, “I think perhaps you might all like to rest here for a few days. Your mother and I will discuss what is best for you all, and I promise that you will all be safe.” We left them alone. Later that day, while Judith was entertaining the children, Majolica and I met with Heathcote, Strewan and Conrad in my library.

“There used to be animal heads on that wall,” Majolica said as we sat before the fire. I had dispensed with all that had been in the room, except my father’s desk and his books. A large tapestry, a coronation gift from the weavers of Kor Tnelis, had replaced the horrendous heads. I explained that I felt more comfortable without the hunting souvenirs. “I wish my husband would allow me to remove his trophies from our great hall. I hate those beady little eyes watching me.”

I explained to Majolica that I wanted only to protect her safety and had consulted with my advisors about the best course of action. “Of course, you are free to go wherever you wish, but because of the knowledge you have concerning your brother’s plans, I think it would be unwise for you to return to Camlan.”

“I never want to return to Camlan or Goremene.” She was emphatic. “All I wish for is the safety of my children and myself.”

“I had considered sending your North to Brak, to my own stronghold of Roth, but Silver Mantle suggested that was precisely where your husband might also begin his search to find you.” As I spoke, it struck me that Majolica had not thought about Tertius pursuing her. Her hand slid to her throat. In that moment, it became clear to her that it would not be a contrite husband seeking his wife but a nervous traitor, anxious to silence her.

“Lord Heathcote is returning to his own lands in The Northern Meeds,” Conrad took over as I reached to hold Majolica’s hand. “His fortified stronghold has withstood many assaults over the years, both from enemies and the elements. He would be pleased if you and your children returned with him."

Heathcote gave her his most reassuring smile. "I have been ill, Madam, and Queen Katherine has been kind enough to relieve me of my duty to travel with her on the journey through The Five Kingdoms. My wife and I have raised seven children, all now grown and scattered far and wide. It would be a delight for both of us to welcome you and your little family."

Majolica was touched. She took his offered hand. "It would be our pleasure, Lord Heathcote. I cannot begin to thank you."

"You have earned all our thanks by making your perilous journey from Camlan to warn your queen of our danger. It is I, and the whole of Magra, who owe you, our thanks." Heathcote had never sounded more like the noble statesman that he had aspired to be, and I was thankful that the whole accession turmoil and his recent illness had left him wiser. I could say nothing that would add to their plans, so I left the two of them discussing preparations with Strewan's assistance.

"I will send Weld along with them as an extra precaution." Conrad told me as we crossed the hall towards the Talarin. It was time for me to have another session with Tory, but this time I was delighted when I saw the straw target in the exercise yard.

"Lord Conrad has appraised me of the secret plans of Camlan and I thought you might like a change of exercise. He told me that you have some skills with a bow." It had been one of my favourite pastimes as a child, while my father hunted in the North. After proving my abilities with the target, I spent my time, practising turning before making my shot, shooting while walking and running, then shooting down from the galleries above. In the final minutes, I caught sight of Judith on her way to her own exercises and Conrad watching from his rooms in the opposite gallery.

"Of course, I suspect that you may never need to defend the city, but it is a good skill to learn." Tory said as I removed my quiver.

"Lord Conrad said we would meet the Goremene army in The Southern Meeds. I assumed it was to be a battlefield." I answered, handing him the bow.

"But you would not be there for the battle, My Queen." Tory began to unstring it.

"Of course, I shall be there." I laughed. "I intend to be at the head of my army. Naturally, I shall be there."

Tory gave me a long, hard stare, then with a brief glance at Conrad, who was watching two Mantles engaged in sword play, he said, "Well, that will mean practising your skills from the back of a horse. We will begin that as soon as possible."

"You can't seriously be considering leading the army?" Judith stopped lifting her heavy weights and came quickly across the practise yard. Sounds travelled easily across this space. I should have known that she would have the same reaction to my comment as Tory.

"I'm their queen. Where else should I be?" I could tell from the looks on all their faces, neither Tory, Judith, nor even Conrad had expected me to lead my men. "We will be defending The Five Kingdoms. Where else would I be?"

I tried to walk nonchalantly away, but they followed, each making their own protests. I stopped at the arch leading to the upper gallery.

"I have made up my mind. It is not for discussion. I hold no one responsible for my decision but myself. I only know that when I am expecting the men of The Five Kingdoms to give their lives, then I should at least offer up the same sacrifice." I started to climb the worn stone steps, wondering how many men had climbed those same steps and not returned from some distant skirmish. I was thankful that only Conrad followed me. I waited for him at the door to his apartment, ready to hand over my sword for his keeping. He took my arm and pulled me inside.

"Are you certain this is the course you wish to take?" There was anger in his voice, our faces close, both our bodies pressed against the closed door.

"What else should I do? Wait patiently in Vellin, fearful that the next person I meet will be the assassin sent by a victorious Goremene army? If we lose, I will pay the price. I'd rather take my place on the battlefield with my people, than being trapped in the palace. I would not want to live if The Five Kingdoms were lost."

He gripped me by the arms. "And what about those you're trying to protect?"

"Anonymity is their best protection." I looked deep into his eyes. "If we lose, life for the common people would not change, except that the yoke might be harder to bear under Goremene, but I will not be alive to see that. I will not only be fighting for my kingdom but also for my life, just like everyone else on that battlefield."

For a moment, we faced each other, breathing hard. The concern in his eyes changed to something else, something I had felt in him but never expected to see. He moved his hands from my arms to my shoulders to my face, bringing me close to him, his lips on mine. I felt enveloped in his arms, in his passion, feeling him as hungry for me as I was for him. Then, from below, someone cried out in anguish. It was Judith. We separated, both shocked at what had just happened. He went to the window, and I followed slowly.

Below us, Judith had sustained a cut on her arm, and Tory was helping her off with her protective vest and linen shirt. Judith's eyes were downcast as Tory set about binding her arm. I could not hear their conversation. My heart was beating so strongly that I could feel it in my ears. When Tory had finished, he handed her clothes back to her, and she gave him a pat on his arm before she left. I felt rather than saw Conrad shift his stance. I gave him an apology of a smile and fled, hurrying back to the palace as fast as I could, to catch Judith and make certain that Grace attended to her, before hiding myself in my library until the pounding stopped and the ache for him began to subside. This turmoil was something that I doubted ever confronted Grandfather Rolland and his Silver Mantle.

XIV PROGRESS

I can vaguely remember my father's Progress through The Five Kingdoms when I was a child. I had to remain in Vellin, but I remember that he set out in spring. I was about to leave the city at the start of autumn. This required an extra wagon for furs and winter clothes. Common sense should have seen us begin in the north to benefit from the warmer winter in the south, but it was imperative that we reach Camlan soon, firstly to protect Majolica by claiming that we had not seen her or her children, and secondly to lull Tertius Norton into believing we continued to trust him. Naturally, there would be no mention of preparations for the coming spring.

Before we reached Wyke, we spent two days at the small but important manor of Lord Taegel, one of my rivals for the throne. Oliver Taegel had earned his place at The Pentangle because he had married the cousin of my mother. It was a tenuous connection, but one that might have prevailed. He welcomed us with civility but was also wary about our reason for singling him out. I knew very little about the man. His small town swelled each year during the holding of a horse fair, and Lord Oliver had been shrewd in his handling of both the traders and the accompanying collection of troubadours and peddlers. Listening to him on our first evening as he explained the small taxes he exerted on the visitors, together with his support of local taverns and wayside inns, I could see that he had impressed Strewan.

The following day, before we departed for Wyke, I walked with him beside the river. He showed me where he hoped to extend the horse fair and his plans to build two new inns to accommodate the growing number of visitors. I asked him how he would have managed all of that if he had been selected as king.

He looked ashamed and spoke to his boots. “Indeed, Your Majesty, it would not have been possible, and I was very relieved when you were chosen. It was Clairstow and Norton who thought I stood a good chance, but to be frank, I never expected to win.” His dimples creased as he confided that both Clairstow and Norton had expected to be crowned. “They had encouraged several other lords to nominate, including myself, Wickstead and Malister. None of us expected to win, but at the same time, they elicited our votes for themselves. I’m not made to be a king,” he confessed. “I have no inclination in that direction. My pleasure, and what I am good at, is recognising opportunities and balancing my ledgers. Norton promised me that if he became king, then he would invite me to be his chamberlain. I might have liked that. I never wanted to be a king.”

I believed him enough to suggest that Strewan remain behind and explain enough about our preparedness for war without giving him details. Strewan had already devised a way of hinting that it was important for each lord to ready their militias for such an eventuality, without alluding to a specific threat. With the promise of reduced taxes for any lord undertaking such an overhaul of his martial might, it was doubtful that any of them would refuse. Already considering himself a possible chamberlain, Strewan was developing a commendable larger view of royal affairs and suggested that Oliver Taegel might also be considered as a councillor to replace Tertius, but that such a plan would remain secret until the spring.

“Thank you, Melchus, that is an excellent idea!” I happily agreed.

His eyes nearly popped out of his head. “That is the first time you have called me by my birth name.” His complexion had gained a deeper shade of pink.

"Really?" I smiled, fully aware that it was true. "Perhaps I am beginning to think of you as a friend as well as a valued counsellor. Is that appropriate, do you think?"

"Without doubt, Majesty!" He grinned, bobbed his head in a bow and crossed the room with a spring in his step.

We were to stay in Castle Camlan for only one night. The excuse for such a short stay was that, as Norton was a regular visitor to Vellin, there was less necessity for time to get to know him. The real reason was Conrad's concern for my safety. He had requested that my room should be large enough to also accommodate my two ladies, Judith and Grace, but in fact, he was going to spend the night sleeping on the floor. Conforming to the best rules of hospitality, we had been given the lord's own bedroom. Tertius greeted us warmly, noting that Strewan and Heathcote were missing. I told him the truth about Heathcote's health and said Strewan had to complete other business before he followed.

"I see you couldn't leave your faithful hound behind," he said as we walked in his garden, while my ladies prepared my room. Of course, he was referring to Conrad.

"Have you forgotten that someone tried to kill me recently?" I said it lightly, as if such an attempt could have nothing to do with him.

"Of course, to tell the truth, I had." He picked a flower and handed it to me.

"I was hoping to see Majolica. Did she return to Goremene with her brother? I suppose it would be a perfect opportunity to see her son. He's staying with his uncle, isn't he?" I gave him the opportunity to pounce on my lie, but he embellished it.

"She did indeed leave with King Florian and took our other children with her. They have never been to their uncle's court. I don't expect to see her until after the turn of the year. It's quite lonely and quiet without them all."

I walked a little ahead of him. "I suppose you could come back to Vellin, but the court has already disbanded until the spring, so I can't think why you would do that." I turned to face him and flirtingly suggested that he might join us on the royal progress.

"Tempting though that is," he said, taking my arm, "Majolica runs Camlan and has left me a long list of things I need to take care of before she returns. So, I must decline your invitation." We walked back to Castle Camlan, like old and dearest of friends.

There was music and dancing that night, and Tertius always set a grand table. It lacked the elegance that Majolica might have invested in the occasion, but it was pleasant. Strewan arrived just in time to join us. It was no surprise that a wandering minstrel had been engaged for the evening.

"He told me he played at your coronation ball," Tertius said as we listened to Findin's harp. It was no accident he was there, of that I was certain, and I wondered just how much of my life this mysterious harper had observed. He led the castle's own musicians in the evening's dances. As Tertius Norton and I moved through the steps of the branle, I could not help but recall the handsome youth with the chestnut curls and ready laughter who had stolen my young heart. I wondered what our future might have been if we had married. He might have made a better king than Brodik, and perhaps he would not have become a vicious husband.

"He has a loyal wife, and yet he keeps a mistress in Vellin. He would not have changed that side of his nature, even if he had married you." Conrad's voice in my head interrupted my daydream. Of course, he was probably right, but for a brief moment, I had wanted to see Tertius as he had been and not the traitor he now was. I glanced at Conrad as we passed. Of course, he was right, but the daydream had been sweet while it lasted.

My ladies enjoyed their evening, although they were all aware of Norton's treachery. They prepared me for bed and were about to join me in the lord's large bed, when Conrad arrived.

"I can protect her myself!" Judith told him.

"I have no doubt that is true, Lady Judith, but there are things about this room that you do not know. Most old castles like this one have secret passages and false walls. The two of us would be better than one, don't you think?" Conrad began to make himself comfortable on the carpet. We settled into the bed, but neither Judith nor I could sleep. Grace did not expect trouble and quickly slumbered.

Judith tossed and turned, eventually getting out of bed and searching the walls for hidden alcoves and doors. She found nothing, except her hunger and went off to find the kitchens. I sensed Conrad was still awake and went to sit with him on the floor. It was dark, but a shaft of moonlight lit patches on the carpet.

"Do you really expect Norton to assassinate me in his own home?" I asked him. He sat up and wrapped his mantle around us both.

"Perhaps not a thief in the night with a dagger, but I think there might be some attempt, something that could not be blamed on Camlan himself."

"I shall be glad when we leave."

"Listen!" he whispered. At first, I could hear nothing, but then, I distinctly heard the sound of something being moved, dragged across the floor above us, or was it a similar sound, a rasping, grating sound above us? It came to us both, suddenly. It was sawing. A small sliver of plaster fell from the ceiling and landed on the bed.

"Grace!" I almost choked on the word.

Conrad leapt to his feet, but the ceiling was already preparing to fall. Without thinking, I held my hands out, raised towards the falling timbers. Everything that Master Jollian and Conrad had taught me coursed through my body in that instant. I managed to hold up the ceiling long enough for Conrad to lift Grace to safety. Then I let it drop.

Grace was shaking, clutching Conrad as Judith sped up the stairs, two at a time. She gaped when she saw what had happened to the bed. She took Grace from Conrad and hurried her away to sleep with Alice. I know neither of them did sleep, but they felt safer together. When Tertius and Strewan arrived, Tertius immediately reminded me that one of the tasks he had been doing during his time in Camlan was inspecting the old building. There was a great deal of rotten timber that he was in the process of replacing. He was only thankful that no one was hurt.

As none of us felt much like sleeping after the accident, we decided to eat a very early breakfast and then depart. Tertius did not object and seemed content that we had all accepted his explanation and apology. It was only as we slowly rode beside the Listi at sunrise that Grace confessed that she saw what I had done and thanked me for saving her life.

"A party trick that Lord Jollian taught me," I replied. "You have been my lifesaver many times, Grace."

She shook her head. "Not quite as literal as that was!"

Camlan behind us, we traced the landward margins of The Great Marsh, Strewan's own domain. The wind tossed sharp sand in our faces, and I could well understand why it was that any tree that was not pollarded survived at an angle. The marsh grasses grew tall in some places, and in others, deep pools of brackish water echoed to the sound of frogs. An occasional ponderous heron stalked through the reeds. I could see that Strewan loved it all, but to me it was a desolate and lonely place.

'The Fen', Melchus Strewan's own home, was a delightful surprise, although we arrived at sunset and left just after sunrise. Set on a rocky outcrop, it defiantly faced the sea, a white bastion whose ancient stone carvings had long since lost definition, scoured by salt water and windborne sand. It was small compared to many lordly manors but unique for within its walls were comfortable rooms of homely familiarity, tapestries of seascapes, woollen rugs created by loving hands in the winter's candlelight and windows, which though small, offered views across the marshes. Within the single bailey, as well as stables, kennels for the hounds and various hutches for rabbits, chickens, and ducks, there was also a sanctuary for ailing wild creatures of the marshes, tended by Strewan's sister Marion, who also presided over our table that evening.

In contrast to the homeliness of The Fen and the ostentation of Camlan, the city of Pellian, Dereculd's capital and Judith's birthplace, spread across the flat land bordering the Weddon River, a lively mix of architecture and pleasing natural vistas. Conrad had ridden ahead and informed Delion of our arrival and of our sleepless night in Camlan. When we arrived, we were shown to our rooms and instructed that no one would expect our presence until the evening, when Delion had planned a celebratory dinner and concert. It gave us all time to rest, and knowing Delion's reputation as a patron of the performing arts, we knew we would be royally entertained. Of course, Delion's favourite harper had been engaged, and I no longer wondered how he had arrived before us. After his departure as an owl, I suspected he would have flown. Perhaps he had been the long-legged heron we passed on our journey.

"It was very courageous of Lady Norton to ride to Vellin and give you a warning. Thorfin has told me how they rescued her children. I do hope they are all safe now.' Delion was a gracious host and would not dream of discussing the substance of Lady Norton's warning until the following day. Leaving most of my entourage to recover and enjoy the relaxing atmosphere of Pellian, Delion, and I rode beside the banks of the Weddon until we reached the small fishing village of Branton beside the sea. He told me that someday he would like to build a harbour at the river's mouth. Sitting on rocks above the shore, I gave him the details of our plan.

"I am more than ready to take Camlan. As you know, while we have enjoyed a long and peaceful existence here, I do maintain a rather large militia to combat the continuous attacks by raiders from the sea. The men are mostly fishermen and coastal farmers, but they are well armed and also well trained. Thorfin's older brothers are in charge, and they are excellent soldiers. Have no fear, we will be ready for any fleet that arrives on the coast, and we can deal with Camlan. Of course, I will also send our people inland if the necessity arises.' He dusted sand from his boots. "Are you recruiting any other lords from this area?"

I told him about my visit to Taegel and my plan to enlist help from Bashiria.

"A good plan, but I doubt you'll get much help from inland. The three fiefdoms between here and The Forest of Lore are all in Clairstow's pocket.' He stood and helped me to my feet. 'He's a vicious libertine with a tongue like a sewer rat, but I doubt he would appreciate an invasion from Goremene. So, unless Tertius Norton has promised him something, it's my impression that he'll sit in his comfortable manor and take no part in any engagements. That way, he'll be the first to flock to the winner, and if there is no clear victor, he'll probably try to organise his own coup.'

Delion had voiced my own assessment of Clairstow. I had no respect for him as a man, but he was a shrewd manipulator, and any support he might give would be carefully weighed against remaining neutral and picking up the spoils. Noris Clairstow had threatened me during the ceremony at The Field of the Pentangle, and I had not forgotten. He was a dangerous enemy and an untrustworthy friend. He had little respect for women, and the two days that we expected to stay at his fortified manor were necessary only because I had to show that I was above pettiness and certainly not afraid of him.

We spent several days enjoying Pelion before our caravan was on the road again, travelling south. Thorfin stayed with Delion. I was sorry to part company with him, but it was clear they had missed each other.

I was not expecting to enjoy the next part of my journey. The Southern Meeds had been dominated by the Clairstow family for many years, and the change in the weather was not auspicious. The rain was with us during the whole of our ride, steady and heavy, turning the road to mud and slush. There was little time or inducement to appreciate the fertile and productive lands of the Southern Meeds. Vineyards clothed the gentle hills while small farms producing vegetables lined the valleys. We bypassed the smaller town of Karstin, famed for its red wine festival and made directly for Clairstow's fortress home.

Unlike most lords, the Clairstow family had built their stronghold in the country and away from the two towns in the area. Their disdain for local people went deep and not without reason. Four generations ago, the town of Nordinay had rebelled against the high local taxes imposed on its market traders and had attacked the stronghold. When the lord went out to confront them, they attacked him, dragged him behind a horse all the way to the town square, where they hung him. It took The High King and a sizeable army to quell the rebellion and help the surviving heir to rebuild his home. Noris Clairstow not only doubted the strength of his queen but also any support offered by the people.

Our welcome was hospitable, if not quite friendly and conversation during our supper was cordial. I discovered that his lady wife was indisposed, as she often was and in her place was his daughter, Sybil. Her elder brother and heir to the vast Clairstow lands was an officer in my cavalry. Sybil was a pleasant and cheerful girl who was clearly excited to meet The Queen and her ladies in waiting. She chattered merrily to us all as we prepared before the supper.

"It must be quite lonely here for you sometimes," Grace commented as she prepared my hair.

"Oh! It is!" Sybil gushed. In the seat beside me. "My father does not allow me to associate with local people, and I have only my mother, her maid and the servants for company."

"You should come to Vellin and visit us!" Shana offered cheerfully as she brushed Sybil's hair. "We could have such fun, and

I could show you the palace and Vellin." The look of longing and enthusiasm on Sybil's face was almost pitiful.

Later, as we dined, I broached the suggestion of Sybil visiting me in Vellin, but Clairstow shook his head.

"Sybil has an obligation to remain here and be a companion to her mother. Besides, as a queen, you probably don't appreciate how much the women of a manor actually supervise everything. My wife is often incapacitated, and I rely on Sybil." The man was insufferable.

"As a queen, Lord Clairstow, I found out quite quickly that women are capable and often expected to manage a manor, when I was taken to Roth! I had to learn very quickly." I hoped I had laced my words with enough indignation to stun him.

"Ah, yes, I forgot," was his reply, with no apology or even regret in his voice. To be fair, Clairstow had not been one of my husband's close friends, therefore my removal from Vellin would have been a surprise to him. Nevertheless, he then added further insult. "Perhaps you are finding that ruling a country is a little harder than managing a manor."

"Absolutely!" I bit back, gripping my knife firmly. "When I was at Roth, all my tenants were supportive, and we worked hard together to bring in the harvest. With a country, a monarch is far less certain of the loyalty of her subjects, who seem to have goals that are at odds with their sovereign."

He gave me a long, hard look, and I matched him, but then decided to take a higher moral path. "Tell me, Lord Clairstow, your wife is of a delicate constitution, is that correct? Is there any way we can help her?"

"My wife is delicate, Majesty," he nodded, then clearly decided to confide more. "She suffers from an aching in her bones and often feels faint. Her headaches are tedious, and her only relief is the application of warm oil on her joints." I saw that his wife's ailments were also tedious to him. “Sadly, there is little anyone can do to ease her condition.”

“The poor lady!”

“She never ventures far from her solar, and as time passes, she has become far less inclined to travel, or even venture into the gardens.” He actually leaned towards me, a sad smile on his face.

“Sometimes she sits outside for a time, enjoying a warm sunny afternoon, but as winter approaches, we will not see her move far from the fire in her room. She finds it tiring to even hold a conversation, and her only pleasure is having Sybil read to her. It is a sad state, but one that my daughter and I must endure.”

It was no small wonder that Noris Clairstow appeared such a lonely figure, and an angry one. I decided that my judgment of him should not be founded on one unpleasant exchange. We both made efforts to spend a quiet evening talking about the neighbouring countryside and his personal preoccupation with collecting local myths and legends. I did not broach the subject of the expected invasion from Goremene.

That night, I heard the sound of sobbing coming from further along the corridor. It continued for some time, accompanied by the sounds of struggles and gasps. Eventually, I could not lie there listening without going to see what was wrong. Inside the solar, there was a frightening sight. Sybil was on the floor, clutching her arm, and it was her sobs that I had heard. On the other side of the bed, Lord Clairstow and another man were holding fast onto a tall, agitated woman, her grey hair dishevelled, her nightdress soiled, her eyes wild.

“See! This must be his other trollop! He has hundreds of them. Leave my husband alone!” she screamed at me. Horror replaced the stern resolve on Clairstow’s face.

“Please take my daughter out of the room!” he appealed to me. I helped Sybil to her feet, and when we were in the corridor, I had to ask her how to get to the kitchens. I had no doubt the servants would be aware of their mistress's state, and I needed to have someone familiar to help Sybil, who was pale and bleeding. After slowly making our way down to the kitchens, I left the girl in the care of a kitchen maid and returned to our rooms to collect Judith and Grace. We returned to the kitchen. Together, we began to repair Sybil's wound. It was not deep but long. She told us that her mother had managed to find a pair of scissors and had attacked her as soon as she was in the room.

"My mother is not a wicked person, and most of the time she remembers who I am, but just sometimes she gets confused. Please don't punish her for this." Sybil recovered her composure quickly. Clearly, this was not the first attack.

When we were almost finished, Noris Clairstow and Conrad arrived. Sybil's father went straight to his daughter and embraced her. Then he turned to me.

"I am truly sorry that you had to witness my wife's condition. It is not something that we can speak of outside these four walls." He put his arm around his daughter. "It is something that we have endured for some time."

"Ten years!" the kitchen maid said over her shoulder as she took away the bowl of water that we had used to clean Sybil's wound.

"My household has had to bear the burden of my wife's madness, too. We are all bound to her, prisoners to her temperaments." His head drooped. "I am ashamed by the spectacle that you had to witness."

"Your steadfastness and the care that you are giving to that poor woman should bring no shame to you or your household. It reveals a loving inner strength that can only be admired." I spoke as I helped Sybil replace her sleeve. She was pale but composed.

"My father thought that if his claim to the throne had been upheld, then we could take her to Vellin and seek the help of physicians and healers. Perhaps even Mantle help." She glanced at Conrad as she took her father's hand. "He was desperate to become king for my mother's sake." She looked me in the eye. "He has been desperate for a long time. His hair has turned grey long before it should have. He's a good man, but sometimes he lashes out at others. He can't help it."

Clairstow put a gentle hand on her shoulder. "You see why I cannot spare her? She is my rock. When I am close to losing my reason, she restores me."

"I see very clearly that both of you have endured a great deal in silence. Why not bring your wife to Vellin and let us try to help her?" I turned to Conrad.

"The mind is a dangerous playground in which to meddle," Conrad faced Clairstow, "but The Souran might be able to calm her ill humours and restore some of her reason. It will take time, and all might not be as it was, but I am certain Black Mantle could help the lady.'

Clairstow sagged into a seat, his head in his hands. This was a very different man from the aggressive bully I had encountered at The Pentangle. He did not speak for some time. Meanwhile, my ladies collected their belongings and left us. Finally, Clairstow looked up.

"I will think on what you have said, Your Majesty, and may I also change my mind about my daughter? I will send her to Vellin to visit you. I have been selfish to expect her to share my burden. It is mine, but it should not be hers."

"Father, no! You need me here," Sybil protested.

He reached for her hand. "I need you to be safe."

"If you truly feel that you can spare her, then I would like to offer her a place among my ladies. They enjoy new company, and I am sure she will learn much from them.' I could see Sybil's eyes widen. "But you do not have to decide now. We have the day to discuss this further, and Sybil will no doubt want to make certain of your own health before she departs. When we continue our Progress, my lord, you should prepare yourself and your lady to leave for Vellin and a meeting with Black Mantle."

XV SOUTH & NORTH

It was with a hopeful heart that I bade farewell to the Clairstows. Sybil would accompany her parents to Vellin, and before we left, Conrad had already prepared Arun Tenregor to receive Lady Clairstow. We had hoped to bypass the town of Nordinay, anxious to be south of The Forests of Lore before nightfall, but news spread fast from the kitchen to the market, and the whole town had turned out to celebrate our passing. It made me wonder just how much the folk of Nordinay had known about Lady Clairstow's condition, for we were often thanked for our kindness without anyone being more specific about what we had done.

"You didn't tell him about the Camlan treason," Conrad observed as the forest came into view in the far distance.

"He has worries enough without me adding one more. I shall call him to arms, but I do not expect him to leave his wife. We had not counted upon his help before our visit, and I don't count upon it now."

The road divides some distance before The Forest of Lore. The northern road skirts around the edge of the forest, rising slowly towards the distant hills. We took the southern route towards Bashiria. Even on the edge of this vast woodland, something was unsettling about it. The trees, birch, oak, alder, beech, and linden, grow so close together that beyond the first trees, only darkness and the vague hints of tree trunks are visible. As we made our camp for the night, the call of the wolves could be heard. They sounded too near for comfort, and guards were set to protect the camp perimeter with fires placed to deter any night visitors. Even with all those measures, it was hard to rest, and I found myself awake long after midnight when the shape of a man in a hood slipped between my tent and the nearest fire. Remembering the night before my election, I called out, waking Grace. She was too afraid to investigate so I reached for my sword and went out.

"Forgive me, Majesty, I did not mean to wake you. I was searching for Silver Mantle's tent." It was Dlin Edgebar, Green Mantle.

"Lord Green Mantle, what are you doing here?" I wrapped my cape tighter about me. The night was cold, and the full moon illuminated the forest.

"I was visiting friends when they told me you were close by." Dlin looked down at the sword. "You will not require that, Majesty. There is nothing within the forest that would harm you." He pointed to the silver leaf that I wore about my neck. "That alone would grant you safety here." He saw me hesitate. "Please put your weapon away and follow me."

Sometimes, the most remarkable things happen when you least expect them. I followed Dlin into the forest. He understood my wariness and gripped my hand. The sounds in a forest at night seem to be louder, as if the trees amplified every footfall, every cry of an owl, every invisible being that snuffles, pipes, whistles, and scratches in the dark hours. We slowed. Ahead, in a clearing, there was no mistaking the creatures gathered there. Moonlight turned their grey coats to silver and their eyes to yellow as they turned to face us.

"Wolves!" I gasped, preparing to flee.

"Not just any wolves." Dlin kept a firm grip on my hand. "The Wolves of The Forest of Lore have always walked close to the shadows of men and honour the great tree. Come and meet my friends. Perhaps tonight they will become your friend, also." He gave my hand a gentle tug, and I found myself walking towards the pack. One huge, pale creature stood and came towards us.

"Lord Fleetfoot, the leader of his race, this is Queen Katherine." The animal showed no fear and came to stand before me. Dlin told me to let him sniff my hand. I did, and the wolf then sat beside me.

"They understand you?" I marvelled.

"I am speaking to you at the same time as using my mind to speak to him. Sometimes they can hear me, but tonight they are wary of strangers, so I want to make sure that we all know what is happening. It is in the tone of your voice and the signs from your body that they perceive you." Dlin looked down at the wolf. "Fleetfoot wants you to enter the clearing, so the pack can see you better."

Even now, when I look back on that night, I become overwhelmed with the memories of that strange and wonderful moonlit glade. I sat with Green Mantle in a circle of wolves, so close that their fur kept me warm, so close we could learn the scent of each other. I stroked their heads and let the cubs lick my hands. Such simple joy as they settled, silent, sharing the moonlight, alas, over too soon. At Fleetfoot's command, the pack began to drift away into the shadows of the forest until he alone stood beside me.

"My friend wishes you a safe journey and wants me to tell you that his kind will always be at your side." Dlin stroked the thick fur of the wolf's shoulder, and so did I. Then even Fleetfoot left, and we were alone. Green Mantle escorted me back to the camp before he, too, melted into the darkness of the forest.

If Pelion had delighted us, the Bashiria capital of Homisag bedazzled us. The buildings were unlike anything in Magra, mostly covered in plaster and painted in vivid colours, rarely uniform and topped with turrets, spires, and dizzily sloping roofs. The spaces between them were filled with exotic vegetation and towering palm trees. Water, though scarce, tumbled, squirted, and bubbled everywhere. In the middle of the city stood a palace. This, like many of the older buildings, was built of stone, no less colourful in its painted exterior but showing elegance in its ornate balustrades and carved, wooden screens.

Our accommodation within the palace compound was simple but very comfortable. Cushions were everywhere, and although the weather was cool and the skies grey during our visit, I could well imagine how valuable the wooden lattice screens would be during the hot summer months. Now, they were covered in heavy woollen tapestries to keep out the cold.

"I hope you enjoy our histories." During a tour of the city, Prince Laydor reminded me of my gift, a history of Bashiria written by the twin princes. We were seated in an open carriage and completely ignored by the townsfolk as they went about their business.

"Thank you, it is a wonderful gift. I began to read it last evening, after our feast." In truth, I was so engrossed in the document that Grace had to take it away after two hours.

"My brother, Likor, did most of the writing. I like to do the research." He stopped the carriage and sent the driver to purchase fruit from a stall. "Try them. They are dates and grow well in our climate. They were one of the things we brought with us from Goremene." The dates were sticky and sweet. I immediately asked if they could send some north for me.

"It is my father's wish that we trade more with Magra and the other kingdoms. Our older brother, Lagrin, has been busy on the great continent setting up trade with Temras." He watched with amusement as I devoured the dates.

"Will Lagrin succeed your father?" I asked, not certain how many children the old king had. During our stay, it had been Laydor and Likor who entertained us. Their father was very frail and saw few people except his twin sons and his doctors.

"No. That is our eldest brother, Beren." From Laydor's face, I could tell that he had little affinity with this particular sibling. "He is with the Kashkie at the moment, trying to woo the royal princess."

"Wooing is a serious business," I nodded. "I have been subjected to some of it recently. Do you think he will be successful?"

"Only if she enjoys combat and hunting." He stole the final date. "Beren's mother was from the warrior caste in Urvik. He is paler than most Bashirians, and the people call him 'the ghost prince' behind his back." Laydor put the stone from the date in his pocket. "For my mother's garden," he added.

Later, in the cool courtyard where the brothers spent their afternoons, I explained the possible invasion by Goremene to them. They immediately volunteered their help. Laydor was certain that Beren would be overjoyed at the opportunity to fight a real battle, and all the more so because it would be against Goremene, which continually tried to influence and bully the Bashirian rulers.

"They are just across the water, and they have long memories." Likor folded his arms. "They can't forget that we were once their property, their slaves. If they gained power in Magra, I imagine they would try to subjugate us once more. Our dark skin set us apart when we were their slaves, and it still sets us apart, even from the rest of The Five Kingdoms. Most of the kingdoms deal with us as equals, different but equal. None of us would wish that to change." He grinned as he turned to his brother. "Send a carrier pigeon to Kashkie and tell the warrior he's needed here." They both laughed.

Leaving Bashiria was a wrench. I had grown very fond of the two brothers and reminded them of their obligation to visit Vellin often. I wasn't certain if Laydor was joking when he remarked that after their father's eventual death, the twins would need to find a new home because Beren would be unbearable to live with.

Our progress north was uneventful, except for the growing chill in the air and the gradual changing colour of the trees. Autumn was creeping quickly south, and behind it the winter would follow. Some distance north of the Bashirian border, Conrad halted our caravan on a wide and windswept valley. Several small streams flowed through the southern part of the valley, and in the north, the land rose steeply in a series of grassy banks and flats towards woodland. He suggested that this would be an excellent place to meet the army of Goremene. The very idea of contemplating a battle chilled me more than the sharp wind, but I agreed that it was a suitable spot. We hurried on towards Rynth.

Ransom Frain made our stay in the Rynth valley very pleasurable, and it was a delight to see again the friends I had made in Silverleaf. I was impressed by all the repairs that had been made and very flattered that a new inn had been built and named in my honour. It marked the centre of the new town of Silverleaf, near the mine of the same name. That had been closed, and new shafts were being sunk further afield. Ransom explained that sink holes would suddenly appear, and each time they were tested, a rich seam of silver, tin and even gold had been found. When we were alone with Ransom, Conrad, and I explained what had happened in Wyke and that we were encouraging the lords to prepare their militias. Thanks to The Souran's ability to communicate across distances, Ransom was well aware of the situation already and had prepared the free towns, as well as sending word to The Kor cities and even distant Kashkie.

From Rynth, we travelled to the free towns of Djengun, Eminga and Jedran, where the local people had petitioned my husband for a garrison to protect them from marauders who came down from the hills. Of course, he had ignored their pleas. Conrad advised me that a garrison would be a good idea. The cutthroats and thieves that hid among the hills were becoming a menace. They were even starting to harry The Meed towns beyond. He had prepared plans to show the townsfolk, and they seemed grateful for our recognition of their plight. We left them with a promise that the first contingent of knights and foot soldiers would arrive the following summer.

While we were in Jedran, news came about devastating storms in Urvik. King Arolan's messenger had been sent to warn us not to attempt to reach them, as snow was already falling, and advised us to proceed directly to Thanis. Always thoughtful, Arolan had sent word to Xerio in Thanis that we would be arriving early.

The Urvik messenger insisted on returning home, so he took my letter with him, warning of the possible invasion of the Five Kingdoms. We passed similar news on to Xerio when we arrived in Thanis. Our welcome there was warm, but our stay was necessarily brief. They, too were expecting snow, and the passes between Thanis and The Meeds would soon be closed. Thus, we began our journey south, through The Northern Meeds. We visited most of the manors, including Heathcote, where my councillor and Lady Majolica were both recovering. Knowing what a burden a progressing monarch could inflict on any manor, we passed quickly on to Wickstead, who was not warned about the Goremene threat because he had been a close friend of Tertius, as was Mallister, whose manor we stayed at and were treated with reserved politeness.

"Time to go to Brak," Conrad told me on our last evening in Mallister. "I will instruct most of our entourage to return to Vellin if you and your ladies would care to return to Roth. Would you like to speak to Lord Elderin, or shall I?"

"I will.' I sounded more emphatic than I felt. "Perhaps you would spend the turn of the year with us in Roth. It is time you met the rest of my household."

"I can think of nothing better, but I must preside at the Talarin for the turning of the year. It is the traditional time for new postulates to arrive, and you and I both know how important it is to test the skills of those seeking admission. Nevertheless, I can think of nothing better than meeting the whole of The Roth household."

XVI ROTH

It was a typical Northern Meed winter's day as we rode south towards Brak. The uplands, naked trees shivering in the wind, our faces flecked with drizzle, welcomed me to the landscape I knew as home. Despite the dreary day, our spirits were high as we rode down through the thickets of hawthorn and rowan towards the market town. Conrad and my ladies sped on to Roth, anxious for the warmth of Martha's kitchen fire and the ever-present cauldron of soup to revive them. I expected a less-than-cordial welcome at The Meed manor house from Ross Elderin.

I was shown into a small waiting room and spent longer than a monarch might expect to be kept waiting by a minor lord. I did my best to be patient. Perhaps he had not received the message telling him that I was about to visit him? Perhaps he was away from home? I had almost reached the end of my list of excuses for him when he appeared, his clothes smeared with blood. He blinked at me and then began to drop to his knee.

"Oh! Please stand, Ross!" I had not forfeited Martha's kitchen fire to watch him kneel. I indicated his appearance as I asked. "Have I arrived at a bad time?"

"A neighbour of mine, and yours, John Potts, fell off a roof this morning and landed on an iron spike. They brought him here, but there was nothing we could do. He was already dead."

"John Potts, the poacher?"

"The same. The fool was trying to escape over the rooftops and lost his footing. He won't be stealing hens from the apothecary again. I've sent someone to tell his wife, and when we're finished, I'll visit the apothecary. For a man with medical knowledge, he was shaken by finding someone impaled on his garden stake."

It was a bad time. Perhaps I should have left, but I persisted. "Is there somewhere more comfortable where we can talk? Perhaps you'd like to change and wash."

"Look!" His voice hardened as he wiped his hands on his legs. "Is it important? I can't imagine why you'd want to talk to me. As you can see, I'm far too involved with the mundane matters of Brak to be of any importance to you. I really would like to get this poacher's death dealt with, so if this was just a social visit, then perhaps …"

I didn't let him finish. "No, not important. I can see you are far too busy to see me!" I moved to the door. "When you have a spare moment, perhaps you could ride over to Brak, and I'll explain then. Give the widow Potts my condolences." I swept out, angry with him, angry with myself and even angry with the poor servant who got in my way as I rushed to leave the manor.

By the time I had ridden past the wood and entered the Roth gates, I had ceased crying, but I knew my face would still betray my turmoil. I took the back staircase to my chamber, where Rosie or perhaps Grace had set out a change of clothes. I could hear the faint sound of people talking, laughing, and as I washed, I could hardly wait to be with those I loved.

Conrad appeared unconcerned about sharing a table with predominantly women, joining in the descriptions of The Progress and offering anecdotes about the places that we had visited. I was content to let them all chatter. I listened, sometimes smiling at their accounts, occasionally verifying some detail that those who had remained in Brak found hard to believe. It was a pleasant evening, and at the end of it, Conrad and I were the last two remaining.

"They are a pleasant company!" He spoke to his glass of Roth mead.

"They are indeed. I could not have survived without them."

"The Lady Judith tells a fine tale, and I can see she is much respected here." He was more relaxed than I had seen him recently. He was admiring the amber liquid in his glass. "Did you speak with the Lord of Brak? You didn't mention it when you returned."

"He was busy." I gulped the dregs from my own glass.

"I see."

"He would probably be too busy to defend the kingdoms. Spring's a busy time for farmers. He will be needed to supervise crop planting." I could feel my anger at Ross Elderin rising again, and I didn't want Conrad to see it.

"Katherine?"

"I need to sleep." I left the table and had to walk past him to get to the door, but he intercepted me.

"You know he cares about you. I'm sure he will come to Roth in the morning."

My fury erupted. "And how would you know, a man who never allows himself to love? How could you know what Ross Elderin feels?" I knew I was being cruel. I knew only too well that Conrad was trying to help, but I was angry and selfish. All through my ride from Brak to Roth, memories of betrayals paraded in my mind, my father, Brodik, Tertius Norton and now even Ross Elderin. I couldn't rely on any of them.

"I know how I feel." He gripped my upper arm and said roughly, "Meanwhile, you are wallowing in self-pity because a man didn't find time to see you, or apologise enough, or whatever it was that he did to hurt you, at least you know he loves you. How do you think it feels to love someone who can never show you love in return because you can't show her, except in your devotion to her as queen?"

I felt my mouth droop open, and all I could do was whisper his name. We stood there, emotionally naked to one another, drained. I reached up to touch his cheek, but he took my hand and kissed its palm, his lips lingering, his eyes on mine. More than ever, the invisible thread that bound us held us there on the edge of a precipice. We were both tired. Perhaps nothing would have happened if one of us had been strong enough to break the thread, but we were weak and fell over the precipice together. In silence, I led him to my chamber, kissing him once at the door, then reluctantly separating to remove clothing. He took my face in his hands, his lips tender, then urgent, before we turned to the bed.

I thought it was only our minds, but it seemed our bodies knew the unfamiliar landscapes of each other with little exploration. The rising urgency, once satiated, took little time to rise again. Neither of us gave thought to what lay beyond those moments of passionate love, a love that might only be shared once in our lifetime. It was enough.

The morning brought a pale sun, and I was tempted to go in search of herbs, not because of Ross Elderin but for the pleasure of walking through the dew in the forest. Instead, I went down to help Martha prepare porridge for the household.

"Well, you're in a cheery mood this morning!" she said, stirring the cauldron.

"I am, yes!"

"So was he, that Mantle fellow. Went out walking, breathing in the fresh Meed air, he said." Martha cast me a sly glance. "Surprising, since you were both up late last night. If I didn't know better, I'd say something was going on between you two.

"He's my Silver Mantle, Martha. We had a lot to discuss, that's all. You heard there might be an attack from Goremene? Well, Conrad and I were discussing it last night." I might have continued to lie to her, but others were trickling into the kitchen to eat.

I joined Rosie in collecting mushrooms after breakfast, and she was also suspicious of my new cheerfulness. I joked that I must indeed be a gloomy soul for the rest of the year. "No," she answered, "but even watching you both last night, there might not be romance between you, but there's something, something deep and beautiful, a deep respect, friendship. I suppose that's a kind of love."

"The best kind," I said, and meant it. I felt no guilt about making love to Conrad, or did he make love to me? For a long time, there has been something that both of us felt might be inevitable. Now that it had happened, the tension was gone. Now, in the soft touch of hands, the gentle pat on the shoulder, there was a memory, perhaps never to be repeated but lasting, which would always enrich those moments.

In the early afternoon, Conrad and I went riding together. Neither of us felt the need to justify what had happened. It had satisfied us both, and while it had felt like a great weight hanging above us before it happened, now it was consigned to our shared past. Not forgotten, but also not important in the breadth of our relationship. When we returned, Judith came rushing out to greet us.

"He's here!" She was breathless. "Ross Elderin! He's waiting in the library, and Rosie is running out of conversation!"

Conrad squeezed my shoulder and took my horse to the stables. Martha never even turned around to face me in the kitchen, merely calling over her shoulder as to who was sitting by the fire with Rosie. The servant's stair was becoming my regular route to reach my room. In the past, I might have spent time choosing my gown. Now, I put on the most convenient, brushed my hair and went down the main staircase.

He stood. He had taken time to spruce himself up, and even his new beard had been trimmed. Rosie prepared to leave, but I took her hand, squeezing it gently, asking her to send some refreshments shortly when I rang the bell. She nodded, a flash of a smile and left. I took one deep breath before I faced Lord Elderin.

He apologised for his churlish treatment of me yesterday, and I apologised for my short temper. We sat by the fire, facing each other. After a few words about the widow Potts and how best to help her, then some explanation of The Royal Progress we had just completed, I began to tell him about Tertius Norton and Florian of Goremene. He said nothing until I became silent. After questions about mustering the lords' militias and how we had hidden the real reason from most except the few we could trust, he pledged his support.

"It was auspicious that Silver Mantle was with you when the ceiling collapsed. He must have responded very quickly to get Lady Grace out of the bed." He coloured when it was clear someone had already told him part of the story. Rosie had certainly struggled searching for topics of conversation.

"I held the ceiling in place until Grace was out of the bed."

A sceptical expression began to form on his features.

"I do remember once telling you about my father's fury when I made his war shield float. Well, this was a more practical application of that skill."

I stood. The moment had come, and now, what I had to tell him would not be easy, although I had practised the words over in my head many times. "I am thankful that you came, and I'm grateful you have pledged your support, if it is necessary. I dearly hope that it is not, but all the evidence tells me that it will happen."

I licked my lips. My throat was dry. "I really needed to talk to you about something quite different, although it is connected." I was already pacing.

"As you know, I was exiled to Roth for a long time and for most of that period, I never saw or heard from anyone in Vellin. Only on two occasions did my husband visit Roth, both occasions on his return from hunting trips in the north."

I looked out of the window, picturing Brodik and his louts dismounting, already inebriated and in need of accommodation." I spoke to the leaded windows. "He was still my husband and in Magra, that meant I was still his wife and expected to perform my wifely duties, even though he had long abandoned me." I looked back at Ross. He sat in the chair, listening, his face without expression.

"To my husband, that included the duties owed to him in the bedroom. When he'd drunk enough wine, he demanded that I lie with him." Now I dare not look at Ross Elderin's face. "I refused him, but my husband never understood or accepted the refusal." I clenched my fists. "The King raped me, twice, each time he came to Roth."

I might have said more, but there was a knock at the door. I called for them to enter. One young man carried a bowl of fruit, and the other a tray with mead and glasses. We exchanged a smile, and they set down their bowl and tray on the table.

Now I faced Ross.

"Ross Elderin, Lord of Brak, may I present to you Cillian?" I placed my hand on his shoulder, "and his older brother, Alexander." I did the same to him. "My sons!"

At first Ross Elderin looked confused, then as the importance of what I had said finally took hold in his mind, he stood and approached them, dropping to his knee before them. "Your Royal Highnesses."

Both boys tried not to laugh. Alexander was less successful and looked to me. He pushed his hand through his blond hair before he offered it to Ross. "Lord Elderin, we do not stand on ceremony here. It is an honour to meet you after so long."

Ross stood. "And to meet you, Prince Alexander." Ross looked to me. "Now everything makes sense. You had to take the throne to keep it for your son."

I hugged both my boys. "My dears, your timing was excellent."

Cillian's face broke into his wonderful smile. "I listened to your mind, and I knew exactly when to knock."

"Of course, you did!" I ruffled his red hair. "Now go and tell Lord Conrad that your mother has announced your birthright, and

Cillian," he turned at the door, "don't pester Silver Mantle tonight, you will have plenty of time to shower him with questions on your way to Vellin." My younger son, still grinning, always sunny, pulled his brother out of the room.

Ross came to me. "How can I ever apologise enough? I should never have doubted your motives. I wish I had known earlier." He took my hand and then tilted his head. "And the king never knew?"

"Brodik never knew, and I had no intention of telling him. I had suffered his cruelty and the indignity of exile. I was not about to give up my children to him. He would have turned them into men like him. Instead, my boys have grown up in the warm and loving environment of Roth. While they might have been starved of male companions and role models, they have been guided by a group of incredible women.

"I intended to reveal my sons' existence when they were older. I planned to have them learn from men I truly respect." We returned to our seats. "Over the last few months, Gwillem, my husband's faithful servant, has been schooling them both on courtly behaviour and the intricacies of court life. It didn't take the old man long to guess that these were Brodik's sons. I remember it quite amused him."

Now it was done, and Ross Elderin knew the truth, too. I felt more relaxed and sat back in the chair. "Alexander has his father's blond hair and fair skin, while Cillian's red hair and round face always remind me so much of my father. I had planned to have Alexander become page to a competent lord or knight who could teach him combat skills and the art of war. I was thinking that I would ask you. Now Camlan's treason has made everything more urgent and dangerous. I have to keep my boys safe next year."

"I'd be honoured to teach the prince what I know, though I've never had a page. It will be interesting for both of us." He stood. "Will you ever forgive me?"

"I will, if you will forgive me." I stood, and before I could take a breath, he took me in his arms, and we kissed.

As this is a journal for posterity, what happened then would not be of interest to future students of our history. It is sufficient for me to say that for a woman whose life had been deprived of physical love for so long, twice in two days was bound to set tongues wagging, even if only among my own people in Roth. Ross stayed overnight and slipped away in the early morning before I farewelled my youngest son and his new teacher, Conrad.

"He's a very promising young man, and I suspect his skills are far from fully developed yet. He will be anonymous among The Talarin novices, and he will be protected by The Souran. Some of them already suspected his existence. He will be safe.' A kiss on my hand from Conrad and a hug from Cillian, and they were off, riding out of sight towards Vellin.

A few days later, with his worldly goods in a clean sack, Alexander left, too. Gwillem was quite tearful until Ross invited him to accompany them, so the young prince would have a familiar face to turn to if he felt homesick. It took little time for Gwillem to pack his own sack, saddle a horse and follow his young master. Martha was heard to grumble that with everyone pinching her potato sacks, she'd have to sew up her knickers to carry the tatties in from the ground.

Within a very short time, my two chicks had flown, and the nest was empty. It could have been a miserable period, but my ladies would not allow me to be idle. We had treats to prepare for the year's end. This year, we will celebrate both at Roth and in Brak. It was an occasion of great merriment and of rubbing Judith's back when she had overindulged.

After year's end, I rode to Heathcote to visit the old man and see how Majolica and her children were coping with the colder winter. It was heart-warming to observe the children, Heathcote and his wife enjoying each other's company and Majolica appeared content and happy. She had gathered some of the local women and was teaching them the Camlan craft of lacemaking.

"Of course, I miss Camlan sometimes," she told me as we walked through Heathcote's small woodland that was inside the stronghold walls. It contained nut trees as well as fruit trees, and Lord Heathcote was very proud of it. He had given the children some chestnuts on strings with which they played a game of trying to hit their opponent's nut off the string. "The market day in Wyke was always full of interest," Majolica mused as we watched the game. "When I first came to Magra, after my marriage, I missed Goremene, and that was replaced by Camlan. Now the Northern Meeds are home. Perhaps there are other homes for me in the future."

Three weeks later, I left Brak with Grace, Judith, Alice, and Shana. Rosie remained as my chatelain. I had one more walk in the woods with Ross. The herbs were hidden under a night's covering of snow and there was a sadness about the place. I think both of us had begun to contemplate the coming spring. He promised he would come as soon as the summons to arms came. It was hard to watch the grey towers of Roth disappear behind us as my carriage left signs of its passing through a white and bitterly cold world.

We stopped at Stovin and visited Lady Grier and her husband, who was ailing and not likely to see out the winter. Their son would follow his father as lord, and his mother was happy to remain as chatelain, as he had no wife. She was eager to promise their quota of militiamen to augment the nearby cavalry barracks.

Halfway to Vellin, one of our wheels broke. Thanks to Judith and a clever coachman, we effected a repair. Two spokes were broken, but with the application of certain items of female apparel tightly wrapped around them and retightened every few miles, we limped into Vellin. There was less snow there, but it was still bitterly cold. We huddled around the large fireplaces and waited for the worst of winter to pass.

There was a change in the weather about six weeks after year's end. The sky was a piercingly clear blue. Although there was no wind and the sun shone, it remained bitterly cold. Nevertheless, I felt compelled to walk in the garden after my session with Tory. It was too early for the spring flowers, but snowdrops appeared in the grass, and it was a welcome sight. I was just bending to see them more closely when someone grabbed me from behind. I had just seconds to react, for he was lifting a blade to my throat. This was no dolt, but a skilled killer, and my sword was sitting in Conrad's rooms in the Talarin. I sent out my thoughts as fast as I could while flinging my arms behind myself before he could pull me close enough to position his knife at my throat. I was grateful that his trousers were thin, for I grasped his genitals with both hands and squeezed them, digging my nails into his flesh. He screamed and released his grip long enough for me to break free.

I could not outrun him, with his longer legs, but I set off dodging between the plants, hearing him close in behind me. Then fortune favoured me. One of the gardeners had left a pitchfork leaning against a tree. I made for it and had it in my hand when he threw the knife at me. It landed in my hip, and I cried out in pain, but swung the fork up towards him as he came at me. His momentum and my anger and fear forced the fork clear into his chest and through his back. His expression was more surprised than pain as he sank to his knees before me. Tory and Conrad both came running up from the Talarin practice yard, only to witness the tines appearing through the man's back. I gave them a pitiful wail of pain before fainting.

I woke in my own bed with Conrad standing at the window, looking out. He turned when I stirred.

"You're probably feeling pain, but that will ease. I've mixed a soothing sedative for you to drink." He indicated the small goblet by the bed. "I wanted to wait until you woke. I think I may have upset your ladies by my staying all night."

"You stayed all night?" I tried to sit up, but the pain in my hip stopped me. "You remained in my bedchamber?"

"I stayed." He gently pushed me back against the pillows. "Surely your ladies have now become accustomed to my staying in your bedchamber. Now, rest. I will leave you to the mercy of those same ladies. You are injured and must sleep. Heathcote has returned. With Strewan, we can manage without you for a while."

The memory of the terror I felt trying to escape my attacker suddenly came back, and with it the memory of his face before he died. "I killed a man!"

"You killed him before he killed you. Your battle has already begun. You drew first blood." He put his hand on my shoulder. "Unless you want to surrender to Goremene and Camlan before they invade, you won't be the last Magran to kill a man." He bent closer. "And if you still intend to lead your army, it won't be your last kill either." He kissed me on the forehead, hesitated, then gently kissed me on the lips before leaving. I began to cry, not sobs of abject misery, but tears, nonetheless. I let them roll down my face as I drank the sedative and went to sleep crying.

The next time I woke, it was when Grace drew the curtains to let in the sun and the cold air. It had snowed, and she wrapped warm furs around me. She refused to allow me to get up and insisted on feeding me soup, although I tried to explain that my hands and arms were uninjured. Then the visitors started arriving, my other ladies, Lord Heathcote, followed by Strewan, Tory, Judith for a second time, and finally Conrad again.

"You look much improved," he said. "Your colour has returned, but it is probably still too soon for you to get out of bed. The wound was not deep, so the flesh should heal quickly." He sat on the bed beside me.

"So, there's no excuse for you to stay all night," I teased.

"None, whatsoever, unless of course Your Majesty commands it."

"Well, I could do that, couldn't I?"

He gave me a sly grin. "You could, but from the dreams you've shared with me recently, I would suspect you'd prefer the Lord of Brak."

"When I recover, I'm going to be practising keeping you out of my head!" I pushed him off the bed, and he left the room laughing.

By the second month of the year, I was able to resume my daily sessions with Tory and the angry gash was already turning into an ugly scar. I could now ride and fire arrows with some sort of accuracy, but occasionally the leg would ache after too much exercise. Tertius Norton had not returned to Vellin but had sent messages informing me that the winter had been harsh and caused much damage both in Wyke and the surrounding countryside. He therefore felt compelled to remain until the repairs to the buildings were completed. When everything was ready, he would return to Vellin.

"Oh, I bet he'll return!" Strewan shuffled angrily in his seat. "With a well-drilled and equipped army behind him!" Strewan, being Lord of The Eastern Marshes, had developed an efficient network of spies along The River Listi that monitored not only the traffic of trade along the river but also watched for any significant changes in the general pattern of life throughout the coast and Camlan region. They were mostly local people holding a long association with Strewan as their lord. They respected him and kept him informed about his region while he was far away in Vellin. They had reported no violent storm damage. Indeed, Strewan himself had travelled to his coastal manor on two occasions over the winter and was not aware of any abnormal weather, even on the coast.

What the spies did report was the gathering of men in Wyke. A substantial but temporary camp had been set out, and clearly, men were being drilled in preparations for war. Provisions were being stockpiled, and a new inner wall was under construction in Wyke. Tertius was certainly busy, not in restoration but preparation. Strewan had also received news from Delion in Dereculd. Unknown vessels had been seen off the coast, and this was verified by Strewan's own spies. A landing had been attempted near the village of Ransom, but the two small, shallow-draft vessels had drifted south into the marshes. Nothing was seen of the craft after that, except the wreckage of one in the marshes.

"Anyone venturing into the marshes in winter shouldn't be expected to survive. Strange things inhabit that wild, inhospitable land, and even the wild fowlers stay on the landward side of the dyke wall in winter." Strewan's jaw was set hard. He confessed that none of the local people would have gone out to find survivors.

"Perhaps he should remain in Wyke,' Heathcote had spent the winter getting to know Majolica Norton and her children, and from what he could gather, their father was prone to using physical violence in his household. Lady Heathcote had grown so fond of her guests and given them so much more of her time and love that the children had asked if they could call her 'Grandmother'.

Conrad rested his lower arms on the table, placing one hand in the other. "If Norton is to remain in Camlan, then it is time to send out messengers detailing the truth about his collusion with Goremene, together with Queen Katherine's command that the lords prepare to assemble with their armies to meet the enemy."

Now it was said, the full weight of what we were about to set in motion frightened me. What if the lords doubted the truth of what the message told them? What if more of them were aligned to Camlan and Goremene that we knew? What if none met us on the appointed day? As they discussed the details of the message, my mind was turning over all the possibilities. I was shaken out of my fear by Heathcote's words.

"She has volunteered to return to Wyke to provide us with clearer details of their plans. I told her it is too dangerous."

"Lady Norton is a brave and noble woman, but the risks for her are too high." Strewan was saying.

"How could she believe that I would condone such a thing?" I interrupted.

Heathcote's features softened. "Because she said that you had never fled from personal risk, and neither would she. She told me that in many ways, you were closer to her as a sister than any of her siblings. You both knew the cruelty of men, and that in this case, you would recognise and understand why she was compelled to do all she could to defeat her husband."

My heart sank. Majolica Norton had held a mirror for me to see us both, and she was right. I had risked a great deal to secure Alexander's future. How could I deny her the chance to fight her own battle against a man who had been a tyrant to his family? For a moment, I could not find the words, but Majolica had been ready for my indecision.

"She has already set out for Camlan. The children will remain at Heathcote. She takes with her carrier pigeons from Heathcote. She will tell Norton that their purpose is to send messages to their children. Once she feels that she can send for them, she will tell him, she will use the birds to call them home. Of course, the birds are my own for communications to Vellin." Heathcote looked down at his hands, knowing that he had shocked all of us.

"We should intercept her. This whole escapade is foolhardy!" Strewan was first to respond.

"No!" I took a moment to copy Heathcote. Looking down at the table, I noticed the ink stains from an earlier time. Then I looked up. "Majolica Norton is no fool, and I will not have her treated as one. This was her decision; one I hope I might have taken in her position. It would not have been made rashly, and she will have prepared some reasonable excuses and lies to account for her disappearance and return. We should not jeopardise her endeavour.

Knowing more details about their plans will make our own stronger. Let us give her this chance to help us." I glanced around at them.

"My father used to say battles are not won solely on the battlefield but in the preparation and careful planning. He also said that reliable intelligence about the terrain, the strength and plans of the opponent and their weaknesses was equivalent to an extra company of knights. Let's allow Majolica to stage her own attack against Camlan. She understands the risk she takes."

We then spent time reviewing the first message to be sent to the lords and free cities. It did not mention Camlan or Goremene, only that intelligence had suggested there was an imminent danger of invasion and that they should ready themselves for my summons. This would alert everyone, even Tertius and his secret allies, but it would not endanger Majolica as she had already set out to Wyke long before the message was sent.

In Wyke, a tearful wife was reuniting with her husband. He had beaten her for removing their children without his permission before realising that having them secretly hidden would ensure their safety when the valley of The Listi might become a battleground. He congratulated her for the foresight while thrusting his manhood inside her. Later that night, she heard him creeping along the corridor in the direction of the east tower, where he had installed his mistress.

XVII The Gathering

Over the intervening months, between gaining strength and replying to messages of support from various lords, I watched the foundations being laid for a new Mantle hostel for travellers on the road north on Lord Scoles' land between Stovin and Vellin. It was close to the village of Kimberwood, which, despite its name, had no trees to speak of and might have been abandoned years before, as the land was scrub and unyielding to the plough. Only its close proximity to the ancient highway north had provided a lifeline for the tired inn, smithy and four cottage farms. With all the turmoil I expected when the Goremene armies appeared, this short excursion to see the foundations laid was welcome.

As the tree buds began to swell in the palace gardens, a final pair of pigeons came from Wyke. Their message warned that Tertius would receive reinforcements from the sea, landing near the village of Ransom. He would then proceed to Vellin and begin his siege of the city. Not expecting too much resistance on his way through Bashiria and the Southern Meeds, Florian and his army would march north to join Tertius. They expected to converge at the very end of spring, possibly east of Nordinay, when the city of Vellin normally hosted its first large market of the year for fresh meat, fruit, and vegetables. It was a time when winter rations were low, and the city was replenished with the much-anticipated summer abundance.

With Conrad's agreement, I sent Weld and Soldin Meganor to Wyke to rescue Majolica. I feared Tertius might already suspect his wife. It was also the time to draft my call to arms for the lords of the land. Ultimately, it would be their response that would save Magra and the Five Kingdoms, not the small but well-trained army Magra possessed, or the swaggering cavalry knights from Stovin. My doubts returned, but spurred on by thoughts of what was going to happen and the sacrifices already made, I signed each message and watched from my window as Mantles set out to deliver them across The Five Kingdoms and the free cities.

The waiting was dismal. I did not choose this war. I did not become Queen to see my country plunged into bloodshed. It was not of my making, and yet I felt the full guilt of it. Perhaps I should never have been a queen. Perhaps I should have told Brodik about my sons and sent them to Vellin. Fears and doubts overwhelmed me every idle moment, so I desperately filled each day with activity. It exasperated my servants and exhausted my ladies-in-waiting. Even Tory would not grant me an extra hour of practice.

'Katherine, be still!' Conrad looked up from his desk. I was pacing about the room as he tried to consider the most ideal placement of our camp, the camp where we would wait for the enemy to arrive. He had sent Mantles back to the plateau between Bashiria and Rynth to make a detailed study of the land.

Strewan returned to his own manor, prepared to defend The Fen if necessary. Just south of the village of Ransom, its promontory position on the edge of old forest lands overlooked the marshland. He had few men he could call upon to stand with him, only his handful of tenant farmers, the fishermen who eked out meagre existences fishing off the coast of the marsh, and the wild-fowlers who knew the marshlands best of all. None of them could be seriously counted upon to protect the Strewan manor. I sent what men I could spare to bolster his garrison, but they were far less than would be needed if Camlan decided to attack. My only hope was that Strewan's lands were unimportant to the Goremene invading force, and Tertius would know how unimportant they were. The only reason he might attack would be out of personal malice towards Strewan. I could not discount that possibility.

When the garrison and knights prepared to leave Vellin, I requested that Heathcote should remain in charge of the city. A limited time would be given to those who wished to flee the city before the gates were closed, but both he and I hoped most would wish to remain to defend Vellin. As it happened, most stayed. I was thankful that inside The Talarin, the novice Mantles, including Cillian, would be safe. I doubted that even Norton would attempt to assail that stronghold. Green Mantle, Blue Mantle and Black Mantle arrived to do their best to help Heathcote. Both Red Mantle and Silver Mantle would be with me on the battlefield.

Three days before we left, three days when I tried to spend some of each day with Cillian, news came from Wyke. It was Soldin Meganor. He was alone. They had tried to steal into the castle to find Majolica but were apprehended by the increased guard, mostly mercenaries from the south. Taken for common footpads, they were beaten but eventually released as harmless undesirables outside the town gates. On their way out of the city, someone recognised Weld. They escaped, but Soldin had left the wounded Weld in Taegel to recover.

I found it hard to quell my fears for Majolica. Had we been too late to save her? I could only hope that she had been imprisoned because Tertius was too engaged in preparations to deal with her. I told myself that fretting would accomplish nothing, that I must direct my focus to what was to come. I was ready to meet the men from Camlan, from Goremene and slaughter them all. From that moment, my doubts were gone.

On the day we left, Grace was stone-faced as she strapped me into the armour Tory had fashioned for me. I insisted I wear it as we rode out of Vellin, to meet and join with the cavalry knights from Stovin. The next time I would don it would be when all the lords and their militias gathered at our place of meeting.

"It will be a fine gathering," Alice said, appraising Tory's craftsmanship as an armour maker as she helped to strap me inside. My armour was light and flexible. It would serve to protect me and yet give me freedom to fire my bow. I appreciated the workmanship and the inlaid rampant lion on the breastplate, but I valued the practical protection more.

Goodbyes were stilted and short. My ladies held back their tears while Heathcote held me close to his chest struggling not to shed tears of his own. The uncertainty of Majolica's fate had weighed heavily upon him. He immediately begged permission to become protector of her children until such time she could reclaim them. We both hoped that time would come.

None of us were good at saying what might be our final farewells. It felt easier to be mounting my horse and riding out of the palace gates and down the Angirat escarpment to the city. From the throng awaiting us there, it appeared that few citizens had left. They lined the streets as they had done when I arrived as a widow. Now, I left as a warrior. Some even fell in behind our company carrying crude weapons. For a moment, I was uncertain what to do.

"Let them come!" Conrad said, at my side. "We will equip them as best we can. They have the right to defend their country."

So, our little army was already augmented by the time the knights from Stovin joined us. It would be the same in every place we passed. Farmers, blacksmiths, taverners and masons, brought their own motley array of weapons to defend their homes. Lord Lamfrik's own contingent accompanied the cavalry, with more men than we expected but also enormous hampers of food, sent by Lady Greer. Later, while still our way to our first night's camp, we were intercepted by Lord Malister and his militia, along with a smaller group of men belonging to Lord Wickstead's household.

"A thousand pardons, Your Majesty, for our tardiness in joining your company." Malister was a tall, thickset man with dark eyes under equally dark, bushy eyebrows and a face that I wondered might look stern even when hearing a joke. At his side, Lord Wickstead, a nervous creature at the best of times, nodded his agreement. Both had been friends of Tertius Norton since childhood. They had even taken his part before and, for a time, after their unsuccessful bid for the throne, but Malister was a man of the north, a neighbour of Heathcote's and whose opinion of The Lord of Camlan changed when confronted by his treatment of his wife. He had visited her while she was in the north and still did not know her whereabouts. Later that day, I rode beside him and told him how Majolica had served her queen.

"Fine lass and a brave one." He sighed heavily. "What fools we were to be swayed by Norton."

I patted his arm. 'We were all swayed by Tertius Norton at some time or another."

We camped the first night beside the river, upstream of Taegel, where Oliver Taegel and his contingent joined us. Before we ate supper, the men of Brak and Heathcote arrived. In the wake of a smiling Ross Elderin came his new and very excited squire. Ross stopped smiling when he saw the expression on my face.

"You brought your squire to a battlefield?" I spluttered as Alexander also stopped grinning.

"It's what squires do," Ross said airily. "He'll take care of my weapons and armour, make sure I'm fed and generally keep himself as far away from the battle as possible. He's perfectly safe, Your Majesty."

"He needs to be sent to safety. How dare you risk his life? He's too young and inexperienced to be here. I would be constantly worried about him!" I could feel my anxiety rising just to know he was among the army. I had not kept him secret and safe for so long only to have him slaughtered on a battlefield.

"I assure Your Majesty that I am where I want to be, serving my sovereign." Alexander dropped to his knee before me. "I am quite capable of carrying out my duties as a squire and would not dare to venture into danger. If I did, I'm sure my dear mother would have

Lord Elderin's head." My son had spoken loud enough for the men sitting nearby to hear and they cheered and applauded him.

"Well said, lad!" Lord Malister cried. "I'm sure your mother would be very proud of you!" Others joined in their praise.

I bent to lift him to his feet. "We will discuss this further." I spoke softly. "Remember you also need to preserve the future sovereign, Alexander. I know it sounds like an adventure to you but it's a place where people will die."

"I promise that I will stay safe." He whispered back to me.

I gave Ross my frostiest glare. "We'll speak about this later, Lord Elderin." I turned to the rest of the seated men. "Enjoy your supper, my lords. We are all grateful to Lady Greer for her generosity. We leave at first light!" I stalked off back to my own tent that I shared with Judith. I don't know if Ross Elderin came to my tent later or that, like me, he was too tired and fell asleep as soon as he rolled into his cot. The night passed quickly and before the day grew bright, we were preparing to leave.

We rode westward, expecting to encounter more lords and their companies but none appeared. There was a heavy mist that dampened more than our spirits and by the time we saw the dark, indistinct trunks of trees announcing the southern edge of The Forests of Lore, I was surely not the only one to fear we had been deserted by the rest of The Five Kingdoms.

"This is an eery place!" I heard one knight say. Another said he had been told there were monsters in the ancient forest and that the sooner we were out the other side, the better. Moments later, we heard our first wolf howl. It reminded me of the last time I had been here with Dlin Edgebar, Green Mantle. That night, the wolves had been welcoming. Today, in the swirling mist, their cries felt more threatening. Suddenly we saw them, ahead of us on the path. I called the company to halt and then rode forward a little before dismounting. Without my helm, I hoped that they recognised me. I had no idea if they were going to attack or simply disappear into the forest.

I sat down and spoke to them, not knowing if they understood my words. Perhaps they could or perhaps just remembering me as Dlin's friend was enough. I recognised pale Fleetfoot, who came to me, and I offered my hand. He sniffed it, then licked it. I told him we were passing through to fight a battle against invaders from the south. I have no idea what he made of my words but when I had finished, he drew his clan to the side of the road, and they watched silently as we passed.

"You're going to become a legend even before you reach the battlefield," Judith chuckled as we left the wolves behind us. "You should have seen the men's faces."

I said nothing. I did not want to be a legend, just victorious and alive with those I loved at the end of it all.

We did not camp until we were well away from the forest. I did not want some foolish young men testing their bravery against the wolves or other inhabitants of the woods. We had passed through in peace and that should be maintained. We finished Lady Greer's hampers with relish and then the men and Judith, shared wine, and ale. I sought out the yeomen archers. They had gathered together around a fire and when they saw me, they dropped to their knees.

"No ceremony here, gentlemen, we are all archers." One of the men gave me his seat. I had noticed many of them had brought small wood and canvas stools that could be packed flat on their packs, or if they were fortunate, on their horse. There were not many who possessed a horse, and they were fascinated to find that I could shoot from the saddle. In all, there were only fifty-six of us. As we shared ale, a contest was agreed upon, when we reached our destination.

"Anyone care to wager who will win?" A tall, gangly fellow asked, leaning against a tree.

"Thorfin of Dereculd, if he's coming!" one said.

“He’s coming,” I told them, “But he’ll not be there when we arrive.”

“Then best have the contest before he comes.” The tall man said, and then to me, “He’s the best among us to be sure.” His eyebrows lifted. “Will Your Majesty be competing?”

“Of course!” I said, certain that I would not be the winner. “I’ll give a purse of four gold crowns to the winner!” At that they all cheered. We talked for a while. I asked them about their lives, their families and then I left them to carouse noisily.

I wandered to where the men of Brak shared mead. They began to rise but I waved them to sit. Ross brought out one of the collapsable chairs the lords favoured. The men wanted to ask me about the wolves, which I tried to dismiss as the fact they had met me before. Then they began to share memories of Roth, seeing it in the distance, encountering Judith and her men repairing walls, Rosie and Grace selling honey at the market in Brak. Most had regarded the place with a strange reverence, ‘The Castle of The Lady’, they called it.

“When this is over, there’ll be a glass of mead and a warm pie for any man who fought with us here.” I told them. “Roth will welcome you all.” I paused. “But don’t all come on the same day!” They laughed. I stood and bade them a good night, then followed Ross into his tent.

“I’m sorry if you think it was dangerous to bring Alexander here, but he has worked so hard.” He had carried the seats back inside his tent. “He’s desperate for you to see how much he has learnt.”

“Obviously, he’s still got some lessons to complete on common sense.” I was halfway through my sentence when my son appeared, saw me, and tried to escape without me seeing him. “Don’t you sneak off, young Sir! It’s both of you that I want to scold.” He stood still and faced me. “How can I give all my concentration to fighting our enemies when I know you are at risk?”

Alexander looked to Ross. “Both of us?”

Of course, I had directed my comment at my son, but in truth, I was already realising how many lives that I personally cared about were in danger, not to mention all those brave men, sitting around their fires, drinking together. My shoulders sagged.

“Yes. Both of you.” I opened my arms, and he obediently filled them. He had suddenly grown taller and looked down at me, a sudden grin emerging.

“Shouldn’t Lord Elderin be part of your embrace too?” His head turned to Ross.

“You young pup!” Ross came towards us. “Away to your bed, or you’ll need me to wake you again. Such a young scamp! The boldness of squires these days!”

Alexander laughed as he fled the tent, relieved I had forgiven him for coming. I had already realised that all the lords had brought their squires. I hoped they would all be safe. This conflict was not of their making and they all deserved a long and prosperous life.

A temporary camp is not the place for romantic assignations, but I was happy that Ross felt the need to put his arms around me. I needed to have them there. It was a tender moment, made sweeter by him telling me again how much he had come to like his squire. I was glad they had met.

Before I left Vellin, I had told Heathcote the truth about my sons. It was important for him to know lest something happened to me. Neither Ross nor Conrad, and certainly not my ladies would be important enough to verify my sons’ claim to the throne, but Heathcote, the most senior of my councillors would. I had furnished him with the proofs, including testimony by the midwife and witness to his birth. It was a sobering train of thought that took me across the camp to my own tent. I passed Judith on the way with Soldin and a few knights. She would not be back until late.

The dawn was bright and clear but the nagging fear that we were still a small army to face the might of Goremene weighed heavily on me as we continued our journey. Very soon we should see the land fall gradually down towards a hollow, beyond which the little hill rose to fall again towards the stream and boggy ground. That hollow, north of the hill would be our camp until the invaders arrived. When they did, we would stream down towards them to engage them in battle.

Conrad knew my fears and perhaps shared them. None of us had spoken much since the beginning of our ride. Suddenly, Soldin pointed to two riders approaching us from the north.

"Is that all there is? Just two men?" Malister couldn't hide his disappointment.

"Two willing men are worth a whole army of cowards!" Lord Clairstow told him.

"It's Mine Master Frain!" Conrad said. Of course, those who knew The Souran could communicate at a distance without words accepted the fact but those who didn't marvelled at the keenness of Silver Mantle's eyesight. We waited for the riders to reach us.

"A good morning, Your Majesty. We hoped you would arrive soon." Ransom Frain had been riding hard. His companion held a hunting bird on his arm. "Harriers are something of a passion of mine," he added, noticing me looking at the bird.

"Is there just the two of you?" Clairstow's face was full of concern.

"How many do you need to fly a bird?" Frain looked a little confused. "Just myself and my falconer."

"Have any others arrived?" Conrad asked him.

"See for yourself," Ransom pointed. "Keep going that way and you'll see." He rode off with his falconer behind him. We followed his directions, coming to the crest of the northern hill.

Below us, in the shallow bowl of rough pasture was a sight that brought unbidden tears to my eyes. Spread in every direction, with tents and awnings, campfires, and hastily erected kitchens, were the armies of The Five Nations. If the gathering at The Field of the Pentangle had evoked the power, ancient traditions and sumptuous majesty of the lords and their retinues, the scene spread before us represented both the diversity and unity of The Five Kingdoms. While each individual army had its own encampment, easily identified by banners, the men drilling or mingling at camp kitchens were indistinguishable. Bashirian soldiers with their distinctive cone helmets lined up alongside the men of Rynth dressed in the same clothes they wore in the mines. Foresters from The Meeds rubbed shoulders with the blond, fur clad men of Urvik. The sight at once gladdened and saddened my heart. Sad that such gatherings of an army, amiable and tolerant, were the harbingers of conflict and death.

"So, they came after all!" Conrad said quietly, casting me a sly glance.

"Yes, they did!" I replied, easing my horse forward. Our movement alerted sentries in the camp and a great cry of welcome rose up to greet us. Riding through the throng of men, I was overwhelmed that such a congregation had come at my behest. I felt that I should acknowledge them.

Sitting on my horse, I addressed them. "My heart is full of pride when I look across this auspicious gathering. People who love their homes, their families, and their countries enough to meet here upon this plot of ground to defend with their lives what they most cherish, hearth and home. I see only heroes before me, and I am humbled. The legitimacy of our birth-right to live free and unfettered from any foreign overlords, the justice of our cause and our right to defend what is ours brings us to this place, at this time. Let it never be forgotten that people of principle and valour, when called to the defence of The Five Kingdoms, assembled here, at 'The Gathering!'

I scarce remember what I actually said, but it has been noted many times and written in memoirs and documents too numerous to mention, not always with accuracy, but with the common purpose to accentuate the importance of 'The Gathering'. Findin, the piper, assured me this was an accurate rendition of the speech. It was the first and perhaps the only time that all those living within or close to the lands of The Five Kingdoms united in the defence of the land. Who knows if it will be remembered after I am gone, except in documents like this, sitting on a dusty shelf somewhere.

Although, as High Queen, I was seen as the focal point for our endeavour, greater and more experienced minds than mine were bent over a large table in a plain, unadorned tent to plan the battle. It was agreed that the site was well chosen and that Conrad's basic plan had been faultless. Now, they worked on the details.

At first, I put myself among them, listening to their suggestions. It was well known that although Urvik and Thanis had never actually been at war with each other, various clans had waged war against each other in the mountains for centuries. The disputes were usually minor, often arising from territory disputes or someone's wife running off with another leader. The resulting skirmishes produced a class of warrior born into a culture of aggression and also stealth. Before our arrival, two parties of men, one from each kingdom had been sent south, scattering along the coast to watch for the Goremene fleet. Bashiria had also set lookouts along their coastline. None was to engage the enemy but to return with reports of the number and movements.

During the explanation for all of this, the men at the table felt bound to lapse into lengthy explanations for my benefit. It was clear that almost everyone else understood their purpose. Partly because I was unable to contribute anything to their discussions and partly to ease several embarrassing moments of unintentional cursing, I excused myself. I was certain there were other things I could do to help.

I was on my way to meet the unsung heroes of the camp kitchens when the sentries alerted the camp to more arrivals from the north. They came like a flood, pouring down the hillside. The free cities had answered the call: Jedran, Djengun, and further west, the three Kor cities, Kor Tnelis, Kor Retniw, Kor Erif. Behind them came the gaudy warrior clans of The Kashkie.

"Where are we going to put them all?" Lord Clairstow exclaimed.

"We'll find room." I told him as we moved to greet them. "They've made the decision to help; we'll find them room."

That night, the valley echoed to the songs and laughter of a united army. Odd disagreements broke out about cramped conditions, food supplies and unfamiliar personal habits but for the majority of our combined forces, it was an evening of discovery and comradery. Among the Kashkie came female warriors, skilled with knives and sword. Judith and Soldin spent the evening at their campfire. After a brief meeting with the two members of The Souran present, I wandered again, greeting weavers turned warlords from Djengun and bakers turned would-be butchers from Bashiria. The cheerful choir from Kor Tnelis were eager to demonstrate their pike handling and I shared a glass of wine with my old friends from Brak.

The archers held their contest, cheerfully offering me commiserations after I failed to move beyond the first round. I nominated the tall forester as my pay master, handing him the prize purse, with six of his fellow archers vowing that they'd see a fair contest.

I was making my way back to my tent when I saw Ross Elderin.

He looked a little flustered. "I couldn't find either you or Judith!"

I reached for his hand. "Judith and Soldin are exploring the intricacies of Kashkie knife wielding." He smiled. It was the smile I remembered from those early mornings. "Come share some Roth mead with me. I know you like it."

He didn't object, nor did he take his hand from mine. "Young Alexander went to bed early after a rather large mug of ale." He saw my expression. "No, I didn't give it to him. The men from Rynth did, and it was Ransom Frain who made certain the lad came to no harm." He stopped. "Does he know who the boy is because..."

"He knows, and we can trust him," I said, leading the way to my tent.

I poured the mead, and we both sat on my cot, a rather larger than normal one as it had been my grandfather's, resurrected by Black Mantle from some dark corner of The Talarin.

"When all this is over...," I began.

"When all this is over, you will go back to your palace, and I shall return to Brak. Let's not deceive ourselves, Kate. The time for us has passed, and you have your boys to think about. I understand that." He put his hand on my cheek.

"Then let us have tonight without thinking about anything beyond that." I finished my mead. "The life of Queen Katherine is out there, beyond this tent. Tonight, I'm Kate, who loves nothing better than those early morning walks in someone else's woods."

"Does she?" His voice was soft and husky.

"You know she does."

He kissed me, lightly at first, but when I responded, he drew me to him and all the doubts about his love for me were gone. Tomorrow was a lifetime away. His arms wrapped around me as one kiss followed another. In the dim light of the tent, I shed my regal status as I removed my hunting clothes. All Kate's become one when gentle hands cup breasts or when a body responds to the growing urgency of another's. We enjoyed each other, then side by side, unwilling to move, touching, exploring, speaking of inconsequential things, until the urge to share our bodies overtook us again.

He left me before dawn. I never saw Judith until after breakfast, which I collected myself, trying to avoid Conrad, knowing full well that he had probably sensed some of what had happened during the night. From the way he dipped his head and looked under his eyebrows at me as we passed, I had not been totally successful in blocking his mind. He left me with a cheerful promise that he would no doubt tease me about it later. As I ate alone in my tent, it occurred to me that I loved both these men in totally different ways. The passion and hunger I felt when I was close to Conrad were balanced by my tenderness for Ross Elderin.

"The one heart is yours forever, but cannot be a husband to you. The other heart needs you to make him whole." The voice came from outside my tent, and at first, I thought it was someone playing tricks. When I peered out, there was the magical harper, sitting in my collapsible chair, eating a large bowl of porridge.

"Master Findin, no less!" I joined him. "And how did you know what I was thinking? Don't answer. It's bad enough that you do!"

"Such deep soul-searching always screams at me." He waved his spoon. "Have them both, if you must, but remember one has sworn his life to the Talarin. The other would gladly swear his life to you."

"Why are you here?" I changed the subject.

"Where else would I be?" He dipped his spoon into the bowl. "The fiercest battle in the history of The Five Kingdoms is about to commence, and you ask me why I'm here!"

I leaned towards him, "Do you know the outcome?"

"Of course not! I don't write history. And don't ask me who will die because I don't know that, either. And I can't stop the carnage before you ask that. I can promise to try and keep my eye on a certain young squire, but that's all." He sat up, looked directly ahead, at the blank canvas wall of my tent and announced, "Ah! Here comes more of your army."

Almost as soon as he spoke, the sentries sounded the alert, and from the direction of The Forest of Lore came the combined might of Dereculd, The Marsh Lords and Taegel. Delion's red lion banner fluttered at their head, the brazen armour of his knights glinted in the sun, his mounted archers followed and then the lords' companies.

"Welcome, Your Majesty!" I said as my cousin dismounted.

"The coast is safe, My Queen." Delion bowed. "We slaughtered them as they landed, and those who escaped were driven into the marshlands. What took them once in there is not for me to say, except that none survived. The fishermen of those parts have been tasked to round up any survivors they find, but I doubt there will be any. The larger vessels were sunk by my fleet."

"That is good news you bring, cousin. And what of Camlan?" I asked as I escorted him to the command tent. He placed his gauntlets on the table and gratefully accepted a glass of wine.

"The city had prepared for a siege, but I suspect the size of our army and the absence of the men from Goremene weakened their resolve. The recently constructed wall had been built in haste and not well. It was easy to breach, and once inside, we had only the militia to contend with."

"What about their lord?" I asked as Conrad came to stand beside my chair.

Delion continued with his account. "There was a sizeable number of knights at the castle gates, but my archers dealt with them. We cleared the city of the people, making them safe beyond the walls. While this was being done, Thorfin made a rather horrific discovery: the body of a woman, a gentlewoman by her clothes, in a criminal's cage. We lowered her, and later we buried her. I brought this to show you." He passed me something wrapped in a monogrammed kerchief. The delicate white linen held a distinctive gold necklace and a marriage ring.

Tears behind my eyes threatened my composure. "These belonged to Majolica Norton!"

Others also recognised the jewellery, wrapped as it was in her kerchief. Malister let his fingers touch the necklace, then backed away, heaving a great sigh. He wept, openly and unashamedly, begging my pardon for his apparent ability to weep 'like a girl'.

"A man who sheds tears for another's death shows compassion, and as I know well, my lord, in my experience, girls are less prone to tears than boys and more like to steeliness and a hunger for revenge."

"If that is so and you have retained your girlish ways, then I am your man. This conflict has become deeply personal for me. I only met the lady once, when visiting Heathcote, but her beauty and sweetness were unforgettable." He drew a heavy breath from somewhere near his ankles and added, "I would gladly strangle Norton with my bare hands."

"Many here knew her." I whispered to Delion, clutching tightly to the small parcel, steeling myself to ask, "And Lord Norton?"

"Ah, yes!" Delion turned as if to leave the tent. "We brought you a gift." I followed him outside, fearing that it might be the head of Tertius Norton. It was indeed the head, and the rest of the body, on his knees and in chains.

XVIII WARRIORS

Presented with a grubby and tattered Tertius, who had the audacity to think an apologetic smile might ease his predicament, I left him and others in no doubt about the metal in my nature.

"I will deal with him later. Chain him to a stout tree!"

"Please, Katherine…," he whined.

"Give him water but no food," I spoke over my shoulder as I led Delion back inside the tent for him to attend the daily meeting with my generals. As they explained their plans to my cousin and the other new arrivals, I needed something to divert my mind from the wretch calling my name as he was being harnessed to a tree. I went out to greet the new arrivals, the men from the east and the volunteers that they had collected as they travelled up the Listi. I thought Strewan would insist on being at the strategy meeting, but instead, he followed me.

"It was rumoured that Goremene thinks you will capitulate when you see the might of their army, but I was not impressed by the example that arrived on our coast. They were large in number but untested and afraid of unfamiliar surroundings. Your cousin's fleet was most impressive in sinking the vessels. The survivors from the water are being held in my castle. They're a sorry lot. The Goremene men who surrendered at Wyke are being guarded there. Should I send word to have them all dispatched?"

I stopped. I had no intention of becoming enamoured with wars and bloodlust. "No, Lord Strewan. If this battle goes our way, we will give them the choice of returning home or starting a new life in The Five Kingdoms. This invasion was not of their making."

"An excellent decision, if I might comment, and Norton? What of him?"

"Tertius Norton is a traitor. I will deal with him myself."

I said nothing more because we were being surrounded by the eager young volunteers from the banks of the Listi. I would dearly have liked to tell them all to go home. This was an adventure that would not end well, but their honest faces as they knelt to me prevented me from saying anything but expressing my gratitude for their presence. Over their heads, I could see that my traitor had been bound in chains to an old elm, far enough away from the camp to avoid his persuading someone to help him.

Judith and I spent most of the day touring the camp, talking to the men. It was a rare occasion for a queen to mingle with her people and speak with them about their lives, their families, their aspirations for the future, and to offer them my thanks in person. When grievances were aired, I asked Judith to note them. When suggestions were made, we kept a list. I might not have been a warrior monarch, poring over battlefield strategies and giving uplifting speeches to the men, but I was a wife and mother, sharing their fears and joys. I was touched by so many who kissed my hand or had tears in their eyes just from our meeting.

In the Rynth encampment, it was heartening to see many of the men and women that I had met at Silverleaf. Jem was there with his new wife, Kaylette, the girl whose life he saved.

"I wouldn't let him come here alone," she told me. "Silverleaf taught me that we live for now, even if we don't have enough money to set up home. We manage." She patted her belly. "Don't show yet, but there's a young Jem in there, and sometimes it feels like he's tunnelling to get out." I begged her to keep safe. "No fear, I've come here as one of our medics. Someone's got to tend the wounded. Mi Mam's over yon tent setting up a kitchen, and we carted all that's needed to make Master Soldin's fine soup." The courage and tenacity of the people of Rynth never cease to amaze me. I left Kaylette setting out the rudimentary equipment of their medics.

"Your Majesty!" We encountered Ransom Frain returning to his people after the strategy meeting, accompanied by a man who was quite clearly not a man of Rynth. "May I introduce Prince Beren of Bashiria. I don't think you've met."

"Indeed not." The man's voice was deep and appealing, like gentle thunder on distant hills, and for some obscure reason it brought to mind winter evenings sitting before a fire. "I believe you are acquainted with my brothers, but I was away on my father's business. It is good to meet you at last, despite the unhappy circumstances." Beren was not the boorish warrior I had been led to expect, and I suspected his younger brothers had misled me. He certainly looked like a warrior. There had not been a finer specimen of strength in the practise yard of the Talarin, and I wondered what Judith would make of him. He was barely out of earshot before her appraisal began.

"Such a handsome face and those muscles have been hard earned."

I smiled to myself. "So, you'd like a practise combat session with Prince Beren?"

"It wouldn't be a practice, and I'm not bothered if he'd prefer a sport other than combat." Judith's cheerful bravado was appreciated on a day of tension and taut nerves.

On our way back through the camp, we spotted Ross giving my son a lesson in swordplay. Judith gave me a cheery wink before she drew her own weapon and joined in the fray. Ross backed away and let Alexander and Judith continue. Occasionally, she would break off and offer him some suggestions.

"She's good!" Ross came and stood beside me to watch them both. "And so is he. Did she work with him at Roth?"

"A little." I couldn't resist the feeling of pride watching them. "She was always concerned that she might hurt him."

"Well, it appears she has overcome that apprehension!" Judith had disarmed him and had him on the ground, telling him what failings he should rectify. Alexander dusted himself off and thanked her for the exercise.

"He's a good boy, sorry, young man," Judith confided as we made our way to the Magran camp kitchens. 'I think he'll make an excellent king.' I said nothing. I knew he was well aware of his destiny and his determination to be a good king. I just hoped that he would have the good sense to stay safe when the fighting began.

As with all things, there comes a tipping point between the novelty of being gathered in unfamiliar surroundings with strangers, a common purpose and the slowly creeping boredom of inactivity. That night, some men drank too liberally, were quick to argue, and fights broke out. By the end of the night there were two broken noses, several minor knife wounds, and some very sore heads the following morning. Judith, for all her weaknesses, retired when I did. We lay on our cots talking of home and memories of earlier days until Judith fell silent and slept.

Most of the kings and their commanders conducted rigorous exercises the following morning. Even the camp cooks were sent scurrying up the hill and back again carrying the heavy cauldrons, an ancient ritual from Urvik, I was told. At noon, everything changed.

I had not spoken to Conrad much since our arrival, so I looked forward to sharing a midday meal with him alone in my tent. He outlined the battle plan and was complementing the way Ross Elderin's squire was conducting himself when Beren of Bashiria burst in.

"Majesty, there is news!" He checked himself and bowed to Conrad. "Lord Mantle, a messenger has come from my spies on our coastline." Conrad nodded for him to continue.

"The Goremene fleet was spotted, and landings began at dawn yesterday on a deserted stretch of beach. My man estimates that the invaders should arrive in the valley below sometime tomorrow. My spies are shadowing the main body of men and will send news if anything delays the enemy or they change their route. They are at some distance from any habitation and shouldn't encounter any obstacles along the way. This valley is on the quickest and easiest route to Velin. They're coming."

Conrad was on his feet. "Thank you, Prince Beren. Forgive me, Majesty, but I must leave you. There is much to do." I watched them hurry to join the small crowd of lords already alerted to some change in the status of the coming conflict. All disappeared into the plain white tent, leaving the rest of the camp buzzing with expectation.

Now preparations began in earnest. Positions and numbers discussed, signals rehearsed, and alternative plans should the unexpected happened such as if the cavalry was overpowered too soon or the flanks providing the pincer movement could not close the gap quickly enough. Once that was done, each company gathered for final exercises. There was no running up hills with cauldrons now. The cooks took up their pikes, knives and short swords, testing each other in single combat. Judith joined The Mantles, and for a while, I watched. They were impressive in their skills and while they might resort to magic in the battle, in their combat drills, they demonstrated an above average skill with weapons and copious amounts of inventive resourcefulness.

Thorfin had sidled up beside me without me noticing him. "My king invites you to join our archers in target practice. He tells me that you can ride and shoot. Is that so?"

"I can, but not as expertly as your company. I would never dare compare myself to the archers of Dereculd."

"Come!" he said, "We welcome anyone to practice with us."

At first, they let me watch. It was a stirring sight, and one unlike any other in our great encampment, for among the mounted company there were women archers. Targets had been rigged, and the normal archers emptied their arrows first. Then the mounted archers took it in turn to gallop past the targets, firing their arrows with short bows, like the one Tory had given to me. When they were finished, the women beckoned me over. I was full of apologies and excuses for I knew my skills were far inferior, but I did my pass and was encouraged to take a second one, after a little advice.

"You did well!" laughed Delion as we unsaddled the horses. "If you intend to really take to the field, we have a spare horse. Take him for they are trained to respond to the rider's whole body as you turn to fire, rather than simply knees." I thanked him and then he added, "Even your light armour will be a hinderance to you. Perhaps take a leather breast plate instead." He handed one to me. "Now you will be able to move freely."

I couldn't wait to try it on. The sixteen women of Delion's company laughed and giggled as they strapped me into it. One suggested, "Try firing your bow now. Stand sideways and swing round to the target." I did and was amazed by how much freedom the breastplate gave me.

Judith was not convinced shedding my armour was a good idea. Certainly, it was protection, but it was also restricting, and it was also easy to identify in battle. The leather breastplate was lighter and far more comfortable. She eventually gave in, leaving me in my tent to find Soldin to spar with.

I was not alone for long. Conrad arrived and with him was Black Mantle. Conrad explained that the older men of The Souran were equal to the task of defending Vellin, but Arun Tenregor felt his place was with us. As he pointed out, Mantles trained their whole life to be warriors and none in three generations had ever faced an enemy. As if to justify his presence, Tenregor insisted that both Conrad and Tory face him. I watched them spellbound. This was not simply swordplay but almost a dance with deadly weapons. They twisted and turned, lunged, and parried with such grace and ease, shifting positions, sometimes defending against two blades at once. Without any apparent signal, they all stopped.

"That was most enjoyable Master Tory!" Black Mantle took a deep breath. "Forgive our pointless display, Your Majesty. We must appear like overexcited youths. It is just that with the exception of Conrad, The Souran have little occasion to visit the practise yard." He drew a kerchief across his forehead. "I am surprised that Ransom did not join us, he is very agile despite his large frame."

"I think there was sufficient Mantle exhibitionism on display!" Ransom Frain had been standing behind me and I never heard him arrive. His lightness of foot was not restricted to swordsmanship and dancing.

Following the indiscretions of the night before, the camp was quiet after sunset. Word had quickly spread that the invaders were already on our shores and making their way north. It was a time for quiet contemplation and thoughts of home, thoughts of what the coming day would bring and for those who believed, to turn to their gods. Most of The Five Kingdoms had never developed a taste for gods but some, like the warriors of Urvik, gathered together to direct prayers to their ancient deity, Accipa, and many of the Rynth miners, whose belief in The Great Tree had strengthened after Silverleaf, found a quiet place to offer up a prayer. I might have done so myself. Ever since my last encounter with the wolves, I felt a sense of closeness to the land that filled me with contentment and a sense of belonging.

Instead, I was drawn to Delion's campfire, where Findin wove his own magic, summoning up music that whispered the echoes of the seashore and the distant beating of waves on rocks. I looked at the faces of his audience, all wrapped in their own thoughts and memories as the notes hovered in the night sky. He acknowledged me with a nod but kept on playing. With the fading music guiding my own thoughts northwards to Roth, I went to my bed. Judith was already asleep.

Shortly after dawn, Conrad woke me. The spies from Bashiria had returned with news that the Goremene army would soon be upon us. It was an eery start to the morning. There was no clattering of cauldrons or queues for porridge. Bread was distributed and men went quietly to their stations. This was Conrad's plan.

Armour was donned, weapons gathered, horses saddled and across the field all was being prepared. Ross and my son came to my tent. We said very little but embraced each other then they prepared to leave.

"Mother!" Alexander looked back. "I will see you in the evening!"

It was the thing we always said to each other at Roth and both Judith, and I replied. Judith tapped me on my arm and began to make her way to join The Mantles. I noticed that the remaining members of The Souran were mounted, too, as was Soldin Meganor. Conrad rode towards me.

"You will not change your mind about taking part?" he asked.

"You already know my answer. If we lose today, death will be my reward, either in battle or at some unknown time and place of Florian's choosing. I choose to die among my own people."

He nodded and turned his horse to join the rest of The Mantles. There was one other obstacle in my way before I could reach my company, Findin, the harper.

"I would offer you my protection, but you would refuse it, and I cannot protect your whole army." He took my hand. "Rest assured, there is one small lion cub that I will protect this day." It was enough and I thanked him for his protection of my son.

The armies assembled before me and shared a moment of humour as I had to be helped into the back of a cart to speak to them.

"My brothers and sisters of The Five Kingdoms, today, we fight for our freedom, the freedom of our children, and their children. Side by side, each of us risks all for that freedom. Today we are equals. Impending death makes it so, but through that equality we share the task. Each one of us…"

I looked down at their faces, all ready to fight for the land they loved and for the protection of their families. It was a moment to remember that every pair of eyes, every beating heart and every life lived had value. No monarch should forget that.

"Each one of us has a part to play and whether we succeed or fail, the gathering of our people on this day, in this place, is testament to the power of The Five Kingdoms. We do not call on mercenaries or slaves. We are free and we fight for that very freedom, not because a king or queen demands it but because we all value the freedom to say," I cried loudly, "We are The Five!"

"We are The Five!" They yelled back to me and did so five times.

I climbed down and was immediately surrounded by a throng of people. Only the horn of the Dereculd herald brought us all to attention. It was time for Conrad, the kings, and the lords to begin to marshal their people.

Judith was at my side. "Who would have thought all those long years back that you and I would be side by side, risking our lives for a kingdom that discarded us. We have proved more valuable than our looks."

"We have indeed," I nodded, "I will see you in the evening!" we both smiled.

After Judith and I had embraced once more, I made my way to join the Dereculd archers.

While I was undistinguishable from the rest of the Dereculd archers, I was perverse enough to wear a tiny gold broach in the shape of a lion, a gift from the men of Rynth. It made Delion smile as we joined the other generals just below the crest of the hill, where the Bashirian men kept watch on the valley below.

"There!" one of them said. He pointed into the distance. A glint of something far down beyond the marshes gradually turned into armour and the purple banners of the Goremenes.

Conrad raised his arm, and The Mantles spread across the hill's crest. Behind them was the Magran cavalry then the mounted archers, followed by any other smaller mounted contingents. The foot soldiers ringed either side of the ridge and also stretched out behind the riders, almost to the tree where the forlorn figure of Tertius Norton was slumped.

The surprise among the Goremene army was what we had hoped for. It must have been a formidable sight in the early light, warriors appearing out of nowhere above them filling the horizon. We heard scrambled commands and a general scattering of people and horses.

I have read many accounts of famous battles between warring armies, when both camps pitch their tents and at some appointed time, they eventually clash. This was not like that. They were the invaders. We gave them no time to prepare. We did not send our heralds to proclaim the challenge. Instead, The Mantles and knights slowly began to ride down the hill, in a sort of loose formation. The archers remained behind, ready to begin with stationery firing. We mounted archers would only enter the fray when the knights had charged.

Florian's knights, unprepared though they were, gathered themselves together quickly and charged towards the hill. Some were caught out by the boggy ground, but many got through. In a matter of seconds, the two armies met in a horrendous clash of metal and the cries of men and horses. The carnage began. Knights collided, horses reared or succumbed to agile pikemen. It was easy to distinguish the black cowls of Mantles, thrown back to reveal their helms and mail. The men of Rynth, swinging axes about their Mine Master, now in his armour rather than his Red Mantle. It was easy to spot Prince Beren, for although he had lost his horse, he still stood head and shoulders above those around him.

From our vantage point, The Dereculd archers began to pick out our targets. The mounted archers directed their arrows at the mounted men, the archers on foot, with their larger and more powerful bows, aimed at the foot soldiers who were pouring in behind their army. I remember an overwhelming urge to vomit, but this was overtaken by the need to fire and continue to fire as some of the Goremene knights made their way through the field and headed up the hill. Now their own archers were involved.

We began to ride, down towards the knot of flailing beasts and men below, firing at the enemy knights intending to stop us. I recall hitting three. The first was felled with an arrow through his helm, and he fell immediately. The second hit a knight's chest and the third slipped across a knight's armour as he turned. Luckily for me, he was already intent on felling the rider ahead of me to my left. A second's glance, and I witnessed the archer being sliced almost in two by the blow from the knight's sword. By now we were reaching the outer edge of the hand-to-hand combat of the pikemen and the wielding of clubs, axes, and pitchforks. I turned my horse to the right, where knights were still finding space to remain mounted and fight with swords, axes, and poleaxes. Being closer, it was easier to pick a target while continuing to ride fast enough to avoid being struck. I had watched the Dereculd archers who managed these things with ease.

Suddenly, two things happened at once. An arrow struck my horse, which fell immediately and as he went, there was a fearsome pain in my left shoulder. The horse fell across my leg, flailing badly in his agony. His head hit mine several times before the pain in both my leg and my arm caused me to faint. I was vaguely aware of being pulled from under the horse and being thrown over the back of a horse. Both of those actions caused me to cry out in pain and faint again.

I awoke in my tent, hearing Judith shouting at someone that now was not the time for modesty. A vile smell of ammonia made me jerk awake. The pain in my arm was unbearable. I was also aware that I was almost naked. My clothes had been removed and Judith was doing something with my shoulder. She was binding it, helped by Soldin, who looked very uncomfortable about seeing more of me than was acceptable. He passed me a blanket that I held in place while Judith completed her work.

"It's the best I can do. Soldin got the arrow out and I've done some of my best needlework. I don't know what to do about your leg." She looked down and I followed her gaze. My leg appeared twisted, and I felt no sensation from it.

"May I be of assistance?" Findin was at the door. "I have some knowledge in these matters. Lady Judith, you, and your good friend may leave Her Majesty to me." Judith did not need prompting. She was out of the tent, her armour rattling as she remounted her horse.

"Now, Majesty!" Findin put his hand on my leg, and something akin to what it must feel like to have fire burn through your flesh spread over my leg. I cried out but then felt nothing, no pain, no sensation of any kind. He looked up at me, "It will be an annoyance for a while, but eventually, it will mend."

I muttered, "Thank you, but why aren't you watching my son?"

"Such ingratitude, Katherine! The last time I saw him he was cheerfully wielding his sword at some Goremene farmworker who had less idea of how to fight than I have to make lace." He patted me on my healthy shoulder. "Don't worry, Kate, it appears that I can watch over two people in a battle."

"Help me into my clothes, I have to be out there." I tried to stand. I was grateful he didn't argue but helped me to dress and managed to find a horse for me, which was miraculously tethered nearby. This time, I donned my armour and strapped on my short sword. I placed the helm, with its distinctive crown on my head.

Back in the melee, word had circulated that The Queen was injured. Some said killed. Some said wounded. Some said kidnapped. They fought on but the doubt about the whereabouts of The Queen hung over them.

Judith rode back into the melee, yelling, “She lives! I’ve seen her!” as loud as she could and was almost felled by a huge man swinging a poleaxe. Close to her, Lord Taegel, now on foot, succumbed to an arrow and a deep gash to his chest. The mounted cavalry and knights were gradually pushing the battle into the marshland. It was becoming slippery underfoot and many floundered not from injury but from being sucked into the slime.

My son, disobeying his mother, and not for the last time, was indeed still mounted on someone else’s horse, swinging his sword at any head that came near enough to be taken off. He first heard the cry, “The Queen!” from a miner beside him who was struggling to overcome a man with a pike. The observation almost robbed the miner of his life, but Alexander slashed at the pikeman as the fellow overbalanced into the mud. Alexander told me afterwards that with the sun behind me, I rode towards the battle like a shadow, with only the edges of my armour gleaming in the light. No one could mistake the crown on my helm. He had little time to see what happened next, for he was defending himself against an experienced Goremene knight. It might have been my son’s last battle if his screaming harpy of a mother had not borne down on the hapless knight with her small, slim sword and sliced through his unprotected throat. That one death spurred those about us to intensify their efforts.

I cried, “For the Five!’ to anyone who would listen and in that moment the cry went up across the battlefield.

“Now please keep out of danger!” Ross manoeuvred his horse next to mine.

That was easier said than done as the fighting around me intensified. I was fortunate that I was mounted and with armour on my legs for the men on foot were pressing tighter. The horse had more experience than I, and it suddenly reared up, kicking men out of its way in front then backing into some unfortunates behind, before it moved forwards with more menace, knocking away foot soldiers with its head. It got me out of the press and heading towards The

Dereculd archers. They formed a protective shield around me, patting me on the shoulder.

"We thought you were gone for sure when the horse fell!" one young woman said. Her name was Lyn, and I stayed with her as she continued to fire her bow until the battle had moved too far into the marsh for the mounted archers to follow. Now the longbow archers took control. Down in the marsh, it was impossible to determine what was happening or who anyone was.

Black Mantle, his tunic and cape spattered with blood, came riding up towards me. "It won't be long now, Your Majesty, we have them surrounded."

"Look!" My archer friend pointed towards the western side of the hollow, where the Goremene wagons had been driven. Several women in gowns were trying to make their escape. They were being pursued by some Bashiria foot soldiers.

"They shouldn't be anyone's quarry!" I turned my horse and nodded to my two companions. "Come with me." I dropped my helm as I rode.

By the time we reached the women, the soldiers were already manhandling them as the women's screams for help were lost in the general clamour. I didn't hesitate but rode towards the men and slashed one man across his back. The archer's arrow felled a second. The others turned on us immediately and would have pulled us from our horses if Black Mantle had not caused all the men to clutch their heads and stumble to the ground.

"They'll have terrible headaches for a few days." Black Mantle assured me, "but they'll still have their heads."

"Thank you, sir, for saving our lives!" A young flaxen-haired girl came to my side. "You and your friends are indeed gentlemen."

"I don't know about her, but I've never been a gentleman!" The archer took off her cap, allowing her long plait of raven hair to fall down her back.

I removed my helm "Neither have I!"

Black Mantle sighed. "I am a gentleman, I hope." He gestured to Lyn, "She is an archer, and this is the High Queen of The Five Kingdoms."

The girl immediately dropped into a curtsey. "I am Celestine, daughter of the King of Goremene."

I beckoned her to stand. "It saddens me that we have had to meet like this, Princess. May I escort you and your ladies to a safer place? You may follow me back to my camp. No one will harm you there."

A great cry interrupted us, and we all looked down into the heaving mess of mud and men in the marsh.

"Father!" Celestine started to run forward, but I barred her way with my horse.

"Better that you wait, Your Highness," I told her. "Stay here with my lord, Black Mantle and my friend, Lyn. They will protect you." I didn't wait for her to agree but rode towards the marsh. I was confident that after seeing how Black Mantle dealt with the Bashiria foot soldiers, he could keep her safe.

Survivors were slowly climbing out of the marsh. A pile of relinquished weapons was already growing on the ground. Conrad and Delion staggered up together, their whole bodies smeared with sludge and blood. Between them was Florian, his head bloody, his arms hanging limply at his side. Delion gave him a not-so-gentle push, and he dropped to his knees.

"I surrender to Katherine, Queen of The Five Kingdoms." His weary eyes looked up at me from out of the mask of mud. "I relinquish all claims and intentions towards the lands of The Five Kingdoms."

That, in essence, was it! The battle won! Some frenzied combatants still struggled until they were brought to their senses by those around them.

The victors cheered and escorted the King of Goremene and all his surviving men into temporary captivity. They would be given access to water to clean themselves, and a formal surrender would be drafted. Meanwhile, on the battlefield, the dead and dying needed my attention.

So many faces! So many lives! As I moved among them, the injured survivors were being taken to The Mantles' sanctuary tent. Inside, friend and foe received treatment with equal dignity. Men gathered the fallen from both sides and took them there. A few knelt beside those too injured to be moved, keeping them company, providing a comforting hand in theirs, a kindly word, anything to ease their death. I did this, too, to anyone in either camp. Celestine, the daughter of Florian, had ignored Black Mantle and followed me to the marsh. She followed my example. When I looked up, she gave me a sad smile. Together, we moved towards where the battle had been the heaviest, at least it seemed so for the bodies were the thickest there. Most had died long ago, in the heat of the battle, and were submerged in the marsh slime beneath others. Celestine stopped suddenly, and I went to her.

"This boy was from my father's stables. He was fourteen." She closed his eyes and used a small kerchief to wipe his face. She looked up at me. "Why do men relish battle so much?"

"It seems to be in their nature." I helped her stand. "When they are not at war, they fight pretend wars at tournaments. This war was never of my making. Your aunt knew that. It's why she came and told me of Lord Norton's plans."

"My aunt? Lady Norton? But she is dead. She died in childbirth." Celestine looked bewildered.

"Your aunt died a slow and painful death only weeks ago. She was tortured as a traitor, by her own husband and left to die in an iron basket in the marketplace of Wyke!" It was harsh of me to tell her anything, and worse in the midst of the dead, but my anger could not even spare her. It was beyond words to think that Florian's daughter did not know the truth. If I could have lashed out at someone in that moment, I would.

"You're lying!" The princess pulled her hand from mine and began to walk back towards where her father was being held. She turned. "You're lying, and I hate you for such a terrible thing to say. She died in childbirth!" I watched her stumble away, adding more mud to her gown as she went. I could not help her. She would have to face the truth eventually, and I wondered, I hoped, she would confront her father.

"Majesty!" It was Arolan, King of Urvik, nursing a bloody arm and being supported by two of his soldiers. I went towards him, to offer my thanks and inquire about his injury, but he pointed, directing my eyes to a spot where several horses' bodies and their riders lay across the field. A small crowd was gathered in a huddle about a chestnut horse, which obscured most of its rider. I began to walk towards the spot, Celestine and Majolica forgotten. My pace quickened as I saw the shining embossed greaves and leather-clad feet of the fallen.

"No! No! no! No!' I kept saying quietly at first, but as I neared the crowd, I was almost yelling. They separated as I approached. When the full horror of the scene confronted me, it was not a word but the howl of some creature from the forests that came from my throat. Soldin was sitting in the mud, cradling Judith's face in his hands, as if she were sleeping, but the enormous gash below her cuirass showed the fatal blow from a pike. Her life had ended swiftly. I dropped beside her and held her hand, feeling the callouses and the bitten fingernails that we had so often chided her about. I wiped blood from the side of her mouth, tried unsuccessfully to push her hair into neatness, and patted her cheek as if to wake her. Soldin gripped my hand to still its frantic movement.

"She can't be dead!"

"She is at peace." He nodded, squeezing my hand before he released it. The crowd encircled us. Some recalled how they'd seen her in battle, others how she could tell a lewd joke or drink a man under the table. All their talk was of her love of life, her hearty friendship, and her strength of purpose. I wished she could have heard them.

Conrad's hand settled on my shoulder. "Let us move her to where she can rest, My Queen." He brought me to my feet, where my son, with a black eye and a cut on his forehead, threw his arm about me. Beside him, Ross reached for my hand. I let them guide me away from the scene, hearing Conrad ask for volunteers to bear the lady gently away to his own tent. I looked back once. Almost too many men were trying to carry Judith. It did not surprise me that later it became a proud boast for many to say they fought beside Judith of Pellion and helped to carry her corpse from the battlefield.

Soldin refused to allow anyone else to clean her. When I later took a gown to dress her in, he took only her undergarments. "She died as a warrior. She would wish to be buried as a warrior." He was carefully cleaning all of her armour. Later that night, the sound of a hammer came from outside the tent. He was beating parts back into shape. He left while I sat with her for a while. I could not speak to her, although I'd tried, reminding her of our clashes at Roth and how we would laugh later. Then I sat, simply holding her hand until Soldin returned. The following morning, I told him of her wish to be buried in Pellion with her family.

"It is fitting!" He nodded. "With your permission, I will take her with me and return to Dereculd with Thorfin and King Delion." We embraced, and I left him sitting beside her.

There was scant celebration that night. With prisoners to feed and guard, food was consumed, and sentries set. For me, it was a lonely evening, looking at the empty cot across the tent. I could not bear it for long, so I visited the injured, taking time to talk to the survivors of both camps. Conrad found me there and escorted me back to my tent. Judith's cot had been removed. This upset me more. He held me close as I wept, then told me he would send some company for me as we both needed rest before the morning. I had expected a female archer, but instead it was Ross who came. We hardly spoke. He lay beside me, cradling me as I cried. Perhaps I did shed tears for Judith. I know that I also shed them for myself in losing her. The woman who had once been my adversary had become a dear and trusted friend.

Dawn brought activity of another kind. The dead were being buried, supervised by Black Mantle. Those who could be identified were noted, and lists of the survivors were collected. Eventually, a stone monument would be erected at this place of death to commemorate their sacrifice. The camp was being disbanded, and I had to bid farewell to many before ever the aftermath of the battle was concluded. My cousin, Delion, and his Dereculd army left immediately. I embraced my fellow archers and watched them all leave, followed by the lowly cart bearing my dear friend's body, escorted by Soldin and the female archers.

XIX VANQUISHED

The battle over, the dead buried, it was time to deal with King Florian, his army, and his court. So many had died needlessly. Florian's invasion had destroyed two remarkable women, both dear to me. No one, no matter which side they had fought for, could claim exemption from suffering and loss. This hung heavily over my thoughts as the kings, lords, the free city leaders and The Souran squashed into the large tent to hear the fate of the invaders. Outside the tent, the survivors sat in quite knots around limp campfires or huddled in chains to await their fate. The dishevelled knot of Goremene generals and officials sat dejected in one corner of the tent. The banners were gone, as were the maps of the battlefield and the huge table over which it had spread.

Only one seat was provided. My leg still gave me pain, and Ross had dressed my shoulder when we woke that morning. I took my place, then Florian was brought to his feet. He was unchained and looking cleaner than when I saw him last. His Bashirian guards made him kneel before me. He opened his mouth to speak but had the grace to realise silence was expected.

"King Florian of Goremene, you are guilty of invading our shores, intent upon taking my crown and subjugating the free people of The Five Kingdoms. I do not wish to hear your reasons nor your excuses." I delivered my condemnation standing.

"As High Queen, I never sought this war. My people did not seek this war. The bloodshed is on your hands. I was never schooled in the protocol of such occasions as this; therefore, my words and my decisions are my own, not set down in some antiquated etiquette of battle."

"You want me to plead for my life?" Florian's misery did not extend to the loss of his pride.

"No!" My laugh lacked mirth. "Why is it that men believe retribution will cancel out harm done? What good would that do? How would any words from you bring to life all those who died here, or feed their widows and orphans?"

"Then just kill me and have done with it!" His words brought a gasp from his daughter and drew swift glances in her direction.

I sighed. There would be no apology from this man. For him, such humility was impossible. I knew he saw it as a weakness. It was for me to show not only compassion but also common sense. "I don't intend to kill you. I never intended harm towards you or your people, many of them now lying dead on foreign soil. I thought about it after Majolica Norton died, but I suspect you were not a party to that murder."

"She died giving birth!" He was impatient for his own demise. "Just kill me, but be just to my people."

Many in that tent had not heard of Majolica's death, so I told her brother the truth, while he knelt, not sparing him any of the details I knew. At first, his impatience discounted what I was telling him, but as the story unfolded, I could see the shock in his face. Tertius had lied to him, too. There were tears in his eyes when I finished.

"I swear I knew nothing of this." He shook his head, his voice barely a whisper, then looked up angrily. "She was my sister!"

"I believe you knew nothing." The faces of those around me displayed the revulsion they felt. "When we met on the battlefield, your daughter told me the same story of her aunt's demise in childbirth. I believe you were told the same lie. It is for that reason that I do not take your life, but know this: it was your secret pact with The Lord of Camlan that brought about her death. Your sister was my friend and my loyal subject, who risked her own life to warn me of your plans. I do not wish to see you dead or pay for the death of a woman that I called my friend. There are too many dead already, too many widows and orphans and for what? Two men's greed for power.

'You and those who wish to return with you will be escorted to the coast of Bashiria and put on your waiting ships for Goremene. The chests of gold intended as bribes, and all your possessions and the possessions of your court will remain here. You will be asked to sign a pledge never to invade our shores again." I lifted the scroll from my seat. There were murmurs among the representatives of The Five Kingdoms.

"You're sending me home?" I detected the momentary smile before he suppressed it. Yes, he was being sent home, and he could continue to live in the lavish luxury he had amassed in Goremene. "I just have to sign a pledge?" It was so easy.

"That is all. It binds you for life to our agreement. If you agree, we will renew our trading agreements with you and offer free passage for your people, as it was before this invasion." As I spoke, I could almost hear his brain clicking over in addition to the murmured disbelief among some of my own people.

"Then I will gladly sign!" He got to his feet, alarming some of the lords. Others were thinking that I had been far too lenient with him and that there should be some further redress.

"There is just one other condition." I held the pledge away from him. He was suddenly on his guard. 'It would be foolish of us here assembled to believe you will keep your word." There was a slight shift in the postures of those behind me. Perhaps I was about to exact some punitive retribution upon him after all.

"I believe that in times past, in order to ensure such a pledge was kept, hostages would remain in the victor's court. It seems a simple way of solving our lack of trust in each other. You will stay in your country and enjoy your life, while your daughter, Princess

Celestine, will remain in Vellin, as my guest. Should you break your word, rest assured that your daughter's life will be forfeit."

There was a general uproar in the tent. Florian and his daughter both objected, while my doubting lords and kings suddenly appreciated my leniency. The important trade with Goremene would continue, and Florian had been dealt his own punishment with the loss of his beloved child, and a sizeable inventory of gold and goods would be shared.

"Enough!" I called, and for once did not need a man to repeat my command. "That is my decision. You may accept it, and I hope you will, or you can die. All of you." I pointedly looked towards the little knot of Goremene women. "There is no alternative. You invaded our lands and have killed many of our countrymen. I'm sure The King of Bashiria, whose home is closest to our present position, would undertake the necessary executions." For his part, Prince Beren nodded, adopting his most formidable stance.

While his daughter collapsed in tears, surrounded by her ladies, Florian the First set his name to the pledge. He was allowed to embrace his daughter, then he was taken away. The Bashirian companies and their temporary prisoners left within the hour. Celestine had been equally shocked when she learnt that her ladies were not part of the bargain. Fiercely angry, she sat on the floor of the strategy tent and kicked out at anyone who came near her.

I beckoned to my son as I spoke to them all. "Lord Elderin of Brak is appointed protector of the Princess Celestine until we reach Vellin. Princess, you would do well to acknowledge and accept your good fortune. Death is never the better option. I have no objection to you corresponding with your father and he to you, but I must insist that you continue to comport yourself as a princess should. This is your fate. Accept it!"

She glared at me but said nothing. I referred to Alexander as the squire of Lord Elderin and asked him to take charge of our royal prisoner. I quietly told him to be courteous and understanding, but not to allow her too much freedom. On no account must she escape.

Later, as the camp began to dwindle until only those returning to Vellin and the North were left, I saw him trying to offer her food. She threw it at him. He shrugged and told her she'd be very hungry by supper.

We left shortly after a noontide meal. The foot soldiers and baggage wagons set out first, followed by the knights. The lords allowed their men to mingle as they themselves did, sharing tales and turning thoughts to their waiting manors. It was a pleasant change from when we arrived. The Souran and the men of Brak were the last to leave. I saw several of them looking towards the tree where Tertius Norton still sat.

"Are you going to set him free, or will you have Ross Elderin kill him?" Black Mantle asked as he mounted. I had told no one of my intentions and had even kept them from Conrad. I was grateful he had not asked.

"Neither," I replied. "I will catch up with you all." I watched them reluctantly follow the way of earlier departures before I rode to the tree and looked down at Tertius. His face was burnt by the sun, and he had not eaten for some days, but he had been kept alive with water. He looked up, screwing his eyes a little to protect them from the sun behind my head.

"Come on, Kate. I've learnt my lesson. I'll be good. Let me go, and we can make a new start." I said nothing,

"Kate! You have to let me go now. I'm sorry about Majolica. It was wrong, I know, but she was going to jeopardise everything. I had to help Florian. He was going to make me king. It's not too late for us, you know. We could make Magra truly great. Now we have Goremene, we could do so much." His attempts to charm me were pathetic. He tried to shuffle towards me, as if being nearer would somehow affect my opinion of him. That might have worked on an impressionable girl, but I was no longer that girl.

"We don't have Goremene. I sent Florian home. I'm determined there should be peace for all of us, including Goremene."

“Then you’re going to release me?” He sat back, resting his head on the tree.

“No, Tertius, I have no intention of releasing you. I think this is a fitting punishment for a man who allowed his noble wife to die like a common thief, in full view of the people of Wyke.” I drew the reins of my horse together and turned his head.

“No, wait, Kate! Kate! Please! Didn’t you say you’d set Florian free?”

“He didn’t torture his wife. In fact, Florian was quite upset when I told him about his sister.” I began to ride away.

“For pity’s sake, please!” he screamed. “Don’t leave me like this! Please Kate! I’m begging you! Come back and run a sword through me, at least! Let me die like a lord! Please! Kate!” His voice grew fainter and fainter as I rode away. Eventually, I no longer heard him.

XX Celestine

I rode away from the battleground, chastened but unrepentant about what I had just done. Condemning Tertius Norton to a slow death would not restore the lives lost, nor help the bereaved. It changed nothing except that it satisfied my own desire, no, my own need for revenge. I promised myself that it would be the last time I would commit such a callous act. It was certainly the only time that I have felt satisfaction in another's death.

Around me, the land showed no anger or disappointment towards me or criticism of my actions. It watched my ride with dispassion. I was just another creature passing through. It cared nothing for my tears. I didn't know if I was crying for the dead or for myself. When the tears subsided, I slowed and allowed the horse to set our pace. I knew Conrad was searching for my mind, but I blocked his thoughts. That alone would tell him I needed this time alone. Emotion eventually drained from me, and in its place came the calm I needed to join the rest of The Magran companies. They were making their way through The Forests of Lore before night fell.

A lone rider attracts unwanted attention in such places, but here, I knew I was among friends. I never saw them, but the wolf's howls told me they were near. Their cries escorted me until I saw the distant campfires on the edge of the forest. As I passed the sentries, they acknowledged me with some relief. Only then did I open my mind to Conrad. He did not ask about Norton. Much later, I told what I had done.

The smell of food overtook all my other thoughts, and I was handed a plate of stew by one of the men of Brak, who took delight in patting me soundly on the back before joining his company. I sat among the lords, welcoming their noisy banter as they retold each other their lighter recollections of the days spent on the battlefield. I noticed that Princess Celestine sat alone, some distance from Ross and my son. When my plate was empty, I placed my camp stool beside her.

"Good evening, Princess!"

"Perhaps for you!" She glared at me venomously.

"Civility always becomes a princess," I scolded, but then added, "but I would feel as angry as you, in your position."

She gave me a look of utter contempt before snarling, "You have never been in my position." I replied that although I had never been a hostage, I had been in exile and forced from my home. I told her about Roth and how hard those early days had been. At first, she stared down at her slippered feet, pretending not to listen, but slowly, as I told her about Judith and the way our friendship changed everything, she dropped the pretence.

"Judith of Pellion was the knight killed on the battlefield." She spoke quietly, almost to herself.

"She was. When she died, I lost a very dear friend. It will be hard for all her friends, especially my ladies in Vellin, to learn of her death."

"You have ladies in waiting?" She was thinking of those she had left behind.

"Indeed, I do!" I got to my feet. "And our conversation has just reminded me of someone that I must speak with. Lord Clairstow has a daughter, Sybil, who hopes to join us. Perhaps she could join us on our way to Vellin. She is a quiet girl with little knowledge of what will be required to become a lady in waiting. Perhaps you could educate her about that."

I detected a glimmer of interest in Celestine's eyes, but she quickly hid it. "I don't think I could have anything in common with such a girl. I have lived all my life in the most sophisticated royal court in the world."

"Of course. Well, a good night to you, Princess." I left her and joined Ross and my son at their small fire.

"She's a stupid, stubborn girl!" Alexander said under his breath. "I've tried being nice to her, but it's no good." He poked the fire angrily. "And you should hear the crude words she knows." He looked across at the lonely girl who stared into the night. "She may be a princess, but she's not a likable one."

"Sometimes it's hard to recognise a person's station in life," Ross told him, offering me a sideways glance. "You have to get to know the person, not judge them by their rank. At this moment, that girl is afraid and lonely, and she needs a friend, even if she rejects that friendship. Keep trying but don't expect too much because right now, she sees all of us as her enemies."

I reached for Ross's hand and squeezed it. He took my hand and kissed it lightly. I left them shortly afterwards and made my way through the large encampment speaking to lords and their men with equal pleasure. I reminded Lord Clairstow about his daughter, and I shared a cup of strong ale with shepherds from the hills above Malister who told me tales of their home after assuring me that it would be their greatest boast to say that Queen Katherine sat at their fire. Before retiring, I came across Conrad, who also appeared to be moving through the camp. He told me that the other members of The Souran had resumed their normal travels. His own men had sustained few injuries. He was concerned about Tory, who had taken Judith's death badly. He was burying himself in caring for the sick among our caravan and refused rest. I was thankful Conrad had induced him to sleep, in spite of his protests. I promised to speak with Tory the following morning. His sadness was as deep as my own, likening Judith to a sister he never had. When we did talk, I could only offer him the same salve that I hoped would ease my own sadness, that of time, and our happier memories.

Our arrival in Nordinay set the pattern for the remainder of our journey. The crowds lining our path were overwhelming. The news had reached the town before our arrival, and at certain points our caravan had to force its way through the jubilant throng. I had to take particular care. People rushed to touch me and my horse. It brought a heavy lump to my throat. People scattered flowers in our path and thrust gifts towards the men as they passed. Not even the austere Mantles were exempt from these attentions. It was pleasing to see their usually restrained faces smiling and nodding to the crowds.

Because Clairstow had ample land around his stronghold, the whole company set up camp there, and we all rested for a few days. I was grateful that he offered accommodation in his manor for me and some of the older lords. I had never regarded a bed as a luxury before. Ross and Alexander were among the guests each evening in the castle's rarely used banqueting hall. Although she may not have appreciated it, I asked that the Princess Celestine be given the room next to mine. She did not refuse and was even civil enough to thank Clairstow for his consideration. She was cold to Sybil's greeting and snarled at Alexander, who took his protection of her very seriously and guarded her door each evening.

"I wouldn't be surprised if that hateful squire was peeping at me through the keyhole!" Celestine told me as we went down to the hall together.

"I think you will find there are no keys to our rooms, Princess, thus no keyholes," I chided her. "Besides, the squire of Brak would never do such a thing. I know his mother."

"The squire might not be like his mother!" she grumbled.

"I hope not!" I stepped in front of her to descend the narrow, winding staircase. "I think he's even better."

During the evening and without prompting from me, Sybil Clairstow did her best to engage Celestine in conversation, admiring her jewellery, telling her about life in The Meeds, and even trying to encourage her take part in the dancing. It was a valiant though not successful attempt. My aching leg prevented my participation, so I watched the interactions of others instead. Now a hero of the battle, the Lord of Brak's squire was a popular dance partner, and I was pleased that he included Sybil among his partners.

The remainder of our short stay was quiet and restful. I toured Clairstow's woodlands with him and found him far more amiable than at our first encounter at The Field of the Pentangle, for which he again apologised. The man had suffered greatly during his wife's illness, desperate to keep her condition a private matter between his household and her trusted physician. After our last visit, when Conrad had soothed her mind and quietened her anxieties, Clairstow had engaged attendants selected for their loving natures, who not only catered for her needs but spent time entertaining her and being her friends. She was not ready to meet with strangers, but watching her from my window, as she picked herbs with two of her nurses, she was relaxed and laughing in their company.

At Taegel, we solemnly buried their lord, Oliver, who I had hoped would one day be a member of my Council. We paid our respects to his family and heir. Our welcome in the town was no less enthusiastic than it had been throughout our journey. Our company spent two days camped beside the River Listi where it joins the River Shreur. There had been little rain recently, and the ground was baked hard, except where the river waters seeped into the banks.

Lady Taegel arranged for me to meet with the widows whose husbands now rested together under the distant battlefield. Sybil assisted me as I handed each one of them a small bag of gold, courtesy of Florian's hasty removal by The Bashirians. The Goremene tents had been left standing and carefully concealed behind bags of oats were chests filled with gold coins. Presumably, it had been intended as payment to someone. Instead, the widows of Taegel would benefit, along with the widows in the five other fiefdoms who had lost their lords.

"Why did you distribute my father's gold? You could have kept it to use in Vellin." Celestine was in a calmer mood, although she would not allow Sybil to take her arm. I had invited both young ladies to accompany me for a walk beside the river.

"The widows can't be supported by their lord, because he is dead, and his successor is little more than a boy. In Vellin, I can personally see to it that the widows there are taken care of. It isn't my gold, and I hardly think your father would object to my using it in this way. He and I might have been enemies when he had designs on my kingdom, but I never thought of him as a mean-spirited man." I reached down to feel the water running through my fingers. Both the girls wore gowns, but I was reluctant to dispense with my archer's riding breeches. All too soon, I would be forced back into appropriate queenly clothing. Celestine had remarked on my unconventional attire to my son, who gleefully relayed her criticism.

"Her Majesty is a widow herself, and while she will not suffer the poverty and stigma attached to that status in life, she understands the sorrow," Sybil spoke without prompting and blushed when we both looked her way.

"It is not your place to interpret the mind of The Queen!" Celestine's nose lifted haughtily.

"Sybil speaks from the heart and has every right to do so." I went to the girls' side. Celestine's rebuke had wounded her enough to make her eyes sparkle. I placed her arm in mine. "I expect nothing less of my ladies, Sybil, and I'm pleased you feel that you can express your thoughts. You will find my ladies equally forthright." I patted her hand on my arm.

In the afternoon, some of the squires organised a strange game of kicking a pig's bladder that some enterprising youth had taken with him to The Gathering. There seemed to be no rules, or teams. The object appeared to be simply to keep the ball moving. At one point, it flew close to where we were seated. The young men halted in their enthusiasm, looking down at the ball, uncertain about how to retrieve it. It was a credit to my son that he also held back. I looked at both the girls. Celestine had her eyes closed, her face up towards the sun, but Sybil had been trying to follow the game. She looked towards me.

"Kick it back, Sybil!" I urged, challenging her. Wearing a broad smile, she stood and kicked it back, up into the air. Several young men complimented her with cries of "Good kick!", "Nice kick!" She returned to her seat, unable to suppress her delight. Naturally, in the course of the next few moments, the ball amazingly returned towards us, and each time, Sybil would stand and kick. Gradually, this lured Celestine out of her indifference, so much so that when the ball rolled quickly towards them both, she leapt to her feet and kicked before Sybil could reach it. Unfortunately, her dainty shoe came off, too. That brought more cheers from the youths, prompting Alexander to retrieve the shoe and bring it back to the princess. Embarrassed, she snatched it from his outstretched hand. He, in turn, smiled broadly at Sybil, who immediately smiled back, blushing.

"Alexander of Brak seems such a polite and thoughtful young man," Sybil said, sitting down. Celestine snorted but said nothing.

That evening was to be the last to be spent with many of the lords from The Central and Northern Meeds. They would leave the following day, each for their own fiefdom. They would return the bodies of their neighbours to their families with a private message from me, as well as their share of the Goremene gold. The evening was a quiet, contemplative time. We sat together, reminiscing. Looking around the faces in the fire's glow, I felt proud of these men, none of them true warriors like The Mantles, but farmers who had fought to protect their homes.

"They feel the same about you," Conrad spoke to my mind. He was beside Malister, who gradually nodded himself to sleep. "They love you almost as much as you love them."

"It wasn't always so, but I'm thankful that it is now," I replied. "We all need time to heal and view our future."

"And what of your future?" Conrad was sitting close to Ross Elderin, both of them listening to an old tale from the mountains of Urvik.

"All in good time. Both my boys need time to grow, and both have wonderful teachers." Sybil, solicitous of her new responsibilities, brought me a shawl against the cooling night.

Conrad glanced across the fire and lowered his head to acknowledge the compliment. "I suspect a certain young squire will be relieved to be free of his prisoner."

Celestine sat beside Alexander with an intentional gap between their seats. She too listened to the Urvik legend about the way dragons chose riders at a ceremony in the mountains. She was tired but relaxed, her hands resting on her lap. A faint annoyance flickered over her face when Sybil placed her own stool between them.

It was hard to part with the men of Brak, not only because Alexander and Ross were with them but because many of them were known to me, and their leave-taking meant farewells to many that I might not see again for some time. The men from Roth also wanted to express their sorrow at Judith's death, for they had known her as a hunter with a keen mind that could build bridges and supervise the distribution of food during harsh winters, as well as drink more ale than most of them.

"What is Brak?" Celestine asked as we watched their caravan move off. "Is it a great city of the North?"

"Gracious, no!" The idea amused me. "It is a very small market town surrounded by woodlands, farms and uplands fit only for grazing sheep." I turned to her. "But I have known it since I was a child. The castle at Roth was my mother's family home, and it was where I was sent in exile. It's a wild and beautiful place."

Without facing me, her eyes still on the trailing baggage wagons, she asked, "Perhaps I could visit it with you some day?"

“Oh! Your Majesty, could we really?” Sybil was on the other side of me, and her enthusiasm for visiting Brak was obvious, as was her reasons for doing so. Celestine gave her a well-practised grimace and marched back to our own baggage wagons that were finally ready to leave.

All previous welcomes paled in comparison to the enthusiasm and the sheer numbers of people packed along the road to Vellin. Children waved lion flags, flowers were strewn in our path, and women handed posies and small tokens to the men as they marched proudly past. News of our victory had reached them through The Souran, and those who had not joined our ranks now offered their hands in welcome to those who had. Old men doffed their caps, and young boys ran alongside the marchers. Some in the crowd dropped to their knees as I rode past with the remaining Mantle escort. Wives greeted husbands who broke from their ranks to hold their loved ones again.

Sadly, not all was joviality. Those whose eyes waited in vain for men returning could not be ignored. Ahead, I saw a woman searching anxiously, then rushing to grip the arm of a man in the ranks, asking him for news. I could not hear what he said to her, but the misery of his news brought her to her knees, her workworn hands thrusting her apron to her face.

I stopped my horse, dismounted, and went to her. “What news, poor lady?” I bent uncomfortably in the armour.

Her fingers drew the apron from her face, but twisted it without her controlling them. “My man is dead, and I have six bairns to feed. He was not much of a man, but he was all I had, and we cared for each other in our fashion.”

I raised her to her feet, as she realised to whom she was speaking, she gasped.

“The loss of a husband is no small thing, and neither are six young mouths to feed.” I looked about me and cried. “We will take care of our widows and orphans. Tomorrow, we will distribute compensation to all those who have lost their men." I turned back to the woman. "What is your name?"

"Anna, Your Majesty." She began to curtsey, but I took her arm. "What did your husband do?"

She raised her head. "He was a carpenter, My Queen, and a good one."

"And he was a true Magran hero." I gripped her hand in mine. "But pride does not put bread on the table, does it? Tomorrow, you will receive his soldier's pension. Do you live in the city?"

"By the river, my Queen." Again, she felt the need to drop, but I held her fast. 'We rent two rooms from The Lord of Camlan. He owns the whole of our street."

"Not anymore!" I called out to the crowd. "All properties in Vellin that once belonged to Lord Norton of Camlan are now confiscated and become the property of The Royal House of Magra. If you are a tenant, then from this day, you will be my tenant. Until the end of the year, all tenants of Camlan will live free of rent. After that time, rents will be negotiated, and repairs will be undertaken." I knew those rickety old buildings. Tertius should have maintained them better. There were, of course, other properties belonging to Camlan, including the elegant house where he had kept his mistress. She was gone, no one knew where, and I intended to possess the building.

Overwhelmed by what had happened to her, Anna returned to the roadside to receive the good wishes of her neighbours. Instead of remounting, I led my horse to be at eye level with my people. We saw each other as I had seen my men at their campfires on the battlefield. There were no barriers. Hands touched. It was something I will never forget, and I am assured it was the same for them. Conrad helped me to remount when we reached the gates of the Angirat. It was here that I dismissed my army. It was only a brief ceremony, with reminders that the paymaster would begin his slow distribution of remuneration the following day. The paymaster was a Mantle who would set up his desk in the courtyard of The Talarin. For several days, men climbed the Angirat to claim their pay. Other Mantles visited widows bearing their husband's pay as well as their share of Florian's gold, a term now in common usage to mean an unexpected windfall.

After many hugs from my welcoming ladies, I introduced them to Celestine and Sybil. Then the three of us enjoyed the luxury of a hot bath before gathering for a quiet afternoon in my private rooms. Shana and Alice immediately took Sybil under their wing and spent a long afternoon of trying on dresses, experimenting with hair and makeup. Celestine had been given her own room, where she remained until Grace invited her to join us for cake. We were about to eat when a knock came on the outer door. Grace answered it and beckoned me.

"You have a visitor!" she said. Before I knew who was there, I waved to let our visitor enter. It was my son, Cillian, grown at least a handspan and was wearing his novice Mantle tunic. Behind him was Conrad.

Despite Celestine being there, I threw my arms around my son. He looked a little disconcerted but responded. I then proceeded to ask all the motherly things that sons probably wished their mothers would not ask. It was Conrad who saved Cillian from any further embarrassment.

"Your Majesty, I thought that perhaps Novice Cillian might like to see for himself that you are safe and well. I have informed him about Lady Judith."

Cillian looked down. "I shall miss Judith. She was always kind to me." He brightened. "She also loved to play tricks on all the children at Roth, and we loved to play tricks on her. She made people laugh."

"Was this the woman who died on the battlefield?" Celestine asked, leaning forward.

I felt Grace stiffen, either because she feared that Celestine might guess Cillian's parentage or that she disliked Judith being referred to as 'the woman'. "The Lady Judith of Pellian was one of Queen Katherine's most loyal ladies-in-waiting. Everyone who went into exile with The Queen knew her for a brave and caring person."

"As did Mantles, who shared the practice yard with her," Conrad added. "We will all miss her."

"I will walk with you back to the Talarin," I took Cillian's arm, "and you can tell me how you are progressing in your studies. Enjoy the cake without me, ladies?" I nodded to Grace as I took the arms of my son and Conrad.

"When will you end the secrecy?" Cillian asked softly as we crossed the garden to the Talarin gate.

"Soon," I assured him. "But you must complete your training, and so must your brother. Then it will be my pleasure to launch you both on an unsuspecting Magra."

I knew my younger son disliked any form of subterfuge, but he also understood its importance. Cillian had never met his father, but Alexander had, just once, when he was quite small. They had met at the time when Cillian was conceived. In less than a week, my husband had terrorised most of the children with his mood swings and wild drinking until Rosie and I decided that she should take them to one of our tenant farms until Brodik was gone. I dismissed the memory. Instead, I embraced my son once more before he returned to the Talarin with Conrad.

The days passed. Summer's brief glory spread into autumn, only to be suddenly ended in a series of storms. The first snow, little more than a flurry and gone within the hour, heralded winter. Despite the journey, we returned to Roth for year's end. Rosie and I had been considering changes to the old stronghold, and I longed to see my son and Ross once more. All my ladies had assembled a large collection of warm clothing and furs, and our caravan north was in strange contrast to the mean little carriage that had taken us south to Vellin at the start of my widowhood. The baggage train would leave three days before our own departure. Everyone was excited to be returning to Roth, including Celestine and Sybil for very different reasons.

"I have never seen snow before," Celestine told Alice. "It must look very pretty when it is on the ground."

"Very cold, too!" Shana clutched her arms as she told them about the dreadful nature of a snowbound winter in Roth.

"What did you do, Princess Celestine, to celebrate year's end?" asked Grace, feeling quite chilled after Shana's memories of rescuing sheep and young lambs after one severe snowfall in early spring,

"Just parties!" sighed Celestine. "The temperature in Goremene is a little different for most of the year. Perhaps a little cooler sometimes when fur is appropriate and warmer when silk and lace are more comfortable." None of us responded to her comments but I'm certain most of us were thinking that the girl was about to discover more than just a variation in wardrobe.

We set out on a beautiful, crisp morning under a cloudless blue sky. The cold pinched cheeks but left bodies feeling alive and energetic. A company of six Mantles escorted us, and it caused Grace a moment of sudden sorrow as she realised that it would be the first time we had travelled without Judith. Grace, Alice, Shana, and Sybil travelled in the coach. I preferred to ride, and I was pleasantly surprised that Celestine requested a horse too.

"My father and I often ride together. I am grateful that you allowed me this freedom, and with one of my own horses." She had insisted upon riding in leggings, too. While mine were somewhat old and weather-beaten leather, hers were a soft kid, dyed blue to match her eyes. I wondered how well they would wear in the rougher landscape of the north.

"We should ride together when we reach Brak. Some beautiful waterfalls and limestone escarpments are well worth seeing." I took my place behind the two leading Mantles, and she followed.

"I don't know what an escarpment is, but we have plenty of waterfalls in Goremene." It was said cheerfully and not tinged with the peevish boasting she had once delighted in.

"Ah, yes, but do your waterfalls freeze in winter?" I countered.

"That, I must see!" She agreed.

We passed the time talking about her memories of Goremene, memories of the opulent but claustrophobic court of her father. Occasionally, she would accompany him to a hunting lodge, where she was entertained by ladies from the court while her father pursued his hunting and fishing adventures. Each year, at high summer, they would retire to the coast. She could not swim and hated the ocean, but spent her days in the shade reading and writing her own poetry. She flatly refused to show me any of it when I asked, but I was pleased to hear that she still wrote it. I could not help thinking that a little wild living at Roth was just what she needed. I also explained that I had an extensive library there with ample vellum for her compositions.

The rowdy courtyard at Stovin brought back more memories of Judith, and I had to spend some time with Shana, who could not erase the evening when Judith drank too much. It was a kind gesture when Sybil took her new friend into the garden to admire Greer's herb and vegetable patch. I took the chance to spend time with the Lady of Lamfrak myself. Her only son, a cavalryman, had died during the battle, her husband was ailing, and she held little hope for his full recovery. His new heir, the son of a second cousin, was already in residence, and although Greer fought hard to retain her authority, the young man was beginning to exercise his inheritance rights before Lord Lamfrak was even in his grave.

"It's so unfair." Greer kicked at a clod of earth that had the audacity to be occupying space on the gravel footpath. "You know that I've been running this place for years and doing it well. Now this young whelp, still wet behind the ears and with no understanding of administration or commerce, wants to change everything. He's limiting the garrison coming for regular evenings, he's cut down on market days, and now he wants to spend good money on setting up a pottery." She ran her hands through her wire-brush hair, curly hair that I had always envied.

"I mean, yes, we have clay here, but not enough to start making our own pots. I told him that he needed to be in The Southern Meeds for good pottery clay. You know his answer?" She turned to me, but I could only shrug. "Course you don't. His answer is to import it from them, make it into pots and sell it back to them." She shook her head. "I told him, they make their own pots, why would they buy ours?" She picked the dead petals from a rose but left the head itself. "He said because ours would be better and painted by professional artists."

She walked backwards, facing me. "Artists! Yes, he's brought three with him, absolutely insufferable creatures who are eating me into penury without picking up a brush. They're looking for inspiration, he says."

Poor Greer, I had never seen her so frustrated. Although she and her son had never been close, he had recognised his mother's strengths as an administrator and had been more than willing to keep her on as chatelain. Now, this distant relative had plans to dismiss her entirely. I promised to speak again with the lords at our next meeting, but I was certain they would not agree to revising the inheritance laws to include women. Unfortunately, it was one of the laws that the monarch had little influence upon, thanks to my great-grandfather, who had been forced to agree to the law as a concession after the lords had supported him in a war. I was thankful that no such limitations towards monarchs had been considered before the Goremene invasion.

We left early the following day because Greer had heard the weather was about to turn unpleasant. Exactly how unpleasant wasn't apparent until we were well on our way to Brak. Beyond Stovin, the road is poorly kept as it meanders through woodlands. Several small fiefdoms claim land here, and despite many attempts to unify their responsibilities to maintain the roads, nothing much has changed. The rain was heavy, and with little shelter save the canopy of trees, everyone mounted was cold and wet. It was at that moment that the back wheel of the carriage broke. With two spokes in splinters, the wheel was beyond repair. We travelled with very few valuables, so we could abandon the carriage for now. Four of our escort, to our immense relief, discarded their mantles and set them about the shoulders of the coach passengers, who were obliged to ride behind a Mantle. Slithering and slipping in the ever-increasing mud, we helped the ladies to climb out, and with much pushing, Celestine and I managed to hoist them onto the horses. It was as we made our way to our own horses that we both slipped and slithered into each other. Now caked in a thick layer of mud, Celestine's eyes being the only clean feature of her face, we regarded each other. Shock, mortification, and disgust erupted into uncontrollable laughter.

"It can't get any worse!" I told her as we trudged back to our mounts. Except, it did. A nearby branch suddenly dropped, frightening both our horses, sending them off in the direction of Brak.

"No!" Celestine screamed and simultaneously slithered, landing on her bottom in a pool of yellow clay. She threw a handful of the disgusting stuff in the direction of the departing horse.

XXI The Year's Turn

We walked on in the soddened gloom. I had no idea how far we were from Brak but very soon the light would fade, and we would be alone in the woods, alone, cold, wet and if not afraid then certainly concerned. Celestine kept close to me, and I wished that I had not left my small sword back in Vellin. We both had our dining knives ready, but they would be useless if we were attacked.

"Are there wolves in these forests?" Celestine looked about her.

"No. Our only danger here is falling in the dark or being set upon by footpads, and they would be desperate indeed to be searching for victims in this weather." The rain had washed most of the mud from our hair and faces, but we still looked like some nightmarish creatures from the swamps.

"I suppose everyone else will be at Roth by now." She moved even closer.

"I hope so." I saw the look of confusion on her face. "To reach Roth, they would have to pass Brak, and hopefully they would inform Lord Elderin of our plight. He will send out search parties."

"I never thought I would be relying on The Lord of Brak and his squire." Celestine didn't appear comforted by the news.

"Ross Elderin is a fine man, and as for his squire…"

She interrupted me. "I know that you know his mother. That must be a comfort to her and to you, but it is not to me. I find him an upstart who is both rude and quite impolite."

"I suppose the young men in your father's court were always polite and never disagreed with you."

"Precisely! I have never had a squire, a squire of all things, be so rude and contradict me. He was insufferable. I hope I don't have to meet him during these celebrations."

"I hate to disappoint you, but I expect Alexander will be there, after all, Roth is his home."

She swept away the hair that continued to fall across her face. "I see, of course, that is how you know his mother. Is she a servant or a gentlewoman?"

"We make no such distinctions at Roth. We are all equals, sharing the work and our leisure, although some of us have special tasks. Our cook is Martha and none of us would want to challenge her authority in the kitchen. Lady Rosemary is my chatelain when I am absent and Judith…" For a moment I had forgotten, and the sudden memory stung.

Celestine moved closer to me. "I'm sure she would have been valuable in whatever she did. The men of Brak spoke highly of her." I nodded and we trod on in silence.

It was not long after that there was a sound of horses moving quickly towards us, the sound of their hooves scattering the mud as they went. One of the riders held a lantern, and they were almost upon us before they slowed, and we both called out.

"What have we here, wood nymphs about their revelries!" a familiar voice said cheerily.

"Ross Elderin! Your Queen is in dire need of your assistance, as I am sure you are well aware." I went to the side of his horse, noticing that the other rider was my son.

"Queen? Is there a queen under all that mud?" He looked across at Celestine. "Lady Grace insisted that we should not delay but ride here as soon as we could. Your ladies have proceeded to

Roth in order to prepare warm baths for you both. If you would both care to climb up, we will be off." He offered me his hand, then looked back at Celestine who had not moved. "Princess?"

I went to Celestine. "Perhaps you would prefer to ride with Lord Elderin, and I shall ride with his squire?"

She hesitated, then shook her head. "It would be disrespectful to expect a queen to ride behind a squire. I shall do it." I watched Alexander help her up without a change of expression on his face. Only when she was securely clutching him about the waist did he give me the briefest of smirks before riding away.

I held my hand for Ross to help me up. Once behind him, I rested my cold chin on his neck. "Kate, this is the most uncomfortable embrace I've ever experienced, and you smell of mud."

"I thought you loved the smell of the forest!" I teased.

"Aye but I like your usual smell better."

Year's End is a strange celebration, which changes depending on geography. In The Northern Meeds, it is a time for drawing closer, hopefully around a huge fire with ample spiced wine and good food. On the eve, we were entertained in Brak, at The Meed castle. It is an old fortress that has spawned several other buildings within its walls. The great hall was hung with garlands and the noble neighbours all gathered for a feast. With the exception of the youngest children, the whole complement from Roth attended. It was a joyful evening with dancing and song as well as fine roasts and large, sweet puddings. Outside in the courtyard, the village of Brak also celebrated, with toasts supplied by both Roth and their lord.

As Queen, I began the dance and for once I could choose the one whose right it should be, The Lord of Brak. Alexander was much sought after particularly during the progressive movements when some indelicate jostling occurred. My son was judicious in his choices. Observing her rank, he deferred from asking the princess but towards the end of the evening, during a progression, they were forced together. For an unpleasant moment I thought she was going to walk away from him, but as she turned, he put out his hand and took hers. By the end the measure she was laughing and when she returned to her place beside me, she was pink and flustered.

"You may tell his mother that I found him an excellent dancer and he has been well schooled by The Lord of Brak in chivalry." She took a deep breath to regain her composure.

"I'm delighted."

Much later, when I was curled in Ross's arms, he told me that Alexander had learnt all he could from him. "He's a fine young man. When will you tell the world about your sons?"

"Patience, my love. Within the year, Alexander will come of age. Perhaps then would be a good time. In the meantime, let him enjoy his anonymity. Once he becomes a prince, the world will expect so much from him. I know how precious it is to be just Kate. As Kate I met the best people." He turned towards me and kissed me again. Our time would come soon enough but even on that cold, winter's night, I could not risk being found in his bed. The following morning, while everyone else returned to Roth on horseback, we walked through the woods. He had a surprise for me.

"You've rebuilt the cottage!" The herbs were still in their wild state but beside them the sad ruins had become a tiny home.

"It's a place that has come to mean a lot to me. I have fanciful dreams that one day I shall meet with an unknown woman and the pair of us would make love here, in secret, away from the world." He showed me inside. There was a bed, a table, and a small hearth.

Year's End passed into memory, and we faced the wrath of the northern winter. Celestine was eager to experience snow but the dry cold persisted. To entertain her, we took long rides and as the winds blew cold from Mount Befell, although there was still no snow, water began to freeze. At last, she was able to see a frozen waterfall. She talked about it all evening and spent several days after trying to paint it.

The Lord of Brak and his squire visited frequently. I caught Shana and Alice discussing which young girl he was secretly admiring. Was it the princess or Sybil Clairstow? Shana knew Alexander was my son because she had lived all her life at Roth, but Alice didn't know. It was to Shana's credit that she kept the secret, but their conversation worried me. I decided that when Lord Elderin and his squire paid their next visit, I would discuss it with Alexander.

"I'm glad you were thinking about it too," he told me. He was sitting in the window seat of my chamber, sitting as he had done as a child, tracing the diamonds of lead holding glass.

"Do you want me to announce it to the world?" I was sitting in my usual place beside the fire. Since returning home I had noticed that I felt the cold more than I had done before.

"Not really, not yet, but I hate for people who come here not to know. If you trust them, couldn't we tell them?" He sat up. "When she's not pouting, the princess is pleasant, and I like Lady Sybil, but I hate pretending that I'm something that I'm not."

I told him that I would consider what to do. It would shatter Sybil's hopes of any future with him but the sooner that happened, the better for her to see him as a good friend. The King of Magra would be expected to take a princess for a wife. As for Celestine, I doubted that she would ever consider him a suitable match."

"Perhaps that is because she looks down on mere squires. At best he could only aspire to become a lord. She is likely thinking that Sybil would be an excellent choice for him, whereas the union of Magra and Goremene would be advantageous for both." Conrad was inside my head, and I marvelled at his power, sending his thoughts all the way from Vellin.

"There was a time that I could easily do that, but you are better at shutting me out. Not that I object as you and Ross Elderin's affections are not something that I wish to share." He continued. "I am within five miles of Roth. I have news that I am sure you would wish to know."

The news was something that I wanted to share with others. Cillian, although he was young had reached the end of his noviciate and was already preparing for his quest, the final step before receiving his mantle. Conrad had also brought suggestions for Tertius Norton's replacement. While Camlan should have been inherited by the eldest of his children, it was being managed by his nephew, Flynn. Flynn and Alice had been close for some time but without his own fiefdom, he would not seek her hand. This had been a bitter blow for her. Conrad had found the solution. Like his uncle, Flynn was well trained in managing the finances of the large area. Conrad proposed that he should replace his uncle as one of my councillors. In that capacity, he would receive a substantial stipend and as the impressive house in Vellin was still unoccupied, it could be offered to all future chamberlains.

I was thrilled by the news and couldn't wait to tell Alice. She was cautious about becoming overjoyed, reminding me that all that supposed that Flynn still cared about her. Poor Alice, she still had doubts about her own worth.

The same afternoon as Conrad's arrival the snow began to fall. It was large flakes at first and then the tiny ones that quickly froze in the cold evening air. In the kitchen Martha was telling everyone that the little snow meant a big snow. It was an old superstition, but in this case, her prediction was correct. Ross and my son had been invited to dine with Conrad and by the time the meal was over, the snow was piled shin heigh at the door. They had to stay the night. Grace and Rosie organised card games in which everyone took part and mulled wine was on hand. In such a cheerful atmosphere, heads became fuddled quickly and laughter made tongues work without heads.

In their corner, Alexander, Shana, Grace, and Alice were enjoying competing against each other. Sparing partners since childhood, my son and Shana were excitedly trying to beat each other. They dropped cards quickly, their shrieks of delight and gasps distracted everyone else. Shana won and while the two observers at their side were grateful for the end of the long duel, Alexander groaned.

Shana cried triumphantly, "Not even Princes can win all the time!"

In an instant, it was done and could not be undone. The room hushed. Dread flushed Shana's face and the poor girl did not have the guile to pretend it had been a joke. Alice looked quizzically at Grace. Grace, in turn was not certain what to do and was fumbling for words. I stood, noticing the shock on the faces about me. Rosie stood too, opening her mouth but said nothing as my hand rose. Slower, Conrad came to his feet.

"Is it, is it true?" Sybil was the first to speak, her eyes threatening tears and her eyebrows knotting.

I placed my hand gently on her shoulder. "It is true. Alexander is my son. He is the son of King Brodik, and he has been kept in secret all his life."

"Why?" It was Alice who asked in a trembling voice.

"You of all people should understand, Alice." It was painful to repeat the events concerning his conception with my son sitting there, but he was well aware of them and if everyone was to understand my reasons, they had to know the cause. When I finished, Alexander came to me and took my hand.

"I'm glad that you have spoken." He looked around the room. "Those of us who grew up here have always known, but my mother was truly fearful for myself and my brother. When she became queen, we knew that at some time in the future the truth would be told and I'm happy that you all are the first to know."

"And you've had to pretend to be Lord Elderin's squire?" Alice shook her head.

"Not pretend, I am his squire." Alexander clasped hands with Ross in the way that lords do when they greet each other. "What better way to learn about being a lord, except from a lord? My mother taught me all she knows about kingship, and Lady Judith taught me about combat. Lord Elderin has been teaching me how to treat men under my command and how to deal with tenants." He looked at me under his eyelids. "And queens."

"Everyone at Roth has kept this secret and now I am asking all of you in this room to guard this knowledge with your lives until I am ready to announce it to The Five Kingdoms." I saw many different reactions to the news. Shana and Alexander hugged each other. Alice was nodding. Sybil was in tears and Celestine's face showed no emotion whatsoever. Was she simply too shocked to respond or was she wearing the carefully controlled face that she had always worn in the court of her father? Shortly after, she retired to her room, inviting Sybil to accompany her.

We returned to Vellin on a blustery day, the final throws of a winter marked by less snow and turbulent winds. Rosie remained at Roth, and Shana begged to stay with her. Although many of us had tried to persuade her that the fault was not hers, she still blamed herself for the incident during the card game. Alexander promised to spend time with her after our departure. We stopped at Stovin to lay flowers on the new grave of Lord Lamfrak and to meet his successor, who was everything that Greer had foretold. He boasted that he would rid his stronghold of indolent cavalry officers and turn his fiefdom into a haven for artists and poets.

Needless to say, we gained another member of our company. Greer, Lady Lamfrak, recognised long before she was told that the new lord had little interest in supporting her, she had been asked to leave, to make way for his intended bride. Greer was pragmatic by nature. At supper, she asked if I might require another lady-in-waiting, and I was happy to welcome her. We had known each other since childhood, when her blunt swords had often been less than complimentary, but as we had grown, I realised that her logical mind and plain speaking had a worth of its own. We successfully squeezed into the carriage and managed to remain on pleasant terms until we reached Vellin, not an insubstantial feat as Greer and the princess appeared to be at odds on every topic of conversation.

I was whisked into the business of the state immediately, meeting my dear old councillors, Heathcote and Strewan, together with Flynn Norton. Installed in his uncle's house, with his widowed mother, he had already impressed both the older men by suggesting several improvements to the taxation laws, even before my arrival. I visited The Talarin for news of Cillian, only to be told that there was no news, which was a good sign. Tory and I discussed a new schedule for myself and for Princess Celestine, who had expressed an interest in learning archery. I greeted guests from Thanis and received a late-year 's-end gift from Rynth. It was a large bronze statue of me, leading several miners into battle. I could tell that Ransom Frain himself was not totally enthusiastic about it, but the project had been started to help rehabilitate injured men who were being taught the art of casting bronze. With that in mind, I was happy to have it installed in the square below the Angirat, with a plaque explaining its origin. I promised to visit Rynth soon.

The weeks passed into Spring. Alice saw more of Flynn Norton, and Greer took Sybil under her wing, encouraging the girl to speak her mind as well as to develop friendships within the palace. Celestine appeared to have settled comfortably into her expected position of being the most beautiful young woman at court, garnering regular praise for her abilities as a conversationalist, as well as a dancer and even a musician. She played the lute. With all around admiring her, it was satisfying to notice that rather than the adulation making her insufferable, it made her more amenable to others. She would often go riding with Greer and Sybil, gradually making it obvious to all that Sybil was her closest confidante. I watched all this during the infrequent quiet moments when the affairs of state gave me time.

With Spring came plans for the annual meeting of all the lords. This year, it was also to commemorate our victory over Florian's army. I insisted that any celebrations should not dwell on glorifying war but on commemorating the dead and celebrating our new beginnings. All my councillors agreed. Messengers were sent, not only to the lords but to all those who participated in the battle to convene in Vellin on the appointed day. A special envoy was dispatched to Goremene to invite their king too. Trade had already resumed, and Florian was delighted for the opportunity to see his daughter.

About a week before the public celebrations, the lords began to arrive for their annual council with the monarch. This was the event that signified the beginning of the wider festivities. Taverns and inns were beginning to fill, and for larger groups, land had been cleared to the east of the river, where tents and temporary headquarters could be established. Pride of place here was for my cousin and his large entourage from Dereculd. I was personally delighted that the mounted archers would be giving a display, and my brief friend Lyn would be among the troupe.

"Where will my father stay?" Celestine asked, following me through my apartments. She had waylaid me at the door of my study and continued to follow me, asking questions about the celebrations.

"Here, in the palace, of course. You will have plenty of time together." I put my hand on her arm, intent on assuring her that I was happy for her to see him.

"Does that mean that I can go home?"

"It does not. You are our guest, but you are also a hostage."

“I’m a prisoner!” She clenched her fists. “I have tried hard to understand and adopt your rustic ways, but I am a Goremene princess, accustomed to better things, better food, better surroundings, better companions!” She folded her arms.

“And yet you adopt the stance of a fishwife!” I went on the attack. “Sometimes you have the manners of a greedy child. You are selfish, no doubt, because you were accustomed to being over-indulged by your doting father. You treat strangers with a rude indifference, and worse, you treat your friends with contempt. Believe me, Princess Celestine, if I had not accepted you as a hostage, I would gladly be sending you home.” I needed to inhale before I went on in a calmer voice.

“It is such a pity because I thought better of you when we first met. I remember a girl who followed me through the battlefield, speaking to the injured and comforting the dying. I don’t know when that girl disappeared. I wish she would reappear more often.” I did not wait for her response but made my way to the white tower, intent on visiting The Talarin. As I unlocked the tower door to gain access to the garden, she was hurrying up the steps after me.

“Wait! Please!” Her face was pinched and white. “You’re right. I know you are. I am selfish and spoilt, and sometimes I say cruel things to people, sometimes to people I know who cannot respond, like Sybil.” She had gripped my arm, and I looked down at her hand. She immediately released me. “I’m sorry.” We stood there, neither of us speaking until she repeated her apology.

“Celestine,” I rested my hands on her shoulders. “I saw a spirited but caring girl on that battlefield. I wanted to know her better. I still want to know her. Over the past months, I thought I caught glimpses of her, but then…”

She looked down. All she said was, “I was shocked about Alexander.”

“Alexander?”

"I thought you were punishing me when you set him to guard me. He was a country squire, little more than a peasant and I hated him for being a peasant, but then I was attracted to him. He offered me nothing but kindness, and even tried to cheer me up. He was chivalrous when he had no right to be. I fought against feeling anything but hate towards him." She sighed and leaned against the wall.

"I knew Sybil was attracted to him too. I knew he felt special to me, a special kind of man, no matter what his origins were, but I couldn't let him see that. He was so lowly." She wrung her hands as she huffed and sighed. "Then you told everyone the truth and he was suddenly a prince and I had treated him so badly that I couldn't even bring myself to speak to him."

I was completely at a loss about what to say. I considered embracing her, but I was too slow. She quickly turned on her heels and sped back to the palace. Stunned, I made my way to The Talarin, where Conrad listened to my version of the encounter with a smile on his lips.

"She'd be a perfect choice for a queen, and it would cement our links with Goremene." He was sitting at his desk, his fingers playing on his beard.

"They're children. It's far too early for any such thoughts."

"He will come of age this year. When were you betrothed?" He rested his arms on the wooden desk. "If I remember, you were about her age." He was right. I had been very young, but my father had engineered my betrothal to Brodik in order to draw me away from Tertius Norton.

"It was so long ago." I sighed. "Should I talk to Alexander?"

That amused Conrad, and he shook his head. "That would be akin to my offering you counsel about Ross Elderin."

"Hardly!" I copied his stance and rested my forearms on his desk. "I'm a grown woman, and you and I have our own history. Alexander is young, and I am his mother."

"All the more reason not to blunder in and never forget that he has been living the life of a squire for some time. I hardly think that the opposite sex is completely unknown to him."

My mouth opened, but I was lost for words. I chose not to consider what encounters my son had experienced and agreed with Conrad that I should allow them both to follow their own paths. If they converged, I would not object. If they didn't. I was powerless to intervene. For a few days, I was overcautious when I was with Celestine. Then other things occupied my mind. I watched the banners of the lords being positioned in the great council chamber, and I set about composing the speech that I was to give to them.

"My Lords of The Gathering, an epithet that I hope remains an indicator of men of valiant dependability, I welcome you to this, our first gathering since we came together in a time of crisis." I looked down at the long and elaborate words that I had so carefully crafted. They were inadequate, and I dispensed with them. The assembled men did not need reminding and would most likely spend the coming days reminiscing among themselves.

"I spent long hours toiling over what I would say to you today, about our past exploits and, more importantly, our future. Instead, I wish to consider that future."

I left my chair and began to walk around the great table. "It is our good fortune that we are all able to be here, together, on this day, a day on which I intend to set in motion the future, our future, yours and mine." I put my hand gently on Conrad's shoulder.

"My Lords." I walked further around the room to where the small huddle of squires sat. Not every Lord had brought servants into the chamber. "I must beg your pardon for a lie that I have lived for some eighteen years. A secret that few knew until this moment." I held out my hand to Alexander. A little stunned, he stood as he took it. Behind me, I could hear muted whispers.

"The Lord of Brak was one of those who recently learnt my secret." Ross was sitting with his back to me, his head lowered. "Now I would like to share it with all of you. It is time that I introduce you all to my son, Prince Alexander of Magra."

There was uproar, a multitude of male voices, exclaiming, questioning, showing indignation and suspicion. Conrad stood and attested to the truth of my words. I raised my hand to silence them.

"I will provide witnesses to my son's birthright, but not at this auspicious time. I have already proved his heritage to Lord Heathcote." The old man nodded, a contented smile on his face.

"Most of you know my history and the history of my husband. I doubt that any one of you could blame me for my secrecy and deception. I am the daughter and granddaughter of kings, and my son has been raised learning the art of kingship from a capable teacher."

Clairstow and others were vocal in their appreciation of the situation that I found myself in and attested to my suitability to train a future king.

"No one could have galvanised our people the way that Queen Katherine did. Even her return for the old king's funeral was supported by the people. They love her and for good reason. No one has shown them more love and dedication. We've all experienced her wisdom and many of us have been touched by her kindness." Clairstow stood as he spoke. "Your Majesty, Prince Alexander!" He bent his knee to my son.

Others followed, one by one; they all bowed to my son. Alexander looked slightly alarmed and was relieved when the men returned to their seats.

Malister remained on his feet. "I saw with my own eyes how our prince earned his spurs in battle, and let us hope that he will never have to repeat that. A man bred in the north has my trust. Especially one schooled by our heroic queen."

Struan, who had only learnt of Alexander's existence hours earlier, was not to be excluded. With a twinkle in his eye, he announced, "I suggest, Your Majesty, Your Highness and My Lords that we adjourn to the antechamber where I believe we can offer a toast to our new prince."

Heathcote raised his eyebrows in delight. "Normally, Prince Alexander, this would be done while you were still in swaddling bands and your mother in her confinement bed. How fortunate that you can both share the toast." So delighted were my councillors with their own surprise, they almost forgot to allow me to lead the way. I did so, on the arm of our 'new prince'.

During the wider celebrations, the people were informed of Alexander's existence, and much feasting and merriment followed. Poor Alexander attended every function and became the focus of most of them. He was welcomed by kings and city aldermen and subjected to admiring glances from every eligible woman in Vellin. He took it all with measured good humour.

On the final night of this first anniversary of The Gathering, the great hall rang with music and laughter, not to mention overflowed with wine, and the tables groaned from the weight of suckling pig, stuffed ducks and pheasants. Findin had accompanied the Dereculd guests and delighted the assembly with his music before making way for the dance. It was the only time that, as Queen, I danced the first measure with my son. Then we separated, I to bring Florian to his feet and Alexander to bow low to Celestine, inviting her to partner with him. It did not go unnoticed that for most of the evening the prince and princess preferred each other as partners. Greer poked her finger into my back and predicted that a royal wedding was sure to follow.

Out on the terrace, which was becoming our usual meeting place, I found Findin, puffing at his pipe and looking up at the stars.

"A fine night!" He pointed the pipe at the sky. "You've made a commendable start to this dynasty."

"I have no aspirations for dynastic power." I sat on the step beside him. "I just wanted my sons to be acknowledged. I shall abdicate in Alexander's favour as soon as I can."

Findin regarded his pipe, put it in his mouth, then removed it. "And what about all the things spinning in your mind, the improvements you would make to your kingdom?"

I winced before giving him a hard stare. "My mind gets very crowded these days with the number of people in there!"

"You still have work to do, necessary work. You began well with your widows and orphans, but there is so much more. I know you've been thinking about the widows of lords, who have managed estates for years but lose everything to a distant heir, or the rights of daughters to decide their own future and the plans you have to educate them better. Then there's the forestry laws that prohibit tenants from removing sick or dead game for their own use, the fair landlords' legislation, the court of small appeals, the welfare of the old, the education of the poor…" He stuck the pipe in the side of his mouth and still managed to say, "shall I go on?"

He had said enough.

I held on to my throne until many of my projects were approved and became real. As soon as I believed that I had set the future prospects of all our kingdoms on a better path, three exhausting years after The Great Gathering on the battlefield, I abdicated in favour of my son. During those years, Alexander and Celestine were learning more about each other and eventually married. I was thankful to leave the kingdom in their capable hands. Florian became a regular visitor to Vellin and when his first grandchild arrived, I wondered if he might stay forever, he was so enamoured with the baby.

Cillian returned from his quest and began his life as a Mantle. Alice married Flynn Norton and the eldest son of Majolica became

Lord of Camlan. Sybil Clairstow married Lord Malister's youngest son and often visits me.

Alexander's coronation was a time of much excitement, and once again, Vellin was filled with visitors from lords to pickpockets. Celestine's gown, Goremene lace adorned with Bashiria pearls was much praised, even by her Goremene family and unofficial celebrations blocked many of the city streets. Across The Five Kingdoms. It was a time to welcome a new beginning. In the time-honoured way, The King received his crown from Silver Mantle at The Field of the Pentangle and on his return to Vellin the bells rang, and Alexander walked among the excited crowds in the great square at the foot of the Angirat. Petitions were collected, flowers and gifts received with much thanks and then the new monarchs returned to the palace in order for the feasting and dancing to begin. I had intended to slip quietly away at this point but suddenly I found myself enveloped by the wedding party and was drawn to stay longer.

My farewell from Vellin was emotional, particularly parting from Conrad. He would steer both my sons through life until he retired in favour of a new Silver Mantle, my son, Cillian. There are rumours that the King and his brother are able to keep in touch with each other over great distances. I know they can communicate with their mother in that way. Most Silver Mantles retain their office until their death, but as Lord of Veldisholm, in The Green Islands, Conrad returned to his birthplace. 'Perhaps when you are no longer queen, you must come and visit us. I think you would like my island, Inserfal,' he told me at our parting.

'We both know I could never cross the seas,' I replied, as I gripped his hands, those hands that had protected and guided me through so much that I thought I could not accomplish. 'Unlike you seagoing islanders and a few brave fishermen on our coasts, we of 'The Five' have a fear of all that salt water.'

He laughed. 'I understand, but I believe that change is coming soon, change that will bring even 'The Five', to extend their horizons. It is already beginning on The Green Islands. I don't quite understand its significance yet, but I am hopeful that it will benefit all of us. That is why I want to see for myself.'

We parted company in his study, that room in which the ghosts of my childhood welcome me each time I sit before the oak desk. I have left my own ghosts there, too. My dainty short sword rests on the windowsill, and to sharp ears come the echoes of Judith of Pellian laughing with her Mantle opponents in the training yard. Conrad himself will leave the order changed but open to the innovations that his successor will initiate. When it was Conrad's turn to leave Vellin, it was done quietly, one early morning, with only Cillian to farewell him. They continued to reach out to each other until the gap between them was full of ocean.

The day after my son's coronation, our small party rode north to Roth. As the distance between Vellin and us lengthened, the heavy burden of the exile years and my days as monarch slipped away. With Grace and Greer beside me and Rosie waiting to welcome me home, I felt my life was beginning anew.

Shortly after, at dawn one morning, in a woodland glade heady with the smell of mint and rosemary, Ross Elderin and I pledged ourselves to each other, and at last I truly became Kate.

GAZETTEER

Angirat: A high escarpment above the city of Vellin and encircled by an ancient wall. The King's Palace and the Talarin of the Mantles are the only buildings.

Bashiria: Most remote of the Five Kingdoms and the one that turned the four kingdoms of Magra, Dereculd, Urvik and Thanis into'The Five'. Governed by a king from the capital of Homisag.

Brak: A small market town in the Northern Meeds. Governed by The Lords Elderin. Close to the stronghold castle of Roth Manor. It boasts a thriving market and a Meed castle of some considerable age.

Branton: The Port of the Kingdom of Dereculd, on the mouth of the River Weddon.

Bredok River: It flows from the southern borders of the lands of The Kashkie, southwards, widening with the addition of several unnamed tributaries. At the northern Bashirian border, it is joined by the River Anawah, flowing out of Goremene from the capital city. The Bredok River widens into a tidal estuary known as The Sul.

Camlan: A fertile region of Magra, still bearing its ancient name. Was once the most powerful and cultured area in the south, long before the unification of Magra. Its principal city is Wyke. The people are proud of their ancient heritage. Governed by the Norton family.

Dereculd: The Kingdom is second in importance after Magra and traditionally ruled by a member of the Magran royal family. Known for its support of the arts, it has been traditionally tolerant of religions and celebrates individuality.

Djengun: A 'free town' in the Western Wastes. Once part of Magra, sometimes considered part of Bashiria, which recognises no formal boundaries. Notorious in its early days for the slave market, abolished by King Rolland. Certain neighbouring countries continue their use of slavery.

Eminga: A 'free town' in the Western Wastes. On the busy trade route between the five kingdoms and the western kingdoms, such as the Kor Principalities and the valley of the Kashkie. It boasts the largest free market outside the capital cities and nine inns. There is a shrine just outside the town to honour its first Mayor, Earlic of Koinsonor. Legend says he brought the first settlers there, commanded to do so by the first king of Magra, Kelin, of the Urvikii. The grotto is said to have strong healing powers.

Erba River: Rises in the marshy uplands to the north of The Forest of Lore and flows east through The Southern Meeds to join the River Listi.

The Five Kingdoms: Magra, Dereculd, Urvik, Thanis, and Bashiria. When the region of Camlan was first created, the land around the town of Wyke was a separate kingdom. Due to several unsuccessful battles between Wyke and Vellin, Camlan became part of Magra.

Gaheil: A town west of the River Listi and north of the Forest of Lore. Famous for its caves.

Goremene: A large kingdom to the southwest of The Five Kingdoms. It shares a border with Bashiria, separated by the long, narrow inlet of The Sul. A kingdom rich in many resources, although it relies upon Rynth for its metals. It benefits from a warmer climate and has been ruled by the same family for generations. Its capital city bears the same name as the country.

The Green Islands / Isles: A cluster of islands to the southeast of the Five Kingdoms. The main islands are Beregstar, Frigisond, and the largest, Inserfarl.

The Grat Hills: Smaller members of the same chain as Mount Befell

Heathcote: A market town in the Northern Meeds of Magra.

Famous for its chestnut trees.

Homisag: Capital city of the kingdom of Bashiria. A vibrant city of colour, vegetation and imaginative wood and plaster buildings. Though water is scarce, fountains are everywhere. A city of beauty and life. Situated on the coast, not far from the famous Sul, the stretch of coastal water that the slaves swam across to escape Goremene to create their own free country on land that had belonged to Magra but was gifted to them.

Jedran Keep: The western border town of Magra with a small garrison of local people and volunteers. It sits in an earthquake-prone region, and before Vellin was Magra's capital, Jedran was the seat of the early kings, prior to the rise of Vellin.

Karstin: A small, Southern Meeds town and centre for the production of red wine. Holds an annual festival when the vineyard owners examine and set prices for the new vintage.

Kashkie, The: The name is generally used for the region, the people who live there and also the principal city. The people are gregarious, favouring colourful clothing and adornments and holding lavish celebrations. The region is also well known for its fortified wines and spirits.

Kor-erif, Kor-retniw and Kor-tnelis: Three independent cities beyond the boundaries of The Five Kingdoms. Occasional seismic activity can damage buildings, and each city has dealt with the problem in its own way. Kor-erif trades with The Five Kingdoms, buys refined ore from Rynth and has a thriving culture of artisan potters, carpet makers and smiths. Kor-retniw trades furs, but the city's religious beliefs forbid much interaction with others, even its neighbours. Kor-tnelis is also governed by the city's religion, although they are welcoming to those who wish to learn more about their beliefs.

Listi, River: Rises in the western mountains, below Mount Befell, close to the shores of Lake Trantor. Flows south through Vellin and reaches the sea at the estuary of The Marshes, the most southerly boundary of Magra and Dereculd.

Lore, The Forests of: Extensive forests in the Southern Meeds that once stretched from the Western Wastes to the sea, dividing the Kingdoms of Magra and Dereculd. Now mainly south of Gaheil and west of Nordinay, although remnants remain in the Meeds. Uninhabited and famous for legends of wolves, giant aurochs and other fables.

Magra: First among equals, Magra is a diverse kingdom covering much of the 'Mid-east-land' of the island known as Toroma to the peoples of The Great Island to the southeast. Magra is traditionally senior to the remaining four kingdoms and its capital, Vellin, is the seat of The High King. Vellin is older than other cities, although it remains smaller than some. In earlier times the capital of Magra was further west at Jedrani, (Jedran Keep). The magi known as 'The Mantles' have their headquarters in Vellin, at The Talarin, adjacent to The Royal Palace. Magra's first recognised king was Kelin of Ulomsk, a Urvikii warrior lord, who set dawn the basic structure of The Five Kingdoms.

Malister: A town on the edge of The Northern Meeds. Famous for deer hunting.

The Marshes: (Also known as The Great Marsh). Extensive marshland from the mouth of the River Listi to the northern part of Dereculd. An old landscape rich in wildlife and myth. Not a place to travel unprotected.

The Meeds: Regions of the Kingdom of Magra, typified by woodland, gentle hills, heathland and marshes, split into Northern and Southern Meeds. The regions are all governed by local lords. A string on market towns spread across the Northern Meeds, towns like Brak, Anardis, Heathcote and further south, Stovin. The Southern Meeds are less populated than their northern cousins with agriculture and vineyards. The main towns are Nordinay and Karstin, plus the southern part of the Forest of Lore. North of the forest and on the edge of the Meeds is Gaheil, a town close to a deep cavern, home of a legendary monster.

Mount Befell: a peak north and west of Brak, the highest peak of the same chain as the Grat Hills.

Nordinay: A Southern Meed town famous for its red wine production. The land between Nordinay and its neighbour Karstin is dotted with vineyards.

Pellian: Capital of Dereculd, on the Weddon River. A centre for arts and creativity.

Rush Bay: A large bay stretching the majority of the Magran coastline from the Jolean River in the north and including The Great Marsh in the south.

Rynth: The region of Rynth lies in a cluster of shallow valleys in the western corner of the lands known as The Southern Meeds and famous for its mining activities. There are no large towns in Rynth. The mining guilds operate their own farms where the wives of the miners can earn extra money.

Sarnmouth: A fishing port at the mouth of the River Sarn. The town is small, its fishing fleet of small boats provides catches that satisfy the needs of the Northern Meeds. The remaining supply for Magra tends to be locally caught freshwater fish.

Shreur River: Rises in the western hills of Magra and flows eastward to join the River Listi.

Silverleaf: The most modern mine in the Rynth valley, at the beginning of this time period.

Stovin: Northern Meed town, prosperous due to its proximity to the military barracks. Governed by the Lords Lamfrik – 'Stovin and the Meadows'.

The Sul: The tidal estuary of the River Bredok. At the northern Bashirian border, it is joined by the River Anawah and widens to become tidal and dangerous to navigate due to shifting sandbars and undetectable, periodic whirlpools.

Taegel: Town situated near the confluence of The Listi and Shreur rivers. Holds an annual horse fair.

Thanis: A small, peaceful kingdom north of Magra, one of the original Five Kingdoms. Home of Kate's ladies, Rosamund and Grace. Has a coastline of fishing villages.

Throdin: The Mantle Sanctuary and Alms House. Perched on a cliff overlooking the River Listi, the sanctuary had been a place of worship long ago when The Old Ones still ruled such wild places. The Alms House offered accommodation and simple healing skills to travellers.

Toroma: Landmass to the north and west of Morica. The eastern and southern coastal kingdoms include Thanis, Magra, Dericuld, Bashiria, Goremene and The Yandill Archipelego.

Urvik: One of the original Five Kingdoms, providing the first High King, Kelin of Ulomsk, after a war with Magra that the Urvikii won. A warrior culture, where children are taught the skills of the hunter as well as the warrior.

Vellin: Capital city of Magra, on the banks of the River Listi.

Weddon River: Rises in the hills of the Kashkie region, flows south, then east through northern Bashiria, into Dereculd, through the capital city of Pellion to the coast at Branton.

Wyke: Ancient capital of Camlan, now a provincial city ofMagra.

AUTHOR'S NOTE

It has been a long time since I visited Toroma and the lands of The Five Kingdoms. It's been good to get back there, although this second visit was in a time long before Megwin and her friends. Megwin's ancestor, Katherine, lived several centuries before her and became the first woman to rule the kingdoms alone.

To tell her story, I have had plenty of help along the way and would like to thank all those who cheered me on, including my family and friends.

Special mention goes to Connie Jagodzinski, writer of historical fiction, who spurred me on and kindly read the first draft, with all its warts and errors. Her suggestions for additional detail and plot changes were duly noted and acted upon. Connie's own books are all available in bookshops and on Amazon. I strongly recommend them. Her stories deal with less well-trodden historical roads, and as such, I always learn more, even in familiar time periods.

Although he is no longer with us, John Marsden, Australian writer of wonderful books, encouraged me to revisit my fantasy world for an adult audience, and I am proud to say, he recommended the original series to his students. He was also instrumental in getting those books published.

To every friend and neighbour who has read, encouraged and shaken their head, thank you. Your cheerful support was wonderful.

Finally, to my family, thank you for having faith in me. To Paul for his IT and creative skills in turning the manuscript into a book, and to my daughter Helen for her continuous support in everything from reading drafts to helping to choose the covers.

Gail Merritt

Gail Merritt is a retired teacher who was born in England, then lived in Dubai and Belgium before settling in Gippsland, Australia. She won her first writing competition when she was nine, with the judge's suggestion that she improve her spelling. Dyslexia diagnosis and the spell-checker have helped a great deal. Her only other prize was a 'Highly Commended" National Literary Award in 1999, for her short story, "Dark". Her first books were Young Adult fantasies, published by Lothian Books, Melbourne. Those were set in the same world as this current adult novel.

When she isn't writing, she spends time in her garden watching the wild ducks on her pond and walking her cairn terrier, Hamish.

BOOKS BY GAIL MERRITT

THE MANTLE CHRONICLES:

SILVER MANTLE

GREEN MANTLE

RED MANTLE

BLUE MANTLE

BLACK MANTLE

Coming soon:

ANARII

(A murder in a Swiss cave uncovers dangerous plans for the future of the world)

and

TO THE KING OF A DISTANT LAND

THE QUEENS of MAGRA Book 2

www.ingramcontent.com/pod-product-compliance
Lightning Source LLC
LaVergne TN
LVHW010643110826
845149LV00014B/2935

* 9 7 8 0 9 9 4 5 8 5 6 9 1 *